HARDBALL

In Chicago, V.I. Warshawski is asked to find a man who's been missing for four decades, but her search turns lethal. Skeletons from the city's racially charged history rise up to force her back: a nun who marched with Martin Luther King Jr. dies without revealing crucial evidence; on the city's South Side, people spit when she shows up. And whilst the elderly sisters who hired her are not completely forthcoming, V.I. finds that her family are also keeping secrets. Then her cousin arrives in Chicago to work on a political campaign and disappears mysteriously. Fearing that her father had been a bent cop, and with deception and corruption every step, V.I. is determined to take the investigation all the way to its frightening end.

Books by Sara Paretsky
Published by The House of Ulverscroft:

TOTAL RECALL
BLACKLIST
FIRE SALE
BLEEDING KANSAS

SARA PARETSKY

HARDBALL

Complete and Unabridged

CHARNWOOD
Leicester

First published in Great Britain in 2009 by
Hodder & Stoughton
London

First Charnwood Edition
published 2011
by arrangement with
Hodder & Stoughton
An Hachette UK company
London

British Library CIP Data

Paretsky, Sara.
Hardball.
1. Warshawski, V. I. (Fictitious character)- -Fiction.
2. Women private investigators- -Illinois- -Chicago- -
Fiction. 3. Detective and mystery stories.
4. Large type books.
I. Title
813.5′4–dc22

ISBN 978-1-44480-622-9

Published by
F. A. Thorpe (Publishing)
Anstey, Leicestershire
Set by Words & Graphics Ltd.
Anstey, Leicestershire
Printed and bound in Great Britain by
T. J. International Ltd., Padstow, Cornwall

This book is printed on acid-free paper

For Judy Finer and Kate Jones

The world, and my words in it,
are poorer for your leaving.

THANKS

I first came to Chicago in the summer of 1966 to do community service for the Chicago Presbytery's 'Summer of Service.' I was assigned to a white neighborhood on Chicago's Southwest Side, not far from where Martin Luther King had been living since January.

My job that summer was to work with kids six to ten years old. My coworkers and I tried to educate them and support them during a frightening time.

My summer in the city was the defining time of my life. My immediate boss, the Rev. Thomas Phillips, saw that my coworkers and I were immersed in every aspect of the city and neighborhood life, from local white citizens' council meetings, the Catholic youth group, and other neighborhood groups, to broader city political and social events.

The White Sox, who were in our backyard, wouldn't return our phone calls, but the Cubs gave our kids free tickets every Thursday, so I became a Cubs fan — a heavy price to pay for a summer of service. We also watched Shaw's *St. Joan*, performed under moonlight at the University of Chicago, which made the university — my current home — seem like a magical place.

Dr. King joined local civil rights leaders like Al Raby in a series of marches designed to protest the city's pernicious real-estate policies. The idea of open housing in Chicago spawned riots all over the city. Marquette Park, eight blocks west of where I was living and working, was the scene of an eight-hour riot, as the neighborhood attacked police for protecting Dr. King and his associates. Slogans with the vilest imaginable epithets were displayed in the park and around town.

Many of our neighbors, especially in the local churches, stepped up to the challenge of the times with courage, openness, and charity. Sadly, some of our neighbors were the bottle- and rock-throwing, hate-spewing rioters of Marquette Park.

The intensity of that summer, the pleasure I had in working with the children, the engagement with the city, despite its flaws, made Chicago a part of me, or me part of it, and it has been my home ever since. *Hardball* takes place in the present, but the heart of the story has its roots in that summer.

As always, many people helped make this book possible. My old coworker Barbara Perkins Wright shared her own perspective on that summer, and helped piece together my memories. Barbara and I heard King speak at Soldier Field, then marched with him to City Hall, where he taped his demands to the mayor's door — what an exhilarating time. We thought change for good was not only possible, but near at hand. Lately, my long-dormant sense of hope has come back to life.

I have relied on Taylor Branch's *At Canaan's Edge* for some details of Chicago in 1966. Jean

MacLean Snyder helped with information about the Illinois prison system and the politics of Cook County's criminal justice system. James Chapman, who teaches at the Stateville Correctional Facility, provided many details of day-to-day prison life there. Linda Sutherland, who corrected some of my U.S. Army mistakes in *Bleeding Kansas*, kindly advised me on the medals Mr. Contreras would have earned from his World War II service. Dave Case, a Chicago police officer and fellow crime writer, gave me helpful details about storage of departmental files. The sisters at the Eighth Day Justice Center in Chicago inspired me greatly. Sonia Settler and Jo Fasen made it possible for me to return to a more normal writing life. The senior C-Dog was helpful as always.

The novel is a work of fiction. I have taken liberties with Chicago police badges. I have tried not to take liberties with Chicago geography, but, of course, every now and then mistakes creep in, and I rely on alert readers to point them out. But most of what takes place between these covers is a work of the imagination, as free and unfettered as is in my power to make it.

CONTENTS

1

Anaconda Fury

Johnny Merton was playing with me, and we both knew it. It was a fun game for him. He was doing endless years for crimes ranging from murder and extortion to excessive litigation. He had a lot of time on his hands.

We were sitting in the room at Stateville reserved for lawyers and their clients. I couldn't believe Johnny was stringing me along, thinking I'd get him out early. It had been too many years since I'd practiced criminal law for me to be a good bet for any convict, let alone someone who needed Clarence Darrow and Johnnie Cochran working double shifts before he had a prayer.

'I want the Innocence Project working for me, Warshawski,' he announced that afternoon.

'And you are innocent of exactly what?' I pretended to make a note on my legal pad.

'Whatever they're charging me with.' He grinned, inviting me to think he was clowning, but I didn't smile back. Whatever else he might be, Johnny Merton was no buffoon.

Johnny was past sixty. During my brief stint as his lawyer when I'd been with the Public Defender's Office, he'd been an angry man whose rage at being assigned yet another new-minted attorney made it almost impossible to stay in the bull pen with him. He'd earned his

1

nickname, 'The Hammer,' because he could bludgeon anyone with anything, including his emotions. The twenty-five intervening years — many behind bars — hadn't exactly mellowed him, but he had learned better ways of working the system.

'Compared to you, my wants are so simple,' I said. 'Lamont Gadsden.'

'You know, Warshawski, life in prison, it takes away so much from you, and one of the things I've lost is my memory. Name does not ring a bell.' He leaned back in his chair, arms crossed. The snakes coiling around his biceps, looping down so that the heads rested on his wrists, seemed to writhe against his dark skin.

'Word is, you know where every Anaconda past and present is. Even to their final resting places if they've left the planet.'

'People do exaggerate, don't they, Warshawski? Especially when they're in front of a cop or a state's attorney.'

'I'm not looking for Lamont Gadsden for my health, Johnny, but his mama and his aunt want him found before they die. Even though he hung with you, his auntie continues to think of him as a good Christian boy.'

'Yeah, every time you mention Miss Claudia, I start to cry. When I'm by myself and no one can see me, of course. You can't afford to get a reputation for softness in the joint.'

'I doubt your tender heart will ever be your downfall,' I said. 'You remember Sister Frances?'

'I heard about her, Warshawski. Now, there truly was a fine Christian woman. And I hear you was with her when Jesus took her home.'

'You hear a lot.' I put just the right amount of admiration into the sentence, and Johnny preened. But he didn't say anything.

'You don't care what she said to me before she died?' I prodded.

'You can make up anything a dead person said. It's a good angle, but I'm not biting.'

'What about the living, then? You care about what your kid has to say about you?'

'You been talking to my girl?' This was news to him, and rage swept him off his feet, making the veins in his throat bulge. 'You been harassing my family, and I hear about it from you in here first? You stay away from my girl. She's living a life any father'd be proud of, and I won't have scum like you bring her down. You hear?'

The guard came over from the corner and tapped his arm. 'Johnny, take it easy, man.'

'Take it easy? Take it easy? You take it easy when this bitch, this cunt, comes after your family . . . I wouldn't run you as a whore, Warshawski, you stink so bad.'

The guard was summoning help. Someone came in with manacles for Johnny.

'The Innocence Project, huh?' I pulled my papers together. 'About the only thing you're innocent of is the smarts to keep your sorry ass out of jail.'

I went through the search even lawyers undergo on their way out of Stateville. I hadn't brought anything in with me, and I was leaving empty-handed, too: Johnny and I certainly hadn't exchanged anything in our forty-five

3

minutes together. Just to be on the safe side, the guards searched the trunk of my car.

As soon as I was clear of the prison grounds, I pulled off the road to stretch my arms. Tension builds in the calmest muscles when those gates close on you, and nothing about time in the Big House made me calm.

Joliet, where the prison stands, lies on the far side of Chicago's heaviest exurban sprawl, and I'd be hitting the road at the same time everyone in the western suburbs was going home. The thought of the traffic knotted my shoulders even more. As I crept forward, I jotted a note in my time log. Forty-five minutes on the Lamont Gadsden inquiry. I'd long passed the point where I was making money on the case, but I couldn't let the inquiry go, not as deeply mired in it as I'd become.

I oozed through the I-PASS lane at Country Club Plaza and finally found myself near streets I recognized, where I could take shortcuts around the expressways. It was almost seven, and the September sun was close to the horizon, blinding me every time the road curved west.

I needed to run in the fresh air with my dogs. I wanted to blow Stateville out of my lungs and hair, then curl up with a drink and the Cubs-Cardinals game. But I had two reports to finish for my most important bread-and-butter client. Best swing by my office and get them done so I could enjoy the game.

Nothing warned me that my drive from Joliet was as relaxed as I was going to be for some time. When I tapped in the code at the entrance

4

to my building, everything looked normal. The lock mechanism released with a wheeze like a dying goose. Nothing unusual about that. I had to use my shoulder to shove the door open. Also normal.

It wasn't until I opened my own door that trouble hit me. I switched on the overhead lights. And saw every paper I owned on the floor. The file cabinets had been dumped, the drawers flung aside so that they perched at crazy angles. My ordnance maps dangled from the lips of their shelves.

'No,' I heard myself whisper. Who hated me so much they'd wreak this kind of fury against me?

I shivered, wrapping my arms across my chest. My office is a big barn with little rooms planted in it, little dollhouse rooms. Lots of places for someone to hide. I backed into the hall and carefully set down my briefcase, as if it were a carton of eggs that needed protecting. I pulled my cellphone out of my jacket pocket and dialed 911. Phone in hand, I tiptoed around the partitions.

The invaders had fled, but they'd vented their rage everywhere. I sidled into the back, saw my daybed had been tossed, the copy machine disassembled. I skirted the upended drawers and went behind the partition where my desk stood. Those drawers had been flung to the floor hard enough to crack the wood. The same violent hands had dismembered my reference manuals. Pages of the *Illinois Criminal Code* were strewn like remains of a victory parade. The frames of my mother's engraving of the Uffizi and my Nell Choate Jones print had been pried apart and splintered, the pictures lying under the shards of glass.

I squatted on my haunches and picked up the Uffizi, cradling it like a child. After a time, my frozen brain started to work. Don't touch stuff, just in case an evidence team takes it seriously.

And what about Tessa, my lease-mate? I crossed to the studio where Tessa welds big metal chunks into space-age sculptures, but everything there was in order. She must have been here this afternoon — a faint sour-sharp smell of solder lingered in the air. I sat at her drafting table, hands sweaty, heart pounding, all those signs of fear and anger, and waited there for the cops.

When I heard the siren, I went out front to meet them. A squad car pulled up, its strobes staining the twilit streets a ghostly blue. Two cops bounced out, a young woman and a middle-aged guy with a gut.

I stopped them at the entrance to show them the keypad. Someone who knew the combination had been here or someone with a sophisticated bypass device. The guy with the gut made a note. He asked how many people knew the code.

'My lease-mate. A couple of people who work for me. I don't know who Ms. Reynolds — my lease-mate — has given the combination.'

'What about the rear exit?' the woman asked.

I led them down the hall to the back door. It was self-locking, with no exterior keyhole or pad.

The woman shone her flashlight around the concrete slab outside the door.

I saw a white band on the slab — one of those rubber bracelets that the kids wear these days to show their support of everything from breast-cancer research to their college field-hockey teams. I knelt to pick it up, but I knew before I looked at it what it would say: ONE. When you looked at it, you were supposed to want to work for a planet unified in love, fighting AIDS and poverty as one. My cousin Petra owned a bracelet like this. It was big on her, and, when she was excited, it flew off her arm.

Petra. Petra here in this office while the tornado from hell whirled through it. My vision blurred, and I found myself sprawling on the concrete slab.

The two cops got me back on my feet, back inside, and asked me what I'd found.

'My cousin.' My mouth was dry, my voice a squawk. 'My cousin Petra. This is hers.'

Young, confident, beautiful Petra had come to Chicago fresh out of college to work as an intern on Brian Krumas's Senate campaign. For another moment, my brain stayed frozen. Then I remembered my video monitor. I have one because the front door is remote from my office and invisible from the hallway. My fingers trembled as I tried to boot up my computer. The modem had been yanked free from the port. The middle-aged cop stood over me while I found the wires and got my system hooked back together. I pushed the ON button. The Apple gave its opening chord, and I breathed a little prayer to the God I don't believe in. Saint Michael, patron of police and private eyes, get me my video files.

While the cops watched, I pulled up the images. My lease-mate had come in at 11:13 and left at 4:07.

Four-seventeen, while I was walking away from Johnny Merton, three people showed up, hats pulled low over their heads, coat collars hiked well up, faces and sexes both unrecognizable. They were all roughly the same height; in their bulky coats, it was hard to tell if they were all the same girth. I thought the one on the left was the stockiest, the one in the middle the thinnest, but I couldn't be sure. We could hear the buzzing as they rang the front door, and then one of them tapped in the door code.

'Who else knows that code?' the male cop demanded. 'Who besides the people you mentioned?'

'I — my cousin knew it.' I could hardly get the words out. 'I let her use my machine one night when she lost her Internet access.'

'Is she in this picture?' the woman asked.

I froze the image on the screen. A professional might be able to decode race or sex from these grainy pictures, but I couldn't make them out. I shrugged helplessly.

I called Petra's cellphone but only got her voice mail. I tried the Krumas campaign, but they'd shut down for the night.

The cops sprang into action, calling codes in — 44, 273, 60 — possible kidnapping, possible assault, possible aggravated burglary. The possibilities were endless and chilling. Squad and tac cars began pouring in while I made the hardest of all the phone calls: the one to my uncle Peter and his wife, Rachel, to tell them their oldest child had disappeared.

2

Wild Parent

'What did you do to her?' Peter grabbed my shoulders and shook me.

'Let go!' I snapped. 'This isn't the way — '

'Answer me, damn you!' He was hoarse, his face swollen with fury.

I tried twisting from his grasp — I didn't want to fight him — but he dug his hands deeper into my back. I kicked him on the shin, hard. He yelped, more from surprise than pain. His hold on me loosened, and I backed away. He lunged for me, but I ducked and moved farther back, rubbing my shoulders. My uncle was almost seventy, but his fingers still held the strength he'd gotten on the slaughterhouse floor in his teens.

The two dogs were making ominous noises in the back of their throats. Still gasping for breath, I put a hand on their shoulders: *Easy, Mitch. Easy, Peppy. Sit.* They had caught my anxiety and were yawning and mewling in worry.

'There's no call for you to carry on like that.' Mr. Contreras had risen to his feet when Peter attacked me. He was an old man himself, close to ninety, but he was ready to fling himself into battle. 'Vic here would never put your gal in harm's way. You can take it from me.'

Considering that Mr. Contreras had flung

10

accusations of his own at me when I reported Petra's disappearance, I was grateful that he was willing to support me in front of her parents.

'You, whoever you are, mind your own damned business.' My uncle was happy to have a fresh target to attack.

'Peter, yelling, this anger, it isn't going to help.'

Rachel spoke from the shadows behind the piano. Peter and Mr. Contreras and I were all startled. In the rage of the moment, we'd forgotten my aunt was there.

When I finally tracked her and Peter down the previous night, they were at a campsite in the Laurentian Mountains with their four younger daughters. It was Peter's secretary in Kansas City who got me the relevant phone numbers and arranged for the corporate jet to fly into Quebec City to pick up the family. Peter and Rachel drove all night to get to the airport. Ashland Meat's jet dropped Rachel and Peter at O'Hare and went on to Kansas City with the other daughters, where they would stay with Rachel's mother.

'Petra was pretty nervous the last few days,' I said to Rachel. 'She said nothing was bothering her, but I'm thinking now maybe this was weighing on her, this plan to let these thugs into my office.'

'Damn you,' Peter roared. 'Petra does not know thugs. You do. You're the one fucking around with the Anacondas, going out to Stateville to see Johnny Merton behind bars.'

'How do you know about Merton?' I was startled.

Rachel gave a strained, apologetic smile. 'Petra and I talk every day, sometimes three times a day. She told us about your meetings with this man in prison. It was interesting news to her.'

'And I heard about it from Harvey, too,' Peter snapped. 'He says Vic here disobeyed a direct order from a local judge to stop looking into the affairs of these old gangbangers.'

If I hadn't been so distraught myself, I would have laughed. 'Disobeyed a direct order? I'm not in the Army, Peter. That judge used to be my boss at the PD. He's afraid I'm going to make him look bad because he did a terrible job on an old case involving one of Johnny Merton's street soldiers.'

'So what if he did? One less gang member on the street for any reason is all to the good.'

'But, Vic, how can you be sure it was Petra in your office last night?' Rachel said.

She'd asked the question before, but she was so worried she kept forgetting the answer. I explained again about finding her daughter's bracelet outside the back door.

'And, yes, it could have belonged to someone else, but I don't think so.'

'Even if it was hers, what makes you think she opened the door?' Peter demanded. 'Maybe it was that sculptor who shares the building. How do you know she isn't connected to some mob operation?'

I opened and shut my mouth several times but didn't speak. Tessa Reynolds is African-American, and I didn't want to find out that her race was driving my uncle's wild suggestion.

12

She's also African-American aristocracy, her mother a famous lawyer, her father a highly successful engineer. They worry that I'm dragging Tessa down into the mud, the cases I get and the people who show up at the building. I'd already had an anxious call from Tessa's mother after last night's break-in made the late news.

I was too tired, and too confused, to pursue that line of thinking. Instead, I booted up my laptop. I'd e-mailed myself the camera footage that showed the trio who'd come into my office yesterday afternoon. Now I showed the images to Rachel and Peter.

'Does any of them look like Petra to you?'

'Of course not!' Peter stomped away from the machine and pulled out his cellphone. 'This is a fucking waste of time. Why are we even sitting here, letting Vic spin us around in circles? She's just trying to get off the hook for putting Petey in harm's way.'

Rachel shook her head; tears were slowly welling and falling along her nose. 'That's Petra in the middle.'

'How can you be sure? Of all the — '

'Peter, it's the Crocodile Dundee hat and outback oilcloth coat she got in Melbourne. She was so proud of them. Even in this picture, I can tell.' She looked at me through her wet lashes. 'Vic, someone must have forced her to do this. We're meeting with Special Agent Hatfield at the FBI in an hour. Give me some names, some people the FBI can talk to.'

'Yeah, cookie,' Mr. Contreras put in. 'This

13

ain't the time to hold your cards close to your chest, the way you like to do.'

'Have you talked to her college roommate, to Kelsey?' I asked. 'I don't know her last name, but she's the person Petra talks about most.'

'Kelsey Ingalls. She called me when she saw the news online this morning. She said she'd tried calling Petra — we all have, and we keep getting rolled over to her voice mail.' Rachel's voice quavered. 'Vic, there must be someone you've talked to who can lead the FBI or the police to Petra. Please, *please* tell me their names.'

I shook my head helplessly. 'My apartment was trashed a few nights ago, and I did wonder if a cop, ex-cop, named Alito had been involved, but I don't have any real reason to suspect him. Other than that, Johnny Merton, the head of the Anacondas, if he was mad enough at me he might do anything, but I was talking to him when this was going on. He didn't lose his cool with me until the end of the meeting.'

Peter seized on Johnny and the Anacondas. If Peter had known I was working with violent criminals, he'd never have let Petra come within twenty miles of me.

'I understand,' I said, when he'd shouted himself hoarse. 'But look at the times recorded on my door monitor. It looks as though Petra was waiting for Tessa — my lease-mate, the sculptor, you know — for her to leave. There's a ten-minute gap. Tessa leaves, Petra types in the code and goes in with those two punks.'

'Vic, coincidences happen,' Rachel said, trying

14

to stay calm. 'How would Petra know people like that? She just graduated from college in May, she's never lived in Chicago, she's been working in an office downtown with a bunch of other twenty-somethings. She's just a suburban Midwest girl who's never seen a criminal in her life and wouldn't recognize one if she did. I'm not saying it's your fault, but you're the one who knows gangsters and people like that. Not Petra. Please, *please* turn your files over to the FBI or to Bobby Mallory. They can look into everyone you've been talking to.'

'Bobby came to my office last night,' I said.

He had pushed his way past the cops filling the entryway and found me underneath my desk, trying to see if anything else of my cousin had been discarded there along with her bracelet. Despite the many good women who have worked for him in the last fifteen years, my presence at a crime scene still gives him heartburn.

'There you are, Vicki. One of the boys who's smarter than he looks saw your last name on a sheet and brought it to me. Who's Petra, Peter's kid? What insane business did you involve her in? Does Peter know? He'll turn your guts into sausage casing if you hurt his kid.'

'Not guilty, Bobby,' I said wearily, crawling out. 'She's working on the Krumas campaign. I don't know why she came here or who she let in.'

I showed him the video footage and explained how she'd happened to have my front-door combination. He frowned over the photos, then demanded of the patrol units if they'd done

15

anything to get the footage over to a video-technology team.

Once Bobby showed up, the tempo of the investigation accelerated. Aggressive cops became subdued and helpful, lethargic ones became energetic, and an evidence team magically appeared and began dusting the whole mess for prints, blood, any trace of anything. Bobby called the FBI, in case it was a kidnapping; they sent a special agent over around eleven, and I had to answer useless questions all over again.

In the middle of it all, I started getting calls from reporters, and a television crew parked outside my office. Brian Krumas himself called while I was talking to the FBI's special agent. The candidate was at a high-end fundraiser in Hollywood, but of course his staff had heard about Petra's disappearance. Krumas talked to Bobby and then to me.

'You're Petra's cousin, right? We met at the Navy Pier event, didn't we? I'm giving you my private number, Vic, and I want you to call me the instant you have any news of her, okay?'

I copied the number into my PDA and went back to the FBI. No matter how mediagenic you are yourself — and Brian Krumas was being touted as a glamorous new Bobby Kennedy — disappearing blond twenty-somethings are national news, and you need to do damage control.

When I finally got home, I didn't sleep much. I kept jolting awake, trying not to imagine what could be happening to Petra, trying instead to think of places I should look for her, and

16

wondering who she had invited into my office.

'You shouldn't be talking to a lowlife like Johnny Merton, anyway,' Mr. Contreras said. 'I been telling you that since the first time you drove out there, but no one except you ever knows right from wrong. The rest of us are too ignorant to have opinions. And now you've got Petra in trouble.'

'I know just how many counts Merton was charged with. It wouldn't surprise me one bit to know he had my girl kidnapped and forced her to open your office,' Peter roared, swinging around the room to put his nose almost against mine. 'If any harm comes to her because of you, whatever it is, I will inflict it on you tenfold. Do you hear me?'

I stood very still, not speaking. If harm came to Petra because of me, I didn't think I could live with myself anyway, but her father's wild rage was impossible to respond to. His phone rang, and he finally backed away from me to answer it.

I turned to face Rachel. 'You go see Derek Hatfield. He's a good field agent.'

'What will you do?' she asked.

'I'm putting my own best agent on the case,' I said bleakly.

My best agent had been unable to find Lamont Gadsden. My best agent had left a trail of desolation at the Mighty Waters Freedom Center. I hoped she could do a better job looking for Petra.

3

No Good Deed Remains Unpunished

Lamont Gadsden and my cousin Petra. It was hard to imagine two people with less in common: an old buddy of Hammer Merton's from Chicago's South Side, a Millennium Gen text messager from an upscale Kansas City suburb. If it hadn't been for me, and some terrible luck, their lives would never have collided.

Petra being my cousin, it wasn't surprising that she looked for me when she showed up in Chicago at the start of the summer, a fresh-minted college graduate with an internship in her daddy's hometown.

It was sheer luck, the bad kind, that I agreed to look for Lamont Gadsden. Sometimes when I want someone to blame, someone outside my family, I snarl unfairly at a homeless guy named Elton Grainger.

Elton was the unwitting deus ex machina who led me into the Gadsden morass. Elton had been working my street off and on for several years. I knew him to say 'Hey' to. I bought *Streetwise* from him, bought coffee or sandwiches for him from time to time. Once, during a blizzard, I'd offered him shelter in my office, but he turned me down. Then, one golden June afternoon, he collapsed in front of my office.

If I'd let him lie, maybe Petra would never have vanished, maybe Sister Frankie would still be alive. There's a lesson in that about the fate that awaits the Good Samaritan.

It happened as I was tapping in the code to my office building.

'Vic, where you been? I haven't seen you in weeks! You're looking good.' He flourished a copy of *Streetwise*. 'New issue today.'

'I've been in Italy.' I fumbled in my wallet for the U.S. money that still looked weird to me. 'My first true vacation in fifteen years. It's hard to be back.'

'Foreign travel. I got all that out of my system at nineteen when Uncle Sam paid my airfare to Saigon.'

I pulled out a five, and Elton fell to the sidewalk. I dropped keys and papers and knelt next to him. He'd hit his head as he went down and was bleeding in an ugly way, but he was breathing, and I could feel his pulse in an irregular, feathery beat, like some fragile ballerina dancing against the music.

The next few hours were a blur of ambulance, emergency room, hospital admissions. They wanted a lot of details, but I didn't know him except as the homeless guy who'd worked this stretch of West Town the last several years. About the only personal thing he'd told me was that he'd lost his wife as his drinking got heavier. He'd never mentioned children. Today was the first time I'd heard about Vietnam. He'd been a carpenter and sometimes still got daywork. As for health care, I couldn't help the hospital with

19

their paperwork. He was homeless. I hoped he had a green card for city health services, but I had no way of knowing.

I wanted to get back to my office — I'd been away ten weeks and had an entire Himalayan range of paper waiting for me — but I didn't feel easy leaving Elton until there was some kind of prognosis or resolution in his care. In the end, it took two hours before an intern who was stretched to the breaking point came in, and that was only because I kept going to the triage nurse and pushing Elton's case: his crisis, asking for oxygen, heart monitoring, something. He had regained consciousness while lying on the gurney, but his skin was cold and waxy, and his pulse was still very weak.

A white woman in her early thirties, who seemed to be caring for an elderly black man, gave me a wry smile the third time I went up to the counter. 'It's hard, isn't it? The staffing cutbacks have been too steep. They just can't keep up with the patient load.'

I nodded. 'I just got back from a long stay in Europe yesterday. I haven't adjusted — to the time zone or our health-care system.'

'Is he your brother?' She pointed toward Elton's gurney.

'He's a homeless guy who collapsed in front of my building.'

The woman pursed her soft rosebud mouth. 'Would you like me to look in on him if they manage to stabilize him? I have friends at some of the homeless agencies here in town.'

I agreed thankfully. Finally the intern, who

20

didn't look old enough for high school let alone an inner-city hospital, came over to the gurney. He asked Elton some questions about his drinking and smoking and sleeping. He listened to Elton's heart and called for an EKG, an EEG, and an echocardiogram. And oxygen.

'He's got some arrhythmia going on,' the intern told me. 'We'll see how serious it is. If he's homeless and drinking, it takes a toll.'

Elton smiled at me and pressed my fingers weakly with nicotine-stained fingers. 'You run on, Vic. I'll be okay here. Thanks for — you know, God bless, all that.'

He produced a grubby green card from an inner pocket, so I knew they wouldn't put him straight out on the street. I caught a cab back to my office and put Elton — not out of my mind, but to the bottom of it. I was exhausted from travel, but I'd been away too long to give myself decompression time before returning to work.

I'd been in Italy, with Morrell, where we'd rented a cottage in Umbria, in the hill country, near my mother's childhood home. Morrell had finally recovered from the bullets that almost killed him in the Khyber Pass two years earlier. He wanted to test his legs, see if he was ready for journalism's front lines — he was aching to return to Afghanistan — despite the death of some three hundred journalists in Iraq and Afghanistan since we began our endless war.

My needs were even more personal: I'd grown up speaking Italian with my mother, but I'd never visited her home. I wanted to meet relatives, I wanted to listen to music where

21

Gabriella had learned it, see paintings in their Umbrian and Tuscan light, drink Torgiano in the hills where the grapes grew.

Morrell and I visited the remnants of Gabriella's family, elderly Catholic cousins who exclaimed how much like Gabriella I looked but who wouldn't talk about the years she'd had to live in hiding with her father, an Italian Jew. They claimed not to remember my grandfather, who had been denounced and sent to Auschwitz the day after someone smuggled Gabriella to the coast and a Cuba-bound freighter.

No one knew what had become of Gabriella's younger brother, Moselio. Gabriella herself hadn't heard from him since he joined the partisans in 1943, and I hadn't been optimistic. My mother's been dead a long time, but I still miss her. I was hoping for too much from her Pitigliano family.

Morrell and I toured the Siena Opera House, where Gabriella had performed her only professional singing role, Iphigenia, in Jommelli's opera, thanks to which I have the most insane middle name in Chicago. We even met a frail diva, now almost ninety, who remembered Gabriella from their student days together in the conservatory. *'Una voce com'una campana dorata.'* A voice like a golden bell, as I knew: Gabriella used to fill our five-room bungalow in South Chicago to the bursting point when she sang.

When she arrived in Chicago, a poor, clueless immigrant, Gabriella answered an advertisement for a singer in a Milwaukee Avenue bar, where the backroom boys tried to take off her clothes while she sang 'Non *mi dir, bell'idol mio.*'

My dad had rescued her from that, my dad wandering in for a beer in the middle of a scorching July afternoon and pulling her away from the groping hands of the bar manager. My father had been a Chicago cop, a kind and gentle man who adored my mother from that day forward.

Looking at the Baroque cupids holding up a plaster banner in the Siena Opera, I felt the gulf between the stage and the music, where Gabriella began her life, and the bungalow in the middle of the steel mills where she ended it. How could my father and I have ever been enough to make up for all that Italy's racial laws forced her to renounce?

That part of the trip had been difficult, but when we left Siena, and Pitigliano, Morrell and I spent a pleasant two months together. It became clear to us both, though, that this trip marked the farewell tour of our affair. We had thought when we planned this vacation that it would deepen our relationship. Since we worked at unusual jobs that kept us from home for long stretches, we'd never spent concentrated time together. As the time came for Morrell to catch his train to Rome and the direct flight to Islamabad, we both realized we were ready to say good-bye.

I flew home from Milan a few days later, sad, wondering what it was that had kept Morrell and me from a deeper, tighter bond. Was I too messy or Morrell too compulsively tidy? Maybe I was too prickly, as some of my friends suggested, for anyone to get close to me. Or maybe, ultimately, each of us reserved our deepest commitments for work. Morrell's career as a journalist covering international human-rights issues looked so much more glamorous than my own, so much more deserving of a deep commitment. After all, I spend my time looking at frauds and sleazy con artists.

That thought depressed me, too, as I left Elton at the hospital and rode a cab back to my office. When the cab reached the rehabbed warehouse I share with my sculpting friend, I had to remind myself again that I was back in America — this time, over the issue of tips, which are never as big in Europe as they need to be here. I took a breath and typed in the code on the keypad at the door. Elton's crisis was over, my vacation was over.

I unlocked my inner-office door. Amy Blount, a young history Ph.D. who's done research projects for me in the past, had organized my documents so rigorously that they just about saluted when I opened the door. The trouble was, there were too damned many of them. My whole worktable was covered with neatly labeled papers, while my desk held a stack of the most urgent papers.

While I was away, I only went to an Internet café twice a week to check for messages. Amy held down the fort for me, handling small projects and responding to routine inquiries. We spoke only when something came up that she couldn't handle.

Right before I came home, Amy suddenly

found an academic position; she'd been looking for three years. She had to leave for Buffalo in a hurry to start the summer term. She'd organized my papers, and left a pot of crimson gerbera daisies, a little wilted from their time alone but a gallant splash of color in my cavernous space.

This afternoon, I poured water into the daisies and pretended to be interested in the mountain range of files on my big, long worktable. Unfortunately, on top of the highest peak stood my credit-card bills. Pay within ten days to avoid loss of credit rating, a kidney, or any hope of filling your car again.

I looked at the AmEx bill out of the corner of my eye, as if that would make it smaller. The dying U.S. dollar meant I definitely should not have cheered myself with those Lario boots the day before I left Milan. Or that Antonella Mason acrylic Morrell and I found on a side trip to Treviso.

I made a face and forced myself to start digging. Fast turnaround on my own past-due invoices had to be my first priority. I put in a call to a temporary agency to find someone to help, and started returning the stack of my most crucial phone calls: those from clients with real money to spend.

A little before five, I had to stop. My body thought it was midnight, and I was starting to forget who I was talking to, or what language I was speaking, in the middle of complicated sentences.

I was putting a few files in my briefcase — the pessimist says the case is half full, the optimist that she'll read them over supper — when the outer bell rang. I have a surveillance camera at the door so that I don't have to run down the hall every time the UPS man is delivering a ton of steel to my lease-mate. I looked at the image on my computer screen.

It's not a sophisticated system, but I thought I recognized the young woman I'd seen at the hospital earlier today with Elton. Elton! I'd completely forgotten him. My stomach tightened. Had she come to deliver bad news in person? I pushed the lock release and moved hurriedly down the hall to greet her.

When I asked about Elton, she took my hand reassuringly. 'No, no. He seems to be okay. I talked to him for a bit this afternoon. He's a vet, Vietnam, so he can be moved to the VA. He'll get better care there.'

I thanked her for coming around in person to tell me, assuming Elton had given her my office address.

She smiled in embarrassment. 'I didn't come on his account, I'm afraid. But he told me you're a detective, and you seem like the kind of person I need.'

Oh, boy. I do a good deed and I get a client. Who says we have to wait for our reward in heaven? When I ushered her into my office, she stood hesitantly in the doorway, looking around, the way people do whose ideas of private eyes are taken from Humphrey Bogart and James Ellroy movies.

'What is it you need detecting, Ms. — ?'

'Lennon. Karen Lennon. It isn't for me but

one of my old ladies.' She sat on the couch and clasped her hands together on one plump knee. 'I'm a chaplain. I work in the Beth Israel system and am assigned to Lionsgate Manor — it's an assisted-living facility that Beth Israel runs — and my clients are mostly old and mostly women. One of my ladies, her son is missing. She and her sister, they're the ones who raised him, they need to find him, it's the only way they can be at peace before they die. I've been trying to figure out what I could do to help them. When I saw how compassionate you were with that homeless man and found out you were a detective, I thought I could probably trust you to treat my ladies right.'

'You know, not to turn down work, but the police have a whole department devoted to missing persons.'

'My ladies are African-American and very old,' Karen said. 'They have bad memories of the police. A private detective wouldn't carry all that baggage, in their eyes.'

'I don't work for free, the way the cops would,' I said. 'Or the Salvation Army — they have a service.'

'The Army says Miss Ella's son's been missing too long for them to do much for her, although they did file a report.' She hesitated. 'She's living on her small Social Security check, didn't get a pension after all her years screwing gizmos together for the phone company. I looked you up online and saw the voluntary organizations you serve — women's shelters, rape crisis, reproductive rights — I thought you probably would do

27

pro bono work if the people were in dire need.'

My lips tightened. 'I *sometimes* do pro bono work but not on missing persons, especially not a person who's been missing for a long time. How long has it been, anyway, that the Salvation Army balked at searching?'

'I don't know the details.' Karen Lennon looked at her hands. She wasn't a skilled liar. She knew, and she thought I wouldn't take the case if she told me. 'Anyway, Miss Ella can explain it to you better than me. Her life's been so hard, and it would ease the last stage of her journey if she saw someone was willing to help her out.'

'Someone will have to come up with money for my fee,' I said firmly. 'Even if I don't charge my full rate, which is a hundred fifty an hour, I cannot afford to pour time and money down a sinkhole in this economy. Does Lionsgate Manor have any kind of discretionary funds you can draw on?'

My old friend Lotty Herschel is the leading perinatologist at Beth Israel. We were having dinner later this evening. I could ask her, both about Karen Lennon and this Lionsgate Manor and whether Beth Israel might cough up money for a good cause. If it was, in fact, a good cause.

'Maybe if you have a conversation with Miss Ella, you can steer her toward a place she could afford.' Karen sidestepped my suggestion. 'What harm can one meeting do you?'

4

Helluva Client

Over dinner with Lotty, I told her about my rescue of Elton and Karen Lennon's appearance in my life.

'Max knows more about the hospital's subsidiaries and their staffs than I do,' she said when I asked what she knew about Karen Lennon and Lionsgate.

Max Loewenthal, Lotty's longtime friend and lover, was executive director of Beth Israel Hospital and on the board of their holding company. Lotty called me the next day with his response. 'Lennon sits on Beth Israel's ethics committee. Max says she's very young, but he thinks she has good judgment. As for your other question, do we have a discretionary fund, we have all kinds of odd funds for odd purposes but none to pay for private detectives to find the missing children of residents in our facilities. You'll have to decide on your own what to do about that, my dear.'

I could have — should have — let Karen Lennon and her old ladies lie, but, after all, Lennon had stepped in to help with Elton. Three days later, when I found a free hole in my schedule, I drove out Roosevelt Road, past the gargantuan buildings the South Side hospital behemoths were erecting, to Lionsgate's tired manor. It was a fifteen-story building, with a locked ward on the top two floors for Alzheimer's and dementia patients, and a variety of apartments and nursing wards underneath. What a grim way to live, knowing the elevator might one day loft you skyward and only bring you down again in a box.

The security guard at the entrance directed me to Karen Lennon's office. The place was so labyrinthine that I got lost a couple of times and had to stop for directions. At least everyone I asked seemed to know who the chaplain was, which meant she was doing a good job of covering her parish.

Lionsgate Manor was clean, but its last overhaul lay a long way in the past. The paint on the walls was chipped, and you could see where walkers and canes had pounded dents in the cracked linoleum flooring. Only a few hall lights were burned out or missing, but management used the lowest wattage possible, so even on a bright summer day the air was a dingy green, making me feel as though I were at the bottom of a dirty ocean.

When I finally reached Lennon's office, she was talking to an older woman, a staff member, but she finished the conversation quickly and got up to escort me to Ella Gadsden's apartment.

I mentioned Max Loewenthal's name to the chaplain as we rode the elevator, and her face brightened. 'So many executive directors are too focused on profit. Max remembers that the hospital only exists because it has a mission to care for human suffering.'

30

We got off on the ninth floor. Lennon led me briskly down the hall. As we went, the pastor warned me that Miss Ella's manner could seem brusque. 'Don't let that put you off. She's been through a lot, as I said at your office, and she puts on a tough veneer for protection.'

Karen Lennon knocked on the apartment door. After several minutes, after we heard the heavy thumping of someone who walked with a cane and the scrape of locks being undone, the door opened.

Miss Ella was a tall woman, and, despite the cane, she held herself ramrod straight. Home alone in the middle of the afternoon, she still wore stockings and a severely cut navy dress.

'This is Ms. Warshawski, Miss Ella. She's here to talk with you about your son.'

Miss Ella inclined her head a fraction of an inch but ignored my outstretched hand.

'Call and let me know how you get on.' Karen Lennon let the comment float between Miss Ella and me. After a few questions about 'Miss Claudia's' condition, the chaplain trotted back down the hall.

I got off to a rocky start as soon as I walked in. The room was tiny and crammed with the mementos of Miss Ella's life — tables and shelves stuffed with Hummel figurines, china vases, glass animals, a large bronze head of Martin Luther King, Jr.. I knocked against a teetery table and rattled a tableau of china gazelles and zebras. Nothing fell, but Miss Ella muttered 'Hmmpf,' adding, 'Bull in a china shop,' in a loud undervoice. Only a small round

31

table near the kitchenette was free of breakables, but it held Miss Ella's workbasket, an enormous wicker affair that sprouted knitting needles like porcupine quills.

Martin Luther King, Jr.'s and Barack Obama's portraits hung on either side of the wall-mounted television, framed religious texts stood among the figurines. '*During your times of suffering and trial, when you see only one set of footprints, it was then I carried you,*' I read, and '*Try to live each day He sends / To serve my gracious Master's ends.*'

The messages seemed incongruous with Miss Ella's bitter mouth and harsh tone, but maybe when she was home alone she was softer, more malleable. She motioned me to a wooden chair next to the porcupine quills and pulled up a second hard chair to face me. When I tried to help her, she gave me a look that could have slit upholstery and told me to sit.

The first few minutes, she only offered the briefest answers to my questions:

I hear you're looking for your son.
Yes.
What is his name?
Lamont Emmanuel Gadsden.
How old is he?
Sixty-one.
'*When did you last see him, Ms. Gadsden?*'
'*January twenty-fifth, 1967.*'

I was startled into silence. No wonder Karen Lennon hadn't wanted to tell me. That was more than a long time to be missing. It was two lifetimes.

Finally I asked if Miss Ella had looked for him at the time he went missing. She nodded grimly but didn't volunteer anything further.

I tried not to sigh out loud. 'How did you search for him then?'

'We talked to his friends. They said he just disappeared.' Her jaws clamped shut, but she pried them open after a moment to add, 'I didn't approve of those friends. It was a hard job to go to them, and they weren't respectful, but I don't think they were lying.'

'And you filed a missing persons report in 1967?'

'We went to the police.' She pronounced the word to emphasize the first syllable: *poh*-leese. 'There we were, two Christians in our Sunday best, and they treated us like we were darkies in a minstrel show.'

'My dad was a cop,' I blurted out.

'What's that supposed to mean?' Miss Ella's jaws worked around her false teeth, as if they were cud. 'That the police are fine, honest men who stand up and say, 'Yes, ma'am,' when a black woman comes into the station looking for help?'

'No, ma'am, of course not,' I said quietly. 'I suppose I thought you should know up front, in case you found out later and thought I was hiding something from you.'

Miss Ella's lips tightened into well-rehearsed lines of bitterness. Not that she didn't have reason: I could imagine the scene, the South Side district station in 1967, when crude racial slurs were part of life and most of the cops were

33

white. But my dad hadn't been like that. It always gets my hackles up when people dismiss all cops as pigs or brutes. Still, it's not a good policy to argue with the client.

'You say 'we.' Was that you and your husband?'

'My sister and me. She came to live with me after my husband passed, when Lamont was thirteen, and I've always said that was when Lamont started to stray — she indulged the boy so much that he lost his sense of direction. But that's water over the dam. My sister is ill now, too ill to live long, and it's a wish dear to her to know what happened to Lamont. That's the only reason I'm opening that box after all this time. Pastor Karen said you come highly recommended.' Nothing in Miss Ella's voice betrayed that she placed any confidence in Karen Lennon's words.

'Very kind of her. Did she tell you about my fee structure?'

Miss Ella pushed herself to her feet. She moved slowly through the maze of furniture to a sideboard. With an audible groan, she bent to open a door and pulled out a small lockbox. She extracted a key from a chain around her neck and unlocked the box.

'My sister's life insurance. It has a face value of ten thousand dollars. When she passes, I will pay you out of what doesn't get spent on her funeral. Unless, of course, you find Lamont. Then the money is his to do with what he wishes.'

She held the policy out for me to read the declarations page. Ajax Insurance had issued it to Claudia Marie Ardenne. Lamont Emmanuel Gadsden was her legatee and Ella Anastasia Ardenne Gadsden his successor. It was a horrible moment, the sense of being a ghoul waiting to feast on her sister's remains. I almost turned around and walked out, but something in my prospective client's face made me think she was hoping for such a reaction, or at least hoping to make me uncomfortable enough to waive my fee.

I pulled out a notebook and started taking down such skimpy details as she could offer: the name of the pastor at her church when Lamont was a child. His high school physics teacher, who thought Lamont had promise and ought to go to college.

'What about his friends?' I asked. 'The ones you didn't approve of?'

'I don't remember their names. It's been forty years.'

'You know how it is, Miss Ella, these things sometimes come back to us in the middle of the night.' I smiled limpidly to show that I knew she was lying. 'In case they do, you can write them down and call me. And the day you last saw him, what was he doing, where was he going?'

'It was at the dinner table. He didn't often come home at dinner-time, but there he was, eating bean soup and reading the paper. We got an evening paper then, and he was reading through it while my sister and I were talking. And suddenly he flung down the paper and headed for the door without a by-your-leave.

'"Is that what you do? Eat and not even say

thank you for the meal?'' I asked. Claudia always thought I was too harsh with Lamont, but I didn't see why a boy couldn't learn manners in this life. He didn't have a job, and there Claudia and I were, me screwing parts together at the phone plant, Claudia cleaning up after spoiled white folks, and Lamont thinking we lived to wait on him!'

She paused, breathing hard, reliving the resentments that hadn't eased for being forty years old. 'So that night, when I said what I said, he kissed his fingers to me and passed some sarcastic comment on the 'delightful repast' before going out the door, just wearing that thin jacket, the kind all those hotshot boys sported in those days. The next day was the big storm, you know. When he didn't come home, I thought he must have taken shelter somewhere. That jacket wasn't enough to carry him through a blizzard.'

Oh yes, the big storm of 'sixty-seven. I'd been ten then, and it seemed like a winter fairyland to me. Two feet of snow fell; drifts rose to the height of buildings. The blizzard briefly covered the yellow stains that the steel mills left on our car and house, painting everything a dazzling white. For adults, it had been a nightmare. My dad was stuck at the station for the better part of two days while my mother and I struggled to clean the walks and get to a grocery store. Of course, the mills didn't shut down, and within a day the mounds of snow looked dirty, old, dreary.

'It was only later we got worried.' Miss Ella's harsh voice brought me back to her living room.

36

'Later, when we could get out and about, and, by then, we couldn't find anyone who had seen him.'

It was when I asked for a photograph that Miss Ella seemed startled. I was surprised, actually, that among all the framed slogans and pictures of Dr. King, Malcolm X, and other black leaders, that I hadn't seen any family pictures at all.

'Why do you need one?'

'If I'm going to look for him, I need to know what he looked like forty years ago. I can scan it and age it, see what he might look like at sixty.'

Miss Ella returned to the sideboard and fumbled inside for a photo album. She looked through it slowly and finally took out a shot of a young black man in yellow graduation robes. His hair was cropped close to his head in the style of those pre-Afro days. He stared seriously at the camera, his eyes hard and bleak.

'That was when he graduated high school. Even though he'd started down a wrong road, I made him stay in school until he was done. The rest are all just baby pictures and such. I want this back, and I want it back in the same condition it is today.'

I slipped it into a plastic sleeve and put it in a file folder. I told her I'd return it at the end of the week, after I'd made some copies and preliminary inquiries.

'But I don't want your sister to imagine this will be easy. I never guarantee results. And, in this case, we may end up with too many dead ends for you to want to continue.'

'But you expect me to pay you even if you don't find him.'

I smiled brightly. 'Just as your pastor expects to be paid even if she can't save your soul.'

She eyed me narrowly. 'And how will I know you're not cheating her? My sister, I mean? And me?'

I nodded. She had a right to know. 'I'll give you a written report. You, or Pastor Karen, can do some spot-checking to see if I've done what I claim I did. But until you give me the names of your son's friends, there's very little I can do.'

When I left a minute later, I heard all the bolts on the door snap shut in reverse order. I stood in the hallway, already depressed by the inquiry.

In the Detective's Absence I

'Hi, Miss Ella. Your sister spent an hour in her chair today. We're going to see if she can get to her feet tomorrow,' the nurse's aide said brightly. 'Have you come to give her her supper? She's tired after working so hard on her therapies today.'

Miss Ella nodded but didn't answer. Claudia, the family beauty: it was harsh to see her like this. Was it a judgment on them, Claudia lying in bed, hardly able to move or talk, wearing diapers like a great big baby? Pastor Hebert would have said so, but Pastor Karen didn't agree. Pastor Karen said God wasn't an angry old man handing out punishments like an overseer or a prison warden.

'But it feels like it, Lord,' Miss Ella murmured, not realizing she had spoken aloud until the aide said, 'What was that, Miss Ella?'

It seemed to happen more and more these days, that she spoke out loud without realizing it. Not a crime, or even a sin, just a nuisance, one of the many of growing old.

The aide carried a tray of mushy food into Claudia's room. The television was on, as if grown women needed to have babble shouted at them twenty-four hours a day. The woman who shared the room with Claudia was rubbing the end of her blanket between her fingers, staring vacantly ahead. Claudia herself was asleep, her breath coming out in fast little snorts. Her hair hadn't been washed, Miss Ella noted grimly, preparing her list of complaints for the head of the ward. That black hair, how it bounced and flipped when Claudia was young, all the way into middle age, really, before it started to go gray and she'd cut it short. She'd let it turn into an Afro, a crown of soft gray curls, while Ella adhered to a life of iron discipline, giving her head over to chemicals and hot irons every month.

Ella sat on her sister's left side, where she still had feeling and movement. Claudia's right hand looked soft, young, the hand of the beautiful girl Ella had been so jealous of all those years back, but her left hand was as knotted and gnarled with age as Ella's own.

'The detective came today,' Ella said. 'She took a picture of Lamont away with her, she'll talk to people, she'll ask questions. Does that make you happy?'

Claudia squeezed Ella's hand: yes, thank you, that makes me happy.

'Maybe she'll even find our boy. And then what?'

''Ate 'n' 'ear,' Claudia spoke with difficulty. ''Ate 'n' 'ear al'ays wron', Ellie. 'Ill e-d-estroy 'ou.'

She had trouble making her lips move to form consonants. The speech therapist made her work on them during the day, but alone with her sister at night she relaxed and did what came easiest.

40

Hate and fear. Always wrong, will destroy you. Ella knew she was saying that because she'd said it so many times in the eighty-five years of their life together. Pastor Karen thought some special gift of empathy lay between Ella and Claudia that helped Ella understand her sister, but it was only habit. She cranked Claudia up in bed and helped her eat a little meatloaf, a few spoonfuls of mashed potatoes, a bite of garish Jell-O.

''Ank 'ou, Ellie.' Claudia lay down, and Ella sat with her until her sister slid away from her into sleep.

5

It's a Bird ... It's a Plane ...
No! It's Supercousin!

Traffic's become like Mark Twain's old bromide: we all whine about it, but no one tries to fix it. Even me: I complain about the congestion and then keep driving myself everywhere. Trouble is, Chicago's public transportation is so abysmal, I'd never have time to sleep if I tried to cover my client base by bus and El. As it was, my trip home took over forty minutes, not counting a stop for groceries, and I only had to go seven miles.

When I'd squeezed my car in between a shiny Nissan Pathfinder and a boxy Toyota Scion, I couldn't summon the energy to get out. As soon as I went inside, my downstairs neighbor and the two dogs would leap on me, all eager for company and two of them eager for exercise.

'A run will do me good.' I repeated the mantra, but couldn't persuade myself to move. Instead, I stared at the trees through the Mustang's open sunroof.

In June, summer comes even to the heart of a great city. Even to the world of the steel mills, where I grew up. The light and warmth of spring always fill me with nostalgia, perhaps more this year because I'd been immersed so recently in my mother's childhood.

After seeing the rich green hills in Umbria, I understood why my mother kept trying to create a Mediterranean garden under the grit of the mills. By July, the leaves, including her camellia, would be dead-looking, coated with sulfur and smoke, but each spring the trees put out hopeful tendrils. This year, it will be different. Maybe the same would be true of my forebodings about my new client. This time, events would prove my pessimism false.

When I'd left Miss Ella's apartment, I stopped at Karen Lennon's office. Miss Ella had signed a contract agreeing to a thousand dollars' worth of investigation — essentially, two full days at half price — to be paid in installments, with seventy-five dollars in cash in advance as a retainer.

A passing nurse's aide told me Karen was making pastoral calls in New Manor's skilled-nursing wing. I sat on a scarred plastic chair in her office for almost an hour; my other choice was an armchair whose springs sank almost to the floor. I wasn't idle: I studied Pastor Karen's books: *Pastoral Theology in African-American Context, Feminist & Womanist Pastoral Theology.* I read a few pages, but when Karen still hadn't shown up I answered phone calls and did an Internet search for a different client, a high-paying law firm. I hate cruising the Net on a handheld — the screen's too small, and it takes forever to load text — but Karen Lennon's computer needed a password to get online.

When Karen finally returned, she was in a hurry, ready to pack up and get out of the building. She tried to give me a welcoming pastoral smile, but she clearly wasn't ecstatic at my demands for time and information, so I said I'd follow her to the parking garage.

'Did you know that Lamont Gadsden hasn't been seen for forty years when you asked me out here?' I asked as she locked her office door. 'Was that why you were so cagey with me?'

Karen Lennon was still very young. Her soft cheeks flushed, and she bit her lips. 'I was afraid you'd say no outright. It's so long ago. My own mother was only a teenager then.'

It rattled me to realize her mother and I were almost the same age. 'Why did Miss Ella wait so long to make inquiries?'

'She didn't!' Karen stopped in the middle of the building's lobby, her hazel eyes large and earnest. 'They asked questions of Lamont's friends at the time, they went to the police, who treated them with total racist contempt. They figured there was nothing else they could do.'

'They?' I said. 'That was Miss Ella and her sister Claudia, right? I told Miss Ella I needed to see her sister and she refused. She grudged every sentence she spoke to me. What is she trying to hide?'

'Oh, Vic, I don't know why Miss Ella didn't tell you, but Miss Claudia had a stroke right at Easter. It's hard for her to talk, and, when she does get some words out, her speech is terribly slurry. Miss Ella's the only person who can understand her completely, although I'm getting better at it. It's been since her stroke that Miss Claudia's become obsessed with this search.

44

Miss Ella tried to talk her out of it because of how long it's been and how little hope there is of learning anything, but Miss Claudia wouldn't rest until her sister promised to find Lamont. Try to find him, anyway. Are you going to look for him?'

I pursed my lips. 'I'll do what I can, but there aren't many avenues to follow. And Miss Ella isn't helping by refusing to give me any names of people who knew her son.'

'I can help with that,' Lennon said eagerly. 'She isn't very trustful with strangers. But I've been here fourteen months now, and she's come to realize she can rely on me.'

'Then maybe you're the one who should try to find Lamont,' I said nastily.

Her rosebud mouth opened in dismay, but she said quietly, 'I would, if I had your skills. I told you I Googled you after we met at the hospital. Your press makes you sound more progressive than maybe you really are. It's why I went out of my way to help your friend Elton, without any expectation of getting paid. I was sure you'd be eager to reciprocate and help someone in Miss Ella's situation.'

'I don't know what her situation is,' I said. 'Maybe you think of her as an old woman worn out by a life of hard work and injustice, but to me she's a woman so bitter and withholding I can't trust anything she says. Even forty years after she last saw him, she is still so angry with her son that she practically chokes talking about him. What if she killed him all those years ago? Or what if he hasn't been missing, and she's

45

ashamed of and angry at the life he's been leading, so she's told everyone he's gone?'

Karen's jaw dropped with shock. 'Vic! You can't think . . . Not Miss Ella! Why, she's a deaconess in her church.'

'Oh, please,' I said. 'The news is full of stories of pastors and priests who've stolen money or molested children. I'm not saying I think Miss Ella did any of those things, not even that I think she killed her son. But I am saying she's hiding something, she's angry, and that she doesn't get a free ride.'

'Are you going to help her at all?'

'We agreed I'd do some preliminary work, and I'm cutting my fees for her, but I am not going to go on if she doesn't keep up her payments.'

Pastor Karen laughed, perhaps relieved that I was going to carry some of the load. 'I think she's scrupulous about money.'

'And remember to ask her for names of Lamont's friends. That's going to be where I'll have to start.'

When Karen said she'd talk to Miss Ella in the morning, I added, 'It would help if I could see Miss Claudia. Do you know where she's living?'

'She's here, at Lionsgate Manor, in our rehabilitation wing, although it's hard for me to be hopeful. She and Miss Ella shared a bed in that little apartment until Miss Claudia had her stroke.' Karen shook her head mournfully. 'All those years of working their fingers to the bone, both of them, and they couldn't afford two bedrooms, even at Lionsgate Manor. It doesn't seem fair.'

Maybe that was what lay behind Miss Ella's hostility: the rank unfairness of life. Life is unfair. Of course it is. When it snows, the rich ski downhill and the poor shovel their sidewalks, my mother used to say. But Gabriella loved life, me, music — above all, music. When she sang, especially Mozart, she moved to a different world where rich and poor, fair and unfair, didn't matter, only sound. What did Miss Ella have that brought her to such a place? What did I have, come to think of it?

A heart-stopping thud on my car window brought me back to Racine Avenue. It was Mr. Contreras, my downstairs neighbor. Mitch, the giant lab-golden, jumped up on the car, his paws on the Mustang's roof, and began to bark. I got out of the car, pushing him out of the way.

'We began to wonder if maybe you had a stroke out here, doll, you was sitting so long. And you got company, cute young gal, says she's a cousin, although she's so young I thought maybe she was a niece or something. But, then, families do stretch out both ways, don't they? She's on your pop's side, I guess, since she says she's a Warshawski. I didn't know you had any relatives . . . '

Mitch punctuated the old man's flood of words with hysterical barks. He and Peppy, his mother, had both been clinging to me since my return home. In my absence, a dog service had run them twice a day, but they needed the reassurance that I wasn't going to abandon them again. Mitch ignored my commands to be quiet and to sit. By the time I'd wrestled him out of

47

the street and into position on the sidewalk, I was panting. Peppy, who'd sat through the whole proceeding with the saintly expression that makes other dogs hate golden retrievers, now started threading herself through my legs, giving little whimpers of greeting.

'Could you start at the beginning?' I asked my neighbor, my hand on Mitch's collar. 'Like my cousin. Who is she? Where is she? And so on.'

Mr. Contreras beamed. He loves family — my family, anyway. He seldom sees his married daughter, Ruthie, or his two grandchildren. 'Didn't you know? Your own cousin, didn't her ma tell you? She's come to work in Chicago, and she's renting a place in Bucktown.'

Bucktown was Chicago's newest Yuppieville, about a mile south of us. Ten years ago, it was a quiet working-class neighborhood, mostly Polish and Mexican, when the ominous happened: young artists looking for cheap studio space moved in. Now the artists can't afford the rents and are moving farther west, while the natives are long gone, to the depressed fringe neighborhoods on the far South Side.

I took my groceries out of the trunk and walked up the sidewalk with my neighbor. If this was a Warshawski cousin, it had to be one of my uncle Peter's kids. He'd been a lot younger than my dad, and had started his family late in life, after he left Chicago for Kansas City, so I didn't know him or my cousins at all. I'd gotten birth announcements over the years, one daughter after another. Petra, Kimberly, and then a blur of Stephanie, Alison, Jordan, something like that.

As we got to the door, a young woman bounced down the steps with all of Mitch's enthusiasm. She was tall and blond, and her low-cut, skimpy peasant blouse, with vest, skirt, leggings, and high-heeled boots, proclaimed her a serious Millennium Gen fashionista, but her wide smile was genuine. It made her look so much like a vibrant, feminine version of my father that I put down my groceries and held out my arms.

'Petra?' I ventured.

'I am, I am.' She hugged me back, bending over my five-foot-eight frame and squeezing hard. 'Sorry to drop in uninvited, but I just got settled this afternoon, and Daddy told me you lived here, near me, and I didn't have any appointments, so I came scurrying up to see you. Uncle Sal — isn't he sweet? He told me to call him that! — he's been feeding me tea in the garden and telling me all the cases he's worked on with you. You're awesome, Tori!'

Tori. My family nickname. Since my cousin Boom-Boom's death twelve years ago, no one had used it, and it was startling to hear it on this stranger's lips. And now Mr. Contreras was her 'Uncle Sal.' And Mitch was slobbering over her. We were just one big happy family.

Mr. Contreras said he knew 'you gals' had a lot of catching up to do, so why didn't we go on up to my place, and he could make us spaghetti later if we wanted. With the dogs racing ahead of us, stopping at each landing to see if we were following, I led Petra to the third floor.

'You should have let me know you were coming to town,' I said. 'I'd have been glad to put you up while you got settled.'

'It happened so fast, I didn't even know I was coming myself until a week ago. See, I graduated from college in May. And then me and my roomie went to Africa for four weeks. We bought a used Land Rover, we drove all over, then we sold the Rover in Cape Town and flew to Australia. Anyway, when I got off the plane in Kansas City, Daddy was, like, do you have a job? And I'm, like, no, of course not. And he says how Harvey Krumas's son is running for the Senate. Daddy and Harvey grew up together back in the Stone Age, so of course they're still best buds. And if Harvey's kid needs help, then Peter's kid will pitch in. So, here I am. My poor body still can't figure out what time zone I'm in.' She laughed again, a loud, husky peal.

'Harvey Krumas, huh? I didn't know he and your dad were friends.'

'Do you know him?' Petra's cellphone rang. She looked at the screen and put it back in her pocket.

'No, sweetie, I don't swim in those rarefied waters.'

Krumas. The name in Chicago meant everything from pork bellies to pension funds. When a new high-rise broke ground here, or in any of a dozen other great cities around the world, you could count on seeing Krumas Capital Management listed among the financial backers.

'I thought maybe since Daddy and Uncle Harvey are such good buds, your dad must've known him, too.'

'My dad was twenty when your father was born,' I explained. 'I don't know if Peter even remembers the row house in Back of the Yards. By the time he started school, Grandma Warshawski had bought a bungalow in Gage Park. Then she moved to Norwood, up on the Northwest Side. That's where she lived when I was a teenager. Your dad took indoor plumbing for granted when he was growing up, but my father and your uncle Bernie — they were the two oldest — they had to empty the slop buckets every morning when they were boys. Between them, Grandma and Grandpa Warshawski didn't make fifteen dollars a week during the Great Depression.'

'It's not Daddy's fault his parents had a hard life,' Petra protested.

'Oh, honey, I wasn't trying to imply that, just explaining what different worlds our two fathers inhabited even though they were brothers. My dad joined the police because it offered a steady paycheck.'

'But Daddy worked hard!' Petra cried. 'He earned every nickel he ever made, down in the yards!'

'I know he did. Our grandmother could never understand why Peter went to work in the stockyards when there were so many better jobs around, but Harvey Krumas's dad offered Peter a job because he and Harvey were friends, and Peter made the most of it.'

If my uncle hadn't become wealthy on a grand scale, he had done well — way better than anyone else remotely connected to my family.

When the stockyards left Chicago in the sixties, Peter had followed Ashland Meats to Kansas City. By the time my dad died, in 1982, Ashland was a five-hundred-million-dollar concern, and Peter was a senior officer. I'd always been a little bitter that he didn't do anything to help out with my dad's medical bills when Tony was dying, but, as I'd just explained to Petra, Tony of course was essentially a stranger to him.

It seemed unbelievable to look at this twenty-something kid and realize she and I shared a grandmother. 'I didn't know Krumas's son wanted to run for office. What are you doing for him with the primary still ten months away?'

Her phone rang again. This time, she answered with a quick, 'I'm busy, I'm with my cousin, I'll call you later!'

She turned back to me. 'Sorry, my roomie wants to know how I am. Kelsey, my college roommate, I mean. In my new place here I'm on my own, which feels really weird after sharing a sorority house and a tent and everything with Kelsey for four years. She's back in Raleigh, and she's bored to *death* after going all over Africa and Australia.

'What were you saying? Oh, what am I doing for the campaign? I don't know. They don't even know! I showed up to work yesterday for the first time, and they asked me what I was good at. And I said, being energetic, which I am, totally. And I majored in communications and Spanish, so they thought maybe I'd do something in the pressroom. But, right now, it's pretty much just wandering around, seeing who's where, and running out to the corner to get people fancy coffee drinks. They could save a *bundle* of money by buying a cappuccino machine for the office, but I like the excuse to be outdoors.'

'What kind of platform is Krumas running on?' I asked.

'I don't know.' Petra widened her eyes in mock embarrassment. 'I think he's green — at least, I hope he is — and I guess he's against the war in Iraq . . . And he's good for Illinois!'

'Sounds like a winner.' I grinned at her.

'He is, he is, especially in his tennis shorts. Women my mom's age get weak in the knees when they see him. Like, my folks took him out for dinner when he came to Kansas City last year, and all the ladies at the country club sashayed over and practically *stroked* him.'

I'd seen plenty of photos on television and in the papers. Brian Krumas was as photogenic as John-John or Barack. Still a bachelor at forty-one, he generated plenty of copy in the gossip rags. Which way did he swing? and Who did he swing with? were perennial favorite points of speculation.

The dogs were starting to whine and paw at me: they needed exercise. I asked my cousin if she wanted to run with us and have dinner after, but she said she had a date with a couple of young women from the campaign, it was a chance to start making friends in her new home.

Her phone rang again when I went into my bedroom to change. In the five minutes it took me to get into my shorts and running shoes, she took three more calls. Oh, youth and the cellphone — inseparable in sickness and in health.

She ran downstairs with the dogs as I locked my apartment. When I got to the door, she was kissing Mr. Contreras good-bye, thanking him for tea, it was totally fab meeting him.

'Come over on Sunday,' Contreras suggested. 'I'll barbecue ribs out back. Or are you one of those vegetarians?'

Petra laughed again. 'My dad's in the meat business. He'd disown me and my sisters if any of us stopped eating meat.'

She flew down the walk. Hers was the shiny Nissan Pathfinder I'd squeezed in front of. She bumped my rear fender twice clearing the curb.

When I winced, my neighbor said, 'It's just paint, after all, cookie. And family's family, and she's a well-behaved kid. Pretty, too.'

'Drop-dead gorgeous, don't you mean?'

'She'll be brushing 'em off with a flyswatter, and I'll be there to help.' He laughed so hard he started to wheeze.

The dogs and I left him coughing in the middle of the sidewalk. Something about all that young energy made me lighthearted, too.

6

Fit for Your Hoof

I woke next morning at five. I was over my jet
lag, but, since getting back, I couldn't seem to
sleep normally. I made an espresso and went out
on the little back porch with Peppy, who'd spent
the night with me. The sky was bright with the
midsummer sunrise. Ten days ago, I'd been
watching the sun rise over the Umbrian hills
with Morrell, yet both he and Italy felt so remote
that they didn't seem to have been part of my life
at all.

The back door on the apartment next to mine
opened, and my new neighbor emerged. The unit
had stood empty for several months. Mr.
Contreras told me a man who played in a band
had bought it while I was away, and that the
medical resident on the ground floor had
worried about whether he would keep everyone
up all night with loud music.

He was dressed in the quintessential artist's
costume: faded black T-shirt and jeans. He went
to the railing to look at the little gardens. The
Korean family on the second floor and Mr.
Contreras both grew a few vegetables; the rest of
us didn't have the time or patience for yard
work.

Peppy went over to greet him, and I got up to
haul her away. Not everyone is as eager to see

her as she is to see them.

'It's okay.' He scratched her ears. 'I'm Jake Thibaut. I don't think you were here when I moved in.'

'V. I. Warshawski. I was in Europe, and can't seem to adjust to the time change. I'm not usually up this early.'

'I'm definitely not up this early. I just got in from Portland on the red-eye.'

I asked if his band had been playing out there, and he made an odd face. 'It's a chamber music group, but I guess you could call it a band. We were touring the West Coast.'

I laughed and told him what I'd heard from Mr. Contreras.

'Poor Dr. Dankin. She worries so much about the noise I make that I'm tempted sometimes to park my bass outside her front door and serenade her. Of course, your dogs and your criminal associates worry her most.'

'My most criminal associate is this gal's son,' I said, petting Peppy. Close up, I could see he was older than I'd first thought, perhaps in his forties.

I offered him an espresso, but he shook his head. 'I have students in five hours. I need to try to sleep.'

I let myself into Mr. Contreras's kitchen to collect Mitch and ran over to the lake with him and Peppy. Mr. Contreras was puttering around his kitchen when we got back, but I turned down breakfast. I wanted to get a head start on Lamont Gadsden. I had a full calendar this afternoon, including a job for my most

56

important client, the one whose fees would pay for those Lario boots and a few other expensive unnecessities.

A forty-year-old trail is a cold one, and Miss Ella hadn't given me much in the way of bread crumbs to follow. In my office, I ran through the databases that make the modern detective's life so easy these days. Lamont Gadsden hadn't changed his name, at least not since those records were automated. As Lamont Gadsden, he didn't own a car in any of the fifty states. He wasn't being sued for child support or alimony. No department of corrections housed him.

I turned to other work and was in the middle of a report for another client when Karen Lennon called. She had visited Miss Ella this morning.

'We talked for a bit, and she finally was able to remember the names of some of the people who knew her son.'

It was a meager list, but it was better than nothing. Miss Ella had provided the names of Lamont's high school physics teacher and a Pastor Hebert from her church. Karen Lennon had somehow persuaded Miss Ella to divulge the names of three of her son's adolescent friends. Interrogation is all about knowing how to ask your question so the subject will answer. Karen Lennon clearly had a touch with Miss Ella that I lacked.

'What about my talking to Miss Claudia?'

The pastor hesitated. 'I think it would be a good idea, if she starts feeling a little stronger. She's been pretty frail the last few weeks, and strangers would be hard on her. And Miss Ella holds Miss Claudia's power of attorney, so that may be an obstacle as well.'

When we'd hung up, I did a search on the list of people who'd known Lamont. Four of the five men were still alive, which wasn't as big a help as the optimistic detective needs. One of the friends from Lamont's youth had died of pancreatic cancer when he was thirty-seven. A second friend had disappeared as thoroughly as Lamont himself. The physics teacher had retired to Mississippi fifteen years ago, and Pastor Hebert, at ninety-three, apparently wasn't quite the ball of fire he'd been in his prime. 'Oh, Pastor Hebert, such a *shame*,' the woman who returned the message I left on his church's answering machine said. 'The Holy Spirit *inhabited* that man's body.'

I asked if he was dead.

'No, no, he's still with us, but not quite *with* us, if you understand. He brought me to Jesus, me and my two boys and my sisters, and we *need* that saintly man's saving voice here now. But the Lord does as He will in His own time, and we must pray to Jesus, pray for Pastor Hebert's healing, and pray for a prophet to lead us out of our wilderness.'

'Yes, ma'am,' I said weakly.

I called the physics teacher, who remembered Lamont but hadn't seen him since his high school graduation. 'He was a bright boy, a good student. I wanted him to go on to college, but he'd turned into such an angry young man, you couldn't talk to him about anything in the white

58

man's world anymore. I suggested Howard or Grambling, but he still wouldn't listen. I didn't even know he'd disappeared.'

The teacher promised to call if he heard anything, which was as likely as seeing the Cubs in the World Series. That left me with a man named Curtis Rivers, who still lived in West Englewood, a few blocks from where he and Lamont Gadsden had grown up. Like the other people on Miss Ella's list, Rivers had done very little that showed up on the Web: he didn't vote, he hadn't been in prison or run for public office, I couldn't tell if he'd ever been married. But he did own Fit for Your Hoof, a shoe-repair shop on Seventieth Place just west of Ashland.

It wasn't until mid-afternoon that I had time to go to Rivers's shop. I spent the bulk of the day cleaning up my job for Darraugh Graham. I was tracing the engineering credentials of a woman Darraugh wanted to head his aerospace division, and my inquiry took me to Northwestern University's engineering school.

When I finished my queries — learning, sadly, that Darraugh's candidate looked too good to be true because she was too good to be true — my feeling of unreality intensified. I seem to be finding more and more job candidates these days who don't care what lies they tell. Maybe politicians and television have so blurred the lines between entertainment and truth that people think no one knows or cares about the difference between a clever story and real experience.

On a summer day, with the lake in the

background and the trees around the fake-Gothic buildings a greeny gold, the campus itself didn't look quite real. I walked down to the water, tempted to join the students who were lounging on the beach behind the engineering building and lose myself in the dreamworld.

My cellphone rang: Darraugh's personal assistant. I sighed and returned to reality, and told Caroline that Darraugh would have to start a new search, that I'd give him full details from a landline. The call broke my mood. I knew it was time to devote myself to Miss Ella and her son. Prickly, unpleasant woman, with her grim forty-year-old past, I didn't want to touch her problems. But I'd agreed to work for her, and that meant she deserved my best efforts, no matter what I thought.

I could hear my mother standing behind me while I practiced the piano: '*Yes, I know you resent this, Victoria, but you make it harder for yourself by refusing to put your best work into it. Engage with the music. It needs you, even if you don't think you need it.*'

I pulled back onto Lake Shore Drive, whipping around the curves, ignoring the lake. I exited downtown and crossed the Loop to pick up the southbound Dan Ryan Expressway. I hate the Ryan, not just because of the traffic, although there isn't an hour of the night or day when all fourteen lanes aren't heavy with trucks and cars. I hate the way it was built, and everything about how it got built.

The road is dug deep into the earth. All you see as you drive are high concrete walls. They're full of cracks with ragweed and crabgrass poking through. If you look up, you get a glimpse of scraggly trees and the occasional run-down tire warehouse or apartment building. Since money for the expressway came from the cronyism in the Democratic machine, they called it Dan Ryan, after the chairman of the Cook County Board who anted up the bucks for it in 1960.

When I left the Ryan at Seventy-first Street, I got an even more depressing look at reality, if that's what it was. Too many of the houses in West Englewood leaned drunkenly away from their foundations. Too many of them had sheets or cardboard filling in for missing windowpanes, and most of the doors would give way to a brisk kick. Vacant lots, filled with urban flotsam and overgrown with weeds, were almost as common as the houses. The only food stores were the kind that prey on the urban poor, hiding a little high-priced, rotting produce behind the shelves of liquor and chips.

Few people were on the streets. I passed a woman clutching an overgrown toddler under one arm, a plastic shopping bag under the other. A couple of men perched on the curb at the corner of Ashland were passing a paper bag from hand to hand. A radio on the sidewalk behind them blared loudly enough to shake my Mustang while I waited for the light to change.

When I pulled up across the street from Fit for Your Hoof, I sat for a minute, trying to dispel the depression I'd let build in me during the drive. A man was sweeping the sidewalk, talking loudly to himself. When he realized I was watching the store, he shook his broom at me, yelling something unintelligible, before scooting backward, crab-like, into the shop. He almost collided with a woman carrying a scuffed pair of white nurse's shoes by the heels who was leaving the shop, but he circled around her in the nick of time.

I stopped to look in the window, where Rivers was displaying goods to 'Help your feet / Feel pretty neat / When they hit that concrete.' Toe pads, arch supports, gel inserts. Above them hung a clotheslineful of dog leashes and collars, and, on the shelves at the back, bright headbands, sashes, handbags, and even a little cache of toys. The tidy, cheery window did its own work for change in a hard world.

When I opened the door, I found myself in a thicket of leather. Ropes hanging from the ceiling displayed more purses, briefcases, harnesses, berets, even work boots and cowboy boots. Behind the ropes, a radio was tuned to *Talk of the Nation*, and I could hear the whine of a belt sander. When I pushed the ropes apart, a steam whistle blew, and a voice cried, 'Welcome to Chicago.'

I stopped, startled. Two men in front of a chessboard looked up at me and laughed. The counter was behind them. A man working on a pair of shoes, his back to the room, didn't turn around but kept sanding the edges on a new heel. I didn't see the man who'd flourished his broom at me.

'Whistle always makes people jump when they don't know it's coming,' one of the chess players

62

said. He was a balding man with a paunch that pressed against an old T-shirt with the Machinists Union logo on it.

'You lost?' His partner was skinnier and older, with skin the color of dusty ebony.

'Often. I'm looking for Curtis Rivers.'

The man behind the counter picked up the second shoe, still not looking at me.

'IRS or paternity suit?' the first chess player said. The savage tone underlying the jokey comment was directed at me, not the man at the belt sander. *What are you doing down here, anyway?*

'My father isn't present, but he's accounted for,' I said. 'Ditto my children. Miss Ella Gadsden is the reason I'm looking for him.'

The sander fell silent. The only noise in the room came from a woman on the radio asking how consumers could ever be sure they were buying clothes made in a factory that respected the workers.

The chess players didn't seem to know Miss Ella's name, but the man behind the counter finally turned around. He placed the shoe he was working on, an old brown Florsheim, in the middle of the counter and leaned over to look at me.

'That's a name I haven't heard for a while,' he said, 'but I don't think I've heard yours at all.'

'V. I. Warshawski. I'm a private investigator. Miss Ella hired me to look for Lamont Gadsden. She said Curtis Rivers was one of his friends.'

Another long pause, before the man behind the counter said, 'We knew each other, a long

63

time back. Miss Ella, what, is she grief struck after all these years? She rented out his bedroom five months after he left. Didn't seem as though she was expecting to see him again.'

'Did you know her sister, too? Miss Claudia? I haven't met her. She's very ill, they tell me. But I understand it's Miss Claudia who actually wants to find him.'

'You got some kind of identification, Ms. Investigator?' Curtis Rivers asked.

I showed him the laminated copy of my license.

'Warshawski. Warshawski. Now, why do I know that name?'

'Hockey?' I suggested. 'A lot of people remember my cousin Boom-Boom.'

All three men laughed at that, as if the idea of hockey itself was a joke.

'A simple no would do,' I said, nettled. Boom-Boom had been more than my cousin; we'd been best friends growing up, proud of our reputation as the wildest kids in South Chicago. Besides, even though he's been dead a dozen years now, they still talk about Boom-Boom in the same breath as Bobby Hull, in that mausoleum on Washington Street.

'Miss Ella couldn't remember many people who might have known her son. You, Mr. Rivers. Two other friends, one dead, the other, Steve Sawyer, I can't find.' I paused, but Rivers didn't fill in the blank. 'A science teacher. Pastor Hebert, from her church.'

'I heard he passed,' one of the chess players said.

64

'No, he's living in Pullman with his daughter,' I said. 'But people at the church are saying he's not too fit mentally, so I don't know what he can tell me.'

'And what can I tell you?' Curtis Rivers asked.

'Anything you can remember about Lamont Gadsden. Anyone else he hung out with, any-place he talked about going, when you last saw him, what his mood was, all those things. If you know where Steve Sawyer is, you could get me out of here so I could ask him those questions.'

'And what will you do if I tell you those things?'

'Talk to more people. Try to find someone who could give me a lead on where he went when he disappeared. Do you remember the last time you saw him?'

Rivers picked up the shoe again. 'It's been a lot of years, Ms. Warshawski.'

'Miss Ella says Lamont left her house the day before the big snow of 'sixty-seven. She says that she and Miss Claudia never saw him again, but did you?'

'The day, the hour, and the minute — trust Miss Ella for that. My memories aren't lined up in formation like that, but if anything comes to me I'll call you.' He turned around and flipped the belt sander back on.

I laid one of my cards on the counter, put two more next to the chessboard. 'If it's any help, I'm not going to faint or run to the State's Attorney's Office if I hear about some old gang connections. I used to represent some Anacondas and Lions when I was with the Public Defender's Office.'

I raised my voice to carry over the belt sander, but none of the men responded. I pushed through the display ropes to the front door, wincing when the steam whistle blew and the recording announced, 'Central Station, Chicago. Leaving now for New Orleans and all stops in between, the City of New Orleans.'

7

Bad Boy Lamont??

I scowled at the dashboard. Did Curtis Rivers know something about Lamont that he didn't want to tell me? Or was it just that the gleam had worn off my winning smile? Even when I was fresh out of law school in the Public Defender's Office, I hadn't been able to 'use my assets,' as my supervisor put it, not too subtly urging me to show cleavage and smirk my way into the good graces of judges and cops. Still, I thought I had been considerate and caring, as well as responsible in what I said, and all those other Girl Scout things in talking to Rivers. He hadn't needed to stiff me quite so hard.

I hadn't had high hopes when I started this investigation, but somehow I didn't expect to hit so many dead ends this fast. Pastor Hebert, who lived with his daughter in Pullman, five miles farther down the Ryan from Fit for Your Hoof, was the last person on my list. Given his questionable mental state, I didn't expect to learn anything startling, but it would wrap up this part of the inquiry. I could go to Miss Ella tomorrow and tell her she either needed to give me more background or end the investigation.

I turned on the ignition but phoned Pastor Hebert's daughter before taking off. I started to explain who I was, but she already knew.

Whoever I had spoken to at the Saving Word Gospel Church this morning had been on the phone to Rose Hebert within seconds. Rose supposed I could come down now, although what anyone could tell me after all this time she couldn't imagine.

'You never know,' I said with determined cheerfulness.

As I pulled away from the curb, the leashes in Fit for Your Hoof's window display twitched. Someone was watching me. But what did that prove? Rivers knew something about Lamont. Or he didn't trust a white woman on the black South Side. Just as I thought. I floored the Mustang so abruptly it fishtailed into a pothole. That would definitely be the last straw if I broke an axle or blew a tire down here.

I couldn't go fast very far, anyway. It was five-thirty, the heart of the evening rush. The line at the entrance ramp to the Ryan took six lights to clear. Traffic stayed bumper to bumper until I oozed off again at 111th Street.

As soon as I left the expressway, I entered a quiet, orderly world that doesn't quite belong to Chicago. Pullman's quiet, tree-lined streets, with their Federal-style row houses painted in greens and reds, stand in sharp contrast to the broken-down tenements just to the north and east.

Maybe its feeling of separateness from the big city is because Pullman started as a company town, a monument to railway magnate George Pullman's ego. The inventor built everything — company stores, houses for his managers,

68

tenements for his workers — who staged a bloody strike over the prices Pullman charged in his stores, coupled with the fact that his houses cost more than they could ever dream of paying. Pullman finally had to give up on his town, but most of the houses remain. They'd been built from bricks made of the durable Lake Calumet clay, which is so highly prized that thieves have dismantled whole garages, if the owners are away, and carted off the bricks for resale elsewhere in the city.

As I continued west, I saw the Hotel Florence on my right. Its turrets and spires had made it seem like a fairy-tale castle when I was little. It's been closed for decades now, but my parents used to eat there to mark special occasions. I stopped, looking at the blank windows, remembering the family lunch on my tenth birthday, right before the city exploded in riots from one end to another. My mother tried to enforce a gay party atmosphere, but none of her attempts at charm or conversation could override my aunt Marie's sour racist harangues.

I hadn't wanted to include Marie, but Gabriella said I couldn't invite Boom-Boom without his parents. Afterward, back in our tiny South Chicago living room, I shouted at my mother that it served her right that Aunt Marie had ruined the party. My father jumped up from the TV, where he was watching the Cubs, grabbed my arm, and hustled me out back.

'Victoria, every day I have to go out on the streets and face people who think their anger counts more than anyone else's feelings or needs.

I don't want to see that anger on your face, or listen to it in your voice, especially not when you talk to your mother.'

My father never scolded me, and for him to do so on my birthday . . . I burst into tears, I created a scene, but he stood by, his arms crossed on his chest. No special treatment for me. I had to calm myself down, apologize to my mother.

The memory still burned in me, my dad's injustice to me on my birthday. The force of the forty-year-old emotion embarrassed me. Staring blindly at the hotel, it dawned on me for the first time that his anger hadn't been solely about me but his fears about what lay ahead. Catholic parishioners defying the cardinal's pleas for charity and peace, taking to the streets with every kind of homemade missile — Aunt Marie's own priest, Father Gribac, essentially inciting his parish to riot — my dad probably was frightened about Gabriella's and my safety. That tenth birthday was the last time Tony was home in the middle of the day for two months.

A horn sounded loudly behind me. I moved forward, threading my way through a patchwork of short, dead-end streets to Langley, where Rose Hebert lived. Knots of commuters were walking home from the train station, most attached to their cellphones. One man was mowing his tiny lawn, while across the street a woman was washing her front windows. Where the street ended at 114th, a clutch of girls was jumping double Dutch. Beyond them, boys were playing baseball in a rubble-filled vacant lot. The girls slid their eyes my way — *Strange white woman on the block* — but didn't interrupt the rhythm of their ropes.

The Heberts lived in one of the original Pullman homes, flat front to the street, red brick with black arches over the windows that looked like surprised eyebrows. Rose Hebert answered the door almost as soon as I rang the bell. She was a tired woman about ten years my senior, her close-cut hair full of gray, her muscular shoulders slumped inside a thin, lavender-print dress.

'I told Father you were coming, but I'm not sure he understood me,' she said by way of greeting. 'It's so hard to believe Sister Ella finally decided to look for Lamont that I called over to Lionsgate Manor to ask her if it was true. People try so many scams against the elderly these days. You have to be careful all the time.'

It didn't seem like a belligerent comment, just the notion at the front of her mind.

'I am a licensed investigator.' I pulled out my identification, but Ms. Hebert didn't look at it. 'Miss Ella got my name from the pastor at Lionsgate, Karen Lennon, maybe you've met her. Miss Ella told me she was hiring me for her sister's sake more than her own.'

'Poor Sister Claudia,' Rose Hebert murmured. 'It's hard to see her like she is now. She was so lively and graceful as a young woman. Daddy was always having to remind her about modest Christian deportment, but my friends and I, we secretly copied how she dressed and how she walked.'

'Miss Ella didn't want me visiting her sister, but it sounds as though you've seen Miss Claudia since her stroke?'

'Yes, oh yes. I drive the van on Sundays and collect our people who can't walk to church anymore, so I bring Sister Ella and some of the other folks from Lionsgate. And I try to visit with Sister Claudia, but she's so weak, I can't tell if she even knows who I am some days, so strangers are hard on her.' Ms. Hebert was blocking the doorway to the house. Loud voices drifted down the dark hall.

I tried to peer behind her. 'And your father? Is he strong enough that I can talk to him?'

'Oh. Yes, of course, that's why you're here . . . But my father, he isn't easy . . . You mustn't mind . . . He's not always . . . ' She kept murmuring flustered comments as she backed away from the door and let me into the house.

A table at the entrance was piled with papers. As I walked past, I saw church bulletins mixed with bills and magazines — sort of like my own entryway except for the bulletins. We followed the loud voices to the living room. They came from a television, where a minister was exhorting us to send him money for letting us know how very sinful we are. The light from the screen flickered on the bald head of a man in a wheelchair. He didn't turn his head when we came in nor move when his daughter took the controls from his fingers and pressed the MUTE button.

'Daddy, this lady here is the one I told you about, the one Sister Ella and Sister Claudia sent. They want her to find Lamont.'

I knelt next to the chair and put my hand next to his on the armrest. 'I'm V. I. Warshawski, Pastor Hebert. I'm trying to find people who knew Lamont, people who might know what happened to him.'

A thread of saliva dribbled from the side of his mouth. 'Lamont. Trouble.'

'He means Lamont was a troubled young man,' Rose said softly.

'Made.' The pastor mouthed the word with difficulty.

'Daddy, he didn't make trouble,' Rose cried. 'He had good reason to be angry, when you think of the terrible injustices we suffer.'

Pastor Hebert tried to speak but only produced a kind of gargling. Finally he choked out the word, 'Snake.'

'Snake?' I repeated doubtfully, wondering if he meant Lamont was a snake in the grass.

'He didn't belong to the Anacondas, Daddy! He helped them protect Dr. King!'

Father and daughter had clearly had this argument many times. His face didn't move, but her lips were trembling, as if she were six, not sixty, and finding it hard to stand up to an unyielding parent.

I sat back on my heels. Lamont Gadsden with the Anacondas — no wonder Miss Ella hadn't approved of her son's friends. In their day, they'd been as notorious as the El Rukns. Weapons, murder, drugs, prostitution: whatever crime was happening in a broad swatch of the South Side, they could claim credit for it. In my three years

73

with the Public Defender's Office, maybe thirty percent of my clients had run with the Anacondas. I'd even drawn their chief once, when Johnny Merton couldn't come up with cash one weekend for his own high-priced mouth.

Merton had been furious that he had to rely on an inexperienced PD. He'd tried to intimidate me into crumpling in his presence. 'You the new snake charmer, girl? You don't have the talent to charm Johnny Merton.'

He'd grown coarser in his insults when I refused to flinch. I was green, but I'd grown up in the steel mills. I might not be willing to sidetrack a judge with my cleavage, but I knew about insults and intimidation. I'd kept my legal pad in front of me, writing down everything Merton said, and when he paused for breath I'd say, 'Let me read your comments back to you, Mr. Merton, and you tell me if this is what you want me to present to Judge McManus.'

If Lamont Gadsden had been an Anaconda, anything could have happened to him. They didn't like members walking away from the gang. Leaving meant you left an ear behind as a token: no one will hear you on the street now when you call for help.

I looked up at Hebert's unblinking eyes. 'What I really am hoping, Pastor, is that you can give me some names, people who knew Lamont, anyone he might have been in touch with after he walked out of Miss Ella's house in 1967. Or if you know anyone, Ms. Hebert. I've been to see Curtis Rivers, and he didn't have anything to say.'

74

Again came the gargling sound, and then the words choked out with difficulty. 'Dead bury dead.'

'Do you know he's dead or are you just hoping no one will stir an old pot?' I asked.

He didn't say anything.

'When did you yourself last see Lamont Gadsden, Pastor?'

He gasped, taking in air. Still without moving his head, he said, 'Stopped church. Said hell bound. No heed. Baptized, no listening.'

'Yes, you baptized him. We took him into Christ's body together, all of us. So how could you say he was hell bound? And why should he talk to you when that was all you would say to him?'

'Drugs. Never listen me, daughter, but drugs. Saw. Know. You, woman, no pants.'

With an effort, he moved his hand to the television control and turned the sound back on. The preacher in the glass box was revealing the true meaning of Paul's letter to the Romans.

'No pants?' I asked Rose, pushing myself to my feet. My thighs were sore from squatting.

'He doesn't approve — our church doesn't approve — of women wearing men's clothes,' she said listlessly.

In Bible pictures, men are always wearing robes. I wondered if that meant women at Saving Word couldn't wear bathrobes, but I decided it wouldn't help my inquiry if I asked. Instead, I followed Rose back along the narrow hall to the front door.

I stopped next to the paper-covered table. 'Do

you think your father knows something about Lamont that he'd have told me if I'd worn a dress?'

She looked down the hall, as if the old man could hear us over the televised preacher. 'He's convinced Lamont sold drugs for the Anacondas, but I never thought so.'

'You said Lamont was angry over the injustices in your lives. What did he do about them or how did he show he was angry?'

'He was part of the group that helped look after Dr. King. You know, during the marches that summer.' She eyed me doubtfully, wondering if I came from one of the white South Side families who created the need for a protective force.

I squinted, trying to remember what I knew about the history of the summer. 'Didn't the gangs declare a truce, a moratorium against fighting among themselves?'

She was still eyeing me warily, but she nodded. 'Johnny Merton from the Anacondas and Fred Hampton from the Panthers and them, they all met with Dr. King and Al Raby to discuss strategy. My father, he felt our church didn't belong in the streets. He didn't like it when Lamont and some of his friends took part.'

'Curtis Rivers.' I said his name involuntarily, thinking about his hostility when I was in his shop this afternoon.

'Curtis was there. Some of the other boys from the neighborhood. And Lamont. They all belonged to Saving Word, and my father denounced them from the pulpit because they wouldn't listen to his authority.'

'But it was six months later that Lamont disappeared. It's hard to think that was connected with the marches.' Something in her face made me add, 'When did you last see him yourself?'

She looked down the hall again. A choir on TV was singing with great gusto. 'Daddy forbade it. Once he denounced Lamont, he said if I went out with him I'd be endangering my own soul.'

'But you saw him, anyway.'

Her mouth twisted in a painful smile. 'I didn't have the nerve. Lamont, he stopped me when I was leaving school. I was over at Kennedy-King — we still called it Woodrow Wilson then — studying nursing, and Lamont, he waited for me after school. He talked to me about the Panthers and Black Pride. I made the mistake of thinking I could explain it to Daddy.'

She looked down at her hands. 'Maybe my life would have been different — could have been different. I got my nursing degree, and I could only get LPN jobs. It was years before I could get hired as a registered nurse. I used to think about that when I saw white women hired over me, and me with just as much schooling and good job reviews and everything and still emptying bedpans. I used to think about Lamont, I mean, and wish I'd paid him more mind. But — '

A bell rang, clear even above the sound of the televised choir.

'That's Daddy. He needs me. I have to go.'

'Are you still working as a nurse?'

'Oh yes. I used to be an oncology nurse, but I had to give that up when Daddy turned so poorly. Now I do the night shift in the ER. I put him to bed before I go on duty, get him up in the morning before I go to bed.'

'And if you'd listened to Lamont, what would you have done different? Or what would he have done different? Would he have stayed around to be close to you?'

In the dimly lit hall I thought I saw her cheeks darken with embarrassment, but maybe that was my imagination. The bell sounded again, a longer ringing, and she pushed me through the open door. I pulled a card from my bag and thrust it into the hand that was holding the door.

'You're an adult, Rose Hebert. You couldn't talk to Lamont forty years ago. But that doesn't mean you can't talk to me now.'

Her lips moved soundlessly. She looked from me to the living room. Habit ruled. Shoulders stooped, she turned back down the hall to her father.

8

A Very Late-Night Call

That night, over dinner at Lotty's, I described my frustrating day. After listening to my description of Pastor Hebert, Lotty said it sounded as though he had Parkinson's disease. 'The fixed staring, trouble talking, those you often see in an advanced stage of the illness. He must be ninety, wouldn't you guess? We don't know enough about how to manage the disease, and these symptoms are hard to control, especially in a man who's that old.'

'Presumably he has other problems or his daughter wouldn't be afraid of him,' I said. 'She's sixtyish, he's dependent on her, but she lets him run her around as if she were a robot.'

'Yes, brainwashing also leaves symptoms that are hard to manage.' Lotty gave a wry smile. 'I saw Karen Lennon at a staff meeting this afternoon. She's worried that she might have made a mistake in introducing you to her patient — her 'client,' I suppose I should say.'

'It's a little late for Karen to be second-guessing herself, not when I've spent a day stirring the pot and getting the phone tree shaking among all the women at Pastor Hebert's church.'

Lotty laughed. 'I think that's what has her worried. Karen's very young. She doesn't know how much excitement a detective can bring to a closed community.'

'She should call me, not try to get you to do it for her. But I'll talk to her in the morning,' I grumbled.

'Don't take her head off as well as mine,' Lotty said. 'If you worked with other people all day long instead of in a hole by yourself, you'd understand how natural it was for her to talk to me during a meeting.'

'After spending a day with people who twitch when they see me coming, I'd be happier in a hole by myself. As long as it had a cappuccino machine.'

'Yes, we'll decorate it and make it *gemütlich*, a cozy hole. I'll send a courier in every day with a fresh bottle of milk and a basket of fruit and cheese.' She squeezed my hand. 'You're still in mourning for Morrell, aren't you?'

'Not mourning, exactly.' I fiddled with the heavy silver. 'More questioning myself, to be my age and not able to keep a stable relationship going. In the back of my mind, I always imagined a child, a family, at this point in my life.'

Lotty raised her brows. 'I'm not criticizing you, Victoria — God knows, I have no right — but you haven't lived like someone who wanted a child.'

'No, I've lived like the pepperpot my father always called me, throwing dust up the nose of any man who came close to me . . . Is that what you mean?'

'No, my dear. So you're irascible, well, so am

I, so are many people. But you put the community ahead of yourself. It's a different form of the female disease, the one you just lamented in Rose Hebert. Your clients need you, the women at the shelter need you, even I need you. Men can put the community first and come home to domestic life, but women, we're still like nuns in a way: if we have a strong vocation, it's hard to meet our private needs.'

Her words made me feel unbearably lonely. 'So I'm a noncelibate nun.' I tried to turn it into a joke, but my voice cracked. 'You've worked things out without Max, though.'

She smiled sadly. 'After many years as lonely as yours, my dear.'

The curved windows reflected the candles on her dining-room table. I watched the multiple flames the glass created. Some of the tension of the day eased out of my shoulders.

We moved the conversation to lighter topics: our planned picnic to Ravinia to hear Denyce Graves sing, Lotty's new perinatology fellow who had cried out that she loved Jane Austen. 'She was the one who went to Africa to study the monkeys, right?' Around nine, Lotty sent me home since she had an early call. She doesn't do much surgery anymore, but she still goes early to the hospital to monitor her fellows' work.

I checked my messages on my way home. Karen Lennon had called to say she'd stopped at the VA and given Elton Grainger the name and address of an SRO, which had rooms for homeless vets. She was a conscientious young pastor, no doubt about it.

81

When I got home, Mr. Contreras erupted from his apartment. 'There you are, doll. I couldn't remember your cellphone number, and you never gave it to your cousin, so we been sitting here, hoping you'd get home before midnight.'

'Vic!' Petra bounced out behind him, Mitch wrapping himself around her legs. 'I feel like such an *idiot*, but I lost my keys and didn't know what to do. So I thought maybe you could put me up for the night, but Uncle Sal said you could probably get into the building, that you knew how to open anything that isn't electronic. So here I am!'

Her cellphone rang in the middle of her hearty peal of laughter. She looked at the screen, then answered it with a breathless account of her life to date, or at least her lost keys, her visit to Uncle Sal and me, and where she planned to meet everybody once she got back into her own home.

'You ever hear of a locksmith, either of you?' I bent to stroke Peppy, who was whining for attention.

'Yes, but they wanted, like, hundreds of dollars to come after hours, and I don't have hundreds of dollars. They hardly pay me anything at the campaign, you know.' Her phone rang again, and she repeated her story.

'I thought your dad had the odd dollar lying around,' I objected when she'd hung up. 'Not that you aren't welcome to sleep on my couch tonight.'

'If Daddy finds out I've been this stupid, he'll

never stop lecturing me on how I'm too immature to be alone in the big bad city.'

'Didn't Peter get you the job on Brian Krumas's campaign?'

'Oh, he did, he did. But he expected me to live, like, in a convent, or at least share an apartment. He pulled a Vesuvius when he found out I'd rented my own place.'

She answered another call. At that point, I decided it would be easier to get her back into her own home than listen to her phone all night long. Mr. Contreras, Mitch, and Peppy announced they'd all like to see where Petra lived, too. I bundled the dogs into the Mustang. The old man was delighted to accept Petra's invitation to ride with her in her Pathfinder.

Petra's place was in a loft building at the tony end of Bucktown, about ten blocks from my office. Parking was at a premium, and I had to cover part of a yellow hydrant line and hope for the best.

Petra held a flashlight on her front door for me. As I knelt on the sidewalk, wiggling my picklocks inside the lock, she answered another phone call. 'My cousin is, like, this detective, and she's breaking into my building,' she shouted to anyone on Wolcott Street who might be listening. 'No, really, she's, like, *NCIS* or *Saving Grace* or something. She solves murders, she has a gun . . . everything!'

I took the phone from her and stuffed it into my back pocket. 'Petra, darling, not while I'm out here doing something highly illegal. Any cop who's cruising around can listen in on your frequency. And, anyway, you're talking loudly enough for everyone on the block to hear you.'

She pouted, an exaggerated, self-spoof of a crybaby, but she held the flashlight steady until the tumblers clicked back. We climbed three flights to her place where I repeated the maneuver. In my hip pocket, her phone rang two more times before I got her front door opened. Her keys were on the floor just inside.

She gave another husky laugh. 'Look at that! I dropped them on my way out. I was so late, I guess I grabbed them with my coffee and my phone and didn't see they weren't in my hand when I left. Oh, Vic, you are a genius. Thank you, thank you, thank you. What can I do for you? Would you like a free invite to our fundraiser out on Navy Pier? It's twenty-five hundred a head. Brian's going to be there. Wouldn't you love to meet him? The president may stop in, although we've been told not to count on it. We've rented the whole east end of the pier, it'll be so cool. And, Uncle Sal, you should come, too.'

I've been to too many fundraisers for my heart to skip a beat at the prospect, but the invitation thrilled Mr. Contreras. An inside seat at a high-end event: it would raise his prestige at his weekly trips to the lodge, where his old union buddies meet to shoot pool along with the breeze.

'Do I need a tuxedo or something?' the old man worried as we turned to leave.

'Wear your overalls and your union badge. Krumas probably wants to look like he's the people's candidate,' I advised.

'Vic! Don't be so cynical,' Petra scolded. 'Although, do you have a union badge, Uncle Sal?'

'No, but I got me a Bronze Star, you know, from getting nicked at Anzio.'

Her eyes shone. 'Oh, wear your medals, that'll be so fab. I'll come over and trim your hair. Kelsey and me, we got pretty good with the shears, primping each other in Africa.'

As we drove home, Mr. Contreras chuckled to himself. 'She's quite a gal, your cousin. She could charm the socks off a rock. You could learn a thing or two from her, you know.'

'Like how to charm socks off a rock?' My memory from this afternoon, my old supervisor telling me to 'flash my assets,' came to mind. 'You think I'm too surly?'

'Wouldn't hurt you to smile more at people. You know what they say, doll: you catch more flies with honey.'

'Assuming you want a whole bunch of flies filling up the place.' I waited while he opened the front door, then took the dogs for a final skip around the block.

Would Petra have charmed Curtis Rivers's socks off, gotten him to tell her all he knew about Lamont Gadsden? I tried to imagine myself skipping into Fit for Your Hoof, a jolly laugh bubbling out of my throat. It was easier to imagine myself tap-dancing backward in high heels.

I poured a glass of whisky and watched a few innings of the Cubs-San Francisco game. Pitching, the perennial Cubs weakness, reared its ugly head again. I went to bed with the good guys down by three runs in the fifth.

I was in the middle of a terrifying dream, Petra laughing heartily as a swarm of flies crawled down my cleavage, when the phone rescued me. I sat up, heart pounding from the horrific image, and grabbed the phone.

'Is this the detective?'

It was a woman, her voice soft and deep, but in my groggy state I couldn't place it. I looked at the clock: it was three in the morning.

'I'm sorry if I woke you, but I've been thinking and thinking about Lamont. If I let it go another day, maybe I won't have the nerve to pick up the phone a second time.'

'Rose Hebert.' I said her name aloud as I realized who she was. 'Yes, what about Lamont?'

A pause, a sucking in of breath, preparing for the high dive. 'I saw him that night.'

'Which night?' I leaned back against the headboard, knees drawn up to my chin, trying to wake up.

'When he left home. January twenty-fifth.'

'You mean Lamont came to you after he left his mother's house?'

'He didn't come to me.' She was speaking hurriedly. Behind her, I could hear the sounds of the hospital, the incessant pages, an ambulance siren. 'I was . . . I was out after church. Wednesday night, you know, midweek church. Daddy was meeting with the deacons after the service, so I left alone. I went for a walk. It was so warm, you remember?'

86

The record heat for January before the big snow began. Everyone who lived through it still marvels at it.

'I went looking for Lamont. I was so confused, I wanted to see him. And I was pretending it was church business, pretending in my head, the way you do, that I wanted him to come to the youth group and tell us what it was like to work near Dr. King, although Daddy didn't approve of churches getting involved in social action.'

She drew a shuddering breath, half a sob, then whispered, 'I just needed to see him, try to get him to touch me again, the way he had that summer. But, like I said, I was pretending I had some bigger, purer reason.'

Once she'd let her shameful memory out, her breathing came more easily, and her voice returned to a deeper pitch. 'I found him, or, anyway, I saw him, at the corner of Sixty-third and Morgan. He was with Johnny Merton, going into the Waltz Right Inn — you know, the old blues joint there? It's been gone twenty years now, but, back then, it was the center of entertainment in my part of town. Not for me, not for Pastor Hebert's girl, but for all the kids I went to high school with — '

'So what were Johnny and Lamont doing?' I asked when she broke off.

'Oh, I couldn't follow them! Daddy would have heard faster than you can spit! I just sat across the street, watching the door, watching kids I'd known my whole life passing in and out. Wednesday was church night, but it was also jam night. Alberta Hunter came sometimes, Tampa

Red, all the big names, along with guys starting out. You don't know how much I wanted to be there, instead of at church.' The phone vibrated from the passion in her voice.

'Did you see them come out again, Johnny Merton and Lamont?'

'Daddy found me before Lamont came out. I was sitting across the street in my coat, even though it was still warm. I couldn't go outdoors in January without my winter coat, not in my family. I remember thinking how stupid it was, sixty degrees and me in that heavy wool thing, and then Daddy came along. He hit me, told me what a common girl I was, what a sinner, what a bringer of shame, to Jesus and to him, lingering outside a bar like a street girl.'

The words tumbled out like water from a fire hydrant, spraying me with their force.

'The next day was the snow. I went on down to school in the morning, even though my face was all purple and swollen from where Daddy hit me. And I was so thankful for the blizzard. I had to spend two nights there at the college, sleeping on the floor with all the other girls. It was the only time in my life where I got to be just one of the girls. White girls, black girls, we all just lay there in the dark, talking about our families and our boyfriends, and I even acted like Lamont was my boy . . . Well, anyway, when the snow ended and I got back home, Lamont was gone. No one ever saw him again, not that I knew. And I couldn't go to Johnny Merton. Someone would have told Daddy, and I couldn't take another — '

Another beating, I filled in silently when she

88

clipped off the sentence. 'Did you ask any of Lamont's friends about him? Anyone who might have known why he was talking to Merton?'

'I did, but not till later. At first, when I didn't see him around, I thought Lamont was avoiding me. I thought God was punishing me. I was so confused in my head, I couldn't decide if God was punishing me for not going off with Lamont when he asked me that past September or if He was punishing me for letting Lamont touch me.' She gave an embarrassed snort of laughter.

'I finally asked Curtis Rivers, but that wasn't until maybe a month or six weeks went by, and he was just as puzzled as me.'

'Was Curtis Rivers with the Anacondas, too?' I asked.

'I never did know for sure who was, who wasn't. I was the preacher's kid, I was the stuck-up girl, they didn't talk to me the way they did the other girls in the neighborhood. I don't think Curtis was — he shipped out to Vietnam, anyway, round about May of 'sixty-seven — he was just the boy everyone trusted. Gang, straight, whatever . . . Curtis, he didn't play sides. Should have been him I broke my heart over, not a no-good street boy like Lamont.' She laughed again, less bitterly this time.

'So is Miss Ella right? Was Lamont dealing drugs?'

'Not the way she meant. I mean, she makes it sound like the South Side was floating on Lamont Gadsden's heroin sales. But she's like my daddy: you move a quarter inch off the straight and narrow, you're Satan's child for sure. And after Lamont disappeared, Sister Ella, she carried on as if nothing had happened. Just held herself straighter, if any back not made out of cast iron could be held so straight. But Sister Claudia, Lamont's going just about broke her heart.'

'Miss Ella says she and Miss Claudia went to the police. Did you ever hear anything about that?'

'Oh, they went. But the cops, they were so ugly. It was like they did this work they hated, looking after Dr. King that summer — 1966, I mean — and then couldn't wait to take it out on any black person who crossed their path. I went with Sister Ella and Claudia to the station house, and the way those cops acted, you'd think those two women had shot the president. Pigs? My, yes, they were pigs.'

I felt the jolt that the insult always gave me.

'You think there's any hope, any chance, you might find him?' She spoke in a soft, shy voice, as if afraid I might mock her deepest feelings.

I wanted to tell her something heartening, hope filled, something that would put life back in her voice. I wanted to spread some honey out for her, but I could only tell the truth, the fact that I thought Lamont Gadsden was either dead or so deeply hidden that no one would ever find him unless he chose to come forward himself.

'I'll talk to Johnny Merton,' I found myself promising. 'It's been forty years, but maybe Johnny remembers what they talked about.'

'Don't use my name,' she begged. 'If Daddy hears about it, or the ladies at church . . . '

'You don't have to go home to him, you know,' I said quietly. 'Even now it's not too late for you to start your own life. I have the phone number for — '

'Oh, once your spirit gets broke, it doesn't matter where you lay your head at night.' Her voice had grown low again with weariness. 'But if you learn anything, call me here at the hospital. My shift runs eleven to seven, Thursday through Monday.'

9

Uncovering History

After she hung up, I tried to go back to sleep, but the conversation had been too unsettling. I lay on the bed, my body so rigid I couldn't even keep my eyes closed. I walked out to the living room and sat cross-legged in my armchair. Peppy, who was spending the night in my apartment, got up from her post by the front door to join me.

Rose Hebert and Petra, both adult women, referred to their fathers as 'Daddy.' When Daddy's in your head, he's the biggest thing there. He doesn't have a first name, or a smaller identity like 'my dad.' You think everyone knows who Daddy is. Did that mean my uncle was himself a bullying presence in Petra's life or just that she was still very young?

Rose Hebert certainly wasn't young. Maybe she never had been. I could see her, nineteen years old, sitting in the shadows outside the Waltz Right Inn, wanting to be part of the group having fun, longing for love. And spending the rest of her life with Daddy, who beat her purple when he thought she was sinning. She never mentioned her mother. When had Pastor Hebert's wife stopped being part of the equation?

The bigger question, at least for the job I'd

agreed to do, dealt with Johnny the Hammer. Lamont Gadsden, last seen entering a blues bar in Johnny's company the night of January 25. Had he crossed Johnny on some drug deal? A fight, a death — killed by Johnny or some hand-picked Anaconda deputy — and then the blizzard, a wonderful cover for any traces of where Lamont had been shot or stabbed.

'Curtis Rivers was at that bar, too,' I told Peppy. 'Why did he stiff me today?'

She thumped her tail softly. I sifted her silky ears with my fingers.

'You never knew Johnny Merton, which makes you a lucky girl. He'd have cut off your beautiful tail for earmuffs as soon as look at you. But could he scare Curtis Rivers so badly that the man won't talk to me forty years later?'

I could imagine the Waltz Right Inn that January night. Open-mike night, local blues greats stopping by, hilarity running high because of the boon of summer in January, everyone happy but the preacher's daughter, sweating in her heavy wool coat. And Lamont Gadsden, who'd left his mother's dinner table to talk to the Hammer.

Over the sound of Alberta Hunter at the piano, Rivers overhears Lamont and Merton. The phone call later that night, or week, the Hammer to Rivers: *If you say word one about what you know, you'll follow Lamont into the river, or quarry, or wherever Lamont Gadsden's body has landed.*

I could imagine it, but that didn't mean it happened. And, anyway, what hold could

Merton have on Curtis Rivers that would keep Rivers silent after all this time? Besides, Rivers didn't strike me as a guy who would faint just because the bogeyman was rattling a chain.

I made a face. Pastor Hebert, Hammer Merton, the enforcers of West Englewood. Both of them beat their followers for infractions against a code only they were entitled to define.

Come to think of it, I'd never checked to see if there were unidentified dead bodies lying around after the big snow. It was close to five now, and the library at my old school wouldn't open for another three hours. I went back to bed. Peppy followed me and curled her soft gold body against my side. She fell instantly into the sweet dreams of the virtuous, but at six I was still lying there, eyelids scratchy from missing sleep, churning over my past encounters with Johnny Merton.

He had scared me when I was with the Public Defender's, even though I was supposed to be on his side. It was because of him I'd gotten an unlisted phone number:

'You don't do your best for me on this rap, bitch, I'll make sure your mama won't recognize your face when they pull you out of the water.'

'Is that why you don't have any LaSalle Street lawyers left, Mr. Merton? Are they all in the Chicago River wearing cement booties?'

I'd been amazed at the time that I could utter those words without my voice quavering, but I'd had to clutch my legal pad to control the trembling in my hands. Even now, the memory of the Hammer's venom could keep me from sleeping. Maybe he could have intimidated Rivers, at that.

I sat up. If I wasn't going to sleep, I might as well get going. I let Peppy out the back door and stood on the small porch, stretching my hamstrings and shoulders, while my stovetop espresso maker heated up.

The midsummer sky was already a deep blue. I drank a coffee, collected Mitch from Mr. Contreras's kitchen — he'd been whining behind the door, indignant at being locked inside while Peppy got to play — and ran the dogs to the lake. The water was still so cold, I gasped when I jumped in, but I swam with them to the first buoy. Maybe if I got my blood flowing fast enough, I'd feel as though I'd spent eight hours asleep.

It didn't exactly work: I was still gritty-eyed and grumpy as I drove south. But I reached the University of Chicago library just as the doors opened. I'd picked up a cappuccino and a croissant at one of the little neighborhood coffee bars and, against all library etiquette, smuggled them into the microform room.

I pulled reels for all the major Chicago newspapers. In 1967, there had been eight dailies, morning and evening editions of four different papers. I started with the *Daily News*, my dad's paper. He liked Royko.

January 25, 1967, the day before the big snow. It's strange how little you remember of events you lived through yourself. Scrolling through the pages, I wasn't surprised that I didn't know the national news: LBJ's war budget; the student protests at Berkeley, which California governor Reagan denounced as a Communist plot against America; or even newly elected Senator Charles Percy's wife's miniskirt. I'd been in fifth grade, and that stuff sailed completely past me.

It was the local news that surprised me. I'd completely forgotten the tornadoes that swept the South Side the day before the big snow, the big storms Rose Hebert had mentioned.

The winds had blown over a half-constructed building at Eighty-seventh and Stony, three miles from my childhood home. A cop had been killed at the scene. I stared at photos of the rubble. Cinder blocks filled the streets, looking like Legos thrown on the living-room floor by a bad-tempered child. A VW bug was buried up to its windows in the debris. And then, the next day, twenty-six inches of snow fell, covering the debris, the mills, the roads, all of Chicago, burying the living as well as the dead.

My memory of the storm wasn't the tornadoes, nor even the dead cop — although every cop's death was an occasion of anxiety for my mother and me — but Gabriella waiting outside for me when school ended. My mother never walked me home from school, and I was scared when I saw her, scared that something had happened to my dad.

That she was worried about the snow seemed funny to me. A blizzard blowing five- and even ten-foot drifts was exhilarating, a game, not cause for alarm. But after a year of riots and protests, where she had sat up night after night waiting for Tony to come home, me sometimes watching from the top of the attic stairs, sometimes joining her at the kitchen table, whenever she did something out of the ordinary I thought first of my father.

'*Tu e Bernardo, spericolati e testardi tutti e dui voi!*' she said to me in Italian, seizing my mittened hand. 'Both of you reckless and head-strong! If I don't stop you, you will get lost in this blizzard. You will do something impossibly dangerous that will cost you your life and forever break my heart.'

'I'm not a baby! Don't treat me like one in front of my friends.' I shouted at her in English, yanking my hand away.

It upset her when I didn't answer in Italian. In my anger, I wanted to hurt her feelings. The truth was, I'd been planning on finding Boom-Boom — Bernardo — who went to Catholic school. We wanted to see if the Calumet River had frozen enough for skating. Being caught out made me sullen, even more so when Gabriella made me play the piano for an hour when we got home.

Sitting in the library this morning, I looked at my fingers, and regret twisted my intestines the way it uselessly does. I could be a decent pianist today — never gifted but competent — if I had acceded to my mother's wishes that I study music more seriously. Why had I fought so against practicing? My mother adored me, and I had loved her fiercely back. Why would I not do this thing that was so important to her? Could it be that I'd been jealous of music? Who could possibly compete with Mozart, my rival for her affections? '*Mi tradì quell'alma ingrata*,' Donna Elvira's aria about jealousy and betrayal in *Don Giovanni*, had been one of Gabriella's favorites.

So lost was I in my memories that I sang the first line out loud and then blushed as everyone in the reading room turned to stare at me. I sank down in my chair and stared fixedly at the screen in front of me.

I looked at reports of homicides starting on January 26 and moving forward to the end of February — they got more play forty years ago when the numbers were smaller — but I didn't see any unidentified bodies. I looked for car accidents and studied gang activity.

The *Daily News* had interviewed members of the Blackstone Rangers, who felt they were the legitimate voice of the black South Side. They were going to do all this good for the community, they told the paper: day care, schools, health care. I made a face in the dark reading room. The gang had started some of their grand projects, but, in the end, all they did was sell drugs and run protection and prostitution rackets.

I turned to the *Herald-Star* and read the same homicide reports there, saw the same pictures of the city up to its rail girders in snow. A week after the *News* talked to the Rangers, the *Herald-Star* played catch-up, running a feature on the Avalon Anacondas.

I sat up straighter, my fatigue forgotten, as I began reading about Johnny the Hammer. In the *Herald-Star*, he described some of the work the Anacondas had performed during the riot-filled summer of 'sixty-six.

I looked at the clock. Reading about Johnny Merton couldn't be charged to Miss Ella's account. I read all five articles in the *Star*'s series: a day inside the projects at Sixtieth and Racine, a day at a clinic that Merton said the Anacondas had started, pictures of the Hammer feeding his own eight-month-old daughter.

'The police are labeling the Anacondas as a criminal gang, and for what? For starting a school milk program for black children? For opening a health clinic at Fifty-ninth and Morgan when there's been nothing in our neighborhood for fifty years? For organizing our people to vote, and getting us a real candidate for alderman in the Sixteenth Ward?'

This was a side of Merton I'd never known about. By the time I'd been facing him in that dreary bull pen at Twenty-sixth and California, he'd moved a long way from community organizer. The only organizing he did by then was where and how to separate small businesses from their money or his opponents from their body parts.

On the other hand, in 1967 he was already head of a powerful street gang. Maybe he'd just been spinning the reporter a line. A lot of white progressives had found street gangs glamorous or hip in the sixties. A lot of white reporters wanted the swagger that being on the inside with a black gangbanger would bring.

'The Man sees us as the threat to law and order on the streets of this city, but we weren't the ones throwing bricks at Martin Luther King, were we? So how come it's the brothers who are behind bars, not the white boys who turned cars over and such? You put Steve Sawyer up for murdering Harmony Newsome on no evidence whatever, no witness, no nothing. The sister went down in Marquette Park protecting Dr. King. And then they want to know why we aren't grinning and tap-dancing for them. What if it was a white boy killed her in the middle of those riots? They were the ones with the weapons, but they are not the ones in jail!'

The *Star* inserted a picture of Harmony Newsome in her high school prom dress, her hair carefully straightened so that it hung to her bare shoulders in a slight bob.

It wasn't the photograph that startled me into sloshing my contraband cappuccino all over my jeans. It was the caption: TRIAL BEGINS TODAY FOR STEVE SAWYER, ARRESTED IN THE MURDER OF HARMONY NEWSOME.

The sidebar explained that Sawyer's trial was the culmination of months of protest by friends and family of the dead woman: they had held a prayer vigil outside the Area 1 police station since her murder the previous August. Sawyer had been arrested at New Year's, which meant the trial was being rushed through like a bullet train.

I sat back in my chair, trying to figure it all out. Steve Sawyer. That must be, or at least might be, Lamont Gadsden's missing boyhood friend. I read through all the papers and finally found a small paragraph in the *Herald-Star*. On January 30th, Steve Sawyer was convicted of

Harmony Newsome's murder. No other details were given. Nothing about weapon or motive and certainly no mention of Lamont Gadsden.

I did a cursory search for John Does. There'd been a good few deaths because of the snowstorm, but even though I skimmed all the papers through the end of April I didn't find any reports of unaccounted bodies.

As I put the boxes back on their shelves, I kept wondering about Miss Ella. She must have known Steve Sawyer had been convicted of murder when she told Karen to give me his name yesterday. Why hadn't she included that information? What was going on with her and her hostility to this search that she herself had initiated? But I had looked for Steve Sawyer along with Lamont in Department of Corrections databases around the country and hadn't found either name. Did that mean that Lamont, too, was actually doing time somewhere?

I hurried past students whose faces were puffy from lack of sleep, pinched with anxiety over exams or jobs or love. In the sunken garden behind the library, I could see a gray-haired woman throwing a ball for her dog. They seemed to be the only happy creatures on the campus.

When I was a student, the war in Vietnam was just winding down. Students with pinched faces were often worrying about the draft, but it didn't seem like today's kids cared much about their own war eight thousand miles away. The thought gave me another idea about Lamont Gadsden. Maybe he'd forgotten to tell his mother he'd been drafted. His bones might be rotting in a jungle in Southeast Asia.

I detoured to Lionsgate Manor before going to my office. Miss Ella opened the door the length of the chain bolt but didn't invite me in. I asked her about Steve Sawyer.

'You knew he'd been sent to prison when you gave his name to Pastor Karen, didn't you?'

'Don't take that tone with me, young woman. You wanted the names of Lamont's friends, and I told you I didn't approve of them. Now you see why.'

It was an effort not to scream at the client. 'What about Lamont? Is he in prison, too?'

'If I knew where he was, I wouldn't have asked you to look for him.'

We went back and forth for a few more fruitless minutes. She didn't know where Steve Sawyer was now or she wouldn't admit to knowing, I couldn't tell. I finally left, cursing her and Pastor Karen — and myself, for agreeing to get involved in their quagmire.

Still, just to cross every *t*, I called the Pentagon when I got to my office to see if they had any record of Lamont. I wasn't expecting any information, so I was surprised when the woman on the other end said Lamont had been called up and told to report to his local draft board in April 1967. He was still officially absent without leave.

'You didn't try to find him, did you?' I asked.

'Oh, honey, I wasn't even born then,' the Pentagon's public-affairs woman said, 'but I expect, from what I've read, that they guessed he was one of ten thousand boys hiding out, either in Canada or somewhere deep inside his own neighborhood. Unless they crossed the legal system somewhere, applying for a driver's license or a loan, or if someone turned them in, we never saw them.'

Which left me back where I'd started, with zero information. Actually, that wasn't true: I had Johnny the Hammer to add to the mix. And I knew what had happened to Steve Sawyer — at least, until January 30, 1967.

In the Detective's Absence II

'The detective lady was here again today.' Ella held her sister's left hand, pressing it to make sure Claudia was listening to her. 'White girl. I think I told you that.'

The gnarled fingers pressed against Ella's own hard palm. *Yes, I'm listening to you. Yes, you told me she's white.*

'She's pretty much used up all the money I agreed to, finding out nothing.'

The left side of Claudia's mouth trembled, and tears slid down her face. Since the stroke, she cried easily. Claudia had always been emotional. 'Such a warm person,' was everyone's favorite description, making Ella feel colder, more bitter against the world at large. Claudia had never been a crier, though. She'd learned early in life, like Ella had herself, that tears were a luxury for babies and the rich. Her heart might break over a dead sparrow in the road, but she wouldn't cry her eyes out.

Now, though, you had to watch what you said. And sometimes Ella felt herself slipping back in time, back to when she was five and Claudia was the darling baby of the block, those soft brown curls, that winning smile, so cooed over in church that Ella would steal Claudia's dolly or slap her when Mama was off at work and

104

Granny Georgette wasn't looking. Pure mean-ness. She knew it then and she knew it now. But sometimes you got tired of always being the responsible one.

'Everything all right here?'

One of the nurse's aides had bustled over. The sisters were out on the sunporch, a kind of enclosed roof garden that held plants and a tiny fountain. The dog that some well-meaning do-gooder brought during the week was drinking from the fountain, to the delight of several of the other stroke patients, but Ella wouldn't let them bring it around Claudia when she was there. She couldn't abide dogs. Cats, either. Why feed and spoil some animal when children were going to bed hungry?

She looked coldly at the aide. 'If I need help, I'll let you know.'

The aide, black herself, stared pertly back at Ella. 'Your sister needs her eyes wiped. That's something you could learn to do for her, Miss Ella, if you don't want me here. But, since I am here, I'm happy to oblige.'

She knelt next to the wheelchair, dabbing at Claudia's face with a tissue.

'What's troubling you, honey? You need something I can bring you?'

Just like everybody else on the planet, soon as she talked to Claudia, she was crooning and singing. Jesus did try His saints, that was certain.

When the aide finally left, Claudia worked hard, forced herself to speak clearly. 'Who 'tective talk to?'

'I told you the names I gave her. She went

through them. I'll say this for her, she's thorough, she's a hard worker. She found Mr. Carmichael — you know, Lamont's science teacher at Lindblom — and he says he never heard from Lamont after the boy graduated. She talked to Curtis Rivers, who says he can't remember when he saw Lamont for the last time. She can't find Steve Sawyer. She knows he got arrested for killing Harmony Newsome, but she says there's no word of what became of him. She says she's been through all those prison records but can't find any trace.'

Ella's mouth worked. She hadn't liked the way the detective looked at her, as if she felt sorry for Ella. No right . . . No right to hand me pity, white girl! You think maybe Steve Sawyer was the only black boy who went through those prison gates and disappeared?

'Not 'Teve. 'Member, Ella? Not 'Teve. New name. Wha' name?'

'What do you mean, not Steve? Of course it was Steve Sawyer who got arrested. I remember how his mother carried on at the trial, even if you don't.'

Claudia's good eye drooped. She was tired, too tired to argue, too tired to be sure her memory wasn't playing tricks on her, the way it did since she'd had the stroke.

She took another breath. ''Hite girl talk Pa'tor?'

'Oh yes, this detective went to see Pastor Hebert. Of course, he isn't talking any more than you these days.' Ella paused. 'She says Rose saw Lamont.'

The left side of Claudia's face came alive. A shadow of her old smile broke through. ''Hen? 'Ere?'

'That same night he left us. After church, Rose was walking home and saw him go into a bar. With Johnny Merton.' Ella folded her arms in grim satisfaction. 'I always told you he was hanging out with those Anacondas.'

'No!' Claudia cried. 'Not drug deal'r. 'Mont not!' She was breathing hard from the effort of making the words come out right and from anger at her sister. 'Wron'! Wron'! Wron'!'

The young aide hurried back over, Pastor Karen in her wake. Ella hadn't seen the chaplain arrive on the terrace.

'What's wrong, Miss Ella?' Pastor Karen asked while the aide began fussing with Claudia.

'I talked to your detective this morning and I'm trying to explain to my sister what she reported. It's not easy. I told Claudia before you ever brought in this detective it wouldn't be easy.'

'Did Ms. Warshawski find Lamont?' The pastor pulled a chair up so that she was sitting between the two sisters.

'She found someone who saw him go into a blues bar with the head of a street gang the night he disappeared. My sister has never wanted to believe Lamont could have been dealing drugs.'

'Not drugs!' Claudia, anxiously following the dialogue, shouted the phrase. 'Oh! Can't talk, can't 'splain. 'Condas, gang, yes! Bad, no. Not bad, not 'Mont.'

She began crying again, tears of rage and frustration at her inability to speak.

10

The Roar of the Hoof

I had hoped that when I left the Public Defender's Office, I had also left Johnny Merton behind. I just didn't know who else to talk to about Lamont Gadsden or Steve Sawyer. I searched some legal databases and was relieved to find Merton easily. I was beginning to think I didn't know how to find people anymore. The Hammer was in Stateville, doing twenty-five to life, for murder, conspiracy to commit murder, and other crimes too heinous to mention in a family paper.

I tracked down Johnny Merton's lawyer. If I could persuade Merton and his attorney to let me in as part of Johnny's legal team, it would be my best shot at seeing him soon. Getting on the visitors' list at Stateville can take six weeks or longer.

The lawyer's name was Greg Yeoman, with an office on Fifty-fifth Street. So Johnny had left the big downtown firms behind and returned to home base in his current round of troubles. That probably said more about his income than his politics.

I drafted a letter to Johnny, with a copy to Yeoman, and returned to more pressing, or at least more lucrative, searches. Even though I was exhausted after my short night and long day, I kept going until almost seven, trying to catch up on paper.

I was finally packing up for the day when the outer bell rang. I saw my cousin on the video monitor and walked outside to meet her. Elton Grainger was there, too, offering Petra a copy of *Streetwise*.

'Vic, you saved my life.' He gave an elaborate bow and kissed my fingertips. He was graceful on his feet but smelled of sweet wine.

'You did?' Petra's face lit up. Perhaps she pictured me stepping in front of a sniper, or some other exciting scene from *Burn Notice*.

'I didn't haul him from a burning building or a sinking ship,' I said drily. 'He passed out in front of me, and I got him to a hospital.'

'I lost consciousness,' Elton corrected me. 'It's my heart. The doctors said I could have died without medical attention.'

'The doctors also said you could die if you don't stop drinking, Elton. And I saw Pastor Lennon this afternoon. She mentioned she'd found housing for you.'

'But I already got my own crib. It's private, and it's a damned sight safer and cleaner than those shelters. And after lying in a tunnel in Vietnam with fifteen other guys, I like being by myself, where I know no one's gonna piss on me in the dark.'

He turned to Petra. 'You ever been in a shelter? 'Course not. Young girl like you, you got your parents to look after you, like I shoulda done with my own girl, but what with one thing and another, I let her down.'

He squeezed his eyes shut briefly, hiding a drunken tear, while Petra shifted awkwardly from one foot to the other. Elton offered *Streetwise* to a couple of passing joggers, then looked at Petra again.

'Trouble with shelters, they rob you blind. You go to sleep for one second, and they steal the shoes off your feet. When you're homeless, your shoes are your best friend. You walk an awful lot and you need good soles under your soles, if you get my drift.'

'Where's your crib, Elton?' I asked.

'It's private. I start telling the world, and it won't be private anymore.'

'I'm not going to give it away to anyone, not even the pastor. But if I don't see you for a number of days, then I'll want to know where to look for you, see if you need a doctor again.'

He looked up and down the street. 'It ain't that easy to find, which is why it's such a good place, but it's over by the river. You get off Honore, and then there's a path. And then there's this shack, hidden way out of the way under the train embankment. Now, don't you go telling no one, Vic. Not your daughter, neither.'

Petra giggled. 'She's not my mother; we're just cousins. But, Scout's honor, I won't say anything.'

I gave Elton a dollar and took a paper. 'I'm coming back in ten minutes with a sandwich for you.'

'Ham on rye, mayo, mustard, no tomatoes, and I'd be real grateful, Vic.' He danced across the street on his light feet to a coffee shop, where people were sitting at outdoor tables.

'What are you doing here?' I asked Petra. 'Lock yourself out again?'

'I saw your car was still in the lot when I was driving home and I hoped you'd let me use your computer for a little bit. Just, like, half an hour, maybe, while you get him his sandwich.'

'They shut down the Net at the Krumas campaign?'

'No, but I want to catch up on my own stuff, and the wireless signal I've been using in my building disappeared today.'

'You've been stealing someone else's signal?'

'It's not stealing when it's just out there,' she said hotly.

I was too tired to argue the point, and, anyway, I didn't really care. I showed her the code to get into the building and made sure I hadn't left any confidential papers lying on my desk.

'Try to remember to turn out the lights when you leave, okay? The outer door will lock automatically behind you, so don't worry about that.'

She gave me her biggest, brightest smile and a warm thank-you. 'Did you really save that guy, Elton, is it? Did you really save his life?'

I felt embarrassed. 'Maybe — I don't know — I got him to a hospital, but he might have recovered on his own. The alcohol doesn't help. He's a Vietnam vet, which I only learned when I picked him off the sidewalk last week. War sure messes with people's minds.'

'I know. PTSD: we studied it in psych.'

'Brian got a plan for them?'

Petra nodded solemnly, feeling responsible for her candidate. 'Of course he does. He ought to be president — after Barack Obama finishes, I mean — but if we get him into the Senate, he'll do everything he can for people like Elton.'

Something about her youth, her solemnity, her faith in Brian Krumas, made me nostalgic for my own youth. I gave her a quick hug and went off to buy Elton's sandwich.

The next morning I started my dance with Johnny Merton's lawyer. Nothing in Greg Yeoman's manner inspired my confidence, but I tried to tread softly around him: he was my ticket to seeing the Anaconda chief. When I met Yeoman at his South Side office, he put on the act of someone who knew the gang world inside out and would run interference for a price.

'I'm not paying for the privilege of talking to Johnny. I only want to know if he'll talk to me. And given how crappy Stateville is, it will be easier if he'll let me come in as part of his legal team. That way, we can meet more easily and talk with a pretense of privacy.'

'Yes, Ms. Detective, but that kind of work costs money. If you want to see Johnny in a hurry, it will help you if you and I become friends.'

Ah yes, becoming friends. A Chicago euphemism for *bribe*.

'After all, the Anacondas still have a street presence, and you wouldn't want word to get out that you were threatening Merton,' Yeoman added.

'But if it does, I'll know where to come for

help, is that it?' I smiled sweetly.

He gave the satisfied smile of a man who sees that the little woman understands how powerless she is. 'If Johnny knows we're friends, I don't think it will come to that. But I can't look out for you for nothing.'

'Then we'll hope it doesn't come to that. Of course, Lamont Gadsden was close to Johnny all those years back when they were protecting Dr. King. Johnny won't be happy if he thinks his own lawyer was keeping him from helping Lamont's mama look for her missing son.' I got up to leave. 'I'm writing Johnny, you understand, writing to ask him to put me on his meeting list. It'll just be easier if he's willing to give me legal credentials — I'm still a member of the bar, after all. But I don't want you to have to do any work that you don't want to, so don't you worry, I'll put it all in writing.'

Yeoman gave me a look that made me glad I was standing near the exit, but he said there was no need to be so very literal-minded, he'd talk to Johnny when he went out to Stateville on Monday.

'In that case, I can send this letter without making changes to it.' I handed Yeoman a copy of the letter I'd written his client. Of course, I didn't say Johnny was the last known person to see Lamont Gadsden alive. I merely wrote that I was making inquiries on behalf of Ella Gadsden and her sister, Claudia, and, since Johnny knew everyone in West Englewood, I was hoping he could give me some names of more people to talk to.

On my way back to my office I stopped at Fit for Your Hoof. The man who'd been there on my first visit was sweeping the sidewalk again, singing to himself, but when he saw me his eyes widened in fear and he bolted into the shop.

When I followed him in, he was clutching Curtis Rivers's leather apron. 'She gonna hurt me. She gonna take away my manhood.'

'No, she's not, Kimathi, because I won't let her.' Curtis folded his newspaper under his arm and led the frightened man into some inner part of the shop behind the repair equipment.

When Rivers came back, he glared at me. 'What did you say to Kimathi to frighten him so badly?'

'Nothing.' I was bewildered. 'He saw me and ran for cover. What's he afraid of?'

'If you don't already know, it's none of your damned business to find it out. What is it you're really after, Ms. Detective Warshawski? Who you protecting or hurting or covering up for?'

No one else was in the shop. I sat on one of the stools next to the tiny chess table. 'What's that supposed to mean? I told you what I wanted and why. Who's suggesting it's something else?'

'That's well done, all innocent indignation. I'm impressed.'

I clasped my fingers under my chin, studying him. 'You're protecting this guy who's hanging around your shop. I don't know how to persuade you I'm not here to hurt anyone — '

He slapped his paper onto the small space between us. 'You can't.'

'But I'm starting to think you know where

114

Lamont Gadsden went all those years ago. Is it his mother who's got you so angry? She is a difficult woman, I know. Is there some secret from the old days that I don't know about?'

'I think I already said more than you needed to hear.' He got up and went behind his counter.

'Rose Hebert saw you enter the Waltz Right Inn right after Lamont went in there with Johnny Merton the night before the big snow. That was the last time anyone knew him to be alive.'

'Now I know you're lying!' He crashed a fistful of tools onto the counter. 'Rose Hebert in the Waltz Right Inn? You overplayed your hand right there, lady.'

I smiled through thin lips. 'You might not jump to conclusions if you listened more closely. I didn't say Ms. Hebert was *in* the bar. I said she saw *you* enter it. Just as she'd watched Lamont and the Hammer a few minutes earlier. Wishing she could be part of everyone else's good time.'

Rivers shifted a pair of shears from hand to hand, measuring me. At least he was thinking over what I said. 'I wouldn't dispute a lady's word, especially not a lady as sanctified as Miss Rose. But I went to the Waltz Right Inn a lot in those days, and I saw Lamont there more nights than not. The night before the big snow doesn't stand out in my mind, Ms. Investigator.'

'Is it Johnny Merton you're afraid of? I don't blame you. He scares me, too. Between him and Ella Gadsden, I don't know which makes me more nervous.'

'Maybe you scare easier than me, and maybe there's a reason for that.'

'What about Steve Sawyer? I know now he was convicted of murder, but he's disappeared, too. There's no record of him in the Department of Corrections. Is he the person you're trying to protect?'

'How dare you! How dare you, bitch, come in here and flaunt him at me!'

My jaw dropped. 'All I know about him is that he's vanished as completely as Lamont Gadsden.'

'You wish. You wish, don't you? Get out of here before I land these scissors inside you.'

The rage in his face was heart-stopping. I parted the handbag-laden ropes, trying to walk naturally, trying not to let the shaking in my legs show. I'd forgotten the train whistle. Its blast made me stumble as I opened the outer door.

A woman passed me at the door, holding a scuffed pair of pumps. 'Noise always gets to me, too.'

I tried to smile, but Rivers's fury made my mouth wobble. I drove slowly to my office, staying off the Ryan: I wasn't steady enough to deal with semis roaring around me.

11

Nothing Like Echézeau for Relaxing

At my office, I found Petra had written THANK YOU in big Magic Marker capitals on a piece of paper with a giant cookie from the coffee shop across the street taped to it. The ingenuous message made me feel marginally better, although I gave the cookie to Elton, who was outside again.

I also found a message from my temporary agency saying they had a Marilyn Klimpton available who met all my requirements including familiarity with legal databases. She'd start in the morning. That was a mercy.

Still, the only thing that would really make me feel better was to understand why Rivers was so furious with me. I spent the rest of the day trying to find out more about both him and Sawyer. My first search had been superficial. Now I went deeper into databases that cost more money. I couldn't charge these to Miss Ella, but I needed to learn what lay behind Rivers's rage.

Nothing came back to link either man to me. Rivers had served in the army from May 1967 through July 1969, with his year in Vietnam sandwiched in near the beginning. He'd been married; his wife died three years ago. They hadn't had any children. He had a sister and two brothers, both living in the Chicago area; I put their phone numbers in my case file. Rivers had never been arrested, and none of his siblings had ties to any of the people whose arrests I'd made possible, at least not in the last six years. Amy Blount had created a database of all the people I'd dealt with during that time, so it was easy to cross-check his name and address against my recent cases.

When I'd exhausted the Net, I dragged out the boxes I'd brought with me from my three years with the public defender. Of course, most of the material had stayed in their offices at Twenty-sixth and California, but my own notes and records still made a tidy pile when I'd emptied them onto my big worktable. I couldn't possibly check all those old cases, but I did pull out my files on Johnny Merton. Curtis's name never came up. Neither did Steve Sawyer's.

I called a friend of mine who had connections to the State's Attorney's Office and asked if they could locate the trial transcript for Sawyer's trial. And, yes, I knew what it would cost me to get a copy and, yes, I would pay for it.

I slid all the papers back into their boxes and tried to turn my attention to other jobs. I was wrapping things up for the day when my friend at the SA's office called back.

'No record of a Steve Sawyer in 1966 or '67, but things were a little sloppy back then. Any hints on the exact trial date?'

I looked through the notes I'd made at the university library. 'The vic's name was Harmony Newsome, but I don't know the trial date.'

He promised to have another look in the

118

morning. Right after he hung up, my cousin Petra phoned.

'Vic, you were a lifesaver to let me use your computer! Did you get your cookie? Do you remember you and Uncle Sal are coming to Brian's big fundraiser next week? I need to get names on a list since the president might come.'

'Yes, indeed, your uncle Sal is counting the minutes. You spell Warshawski W . . . A . . . '

'Yeah, I know. It's like a *warrior* in a *rickshaw* going *skiing*. How do you think I passed first grade? I was the only kid in my school who knew what a rickshaw was.'

We both laughed, and I felt better when I'd hung up. Maybe Mr. Contreras was right. Maybe I did need to be more like my cousin, learn to charm the socks off rocks.

The next day, I resolutely put the whole Gadsden case out of my head. Lotty and I were having our weekly dinner that night. I arrived a bit late, since a job had taken me to the DuPage County Courthouse, and the traffic back to the city was typically sludgelike. When Lotty let me into her apartment, I was surprised to hear voices in the background. She hadn't told me anyone else was coming.

Max Loewenthal was on the balcony that looked across Lake Shore Drive to Lake Michigan. He and Karen Lennon were both holding wineglasses. She was laughing at something he was saying.

'Ah, Victoria!' Max came forward to kiss me. We hadn't seen each other since my return from Italy. 'How good it is to see you again, and looking so very refreshed from your trip.'

That was typical of Max. I looked about as refreshed as a month-old jar of dandelions. He poured wine for me — Lotty doesn't drink, except for the occasional medicinal brandy, but Max keeps part of his important cellar at her apartment. We chatted over the Echézeau, while Lotty heated up some duck she'd bought at a carry-out place near the hospital.

Max knows Italy well. Over dinner, we talked about the wines of Torgiano, and the Piero frescoes in Arezzo. When I described the stage in Siena where my mother had trained and sung, Lotty and Max got into a side argument about the production of *Don Carlos* they'd seen there in 1958.

Finally, over coffee, Max came to the point. 'I saw Karen this afternoon at an ethics committee meeting, and when she told me she needed to see you I asked Lotty to include her tonight.'

'Not that I object, but I'm not hard to reach. Or has Miss Ella asked you to slip me some poison?'

Karen had drunk her share of the heavy burgundy, and she giggled with more hilarity than my comment merited. 'I guess you and she had kind of a quarrel yesterday morning.'

'You could say that. She's annoyed with me for trying to find one of her son's friends, and I'm annoyed with her for hampering the investigation and keeping me away from her sister.'

'I think Miss Claudia would like to talk to you, if she can get the words out clearly enough for you to understand. She had her own fight with her sister after you spoke to her, and it had something to do with that friend of Lamont's. That's why I wanted to see you as soon as possible, to talk to you about him.'

'You've run into Steve Sawyer?' I couldn't disguise my surprise.

'No. But one of my projects is serving on the Committee to End the Death Penalty, and the chair, she's a Dominican nun named Frankie — Frances — Kerrigan. She may know something.'

'I didn't think he got the death sentence, but maybe he was executed, and they didn't keep a record.' Maybe that was why Curtis Rivers was so furious.

Karen shook her head. 'No, no. Today's my day for racing around Chicago doing good works — death penalty this morning, hospital ethics this afternoon. I had just come from seeing Miss Ella, so she was on top of my mind. And while we were waiting for the rest of the group to arrive, I told Frankie how frustrated I felt, having sicced you on the case, and how it was impossible to figure out what was going on with Miss Ella. Well, Frankie asked a few questions, the way people do to be polite if they see you're troubled, but when she realized it had to do with that civil rights time she got really interested. It turns out she was in Marquette Park the day the girl was killed, the one Steve Sawyer was arrested for murdering.'

'What?' I was startled into sloshing coffee over Lotty's linen napkins.

'Yes, Frankie had really bucked the tide of the

121

South Side. Her family lived in Gage Park, and her father was furious when she got interested in the civil rights movement. But her mother kind of quietly supported her. That's when Frankie found her vocation as a nun. They were so brave, those sisters. They still are, actually. She lives and works at something called the Mighty Waters Freedom Center.'

'Harmony Newsome,' I interjected, trying to steer her back on course.

'Sorry, right. Frankie had been in Selma with Ella Baker, and she was marching with King and the others in Chicago. And she was with Harmony Newsome when Newsome was killed. Isn't that incredible?'

'It's extraordinary. Did she . . . What did she . . . the killer . . . Did she see . . . '

'I don't know what she knows about it. All she told me was that Steve Sawyer's arrest had always troubled her, and she'd like to talk to you.'

I bombarded Karen with questions: why had the arrest troubled the nun, had she seen the actual murder, had she stayed in touch with Sawyer?

Karen held up her hands, protesting. 'Ask Frankie. I don't know any of that stuff.'

Max laughed. 'Victoria, I seldom actually see you at work, but now I understand why you are so attached to that large dog of yours: you are very like a retriever trying to flush a rabbit, you know.'

I joined in the general laughter, and in Lotty's effort to turn the conversation in a different

122

direction. Max brought out a bottle of Armagnac, and even Lotty drank a little. We lingered late, unwilling to give up the warmth around Lotty's table, unwilling to go back to the world of coldness, of homelessness, of desperation, where Karen and I both worked.

As we rode the elevator down, Karen brought me abruptly back to that world.

'I checked with the SRO where I found a room for your homeless friend. He didn't show up, and I wondered about that. It wasn't easy finding a place. Low-income housing is disappearing faster than the rain forests.'

'It was good of you to go out of your way, but he seems to be a guy who's so allergic to other people that he'd rather take his chances on the street.'

We had reached her car. As she got in, I commented on how packed her life was, her work at Lionsgate, with the homeless, the death penalty. 'What do you ever do to relax?'

'What do you do?' she said pertly. 'Except for your Italian trip, it sounds like you're at it morning, noon, and night.'

I laughed it off. But as I walked the two blocks farther to my own car, I had to agree, I wasn't living much of a life these days.

12

Meeting the Hammer in the Tank

The first thing I did in the morning was to call the Mighty Waters Freedom Center and ask for Sister Frances. The woman who answered said Sister wasn't in the center that day but gave me her cellphone number.

'She's out of town, trying to find housing for the families of some of the immigrants who were arrested in Iowa last week. They can't find enough homes for them over there.'

I dialed Sister Frances's cellphone and wasn't surprised to get her voice mail. I left as concise a message as I could: Private detective, Steve Sawyer's trial. If she remembered any details after all these years, would she call me.

Marilyn Klimpton arrived from the temporary agency. I spent most of the rest of the day working with her on my files and creating a list of key clients. If one of them called, Marilyn needed to find me and get me a message at once.

Late in the day, I heard from Sister Frances. She wasn't sure when she'd be back in Chicago, she said, but she'd arrange to meet me as soon as she returned.

When I pressed her to tell me about Steve Sawyer, she said she wasn't sure that what she knew would be useful to me. 'I didn't know him, and I was so shocked, so overwhelmed, when

Harmony collapsed, I wasn't thinking at all. It wasn't until much later that I started to try to remember details about the march, and what I do remember is too . . . too . . . insubstantial. If I try to talk about it now, I'm afraid it will all evaporate. Let's wait until we can meet face-to-face.'

That was frustrating as well as disappointing: I should have realized that if Sister Frances had seen who killed Harmony Newsome, she would have spoken up forty years ago. I had to put the Lamont search on a back burner where the flame was just about ready to go out. I had to wait, anyway, for the trial transcript, for a chance to see Miss Claudia. In a bitter irony, Johnny Merton was beginning to look like my last hope.

Because nothing happens fast in Stateville, I was surprised that my visit to Merton happened ahead of the transcript and seeing Sister Frances. Inmate letters typically sit in bags for weeks, sometimes months, waiting for someone to get around to sorting them. When Johnny's lawyer Greg Yeoman called me a scant ten days after I sent my letter to Johnny with the news that the old gang leader would see me, I knew the Hammer still had plenty of influence.

My visit to Stateville was scheduled for the day before Brian Krumas's big shindig on Navy Pier. Before driving to Joliet, I took Mr. Contreras to his safe-deposit box in his old neighborhood so he could pick up his medals.

Even though he was keyed up almost beyond bearing, talking nonstop about the fundraiser, what he thought I should wear, whether he should call Max Loewenthal to borrow a dinner jacket, Mr. Contreras took time to warn me — again — against getting involved with Johnny Merton.

'He's got a lawyer, you said so yourself. Let the lawyer ask him your questions. If those black friends of his ain't talking to you, there's a good bet Merton won't, either. Would you trust some black detective who came around asking questions about your childhood friends?'

It wasn't our first go-round on the topic. 'I hope I'd have enough sense and skill to evaluate their sincerity and skill. And not judge them or any person on their race.'

'Yeah, well, if you have to have a dish perfect before you eat it, you're always going to starve to death, cookie, and that's a fact. It's pretty darned hard for the rest of us to be perfect enough for you.'

I was just perfect enough not to tell him he could get himself to Petra's damned fundraiser. At the bank, I waited in the lobby while he went to his safe-deposit box. He returned, glowing with justifiable pride over his collection: a Bronze Star, a Purple Heart, his Good Conduct Medal with stars, and his ETO medal, also with stars. I left him polishing them while I drove west to the Big House.

It wasn't even as though I wanted to visit Johnny, certainly not that I wanted to go to Stateville. I had been locked up once myself. It had almost killed me, and the helplessness and pain from those two months still haunt my nightmares. Prison is one endless round of violations of every human boundary — your mail, your time alone, your time with others. All these are invaded. Someone listens to your phone calls. Toilets and showers are open to any prurient guard. And your body itself is constantly violated, you being powerless to protest the frequent strip searches.

As I left the interstate for Route 53, my stomach twisted so hard that I doubled over at the wheel and had to pull off the road. I knew I would be searched, and that was the problem. I kept telling myself that it was impersonal. Too many people — civilians, lawyers, guards — had smuggled in weapons and drugs to exempt anyone from a thorough inspection of person and property. But the thought of willingly submitting to it turned me so cold I was shaking. I switched on the heater despite the warmth of the July day. Gradually I calmed down enough that I could drive through the gates.

I showed the sentry my letter from Greg Yeoman announcing me as part of Johnny Merton's legal team. I showed my letter from the warden authorizing my visit this afternoon. The guard did a thorough inspection of my car, including the old towels I keep in the backseat for the dogs.

When I passed through the three sets of razor wire, the electronic security, and the body search, I felt myself shriveling, disappearing into a numb place so I couldn't feel pain. I was panting when the search was finished and I was escorted into the lawyers' holding pen.

Like everything at Stateville, the room was old

and poorly lit. The sagging deal table where I was going to meet Merton might have been manufactured in 1925, the year the prison opened. Stateville consists of a series of circular cellblocks, with a guard station in the middle of each. Guards, in theory, can see all the cells without the prisoners being able to tell if they're observed.

As it stands today, the lighting in Stateville is so bad that no one can see much of anything. Many of the inmates spend days in the dark. Pigeons fly through their cells and along the corridors, getting in easily through the cracks in the windows and walls, but, like many of the humans, never finding their way out again.

Because of staff shortages, the men are essentially in a Supermax facility, allowed out briefly once a day, often going weeks without getting to use the exercise yard. Their starchy meals are slapped through the bars at them. I guessed that's why Johnny agreed so readily to let me be part of his legal team. Even if the state wouldn't let him use a gym or a library, they had to let him see his lawyer.

I'd been in the meeting room more than an hour before the locks scraped back. A guard came in with Johnny in cuffs and seated him at the scarred table. He left us alone for a minute, then returned with two Styrofoam cups of coffee. Johnny clearly had clout! The guard stepped to the corner of the room, supposedly out of earshot.

'So, little white girl lawyer couldn't take the heat at Twenty-sixth and California.' Johnny gave me an evil grin. 'Had to jump to the pig side of the fence, huh?'

'Good to see you again, too, after all this time, Mr. Merton.' I sat down across from him.

Actually, seeing Johnny was a shock. He was almost bald, and what remained of his close-cropped hair was white. He had once been lean and lithe, as supple as his anaconda namesake, but the loss of exercise and increase of heavy food had weighed him down. Only the anger behind the tearing in his bloodshot eyes was familiar. That, and the coiled snakes tattooed on his arms.

'And what brilliant new insights are you bringing to my legal team, little white girl?'

I narrowed my eyes at him. 'The pleasure of knowing I don't have to try to make you look good to a judge again.'

That silenced him. I hoped he was remembering the time I represented him all those years back. In our meetings, after showering me with the barrage of insults that had become his second skin, he had raged against the rampant racism of the courts, the cops, the economy. I somehow persuaded him to tone it down, to speak civilly to the judge and opposing counsel, and, in the end, we got an aggravated assault charge reduced to a sentence for battery.

'I read through your file over the weekend. I expect the cops could have got you anytime they wanted you for the rackets, but they were waiting for you to make a big mistake and do it in front of a guy with a wire.'

He smacked the table with his palm. 'You

think I'm admitting to anything in front of you, bitch, you are so wrong!'

I pulled *Suite Française* from my briefcase and started to read. After watching me in mounting fury, Johnny suddenly gave a bark of a laugh. 'Right. *Ms. Detective*, I should have said.'

'Close enough.' I closed the novel but didn't put it away. 'I'm looking for an old pal of yours. Lamont Gadsden.'

The ugly look, never far from his face, came back full bore. 'And what do you want to frame him for, Ms. Detective?'

'I'm the wrong kind of detective for that, Mr. Merton. I only want to find the guy.'

'So someone else can stick him in here next to me?' His face was mean, but he knew the prison system: he spoke in a jailhouse whisper.

'Is there a reason he should be? Was he complicit in one of those murders they booked you for?'

'They booked me but never proved anything. No evidence but a high-wire act, and that acrobat ain't soaring too high these days.'

The man who'd fingered Johnny for three gang-related slayings had been Johnny's second-in-command at the Anacondas. He'd been found dead in an alley the day Johnny's trial started, as I'd read in the *Herald-Star*'s account of the trial. They'd never arrested anyone for the man's murder, although his ears were missing, the telltale sign of an Anaconda who'd been abandoned by the gang.

'Booked you and convicted you. I'm sure Greg Yeoman did his best, but you didn't give him a

130

whole lot to go on with, did you?' I paused for a beat, let him smolder anew over his adjutant who'd flipped for the state. 'Lamont Gadsden. His mother is old, the aunt who doted on him is dying. They want a chance to see him before they pass.'

'Ella Gadsden? Don't make me start to cry, Detective. There is no guard in this prison — hell, no guard in this whole system — as hard as that pious lady. Only person who can match her is that reverend of hers.'

'What about Miss Claudia? She's having trouble holding her head up, has trouble even forming words. She wants to see Lamont again.'

He folded his arms in front of him in a deliberate gesture of disrespect. 'I remember those two sisters, and Miss Claudia was always a ray of sunshine on South Morgan. But I don't remember any Lamont.'

'He was with the Anacondas during Freedom Summer, helping look after Dr. King in the park.'

'His ma tell you that? No disrespect to an upstanding pillar like Ella Gadsden, but maybe her memory ain't what it once was. She must be somewhere near a hundred years old.'

'Eighty-six, and I don't think there's a thing wrong with her mind.'

Johnny laid his arms on the table so that the coiled snakes were under my eyes. 'I am the Anaconda, and if I say I never saw any Lamont Gadsden then he wasn't with us, Freedom Summer or not.'

His menace was palpable, but I couldn't

understand why he would be disowning one of his homeys. 'Funny, other people remember him well. So well, in fact, that they remember seeing you go into the Waltz Right Inn with him the night before the big snow. The last night anyone saw him alive.'

The words hung between us for a long moment before he said, 'Lot of people went through those doors, girl, hard for me to remember who I might have seen forty years ago. But I'll ask around. Maybe some of the brothers have a better memory than me.'

'And while you're asking around, see if any of them remember Steve Sawyer, too.'

He laughed, if that's what you could call the raw and raucous sound. 'I heard you were asking for Steve Sawyer. It's funny, *damned* funny, *Detective* Warshawski, that you of all people don't know where that brother ended up.'

I looked at him with so much bewilderment that he laughed again, then signaled to the guard. 'Time's up, white girl. Come again sometime. I always enjoy the chance to shoot the shit about the old days.'

13

A Wild Night at the End of a Pier

The police had cordoned off Navy Pier. As Mr.
Contreras and I showed our invitations at the
barricade and were passed through, I couldn't
help thinking of Stateville. It's true that the cops
here treated us with deference since we had the
VIP reception tags for people who gave ten
thousand or more or who had connections to the
campaign, but the barricades, the very idea that
we were never far from a police guard, made me
tense.

'You okay, doll? You want to ride?' Mr.
Contreras looked at me anxiously and pointed to
the trolley cars waiting to take guests to the east
end of the pier.

I realized I'd come to a halt in the middle of
the street. I smiled at him, determined not to
ruin his pleasure with my fanciful fears. The
evening was soft and warm, with the reflected
sunset painting the eastern sky a rosy gray. I took
his arm and said I needed the walk.

The pier is a strange, honky-tonk place, a
tourist version of what Chicago means: gimcrack
souvenirs of our sports teams and of the pier
itself, the big Ferris wheel where you slowly rise
above the city while listening to ads, the usual
high-fat eateries, and the endlessly blaring,
pulsing music. Loudspeakers placed on poles

every ten feet guarantee that you can never escape the noise.

'Krumas for Illinois' had taken over the pier, with the small donors partying at the west end under the Ferris wheel, and the VIPs a quarter mile east. In a signal of Krumas's star power, the state's celebrities were moving around us: the Illinois house speaker, the attorney general, county officials, corporate chiefs, big lawyers, local media luminaries.

You can't be a player in Chicago without crossing paths with many of the usual suspects. It pleased Mr. Contreras no end to have a number of people come out of the crowd to greet me by name. I saw Murray Ryerson from the *Herald-Star*, with a carefully fit young woman, and Beth Blacksin, who anchors Global Entertainment's evening news.

'See, doll? I said you needed to be dressed up. And, look at you, best-looking gal in the place, and everyone knows it.'

I'd worn my mother's diamond drop earrings and an ankle-length scarlet sundress I'd bought for a wedding last summer. I did it partly to please Mr. Contreras and partly, I confess, to flaunt myself. I wanted my young cousin to see that you could be circling my age and still be sexy. Dominatingly sexy. At that thought I gave an involuntary grimace. I hoped my time with Johnny wasn't rubbing off on me. How depressing for a feminist to feel the need to dominate anyone, let alone do it with a red dress.

Still, I enjoyed it when my once-upon-a-time husband, a player himself, partner at one of

Chicago's international law firms, gave me a silent whistle in greeting and kept an arm around my bare shoulder a moment too long for his current wife's peace of mind. When I introduced him and Terry to Mr. Contreras, the old man recognized their names and laughed with pleasure.

'He's thinking maybe he made a mistake letting you go, cookie,' he whispered audibly as we moved on.

'Not when he remembers how I've treated some of his important clients.' I laughed, too, though, happy at the attention.

Mr. Contreras was jaunty in his one good suit. His battle medals and ribbons attracted their own attention from men like my brief husband, who had carefully constructed their lives to avoid any public service, especially the kind where other people shot at you. Now too old to serve, they had a wistful longing that they, too, could brag of their military heroics.

At the east end of the pier, we showed our VIP tags again and got admitted into the grand ballroom. The outsize space with its star-studded ceiling had been designed back in 1916 with this kind of event in mind. A band, lost in one of the alcoves, was playing a rumba, the music barely audible above the hubbub of the crowd. White-jacketed waiters offered us little snacks, members of the legislature and the governor's entourage huddled with lobbyists and lawyers, PR staff and journalists kept firing camera strobes at obligingly grinning guests, and, near each entrance, city cops stood at grim attention.

We were handed Brian Krumas lapel pins by a twenty-something volunteer when we entered, and, everywhere we turned, Brian's smile gleamed at us, tacked to tables, chairs, the support columns in the room. Topping it all was a floor-to-ceiling portrait of the candidate with his slogan, KRUMAS FOR A CHANGE IN ILLINOIS. He was flanked by the president of the United States, the governor of Illinois, and the mayor of Chicago.

We were working our way to the drinks table when I felt a tap on my shoulder. I turned to see Arnold Coleman, my old boss at the county criminal courts. He'd been a political flunky who made sure not to step on the toes of a powerful state's attorney, and he'd been given his reward: a state appellate judgeship.

'Vic! Good to see you have time to turn out for young Brian, even if a judicial campaign is beneath you.'

'Judge Coleman, congratulations on your election.' I had turned down my invitation to a fundraiser for Coleman's campaign — Illinois treats its judiciary like any other commodity for sale — and Arnie clearly had kept a list of friends and foes. Another Illinois tradition.

'You keeping your nose clean, Vic?' the judge asked genially.

'Wipe it twice a day, Judge, on my sleeve, just like we used to do at Twenty-sixth and California . . . Judge Coleman, this is Mr. Contreras.'

My old boss gave a fake laugh and turned back to his own party, ignoring my neighbor's outstretched hand.

136

'Cookie, that's no way to talk to a judge,' Mr. Contreras scolded.

'I don't know. From what I hear from my old pals at the bar association, justice in Coleman's court isn't just blind, she's deaf and lame, too. The only one of the five senses she has left is touch, to feel how big the bills you're pressing into Coleman's hand are.'

'That's terrible what you're saying. It can't be true. People wouldn't stand for it.'

My mouth twisted in an involuntary grimace. 'When I was with the PD, Coleman and the state's attorney — Karl Swevel, it was then — fell over each other to see who could line up the most support for the local Dems. Who we defended and how we did it, that took a far distant backseat to licking local asses. Nobody minded then, and nobody seems to care much now.'

I saw that my neighbor was looking seriously aggrieved — as much at my choice of words as what I was saying — and patted his arm consolingly. 'Let's find the kid. We need to prove to her that we showed up.'

We worked our way through the press of people until we stumbled on Petra near one of the bars. She was talking to an assorted collection of lobbyists and legislators, who all had the round shiny faces of people who've spent too many years with their heads in the public trough.

Petra squealed with delight and flung her arms around Mr. Contreras. 'Uncle Sal, you made it! Look at you with all your decorations! And, Vic, you're so splendiferous! I wondered for a second who Uncle Sal's gorgeous date was.'

She gave a peal of laughter, and the group she'd been talking to, jaded old party hacks though they were, joined in. Mr. Contreras brightened instantly. Petra herself was wearing a chiffon flower-child dress over shimmery tights. In her spiky heels, she towered over almost everyone around her, including me.

'I have to find the senator, I mean Mr. Krumas — I keep forgetting we have to elect him first! — I know he'll want a picture with Uncle Sal,' she explained to her group, adding to Mr. Contreras, 'I'm going to take you to Uncle Harvey's table so I know just where to find you.'

She linked her arm through Mr. Contreras's and started to steer him through the crowd. I followed meekly in their wake. Twenty-three years old and she was already a pro, tapping shoulders, laughing, stooping to hear what an old woman with a hearing aid was shouting up at her.

About a dozen numbered tables, festooned with red, white, and blue balloons and giant RESERVED signs, stood near the band and a podium. Pretty soon, we'd get to hear a bunch of soul-stirring rhetoric. The tables were set aside for the people who had really come through for Krumas. According to the program, they cost a hundred fifty grand, fifteen grand a chair. Which just proves that adage about real-estate prices being all about location; the chairs were the same metal folding kind you can pick up at any church rummage sale.

The seats would fill when the speeches started. Right now, only a handful were taken. Petra took Mr. Contreras over to Table 1, right in front of the podium. Jolenta Krumas, the candidate's mother, was sitting with a small knot of older women who were all talking at the same time. Two younger women sat across from them. I recognized Jolenta from the newspaper photos of Brian with his family. I think the younger women were a sister and sister-in-law, but they weren't as striking as Jolenta. Her thick dark hair, well streaked with gray, was swept back from her face with a couple of diamond butterflies. At sixty-something, her posture was still perfect. She was intent on what the woman to her left was saying, but she looked up with a good-humored smile when Petra bent down.

'Aunt Jolenta! This is Salvatore Contreras. He's, like, my newest honorary uncle, and I know the senator-to-be would adore meeting him and having his picture taken!'

Jolenta Krumas, glancing from Petra to the row of polished medals on Mr. Contreras's suit, gave a wry smile. 'You are doing a splendid job, darling. I'll make sure Harvey tells your papa the next time they talk. And so, Salvatore, is Petra exhausting you? Come, sit down, rest! Brian will be along in a while. He's in back with some of Harvey's friends. Now that he's running for office, I'm lucky if I see him at Mass on Sunday mornings. This fundraiser is our first meal together in months!'

Petra turned around and saw me behind her. She made a grimace of mock contrition. 'Oh,

Aunt Jolenta, I'm sorry, I forgot to introduce my real cousin, Vic, Victoria. She's Uncle Sal's upstairs neighbor. She's a detective. Vic, this is the senator's mom.'

'Senator-to-be, dear, senator-to-be, we all hope. The election's a long way off. Let's not jinx it, okay?'

She patted Petra's hand, then indicated a chair near her for Mr. Contreras. Everyone swarming nearby stared at him, trying to figure out what he'd done to get a seat near power. I picked up a glass of wine from the Krumas table. As I moved toward an exit, I heard a woman say to her partner, 'Oh, that's Brian's grandfather. The guy behind me just told me that.' I laughed a little. So stories start.

I moved away from the building and walked to the east edge of the pier, remote from the pounding loudspeakers and the endless preening conversations. See and be seen, see and be seen.

I stared down at the ripples that gleamed on the black water. The pier was awash with money tonight, with everyone hoping some would drift their way. Or at least some glamour or a tiny snippet of power.

Like my old boss. I hadn't thought about Arnie Coleman for a long time, but he was the main reason I'd left the criminal courts. If you had a high-profile case that State's Attorney Karl Swevel wanted to ram through, you were supposed to put on the brakes when it came to questioning the cops or finding witnesses who might support your client. I'd ignored the directive once, and Coleman told me then that if it happened again I'd be on report to the state bar's ethics committee.

My dad had died six months earlier. My husband had just left me for Terry Felliti. I felt unbearably alone and scared. I could lose my license to practice law and then what would I do? The next morning I handed in my resignation. I went around to the private criminal defense lawyers and starting doing odd jobs for them. And one thing led to another, and I became a PI.

I started to feel cold in my backless dress. When I returned to the melee, the band was playing a martial medley. The candidate and his inner circle had appeared. Krumas was working his way through a wildly cheering crowd, shaking hands here, kissing a woman there — always choosing a woman hovering on the fringes of a group, never the most striking in the knot he was passing through.

He was, as Petra said, extraordinarily beautiful in person. You wanted to lean over and stroke that thick head of hair. And, even at a distance, his smile seemed to say, *You and I, we have a rendezvous with destiny.*

I craned my head to see if Mr. Contreras had been allowed to stay at Table 1. I finally saw him, looking a little forlorn, squeezed between Brian's sister, or maybe sister-in-law, and a stocky young man who was talking across my neighbor to another man on Mr. Contreras's left. I threaded my way to his side, prepared to rescue him, if that's what he wanted, or to stay on the sidelines until he was ready to leave.

Harvey Krumas appeared from some place in the crowd and stood behind his wife, with a small fist of cronies in attendance. I recognized the head of the Fort Dearborn Trust but none of the others, although a stocky Asian man was probably head of a Singapore company in which Krumas had a large stake.

The candidate's father was in his late sixties, with a thick head of curly gray hair and a square face that was starting to give way to jowls. When he saw me near Mr. Contreras, he bent to ask his wife about me. His heavy face eased into a smile, and he beckoned to me. It was only when I crossed to his side of the table that I realized Arnie Coleman was part of the group around him.

'Little Petra's talked about you — her big cousin, Vic, the detective. You're Tony's girl, right? Tony Warshawski was the staid and steady guy on the street,' he explained to his friends. 'Bailed me and Peter out more than once, back when we were wilder than we can afford to be these days. Bet you don't know that old Gage Park neighborhood, do you, Vic? Not much to detect there these days, except a boatload of poverty and crime a pretty gal like you shouldn't touch.'

'Warshawski used to work for me in the PD's Office, Harvey,' Arnie Coleman said. 'She was always getting her hands dirty up to her nose.'

Krumas was surprised to have Coleman turn his party chitchat into something so venomous, and I was astonished, too. Who knew his animosity ran as deep as that after all this time?

142

'We had a pretty rough crew as clients, Mr. Krumas,' I said. 'People like Johnny 'the Hammer' Merton. I don't know if you remember him from the roaring sixties, but I guess he was quite a figure on the South Side in his day.'

'Merton?' Krumas frowned. 'Name rings a bell, but I can't . . . '

'Head of a street gang, Harvey,' Coleman said. 'You probably saw his name in the papers when we finally got him locked up good and proper. After Vic here kept him loose for too many more years.'

'Is that the man you went to see yesterday?' Petra had popped up next to Krumas. 'Vic drove out to the prison to visit him, and he's, like, covered with snakes or something, didn't you say?'

'Tattoos,' I explained to a startled Harvey.

'You haven't taken up the baton again for Merton, have you, Vic? He's locked up for a reason. No maverick investigator is going to come up with any evidence that will overturn his convictions.' Coleman announced.

'Oh, she's not trying to get him out of jail,' Petra said. 'She's just working on a case that goes back to when you and Daddy lived in Gage Park, Uncle Harvey, some guy who went missing in a snowstorm or something. I made her drive me down to see the house Daddy lived in, and I couldn't believe it! Like, it would totally fit into our basement in Overland Park.'

'A guy who went missing in a snowstorm?' Krumas was bewildered.

'The big snow of 'sixty-seven,' I explained,

wondering at my cousin's capacity for burbling forth disjoint news. I looked at Coleman and added, just to be malicious, 'Black guy, a friend of Johnny Merton's. They were protecting Dr. King from the rioters in Marquette Park in 'sixty-six. Were you already with the PD then, Judge? Did you make sure those good boys who threw bricks and stuff got acquitted?'

'That's when this city began to go to hell,' Coleman growled. 'If your father was with the cops, he probably told you that.'

'Meaning what, Judge?' I could feel my eyes glittering.

'Meaning men ordered to turn on their neighbors, on decent churchgoers, trying to protect their families.'

'Are you referring to Dr. King?' I asked. 'If I remember correctly, he was a churchgoer — '

'That's enough!' Jolenta Krumas turned to look at us. 'This is Brian's big night. I don't want a lot of sniping and backbiting to interfere with it.'

'Jolenta's the boss.' Harvey crossed his arms over his wife's shoulders. 'And she's right as always. Vic, good to meet Tony's girl. I can't believe you've been stirring up the South Side all these years, and we never met. Don't be a stranger from now on.'

The words were pleasant, but they were a definite dismissal. Coleman smirked as I retreated to Mr. Contreras's side, while he got to stay next to power and glory. A moment later, though, the candidate appeared. Brian kissed his mother, embraced his father, and then was taken by Petra to meet Mr. Contreras. She was flanked by the campaign's PR staff, and it was my side of the table, not Arnie's, that Beth Blacksin's Global Entertainment cameras began shooting.

14

Dreams of Olden Times

There was a blizzard, a white wall of snow. I was choking as I fought my way through it. I needed to find my father, I needed to make sure he was safe. Someone had blown up St. Czeslaw's. Even though they were Christians they had blown up their own church. Father Gribac was standing in front of the burning building, waving his arms, shouting that the cardinal had it coming. 'If he wants to give the church to the niggers, we'll see there's no church left to give them!'

Every time I tried to pass him, the priest shoved me backward. My father was a policeman, he was trying to protect the church, they might have blown him up, too. 'Papà!' I tried to shout, but, dream-like, I had no voice.

I sat up, sweating and weeping. I'm a grown woman, and there are still nights when I need my father so badly that the pain of losing him cuts through and takes my breath away.

I supposed the dream came from seeing my ex-husband the night before, that and meeting Harvey Krumas. Dick Yarborough had loved my father. Tony was what kept our brief marriage together as long as it lasted. Even though Dick left me almost as soon as the funeral was over, whenever I see him he brings my dad to mind.

And then there was Harvey Krumas, the

candidate's father. Tony used to keep him and my uncle Peter on the straight and narrow, Harvey said last night, as if my dad being a cop meant he monitored people's lives. It had been a misery of my childhood, parents saying to my playmates, 'Victoria's father is a cop. He'll arrest you if you don't behave.' Apparently that was also how Harvey and Peter had seen Tony, not as a person, just a uniform.

'But if you hang out with a prize creep like Arnie Coleman, you probably need someone to keep you on the straight and narrow,' I said out loud.

My voice startled Peppy, asleep on the floor by my side. She twitched and whimpered.

'Yeah, you haven't seen your birth father for years and years, either, have you, girl?' I leaned over to rub her head.

Father Gribac had been the pastor at St. Czeslaw's, the church my aunt Marie attended. Actually, nobody had blown up St. Czeslaw's, but Father Gribac sure had fanned fires of hatred in South Chicago after the riot-filled summer of 'sixty-six. Marie was just one of the crowd of furious St. Czeslaw parishioners who vowed to do everything they could to show King and the other agitators he'd brought with him that they should stay in Mississippi or Georgia where they belonged. She was furious that the cardinal made every priest read a letter to the parish on brotherhood and open housing.

'Our Chicago Negroes always knew their place before these Communists came to stir them up,' Marie fumed.

Father Gribac read Cardinal Cody's letter, since he was a good soldier in Christ's Army, but he also preached a thundering sermon, telling his congregation that Christians had a duty to fight Communists and look after their families. We heard all about it from Aunt Marie when she dropped in on my mother a few days after my tenth birthday.

'If we don't stop them in Marquette Park, they'll be here in South Chicago next. Father Gribac says he's tired of the cardinal sitting in his mansion like God on His throne, not caring about white people in this city. We're the ones who built these churches. But Cardinal Cody wants to let those ni — '

'Not that word in my house, Marie,' my mother had said sharply.

'Oh, you can be as high and mighty as you like, Gabriella, but what about us? What about the lives we worked so hard to make?'

My mother had answered in her ungrammatical English. 'Mama Warshawski, she tells me always the hard times Polish peoples have in this city in 1920. The Germans are here first, next the Irish, and they are not wanting for Polish peoples to work at their work. Mama Warshawski tells me how they are calling Papà Warshawski names when he looks for work, stupid Pollack and worse. And Tony, he must do many hard jobs at the police, they are Irish, they not liking Polish peoples. Is always the way, Marie, is sad, but is always the way, the ones coming first want to keep out the ones coming second.'

I hugged my knees, shivering as my sweat

148

dried. It seemed as though everywhere I turned these days, I was being forced to think back forty years to those hot riot-filled days. Or to the January blizzard that followed. Johnny Merton, Lamont Gadsden, and now, tonight, Arnie Coleman, with his veiled racist comments: *That's when this city started going to hell . . . cops forced to turn on their own neighbors.*

They had busted up the South Side, those riots. My father, coming home after four days on shift without a break, had been shaken by the hatred he'd experienced, directed at him and his fellow officers, and even at some nuns who were marching with Dr. King. *'You can't believe the insults these Catholic boys shouted at the sisters. People I went to Mass with when I was a boy,'* I'd heard him tell my mother when he finally got off duty.

I pulled on a sweatshirt and shorts. Peppy followed me into the dining room, where I knelt in front of the built-in cupboards and pulled out the drawer where I keep a photo album of my parents.

I brooded over their wedding picture: City Hall, 1945. My mother, in a severely tailored suit, looking like Anna Magnani in *Open City*. My father, in his dress uniform, bursting with astonished pride to be marrying 'the most extraordinary woman I ever met.'

Petra's father, Peter, a late thought in my grandparents' life, was a child in a sailor suit in the family photo. My grandfather, who died when I was small, was there, tall and big-boned like all the Warshawskis. Boom-Boom's parents appeared in several photos, my aunt Marie characteristically looking sourly at her immigrant sister-in-law, my uncle Bernard giving Gabriella a most unbrotherly kiss. I looked more closely at that picture. Maybe that explained some of Aunt Marie's sourness.

Pictures of me didn't appear until much later. I was a late thought, too, in a way. My mother had three miscarriages before I was born, and two more after, a sign, or maybe a cause, of the cancer that grew inside her and silently overwhelmed her.

I found a family shot at the beach when I was three: my mother, in a rare moment of relaxation, looking more like Claudia Cardinale than Anna Magnani; me, grinning over my sand bucket; my dad, in swimming trunks, bending over her and me. His two pepperpots, he called us.

I flipped the pages. Softball in Grant Park. My dad played on one of the teams the department fielded. I used to know most of the men he played with. I frowned over the team picture now, reading the names printed underneath in my father's curious boxy script. Bobby Mallory, in his rookie year on the force, playing shortstop. Two men who'd died in the last few years had been in the outfield.

My eyes widened in surprise as I looked at the man next to Bobby: George Dornick. He'd been part of Brian Krumas's entourage last night. After the drumrolls and trumpets gave Krumas a royal fanfare, those of us lurking around his father's table met the candidate and entourage.

Dornick was running a big private security firm these days. He was advising the candidate on terrorism and Homeland Security issues.

It's not strange to find ex-cops running private security firms. It was strange meeting him last night and now seeing him forty years younger, with his hair still brown and thick, grinning with my dad and Bobby and the other men I'd known. If Tony hadn't died, maybe he'd have gotten rich doing private security, too.

I finally put the album away and went back to bed, but I couldn't relax into sleep again. I found a bottle of blueberry juice in the cupboard and took a glass out to the back porch. Peppy, who'd wandered down into the yard, gave a short bark. I leaned over to see the back gate starting to open. Peppy stood stiff-legged, growling. I called to her, but she stayed at attention, growling more loudly as a luminous white shape appeared.

I started down the stairs in my bare feet but stopped on the second-floor landing when I realized it was my new neighbor returning home with his bass in its large white case. Peppy changed at once from warrior to cheerleader, circling around him as he came up the stairs.

'That's a good feeling, someone to greet you at the end of a hard day. I was feeling sorry for myself just now, coming home to an empty apartment.' He was in black tie tonight, but he'd put the tie in a pocket and undone his shirt. 'What are you doing up so late?'

'Indigestion. I ate too many politicians for dinner last night. What about you? Isn't it three or something?'

'We finished at Ravinia, and one thing led to another,' he said vaguely, making me suppose he'd been with a lover. He leaned the bass against his kitchen door. 'What politicians were you eating?'

'My cousin — the tall kid you may have seen around here — she has a bit part in the Krumas machine. She dragged me to a high-end event. At least my ex saw me looking my best, not the way my clients will in a few hours.'

'Oh, these exes! At least yours probably isn't an oboe player. Their main relationship is with their reeds.'

'Mine was wound up most in his billable hours. But I brought my own faults to the table,' I added somberly, thinking again of Morrell and my failure to make that relationship work.

I left Jake Thibaut at the third-floor landing and went back inside. I tried to sleep the few hours that remained before I had to go downtown for my seven-thirty meeting. After I finished my presentation — more by luck than skill — I went to my office to check in with Marilyn Klimpton from the temporary agency. I tried to focus on reports and e-mail, but I was too sleep-deprived. I went back home to bed.

15

Old Trial . . . or Something Like It

I was awakened a little before three by another family drama: Mr. Contreras's daughter, Ruthie, arriving from Rolling Meadows with her two sons, was shouting at her father from the doorstep. Mitch and Peppy were barking furiously.

Once again, I went to the street window to look down. The dogs were waving their tails as they barked to show they didn't mean serious harm. Ruthie was standing on the cement slab in front of the door while her teenage sons lingered behind, looking as though they'd rather be anywhere than here. From above, I had a clear view of the black roots sprouting in Ruthie's bleached hair.

'We have to find out about you on the news. You don't have the common decency to call and say, 'Oh, by the way, I'm going to meet all the bigwigs on earth,' let alone invite me and your grandsons to go with you. Your own flesh and blood, and you show up on TV with that so-called detective.'

My cousin Petra suddenly appeared in the scene, dancing up the sidewalk, in stovepipe jeans and her high-heeled boots, clutching a sheaf of newspapers. The dogs ran to greet her, barks turning to squeaks of pleasure.

'Uncle Sal!' Petra's husky voice drowned out

Ruthie's nasal whine. 'Uncle Sal, just look! Wasn't that a fabulous party? Weren't we all incredibly brilliant? And you are a *star*, Uncle Sal. Did you see the *Herald-Star*? And the *Washington Post* used the same photo.'

I ran to the bathroom and stood under a cold-water shower for a minute. I hadn't bothered with the papers on my blear-eyed way to and from the Loop this morning, but I'd tucked my copy of the *Star* into my briefcase. I looked at it now.

There Mr. Contreras was with Brian Krumas, on the front page of the ChicagoLand section. Krumas, a lock of hair falling over his forehead à la Bobby Kennedy, had one hand on Mr. Contreras's shoulder, the other clutching Mr. Contreras's arm just behind the elbow, so that the camera's focus was on my neighbor's medals. His Bronze Star gleamed as brightly as the candidate's smile. Petra's value to the campaign must have quintupled overnight when she got that photo staged.

I pulled on my jeans and a T-shirt and went down to join the party, or whatever it was. 'Autograph, autograph.' I thrust my copy of the paper at Mr. Contreras. He was smiling so widely I thought his ears might split open.

'Isn't he wonderful?' Petra said. 'Uncle Sal, you're a hero! There's no stopping you now!'

She was oblivious to Ruthie's broad insults: '*What hole did you crawl out of? I don't remember no cousins called Petra. This here is his real family.*' Her sons were embarrassed and her father offended, but Petra ignored her,

154

demanding that I let them go up to my apartment to look at my computer.

'He's on YouTube. He'll want to see that. And you guys will, too, won't you?'

The grandsons shuffled their feet and mumbled, adolescents unnerved by Petra's Valkyrie sexuality. Her cellphone rang as we were clambering up the stairs. Petra looked at the number, then announced it was her office, she had to take the call.

'He does? Really? . . . No, I'm at my cousin's . . . Yeah, my cousin Vic . . . I suppose in half an hour.' She hung up and turned apologetically to Mr. Contreras. 'That was Tania, my boss at the campaign. They never need me for anything. Anything important, I mean. In fact, Tania told me I worked so hard last night I could take today off, but now I'm supposed to go to the office right away for a meeting. Vic, can you show Uncle Sal the YouTube footage? All you have to do is search for last night's event. I gotta run.'

She clattered down the stairs in her high-heeled boots, leaving Ruthie fuming even more. *Who did she think she was?*

'She's my cousin, Ruthie, so let it ride, okay?' I took the unhappy family up to my apartment and set up my laptop for them. The grandsons could navigate YouTube for their grandfather, but, while everyone was shouting out on the walk, I'd gotten a text message of my own. The transcript from the Harmony Newsome murder trial was ready for me to pick up.

I rode the El downtown. Finding the trial record hadn't been hard: they're all on microfilm

155

down at the county building. Getting it translated had been tougher. The reporter who'd transcribed Steve Sawyer's trial was long gone. Her machine and her shorthand notes were also long gone. Finding someone who could make sense of the document hadn't been cheap: I had to shell out almost two thousand dollars for the transcript. I handed in my credit card with a sour face. Miss Ella, allegedly, was paying me a thousand dollars for my initial inquiries. I was now close to that much in the hole. How much further could I really afford to go?

I rode back to my office, feeling so bitter about the money I was losing on Miss Ella's business that I couldn't bring myself to look at the transcript. The temp was typing letters and e-mails that I'd dictated during the last few days. She handed me a list of a half dozen phone calls to return.

While I was holding for Darraugh Graham, I finally flipped through Steve Sawyer's trial record. For a murder trial, it wasn't very long, only nine hundred pages, many of them filled with yes-or-no answers. Not much defense. As Darraugh's PA came back on the line to apologize for keeping me waiting, my own name suddenly jumped out at me.

Testimony of arresting officer, Tony Warshaw-ski. My father sent to pick up Steve Sawyer? This couldn't be, my dad, back in my life, in this unbelievable coincidence. Johnny Merton's bitter comment suddenly came to me, that it was damned funny that *I*, of all people, didn't know where Sawyer was.

'Vic? Vic, are you still there?'

'Caroline,' I said weakly. 'Tell Darraugh I'll have to call him back. Or if it's urgent, he can reach me on my cell tonight.'

I hung up without waiting for her response and took the file over to my couch. I couldn't make sense of any of it. Merton, Sawyer, my dad: they began to whirl in my head like an old top until I felt so dizzy I couldn't see anything at all. 'Enough melodrama!' I said out loud, startling Marilyn Klimpton: 'Shape up, Warshawski. Pull yourself together!'

I went to the little kitchen I share with Tessa and made myself a black coffee. Sitting cross-legged on my office couch, I went back to the beginning and read the whole transcript. The trial had lasted a day and a half.

Harmony Newsome had died in Marquette Park on August 6, 1966. The day of the civil rights march, accompanied by an eight-hour riot performed by the local community.

At first, police and fire officials thought Newsome had fainted. It wasn't until they couldn't revive her in the ambulance that the fire department realized she was dead. Because of the confusion in the park and the amount of debris left behind, police had been unable to locate exactly where she died or to find the murder weapon.

The medical examiner testified that Newsome had been killed when a sharp object penetrated her brain through the eye. The detectives in charge of the case, Larry Alito and George Dornick, testified, claiming that right after

Christmas, 1966, an unnamed neighborhood informant led them to Steve Sawyer. Otherwise, given the crowds in the park when Newsome was killed, they probably would never have made an arrest.

Marilyn Klimpton was leaning over me. It was five-thirty, and she was leaving for the day. 'Sorry to interrupt, but I called your name three times, and you didn't hear me. I've left letters for you to sign. And you still need to get back to Darraugh Graham.'

I smiled as best I could and attempted to follow her report on her progress today. As soon as the door closed behind her, I went back to the transcript. After three days in custody, Sawyer had confessed to the murder. Alito read the confession out in court. Sawyer had been in love with Newsome, but she wouldn't pay attention to him. She got 'hincty' when she went away to college.

JUDGE GERRY DALY: Hincty? Is that some kind of colored word?
ASST. STATE'S ATTORNEY MELROSE: I believe so, Your Honor.
JUDGE DALY: Could I have that in English, Counselor? (Laughter in the courtroom.)
ASST. STATE'S ATTORNEY MELROSE: I believe it means 'stuck-up,' Your Honor, although I don't speak their lingo, either.

According to Sawyer's confession, he thought he could kill her during the riots and have the murder be blamed on the white people in the park. Judge Daly questioned Sawyer briefly. The public defender assigned to Sawyer raised no objections, either during the reading of the testimony or during the judge's questioning. He didn't call any witnesses. He didn't try to get the name of Alito's and Dornick's snitch.

Sawyer's responses to the judge seemed vague and unconnected, and he kept saying, 'Lumumba has my picture. He has my picture.'

The jury deliberated an hour before returning their guilty verdict.

I reread my father's testimony, shivering. It was as though my nightmares of the early morning had been a prophecy of what I would find here. My father, sent to execute the warrant, described Sawyer's shock and his attempt to flee, described cuffing him, described telling him his rights. Miranda was new that year. The transcript included some ribald byplay between State's Attorney Melrose and Detective Dornick over Sawyer's rights.

Dornick and Alito, the detectives in charge. Larry Alito had been my dad's patrol partner for a year or so around 1966. My dad hadn't liked him much, and I could remember him complaining about Alito to my mother. There was one night when he came home depressed: Alito had been promoted to detective, while he, Tony, with ten times the experience, was still in uniform. My mother consoled him, saying, 'At least you don't have to work with that *prepotente* any longer.'

The sky outside my high windows darkened as I sat on the couch, staring into nothingness.

When I finally turned on a light, I saw it was after eight o'clock. I signed my letters and took a last look at the transcript before putting it into the Gadsden file. I'd been brooding so much over my father that I hadn't noticed the name of Steve Sawyer's lawyer. Arnold Coleman, my old boss, now a judge. He'd been a green, young public defender in 1966, but he couldn't have been so green he didn't know he was supposed to raise an occasional objection. Like to the racially charged language in the court.

And why hadn't he demanded the identity of Detective Alito's snitch? Could that have been Lamont Gadsden?

16

Alito Off Guard

'Is this your idea of a joke, Vicki?'

I'd waited an hour for a word with Bobby Mallory. Dropping in unannounced on a senior police officer is never a really brilliant idea, but at least he was actually in the building. The sergeant guarding access to those shiny new offices in Bronzeville didn't know me, but Terry Finchley, one of Bobby's aides, was nearby. He isn't exactly a fan of mine, but he did grunt at the sergeant that it was okay to send me upstairs to wait for a break in Bobby's schedule.

I'd brought a stack of work with me. As the wait dragged on, I managed to answer a bunch of e-mails and finish a report, on the fraud burdening a small tool-and-die company, before Bobby came out of his office to see me.

He'd greeted me with a mix of affection and wariness. He knew I wouldn't have come to police headquarters unless I had a favor to beg. Still, he put an arm around me, called to his secretary to bring in a cup of coffee for me, and started with family news. He'd become a grandfather for the seventh time, but he was as pleased as he'd been the first time round. I made suitable noises, and wrote a note in my PDA to remember a christening present.

'That boy you're dating, I hear he's back in

Afghanistan. He didn't go halfway round the world to get away from you, did he?'

'That boy is a fifty-year-old man, and we both realized he finds Afghanistan way more exciting than he does me.'

I startled myself as well as Bobby with the bitterness in my voice. Before Bobby could probe, or, worse, comment that my lack of domestic virtues was what drove men from my side, I quickly started to explain my story: the trail I was trying to follow, how Ella Gadsden's inquiry had led me to the old Harmony Newsome murder trial.

Bobby shook his head. 'If it was one of mine, I've forgotten it.'

'It was high-profile at the time. Civil rights worker, killed in Marquette Park. Her family brought a lot of pressure on the department until they made an arrest.'

'I still don't remember.' He smiled bleakly. 'Families are always pressuring us to make arrests. This time, we made an arrest, right? And got a conviction? So where's your beef? You saying now that the verdict was tainted? You're Madame Zelda who sees all, knows all?'

I pressed my lips together. 'I wasn't planning on overturning the verdict, although maybe I should try. Reading the trial transcript was like reading Mistrial, Malfeasance, and Nonfeasance 101. The state couldn't produce a murder weapon, and the public defender didn't call any witnesses. The detectives, the state's attorney, and the judge had a good old time laughing over language and customs on the black South Side, except they used far-less-polite words.'

'So the justice system in 1967 had its flaws. I can't fix the past. Tell me one of my cops is using filthy language today, and I'll do something about it.'

'My dad was the arresting officer.' I got the words out with difficulty. 'I'm trying to find out what happened. People are hinting that Tony crossed a line — '

'I don't believe this!' Bobby thundered. 'I don't believe even you would have the nerve to come in here and smear Tony's name. Two things mattered to him: Gabriella and you . . . you for what reason I've never understood. The best officer, the kindest man, the closest friend, and you . . . you . . . you have the *damned* gall to — '

'Bobby!' I stood and leaned over the desk into his angry face. 'Shut up and listen to me! I don't want to think any bad thing about my father, ever. I know better than you what kind of person he was. He trained a gazillion cops. A lot of them did like you, went on to big careers, but he wouldn't put in for promotion himself because he didn't want to make compromises in his . . . his code of honor.

'Something happened to Steve Sawyer after my dad picked him up. The men who know Sawyer won't tell me, but they keep passing hints, and I need to know.'

'If I knew, which I don't, I wouldn't tell you. You'd put it out in the *Daily Worker* or some other left-wing pile of crap and smear — '

'Enough!' I sat down wearily. 'It is not easy to be a cop's kid and date cops and have cop friends, all the time knowing what some people do with that badge in front of them. But if Tony didn't talk to you about the Sawyer arrest, he didn't. Maybe that means it went by the book. I guess I'll see if George Dornick will talk to me. Or Larry Alito.'

'Dornick? Alito?' Bobby leaned back in his chair, suddenly quiet, even wary. 'Why . . . Oh, were they the detectives in charge? Well, well, well. Dornick is a big SOB now out in the private sector. I'd love to be a fly on the wall listening to how you figure out a way to talk to him.'

'And Alito?'

'Last I heard, he retired up to Chain of Lakes. You let me know how you make out with him and Dornick. If you end up with your nose broken, I'll send them a personal commendation on department stationery.'

I stood up to leave. In the doorway I turned to look at Bobby, who was still breathing hard.

'Guess who Steve Sawyer's PD was, Bobby. Arnie Coleman!'

'So?'

'So, when I worked for him in the criminal PD's Office, he cut so many deals with the State's Attorney's Office, he looked like the SA's chief assistant. You know he got his reward: a state appellate judgeship. Judge Coleman was hanging around Harvey Krumas at the big shindig on Navy Pier the other night.' When Bobby didn't say anything, I added, 'And George Dornick is young Krumas's adviser on Homeland Security and terrorism.'

'What's your point, Vicki? That Krumas knows a lot of people?' Bobby smacked his forehead in mock comprehension. 'Oh, I get it. Harvey Krumas fixed the Steve Sawyer trial forty years ago, even though he was just a twenty-something guy from the South Side without any power?'

'His father owned Ashland Meats,' I said.

'Yeah, that was a two-bit outfit before Harvey took over and turned it into the operation he's got today. When I joined the force, Dornick used to razz Harvey about having the bulls with the smallest . . . Never mind that. But in — '

'Dornick used to razz Harvey?' I asked. 'Harvey was never a cop. Or was he?'

'No, no. He and Dornick grew up in Gage Park together. Ran around with Tony's brother, your uncle Peter. Are you trying to say that somehow Harvey got Arnie Coleman to turn on his own client while Dornick got the perp to make a phony confession and now Harvey's rewarding them by letting them lick his son's ass, if you'll pardon my French? Do you imagine if Tony was still alive he'd be part of that inner circle, too, because he tortured Sawyer for Krumas?'

It was my turn to be discomfited. I left without trying to say anything else, but when I returned to my office I looked up Dornick and Alito. Bobby had made me feel defensive, but when I first said their names he'd grown quiet. At full strength, the CPD includes some thirteen thousand officers. It's true Bobby's been with the force a long time and he knows a lot of people, but he doesn't know all thirteen

165

thousand. Yet those two names had stood out for him.

Of course, Bobby would have met Harvey Krumas and my uncle Peter through my dad. If Peter and Harvey had grown up with George Dornick, I guess it wasn't surprising Bobby would have met Dornick, too. And since Alito and Dornick worked together, Bobby would have known Alito as well.

Maybe I was reading too much into Bobby's reaction to their names. But that didn't stop me from digging around on the Web.

There were hundreds of hits for George Dornick. Dornick had started Mountain Hawk Security when he retired from the force. His website told me that the firm specialized in training police officers around the world in how to do everything from recognizing and combating terrorists to identifying clandestine drug labs. Mountain Hawk provided tactical training for officers needing help with close quarters combat, use of Tasers and other 'restraining devices,' wilderness survival for desert- and mountain-based forces, and how to use cars as offensive weapons in urban environments.

'Our clients expect total confidentiality, and we provide that, along with world-class training, so we regret that we can't supply you with a client list. We have worked with police forces throughout the Americas, in cities, in jungles, and in the punishing Sonoran Desert. We have also sent our experienced personnel into combat zones to provide support for American troops. With offices and equipment in nine strategic locations around the globe, we can be at your next training meeting within hours.'

I found pictures of Dornick, looking alert and combat ready, with everyone from Chicago's mayor to the president of Colombia. I saw Dornick demonstrate the use of Tasers to women at a domestic-violence shelter and read articles about contracts he'd received from San Diego, Waco, and Phoenix to conduct special border-patrol training sessions. I couldn't find information about his life as a policeman, but he'd left the force some fifteen years ago.

Alito looked more like the average cop. Forty years on the force, retired to a small lake in northern Illinois. The little bit of press he'd gathered showed a mixed picture. He'd been cited for bravery during a hostage crisis involving armed robbers at a strip mall on Roosevelt Road. Then, six months later, he was accused of using excessive force at the same incident, for killing both robbers, as the situation unraveled. He'd injured one of the hostages, which was why he'd been censured, and an unnamed coworker quoted him as saying, 'She's lucky to be alive, and they're better off dead, so what's the beef?'

Since a lot of the citizenry agreed that a dead armed robber saved the city the expense of a trial, the letters to the editor were predictably pro-Alito, with a segue into the importance of every American being fully armed at all times.

I stared blankly at the computer for a few minutes, then pulled up a map of Alito's home. He lived just a mile south of the Wisconsin border, near one of the little lakes that dot the hills northwest of Chicago. A lot of Chicagoans have weekend homes up there. Some, like Alito, retire to live there year-round.

According to MapQuest, the sixty-mile trip from Western and North to Lake Catherine should take about eighty minutes, but they were assuming you were driving at three in the morning during a rare period when neither the Kennedy nor the Edens was under construction. I reached the north shore of Lake Catherine two and a half hours after leaving my office.

It's true the birds were chirping, the sun was shining, and the air was clearer than on Milwaukee Avenue, but my mood was much grumpier, and I was desperate for a bathroom. That involved backtracking to the nearest service station, where I spent a little fortune filling my Mustang, used the mercifully clean washroom, and bought a chili dog to tide me over. I'd been so intent on my searches that I'd forgotten lunch, a major violation of the Warshawski family motto: 'Never skip a meal.'

It was close to five o'clock when I finally pulled off the road at the top of Queen Anne's Lace Lane and walked down to Alito's house. He lived in a yellow split-level shoehorned onto a tiny lot, his neighbors as close as they would have been on the South Side of Chicago. But here, he was just a few steps from the water.

As I'd sat in the tollway traffic, I'd tried to come up with a strategy for getting Alito to talk to me. At one of my PI training seminars, we'd reviewed 'techniques for conducting a successful interview.' Get your subject to think you're on his side. Don't be confrontational. Establish some common ground that he has to assent to. *'So, Larry, did you torture Steve Sawyer?'* would not be a good opening gambit. Instead, try, *'So, Larry, let's agree that it was a necessary and good thing to torture Steve Sawyer.'*

Alito's wife answered the door. She was about her husband's age, somewhere in her sixties, in Khaki cargo pants, with faded red curls that reminded me a little of the aging Gwen Verdon. She didn't smile or greet me with any warmth, but she didn't slam the door in my face, either. When I explained that I was the daughter of one of her husband's old partners on the force and hoped Detective Alito and I could talk, her expression lightened minimally.

'Larry just got back from golf. He's showering. He'll be down in a minute or two. I'm making supper right now . . . '

The sentence trailed away vaguely, as if she were afraid I might want to be fed. I assured her that I didn't need food, or even very much time. Should I wait in my car? That galvanized her into inviting me to come out back, where she was getting ready to put burgers on the grill.

The cramped family room made me think of Miss Ella. Like her home, this one was filled with small china figurines. Ms. Alito seemed to collect angels and kittens rather than African jungle creatures, but everything was clean and carefully arranged, down to little dishes of play milk in front of the kittens. I felt my scalp twitch. There was a sense of desperation in the displays. Still, as I trailed after her through the family room to the kitchen, I made appropriate noises about charm and so on.

'It's small, of course, but it's just Larry and me. We have the one son, but he lives in Michigan, and, when he comes to visit, we just put the grandkids in bunk beds on the sunporch. You sit out here on the deck, and I'll go tell Larry you're here.'

I walked to the railing and looked around. Lake Catherine was at the end of the road, about thirty yards south of the Alito place. You could just glimpse the gleam of sun on water through the willows and bushes that grew around the shore. The neighbors to the north were grilling; the lots here were so small that the hamburgers and chicken legs were practically under my nose. Despite the chili dog, I was still hungry. I wanted to jump over the fence and grab a drumstick.

A man's voice came clearly through the open window above me. 'You didn't even get her name? Sheesh, Hazel, don't you ever think?'

'Oh, for heaven's sake, Larry, you think every person you meet is going to scam you.'

'And you didn't find out what she wants?'

'You gotta pay extra if you want me to be your secretary, Mr. Alito.' Hazel's voice was part sarcasm, part seduction, a disturbing window into their relationship.

Alito grumbled, but the conversation faded, and, a moment or two later, he joined me on the deck. He was fresh from the shower, his thinning hair still dark with water, but his eyes were almost as red as his sunburned nose. He was carrying a can of beer. From the smell of his breath as he came up to me, it was his fifth or sixth of the afternoon.

'Detective Alito, I'm V. I. Warshawski, Tony Warshawski's daughter.'

'That a fact.' He looked at me without enthusiasm.

'Fact,' I said brightly. 'I found a picture of your old slow-pitch team the other night. My dad played first, I think . . . Is that right?'

'How should I remember? Tony Warshawski on first, what's on second, that right?'

I laughed dutifully. 'You know my dad's been dead for some years now.'

'Yeah. Sorry I forgot to send flowers, but we didn't stay in touch.'

'And I became a detective, but private. I'm not with the force.'

'Private dicks, they give me a pain in the whasis.' He swallowed deeply from his beer can and set it on the deck railing.

'I'm looking up an old case that my dad and you both worked.'

He didn't say anything, but a pulse in his neck started to jump.

'Steve Sawyer.'

'Don't ring a bell.' The tone was indifferent, but he grabbed the beer can and took another deep swallow. 'Hazel! Bring me another!'

His wife had been standing at the grill with her plate of raw meat, waiting for me to finish so she could make dinner. She reached into a cooler by the grill and brought out another can. What a fun evening for her.

'You and Tony had been partners on patrol in

'sixty-six, and then you got moved to the detective branch at — '

'I can read my own history in the obituary pages. What's your point?' He grabbed the can from his wife and popped the top.

'It was a high-profile case at the time. A young civil rights worker was murdered during a demonstration in Marquette Park, and months went by without an arrest. Then you picked up Steve Sawyer.'

'*Tony* picked up Sawyer,' Alito corrected me.

'I thought you didn't remember Sawyer.'

'All those shines marching in the park, you saying that brought it all back to me.' He smirked.

'I didn't say that,' I said sharply. 'I said a civil rights demonstration.'

'Yeah, it was a demonstration full of shines.' He laughed, and, in the background, Hazel laughed tinnily, too.

I gritted my teeth but said, 'So if it's all come back to you, who was the snitch?'

'Snitch? What snitch?'

'At the trial, you said your snitch had pointed you to Sawyer. No one ever asked for your informant's name. I'm asking you now.'

'Ah, jeez, what a dumb-ass question! Like, I remember every two-cent junkie who wanted a fix bad enough to finger his friends.'

'What about Lamont Gadsden? How well do you remember him from your old beat?'

The question took him off guard, and he slopped beer down the front of his Sox T-shirt. He hollered to Hazel to bring over a towel. When

172

she'd mopped his shirt, he said, 'What were we talking about?'

'Lamont Gadsden.'

'He another of your shine friends? Name doesn't ring a bell. If that's what you came for, you wasted a tankful of gas.' The words and tone were right, but his forehead was beaded in sweat.

I looked at him steadily. 'When Sawyer came into court, he was badly disoriented, didn't seem to know who he was or where he was, going by the trial transcript. What do you remember about that?'

'He tripped and fell against the bars of his cell. You could ask Tony, if he hadn't croaked, and he'd tell you the same. Now, get the fuck off my property.'

'What do you mean, Tony'd tell me the same?' I felt as though someone had punched me in the gut.

'What I said. Everyone says your father was too good to be true, right? The level cop, not the cop who had community complaints or IAD smelling his shorts before he put them on? Well, I could tell you a thing or two about Saint Anthony.'

'Maybe the whole South Side had reason to hate your guts, but Tony Warshawski was the best damned cop in Chicago. You were lucky you had the chance to work with him. But you got hincty, like you claim Steve Sawyer did, didn't you, and bought yourself a — '

I saw his fist coming a half second too late. I swerved, and he missed my jaw, but the blow socked my right shoulder. I kicked him on the shin and went for his solar plexus, but water suddenly poured over my head, my eyes, my mouth, and I was choking: Hazel had turned the hose on us, spraying her husband as thoroughly as she was me. Alito and I backed away from each other, breathing hard. I stared at him for a long second, then turned abruptly and opened the door to the kitchen.

'You can't go through the house, you're all wet,' Hazel observed in her unemotional nasal voice.

I followed her off the deck without looking again at her husband. She pointed me toward a narrow path that separated her house from the one next door. As I walked up the lane to my car, I could see curtains twitch at windows along the way. If I had to live with Larry Alito, I wouldn't fill the house with china kittens. I'd have a large collection of axes.

17

The Friendly Man from Mountain Hawk

Going home, I drove east all the way to the big lake before starting south. I stayed on the local roads. It made for a longer trip, with all the stoplights in the little towns, but the breeze off Lake Michigan was cool, and it was easier to think without the congestion and impatience that clogged the tollway.

Partway down the coastal road, I stopped to walk over to the lake. The water was purply gray in the summer twilight; I could see running lights away from the shore, but I was alone on the beach. Crickets and frogs chirped around me.

Alito hadn't been surprised to see me. Who had warned him? I didn't want to think it was Bobby. That opened the door on a kind of ugly possibility that I couldn't bear to examine: my father's best friend in league with a drunk, abusive cop.

Maybe Arnie Coleman had called after seeing me at the Krumas fundraiser. I tried to remember what I'd said when we were sparring at the Krumas table. It was Petra who blurted out that I was working on a case going back to Gage Park in the sixties. And I had mentioned Johnny Merton. If the Sawyer trial lay heavy on

Coleman's conscience, he could have connected the dots, although I had a hard time imagining anything lying heavy on my old boss's conscience.

The other thing that this afternoon's interview showed was that Alito knew Lamont Gadsden's name. Had Lamont been his snitch, then, after all? Had Merton killed Lamont to punish him for fingering Sawyer? The Hammer was capable of anything. Murder was all in a day's work for him.

Tony would have said the same thing, Alito claimed, that a prisoner in his custody with a bloody nose and a black eye had tripped and fallen against his cell bars. 'He would not, you lying little two-bit scumbag. You think because Tony's dead you can drag him down, but you damned well can't.'

My heart was pounding. I thought I might choke to death, there on the shores of Lake Michigan. Christmas Eve, it came back to me suddenly. Christmas Eve, when I was in bed and my parents were in the kitchen, their reassuring laughter coming up the stairs. Had Bobby been there? Someone, a friend, having a glass of wine, and Alito stopped by. He and my father were arguing.

'You got your promotion. That's enough, isn't it?' my father said, and Alito replied, 'You want to see him in prison?'

I had crept down the stairs, anxious, and heard my mother sharply call my name. I scurried back up the stairs, lying on the attic floor, straining to hear, but my dad and Alito lowered their voices.

Who would have gone to prison? What were they fighting about?

My shirt was still damp from Hazel's soaking, and the evening breeze rising across the lake was making me shiver. I walked slowly back to my car, trying to dredge up any more remains of that fugitive memory.

I stopped in Highwood for supper. The little town, halfway between my home and Alito's, had been settled in the nineteenth century by the Italian artisans who built the North Shore mansions. It's become a kind of foodie heaven, but I chose one of the old Italian restaurants, where you got a straightforward pasta and the chef was called a cook. I spoke Italian with the owner, who was so pleased he gave me a free glass of Amarone.

For an hour, while we talked about food, and I described a memorable meal I'd eaten in Orvieto, across the square from the cathedral, roast pigeon with fig terrine, I forgot my anxieties. On the way home, though, I kept worrying about my father, and Larry Alito, and Steve Sawyer, the way you do with a sore tooth.

Curtis Rivers and Johnny Merton both thought my father had beaten up Sawyer. That was the only credible explanation for the way the two men reacted to my name and my questions. But Tony would never have done that, not unless Sawyer had jumped him and he'd had to subdue him. But Sawyer had been confused, and badly represented, at his trial. What if —

'What if nothing!' I said aloud. 'Tony didn't beat people up. Ever.'

177

George Dornick had been the senior detective in the Harmony Newsome investigation. I would call him first thing in the morning, see if he could set my mind at rest.

Despite Bobby's jeers, it proved easy to get an appointment with Dornick. The Warshawski name doesn't open many doors in the world, but men who had served with my father were usually willing to see me. At least once, anyway.

When I called at eight, as soon as I got back from running the dogs, Dornick's secretary said he could fit me in between nine-thirty and ten a.m. meetings. I dressed carefully in an amber jacket over beige slacks — feminine but severely professional — and rode the El into the Loop.

Mountain Hawk Security's headquarters occupied four floors in one of the glass towers on Wacker that line the Chicago River, and their reception area actually overlooked the river. I got there at nine-thirty to be safe and ended up waiting for over an hour. For a time, I amused myself watching the barges and tour boats while Mountain Hawk personnel passed between elevators and locked glass doors leading to offices. They spoke in urgent tones that stressed the importance of their work. A few clients arrived and were whisked inside.

I was getting bored, and there wasn't much to read in the waiting room: *The Wall Street Journal, SWAT Digest*, and company brochures. I spent fifteen minutes on the phone with my temp, Marilyn, and sent a few e-mails, but I was getting restless by the time Dornick came out to greet me.

Dornick was a vigorous man in his sixties. The brown hair in the softball-team photo had turned gray in the way that gets labeled distinguished. Seeing him in his pale summer worsted, I found it hard to believe he could ever have been covered with mud from a slow-pitch game in Grant Park.

He held out a hand and shook mine energetically. 'So, you're Tony's girl. I should have recognized you at the fundraiser the other night. You look just like him around the eyes. He was a sad loss, a very sad loss. One of the best cops I ever had the privilege of serving with.'

The contrast to Alito couldn't have been more pronounced. Dornick put an arm around my shoulder and told 'Nina' to get us coffee and hold his calls. He steered me into the kind of office you want to see when you need a good program in subduing and manacling the restless masses. Everything was made of polished wood and stone, much of it gleaming black. No paper was visible, but an array of computer consoles kept Dornick in touch with his team. On the wall were the pictures of Dornick that I'd seen on Mountain Hawk's website.

'This is really impressive,' I said. 'How did you put it all together?'

'Twenty years in the Chicago PD got me my law enforcement know-how, and then it was a matter of scrabbling and scrambling. Some of my childhood buddies pitched in their nickels. I had a lucky break early on, busted a Hamas training camp on the Peru-Colombia border. It was a fluke, the way things often are in police work: we were only looking for drugs, and we found armaments that made our eyes pop.' He laughed. 'You'd think after being on Chicago's streets, nothing could surprise you, but that's until you get into those Latin American jungle outposts.'

Nina brought in coffee — lovely, smooth coffee — probably hand-knitted in one of those jungle outposts.

'Nina tells me you're in private security yourself, that you have a one-gal shop. You interested in moving up to the majors? I'd be pleased — privileged, really — to bring Tony's daughter into my organization. I learned more from him in two years on the streets than I ever did anytime after.'

'Yeah, my dad was a great guy. I still miss him. But I'm better on my own. I've been my own boss too long to be happy in a big organization. Besides, you probably know that I started in a big outfit, the county Public Defender's Office.'

Dornick nodded. 'I saw your old boss at the Krumas event. You were right to chafe against an SOB like Arnie Coleman, and you were young at the time. A big organization can be a chance to spread your wings rather than have them clipped. You keep Mountain Hawk in the back of your mind the next time you're out doing surveillance in the rain and know you have to race back to your office to file a missing persons report.'

I was startled: it was as if he had spent a week watching my workload. No doubt about it, he was as smooth as his coffee. I thanked him awkwardly.

Dornick ducked a discreet look at his watch. 'So what is it you need today, Vic?'

'I'm following an old cold trail,' I said. 'A person who's been missing for forty-plus years. My closest lead to him is also hard to track down. You were the detective who handled the interrogation when he was arrested for murder: Steve Sawyer, the Harmony Newsome trial.'

Dornick put his coffee cup down and whistled silently. 'That is an old cold trail. My God, I do remember the case, though: it was the first murder investigation I'd caught on my own. I was working with Larry Alito. You talk to him? I think he's up in Wisconsin now.'

'I saw him yesterday. He's on Lake Catherine, in the Chain of Lakes. He said he didn't remember any of the details, although I got the feeling that he was hiding a lot behind a can of beer.'

Dornick laughed. 'Behind a can? Make it more like a case . . . One of the reasons I wanted to leave the police. Larry Alito was not a good boy to partner with, I'll tell you that between you, me, and the kitchen sink. No one could forget the Newsome case. It was so high-profile, the mayor was calling me personally. The dead girl was a really important person in the civil rights movement. We couldn't afford a black eye as a city, not after the way the riots had played on national TV the summer before.'

'You didn't have any doubt that you arrested the right man?'

Dornick shook his head. 'We had a good snitch on that one. Not a jailhouse snitch, a guy who was undercover for us in the Anacondas.'

'Was that Lamont Gadsden by any chance? He's the man I'm trying to find.'

A funny look crossed Dornick's face, the expression Boom-Boom used to assume when he was deciding whether to dare me to do something really insane, like jump off the breakwater into Lake Calumet.

'What the heck, Vic, it's been all this time. Yes, Gadsden finally turned Sawyer in. We'd been leaning on him for a name, and I guess he and Sawyer were good friends in the Anacondas. You're not trying to suggest that Sawyer didn't do it, are you?'

'I'm just trying to find Lamont Gadsden for his mother. You don't know what became of him, do you? He disappeared the night before the big snow.'

Dornick shook his head. 'We wondered, too. We wondered if Hammer Merton found out Lamont was a flipper and had him put away, because we never saw Lamont again. We checked with Hammer, but you know yourself how tough he is to talk to. What do you want with Sawyer?'

'I'm hoping he can tell me something about Lamont. But I'm meeting with a nun from the Mighty Waters Freedom Center. She was with Harmony Newsome when Newsome was killed, and she does have some doubts about whether Sawyer was the murderer.'

Dornick laughed. 'Oh, the sisters. The ones who didn't try to beat our balls off at school look at the world through such rosy glasses. Or they imagine they can be another Sister Helen Prejean, even get hard-asses like me to oppose the death penalty.'

Nina came in. The meeting was over. Dornick ushered me out with a renewed assurance that 'Tony's gal' was always welcome at Mountain Hawk. 'And you tell your nun that I'm darned sure we sent the right guy to Pontiac.'

'There isn't any record of Steve Sawyer in the Department of Corrections,' I said as Dornick turned to go back to his office. 'Are you sure it was Pontiac?'

Dornick paused in the doorway. 'It might have been Stateville. Not every detail sticks, this far from the trial, and your dad probably could have told you, or Bobby, that we cops don't follow our perps once they're sentenced.'

I made appropriate sounds of gratitude for his time. 'There's one last thing, George, and it's very hard for me to bring up. One reason I'm having trouble on the street with my search is, the guys who grew up with Gadsden and Sawyer think Sawyer was roughed up pretty bad during the arrest.'

Dornick turned again, hands on his hips, eyes bright with anger. 'They always say that, Vic. You should know from your time in the PD's Office, they always bleat about excessive force. We operated by the book, and I mean we dotted every *i*. We had too much riding on the arrest. And don't you go dragging Tony's name through the mud on this. He was the best, Tony Warshawski, and those scumbags were fucking lucky to have him bring them in.'

183

That was the end of the interview, but his reassurance lingered with me all day, gave me more confidence, as I did a document search at the county archives, as I organized a freelancer I work with to do surveillance at a warehouse in Mokena in the southwest suburbs. On my way back to the city, I toyed with the idea of signing up with Mountain Hawk Security. It would be great to be part of a big operation where someone else went to Mokena.

Dornick had been right about a lot of things, most especially his appreciation of my dad. I'd liked him. So why had I come away with an uneasy feeling, as if something he'd said had triggered not an alarm — that was too extreme — but a warning?

I was sure, in the kind of operation Mountain Hawk Security conducted, that all meetings were secretly recorded. If I could get a copy of the disc Nina made of my conversation, then maybe I'd be able to figure out what was bugging me. I laughed, picturing myself scaling the green glass tower, cutting a square out of one of the windows on the forty-eighth floor, disabling Mountain Hawk's security measures.

Movie heroes have it so easy. Clint Eastwood would pull out his Magnum and blow people away. 'Make my day,' he says, taking out someone's brains, and we all cheer. Soon the survivors are so nervous, they tell him everything. In life, when you're scared or being tortured, you'll say whatever the terrorist wants to hear.

Like Steve Sawyer, coming into court

disoriented, confessing to Harmony Newsome's murder. At that thought, my foot came off the gas, and I slowed so unthinkingly that a van behind me honked furiously. I held up a placatory hand and pulled off at the next exit.

I sat at the curb at the end of the ramp and tried to think. Lamont had flipped on Sawyer — Dornick said that — and Johnny had been furious and killed him, or Curtis killed him for Johnny, and they'd disposed of the body.

Make my day, one of you, make my day. Tell me what happened. I couldn't imagine a threat or a bribe that would make either Dornick or Alito open his secret diary to me. I didn't have an in with the state's attorney, to offer Merton immunity or even a reduction in sentence for talking to me. And, even if I did, Merton still might not talk to me.

Maybe Judge Coleman would explain why he hadn't called any witnesses when he'd represented — or misrepresented — Sawyer forty years ago. Maybe there had been damning evidence that he kept out of the trial. I looked up the number for the Cook County judges and called Coleman.

Naturally the judge wasn't available for my call. A clerk said she'd be glad to take a message, in a voice that sounded like she'd be glad if she never used her telephone again. I wanted just to leave my name and number, but the clerk wouldn't take a message unless I explained my business in some detail. I used to work for the judge, I said. I wanted to go over an old trial, one that dated to his early years in the PD's Office. I

185

left my number without any expectation of ever hearing from him.

I'd pulled off the road at 103rd Street. Pullman was just a few miles to the east. Maybe Rose Hebert could shed some light on all these players.

18

Dubious Judge, Frightened Woman

Rose answered the door in another sober dress, this one a navy dotted Swiss. She looked at me with a flicker of eagerness.

'Have you learned something about Lamont?'

It was painful to tell her no, to watch the dull, heavy expression settle on her face again. 'I need some advice or insight — something like that — into Johnny Merton or Curtis Rivers.'

She gave a self-derisive bark of laughter. 'I don't know enough about life or those two men to have insights into their minds.'

'You're selling yourself short, Ms. Hebert,' I said gently. 'I don't have news for you, but I've been to see both men, and I've talked to people who knew Steve Sawyer. There's been a suggestion that Lamont might have flipped on Steve, might have led the police to Steve Sawyer, might have said Sawyer was Harmony Newsome's murderer.'

'Oh no! I . . . Oh — '

The house bell had begun to ring behind her, and she turned fearfully away from me. 'He wants to know who's at the door, what's keeping me so long.'

I grabbed her wrist and led her down the shallow stone steps. 'Maybe he's ninety-three, but he's not too old to learn how to cope with frustration. Where can we sit where you'll be comfortable?'

She looked back at the house but finally muttered that there was a coffee shop on Langley where she often stopped for breakfast on her way home from the hospital. We drove over to the Pullman Workers Diner in my Mustang, where the waitresses greeted Rose by name and looked at me with frank curiosity. Rose ordered coffee and blueberry pie. I had a slice of rhubarb to keep her company.

'I don't even know where to start,' she murmured when we'd been served. 'It's all so wrong. Steve, Harmony, I don't believe that. But even if he did kill her, Lamont — oh, he and Steve were best friends growing up — Lamont would never have turned him in to the police.'

'Did Harmony live in your neighborhood?'

'She and her family, they were up the street from us, but they went to a Baptist church that Daddy said wasn't a true church. And they were rich. Mr. Newsome, he was a lawyer. And Harmony's brother, he went off to law school and became a professor out east someplace. Harmony was in college down in Atlanta. She got involved in the civil rights movement down there, and, when she came home for summer vacations, she talked it up in her church's youth group. She talked at a lot of the churches in our neighborhood, but not at Daddy's church, because he thinks women don't belong speaking up in church, like it says in Saint Paul. And, besides, he doesn't think church people belong marching on the streets. We belong in the pews.'

She bent over her coffee, stirring it as fiercely as if it were her father, or her own life, she were attacking. 'I shouldn't say this, but I was so *jealous* of Harmony. She was so pretty. She got to go to a fancy college, Spelman, while I had to scrimp to put together money for nursing school. And, then, the boys were all *spellbound* by her. When I first heard she was dead, I was glad.'

I reached across the table and pressed her free hand. 'You didn't kill her by being jealous of her, you know.'

She looked up briefly, her face contorted in pain. 'All the boys followed her around, even the ones who went to our church, which is why I never could believe Lamont really cared about me. I figured he thought I'd be an easy mark, big old ugly girl like me no one else wanted. If he couldn't have Harmony, he'd make do with me. But I don't think any of the boys would have killed her, not out of jealousy like they claimed Steve did. She never went out with him, never went out with any local boys. Far as I knew, she was in love with the movement, not with any boy, not even some college boy in Atlanta with her same background.'

'Were Steve and Lamont at the Marquette Park march?'

'Daddy ordered everyone in our church to stay away, but Lamont and Steve, they ignored him. Johnny Merton, he'd taken part in the deal the gangs made with Dr. King, that they wouldn't fight that summer, and, in exchange, they provided protection along the march routes.'

She sucked in a breath, remembering, and

189

continued very softly. 'Oh, Daddy was angry. He hated having his authority crossed. When Steve and Lamont did what Johnny wanted, not what their own pastor said, he read them out of the congregation. It was a terrible, terrible Sunday, and after church Daddy told me my own soul was in danger if I ever even spoke to Lamont Gadsden again. Even so, if I had to go to the store or something, I'd take a route that led me past his home, or Carver's Lounge, where he and the other Anacondas shot pool . . . ' Her voice trailed away.

This morning, George Dornick told me Lamont had been the person who fingered Steve Sawyer for him and Alito. I remembered the funny look he'd given me when I'd asked. Maybe it had really been Pastor Hebert, furious with his two parishioners, wanting to get the police to take care of them for him?

'How angry was your father with Steve and Lamont?' I asked Rose abruptly. 'Could he have turned them in to the police?'

'What a terrible suggestion! How dare you even think a thing like that!' She pushed her chair away from the table. 'Daddy is the holiest man on the South Side!'

Like Tony had been the best cop on the South Side? Were we daughters always like this, always ready to leap to our fathers' defense even against the evidence?

I looked into her flushed face. 'Ms. Hebert, I apologize for speaking so bluntly. I shouldn't have said the first thought that came into my mind. You say you don't believe Lamont was a police informant, and certainly not your father. Who, then?'

She twisted her fingers together. 'Does it have to be one or the other?'

'No. It could be someone I haven't even heard of, some two-bit player in the Anacondas. But I went over to Stateville to see Johnny, and he's pretending he never heard of Lamont. That makes me think, well, I'm sorry to give you the harsh unedited workings of my mind again, but — '

'You think Johnny murdered Lamont? I wondered, too, when he disappeared . . . But it's hard for me to see a reason . . . Unless Lamont snitched out Steve . . . Yes, that could be a reason . . . But . . . ' Her words twisted around with as much agitation as her fingers.

'Oh, that Johnny Merton, there's nothing I wouldn't believe of him. And yet, he set up a clinic in our neighborhood. He made the government give our children the same milk they handed out in the white schools. He looked after his little girl like she was the crown jewel. Dayo, that was what Johnny called her. And that made Daddy mad all over again because it was African. It means 'joy arrives.''

She gave an unhappy bark of laughter. 'My daddy would have looked at me and said, 'Joy departs,' so why am I standing up for him?'

'Where was your mother when you were growing up?' I asked.

'Mama died when I was eight. My granny, she took me in for a while, but her heart was bad. And, anyway, Daddy wanted me home where he could keep an eye on me.'

I paid for the pie and the coffee and drove Rose back to her home. During the short ride, she tried cleaning her face with a tissue. She couldn't face her father looking distressed.

'He'll think it's about sex. At my age, with my life, he's still sure I'm off having sex with strange men.'

'Go for it,' I said mischievously, pulling up in front of her house. 'It's not too late, you know.'

She looked at me, startled, almost afraid. 'You are a very strange woman. Where would I even find a man who'd look twice at me?'

As she got out of the car, I remembered a final question. 'Do you know where Steve Sawyer is now? I think Curtis Rivers and Merton both do, and they won't say.'

She shook her head slowly. 'He was in prison a long time. I know Curtis, he visited Steve. But I heard, maybe he even died there. Don't be thinking Curtis would tell me. He doesn't like me any more than, well, he seems to like you. He thinks I was always carrying tales back to Daddy when we were in high school. He can't forgive that.'

She hesitated, then leaned back into the car. 'You're a good listener, and I appreciate that. I'm grateful.'

'That's good. I'm glad.' I was a good listener because I needed her to tell me things, a thought which embarrassed me enough that I added, 'You can always give me a call, you know, and talk to me again.'

She walked heavily up the steps, her shoulders

stooped. No one would look at you with love, or even lust, if you were so bowed over, but she didn't need me to tell her that.

I turned around and headed back to the expressway. By now, it was the height of the afternoon rush, and the Ryan was about as express as a turtle with corns. I was stalled on the overpass above the Sanitary Canal when my cellphone rang. I figured the risks of talking while driving didn't extend to talking while parking, but I did almost hit the car in front of me when the woman at the other end said she was Judge Coleman's secretary and could I hold for him.

'Judge! Thanks for returning my call. I'd like to stop by to ask you about one of your old clients.'

'We can do this by phone. I told you the other night to leave Johnny Merton alone.'

I ground my teeth. 'Not the Hammer. One of your first clients, Judge, when you were a new-minted PD. Remember the Steve Sawyer trial?'

He didn't say anything.

'Harmony Newsome's murder. Do you remember her?'

He turned so quiet that I thought at first the connection had gone. Someone behind me honked. A gap of four feet had opened in front of me. I scooted forward, glancing at the oily surface of the canal. The day was hot and humid, and the water looked as though every person murdered in Cook County in the last century had rotted in it.

The judge suddenly spoke again. 'Why this

interest in ancient history, Warshawski?'

I thought my answer over carefully. If I'd been able to meet with Coleman in person, transcript in hand, I would have tried to ask about all the gaps in the record — why he didn't try to find out the name of the snitch, why he let the obvious collusion between the cops and the state's attorney go by unchallenged — but, on the phone, I didn't have any way of pressuring him.

'Steve Sawyer's name keeps coming up in a missing-persons search I'm doing, but he's disappeared as well. In fact, there's no record of him at all after his trial. I'm hoping you have your old notes. I'm trying to find which prison he was sent to.'

'That trial was forty years ago, Warshawski. I remember it, my first high-profile case.' He laughed thinly across the airwaves. 'I learned a lot from that trial, but I couldn't possibly keep track of all the lowlifes who went through Twenty-sixth and California during my time there.'

I was finally on the farside of the canal. 'Of course not, Judge, but the transcript did raise a number of interesting procedural questions.'

'Why did you read the transcript?' he demanded.

Of all the questions he might have asked, that was the oddest. 'Looking for traces of Steve Sawyer, Judge. It was exciting to see your name there. Mine, too. My dad was the cop they sent to make the collar.'

Cellphones don't give you good reception, but

I thought I heard a quick intake of breath, almost a gasp. 'You have questions about the trial, ask your father.'

'He's been dead for years, Judge, and I'm not a big believer in séances.'

'You were a smart-ass know-it-all when you worked in the courts, Warshawski, and it doesn't sound to me like you've changed any. I don't owe you a damned thing, but I'm still going to tell you for your own good to leave all that old history in the archives. Merton, Newsome, the boy who killed her, leave it alone.'

He cut the connection before I could thank him. Just as well. I couldn't have kept the savagery out of my voice much longer.

19

Exuberant Cousin

When you get home feeling that you've been pummeled by all sides in the Hundred Years' War and you're longing to lie in the tub for a decade or so to soak away your wounds, the last thing you want is to see your high-spirited cousin's shiny Pathfinder parked out front. I tried to slink past my neighbor's place unnoticed, but the dogs betrayed me, whining and scratching at his front door. A moment later, they all bounded into the hall, dogs, cousin, and Mr. Contreras.

'Uncle Sal's picture got me a kind of promotion,' Petra called. 'We're celebrating! Come on in.'

I protested feebly that I was exhausted, but they ignored that. Mr. Contreras bustled inside to get a glass of Spumante while the dogs circled me, yipping as if I really had been away for a century. The commotion brought the neighbor across the hall into the entry-way. She's a plastic-surgery intern who is perpetually affronted by the dogs. She keeps trying to get the co-op board to declare the building pet-free, but the Korean family on the second floor, who have three cats, was so far fighting on Mr. Contreras's and my side.

'Really, the dogs won't hurt you, they're super-friendly!' Petra called to the doctor. 'See

196

Mitch? He'll take food right out of my mouth, won't you, boy?'

She put a taco chip between her lips and invited the dog to jump up on her. Before the intern had a stroke or called the cops, I bundled my team into Mr. Contreras's living room.

'The coals are just about ready,' the old man beamed. 'We wasn't going to wait more than five minutes longer for you, doll, but now I can put the steaks on.'

I don't much like Spumante. While Mr. Contreras took the steaks — a gift from Uncle Peter — out to the grill, I poured my glass down the sink and went upstairs for whisky. I looked wistfully at my bathtub, but settled for a quick shower. With clean hair and clothes and a glass of Johnnie Walker, I felt, if not revived, at least strong enough to cope with the outgoing personalities on the first floor.

They were all out back now, the dogs sitting at attention around the grill in case one of the steaks dropped to the ground. Petra's hearty laugh floated up the back stairs to me. I could hear Jake Thibaut playing his bass next door. It would have been pleasant just to sit on the steps, listening to the music, drinking my whisky, but I let duty be my guide and went down to the garden.

I asked Petra about her promotion. 'Does this mean you're working directly for Brian Krumas now?'

'Don't I wish! Although, maybe I don't. There's so much responsibility at the high levels of the campaign, making sure all the facts are right, the speeches are just so, that Brian knows who's saying what about him and what he needs to think about. I'm happy to be a worker bee, although Mr. Strangwell — he's, like, Brian's most important adviser — he met with me personally. He wants me to brief him about the same stuff I tell my real boss.'

'That sounds like a serious jump up the ladder,' I said. 'How does your real boss feel about it?'

'Oh, Tania's used to people moving around in the operation. She's totally cool. I wish you'd met her at the fundraiser, but she was pretty much spending the whole night with national media types.'

'What's Strangwell like?' I'd never met him, but you can't operate on even the fringes of Chicago politics without knowing about him. If he was advising Brian Krumas personally, it meant the national party might well be grooming Brian for a post-Barack Obama presidential run.

Petra gave an exaggerated shudder. 'He's kind of scary, he's so serious. Everyone else in the campaign, we're all young and we joke around, it's how we get the job done, but he's Mr. Serious. In my pod, they all call him the Chicago Strangler. And when he looks at you and tells you he wants something done, you feel like, gosh, better drop everything and do this *now*. And, even then, you're afraid it won't be good enough.'

'What does he have you doing, then?'

'Really, just more of what I've been doing, looking for attacks on Brian, seeing what's out there, but getting more focused, you know?' She gulped down her Spumante. 'That's enough of the boring old campaign. Did you go see any more snake charmers today?'

'Snake? Oh, Anacondas! Very good, little cousin. I'll call Johnny Merton that the next time I visit and see what kind of reaction that gets me. No, just burrowing around in the past. Even more boring than the campaign, I assure you.'

'Why would you want to do that? Are you, like, trying to get on *America's Most Wanted*, find some criminal who's been on the run for forty years or something?'

'If Vic ever went after one of them old crimes, she'd only be doing it to prove the FBI or the cops or someone had arrested the wrong person. Nothing gets done right if she ain't done it herself.' My neighbor's tone did not make his words a compliment.

'So do they have the wrong man in prison for murder or something?' Petra asked, eyes so wide that her long mascaraed lashes were flat against her brows.

'I don't know if the guy I'm looking for is guilty or innocent. He's disappeared.'

'So leave him lay,' Mr. Contreras said roughly.

'I would,' I answered slowly, 'but . . . I read the trial transcript . . . and my dad was the person who arrested him. And . . . and I want to know what went on when he picked up the guy.'

Mr. Contreras insisted that that was all the more reason for me to leave it alone. 'Who knows what your pa faced when he was on the job. With your cockeyed way of looking at things, you'd put the worst interpretation on it.'

'What if he beat up a helpless man? What good interpretation could I put on that?' I cried.

'I'm saying, what if he did? People look all helpless and defenseless in a courtroom, but, you don't know, did he pull a gun, did he attack your pa, maybe threaten his life? You can't go by only the end of the story, cookie, you got to know the beginning and the middle, too.'

'Uncle Sal is right,' Petra chimed in. 'I never knew Uncle Tony, but Daddy talks about him a lot. He was a good person, Vic. You can't go around making up stories to say he wasn't.'

'I'm not. I know better than either of you what a good man he was. I grew up with him.' I rubbed my eyes wearily. 'Was Peter still here in 1967, Petra? I can't remember when he moved to Kansas City.'

She flashed the smile that made her look like my father. 'I wasn't around so I can't be sure, but I think it was in 1970 when Ashland Meats moved down, or maybe 'seventy-one. I know Daddy didn't marry Mom until 1982. She was some kind of local debutante or something. Queen at the American Royal. You know, the big livestock show. The Queen and King of Meats, that's what I call their wedding photos.'

I laughed dutifully, but said, 'I wonder what Peter remembers from the summer of 'sixty-six. He was still living with Grandma Warshawski over on Fifty-seventh and Fairfield. He must remember the Marquette Park riots.'

'He always says that's what ruined the South Side. The neighborhood started to change.

200

Grandma Warshawski had to move north to get away from the crime.' My cousin shifted uneasily on the grass as she caught my expression.

The fault lines of race in the city, they run through my family, along with the rest of the South Side. My grandmother had wept when she moved. That unnerved me, as a child, to see an old woman cry.

Granny Warshawski tried to explain her own confused and conflicted feelings about race, about the changing neighborhood. 'I know how hard it is to be the stranger in the land, *kochanie*, but I don't know these black people. And Grandpa is dead. Peter will find himself a wife someday soon. My friends are gone. I can't be alone here. I'm scared to be the only white lady on the street.'

I'd been eleven at the time. I'd argued with her, belligerent, self-righteous, even then. Was that what made it hard for me to live with someone else? Was it what Mr. Contreras had just accused me of: that, in my book, I was always the only one who knew anything?

'I don't suppose Tony confided in Peter, or that your father would even remember after all this time. He's had meat to worry about, not to mention you, which must be a full-time job. But maybe I'll give him a call, ask him.'

'I can do that, Vic. I talk to him or Mom just about every day. But maybe Uncle Tony left some kind of record. Do you still own the house he lived in? We could go exploring for secret closets or something.' Petra's eyes sparkled with excitement.

'Sounds like you want to be a detective yourself,' I said. *'Petra Warshawski and the Secret of the Old Closet*. No, sweetie, houses in South Chicago were built pretty close to the lath. Not much room for secret hiding places. Anyway, I sold it after he died. And I was lucky to find a buyer, the neighborhood was so depressed.'

'What did you do with his stuff? Did he keep a diary?'

I laughed. 'You're thinking of storybook cops like Adam Dalgliesh or John Rebus, endlessly second-guessing themselves. When Tony needed to unwind, he'd watch the Cubs or play ball himself, have a beer with your uncle Bernie. He didn't brood or write poetry.'

'But didn't he leave you anything?' Petra demanded. 'Like, I don't know, his prize bowling ball or something?'

'Neither that nor his polka-playing accordion. Where do you get your stereotypes, Petra?'

'Take it easy, doll,' Mr. Contreras admonished me. 'Lots of guys bowl. Not that I liked it much. Pool for me. That, and the horses. Although my ma thought it'd turn me into a dropout and a drunk.'

My dad hadn't left much. Unlike a lot of cops, he wasn't a gun collector: he'd had only his service revolver, which I turned in when he died. I'd kept his sole backup, a 9-millimeter Smith & Wesson, for my own use. I'd given his shield to Bobby Mallory.

I had the photo album I'd looked at the other night, some softball memorabilia, a plaque

featuring the eight-pound coho he'd caught in
Wolf Lake. I'd kept some of the tools from the
little shop he'd had behind our old kitchen. I
even used them occasionally to repair a broken
sink trap or build a simple piece of shelving.
Other than that, all I could remember keeping
was his dress uniform, which I'd stored in a
trunk with my mother's music and her burnt
velvet concert gown.

Petra was all for digging into the mementos
then and there. When she heard I hadn't looked
at the trunk for years, she was sure there was
something I'd forgotten that would explain
everything. Mr. Contreras agreed with her. 'You
know how it is, doll, you put things away, you
forget what they were. Same with Clara's things.
When I went to look for her jewelry to give to
Ruthie, I found I'd put all kinds of things in
boxes, even her false teeth!'

'I know, I know,' I agreed wearily. 'My dad
probably had the secret plans for building a
gasless car, but I'm not going to look for them
tonight. I'm beat. I'm going to bed.'

Petra had drunk a fair amount of Spumante,
which made her argumentative and insistent on
going to the third floor at once. I got tired of
arguing long before she did, and announced I
was going to bed. I suggested that she stay the
night. I didn't want her driving in the state she
was in. Finally, around eleven, when Mr.
Contreras chimed in on my side, she let us put
her into a cab.

I helped him clean up, letting his waterfall of
talk wash over me. Yes, Petra was a good kid,

wonderful news about her promotion. Yes, maybe I was too hard on her. Didn't I remember being young and enthusiastic? And then he was off to the races on his own youth. I left him in front of the television with a glass of grappa and took Peppy upstairs with me.

In my dreams, though, a saber-toothed tiger was charging me. When I fell helpless to the ground in front of it, it changed shape and became my father.

20

Trunk Show

Petra showed up the next morning just as I was returning from the lake with the dogs. She'd come to collect her Pathfinder, but when she saw us she climbed out of it and jogged over. The dogs raced to her, fawning and barking, covering her white cargo pants with water and sand. She was as bright as ever, showing no after-effects of her evening with Spumante.

'You know, we could look at that trunk of yours before I go to work,' she said, playing with Mitch's ears.

'What's with you and my trunk?' I demanded. 'Do you think there are going to be false teeth or rubies or something?'

She grinned at me. 'I don't know. I guess since coming to Chicago, I've gotten more interested in my family's history. I mean, my mom's family, they've been in the Kansas City area for *centuries*. One of her ancestors was a colonel in the Confederate Army, and another came out to Kansas with the anti-slavery pioneers in the 1850s, so I grew up on all her stories. And her family is, well, so WASPy that Dad's story was always kind of looked down on. You know, Polish meat-packers. Now I want to know more about the Warshawskis. They seem more interesting since I've been in their city, and met you and so on.'

I'd taken her to look at the bungalow on Fairfield Avenue where my grandparents lived when they moved from Back of the Yards. Now Petra wanted to see the house on the city's Northwest Side, where Grandma Warshawski moved after the 'sixty-six riots, and the tenement in the stockyard district where my dad grew up and her own father had been born.

She followed me up the stairs, energetically planning an outing for the end of the workday that would include Back of the Yards, my childhood home in South Chicago, and Norridge Park, where our grandmother lived out her old age.

'Petra, darling, calm down. How about one house at a time, being as how just getting from Norridge Park to South Chicago will take us a couple of hours?'

She gave her self-mocking pout. 'Sorry! Mom always says I take off like a rocket ship when everyone else is still riding in buggies. Let's go see Back of the Yards and your house today. We can go to Norridge Park tomorrow.'

'Or even on the weekend, my little Saturn booster. I have plans for tomorrow night.'

I put my stove-top espresso maker on to heat, asking my cousin to turn it off when the pressure built up, while I rinsed sand out of my hair and off my skin. When I returned to the kitchen, there was espresso all over the stove and floor and no sign of my cousin. I turned off the flame, cursing loudly, and began mopping up coffee.

'Oh! Sorry!' Petra suddenly appeared in the doorway. 'I didn't know how long it would take, so I thought I'd just try to find your trunk.'

'Damn it, Petra, why couldn't you stay in here long enough to turn off the stove?'

'I said I was sorry!'

'That doesn't solve the problem. I don't want you helping yourself to my home, especially not when you don't do a very simple task that would have kept this explosion from happening!'

'I'll clean it up while you get dressed,' she muttered.

I'd used the towel I'd dried off with after my shower to soak up the worst of the mess. I put it in her arms, wet grounds and all, and stalked back to the bathroom to rinse coffee from my hands. When I returned to the kitchen dressed for work, Petra was standing in front of the stove, anxiously monitoring my little espresso pot. The floor was washed and the bath towel I'd dumped on her was hanging on the porch railing outside my back door.

She looked at me with an expression so much like Mitch's after he's been caught digging up the backyard that I couldn't help laughing.

Her own face relaxed into a smile. 'Gosh, Vic, do you know how scary you look when you get mad? I hope I'm doing your coffee thingy the right way.'

I turned the flame off as the pot started to burble, and offered to lend her some clothes; her own were stained with coffee, both from the towel and her energy in diving in to clean up the kitchen. She took a T-shirt, and trailed after me into the living room.

I felt my temper rise again when I saw that

she'd been rooting through my big walk-in closet. She'd pulled out my winter boots and my bike to get at the trunk, which stood open. She'd ripped apart the protective tissue in which I'd wrapped my mother's velvet concert gown. The dress itself was flung over my armchair so that a sleeve and the skirt were on the floor; my dad's dress jacket lay open on the piano bench.

'I guess I'm so used to living with my sisters and my roomie, I forgot not everyone wants to share,' Petra said in a small voice after a glance at my face.

'It's not about sharing, it's about consideration, empathy.' I picked up the evening gown and started to fold it back into the sheets of tissue, my hands shaking. 'Do you know how many hours of lessons my mother gave so that she could buy this dress? How many evenings we ate pasta without sauce?

'Do you know what it's like to live with so little that each possession has to be cared for and cherished? My mother started to rebuild her career in this gown. After each performance, I helped her hang it up, with dried apples and cloves to keep moths out of it. She could mend little tears in it, but, if it had been badly damaged, she couldn't have afforded another. My mother died when I was sixteen. I don't have much left to me that has her hands on it, her touch. I don't want you near this trunk or her clothes.'

'I'm sorry, Vic. I was thinking about your dad, and you wanting to find something to show what he was doing in 1966. I didn't think how this would look.'

I took a breath and tried to steady my voice. 'I think it would be a good idea if you left now.'

'But aren't you going to look at your dad's stuff?' she asked as I started to fold Tony's jacket.

'By myself. When I feel up to it. I'm late now for a meeting with a client.' I tried to find a lighter note. 'Doesn't the Chicago Strangler expect you to show up some time? Even if you were yesterday's hero, you could be today's goat. Campaigns aren't forgiving places.'

She started to explain how relaxed her work atmosphere was. ' . . . And, anyway, because Brian's dad and my dad were, like, homeys, Brian knows that family comes first.'

'Brian told you to come look at my dad's dress uniform because he and Peter grew up together?'

She turned red. 'No, of course not. I just meant . . . Oh, never mind. I'll see you tonight, okay? We can go look at Back of the Yards!'

I looked at her wearily. 'I've had enough family for today, Petra. I'll call you when I feel up to spending an evening with you.'

'I cleaned up your kitchen, I apologized for taking out your mom's dress, I think you could show some kind of response.'

'Do you?' I was kneeling by the trunk to lay my mother's gown inside but turned to look at Petra. 'My response is that you are a wonderful young woman with a lot of energy and goodwill, but you've lived your whole life in a privileged bubble. Come back and see me when you've thought through how you'd feel if your mother was dead and your only memento of her was treated like . . . like a towel for mopping up coffee.'

She stared down at me, her face a mix of surprise and anger. Her cellphone rang. She pulled it from her shirt pocket, looked at it, looked at me, and bolted from my living room. I heard her cluntering down the stairs in her heavy shoes, the sound drowning her voice as she answered her phone.

I sat for a time on the floor, my mother's dress still in my lap. I smoothed the tissue, my throat tight, remembering how Gabriella looked onstage at the old Athenaeum Theatre, her only major recital before she became too weak to perform. She had been luminous in this gown, and her voice had filled the theater.

I looked at my watch. I had about an hour to get downtown. Instead of replacing the gown and my dad's dress uniform jacket, I started rummaging through the trunk myself. My mother's music, a box of my old school report cards, my birth certificate, my parents' marriage license, my mother's naturalization papers.

Another thin box held reel-to-reel tapes. My mother had recorded herself when she began training seriously again. She went to a professional coach but could afford only a single session a month. Mr. Fortieri, the instrument maker, had a Pioneer recorder, a beautiful piece of machinery, that he let my mother borrow. It weighed a ton, and I remembered helping her carry it home on the train.

Mr. Fortieri lived on the Northwest Side, and it was a day trip for us to go there and back: the

Illinois Central downtown, the Ravenswood El to Foster, and then the long bus ride across Foster to Harlem, where Mr. Fortieri lived in an old Italian enclave. While he and my mother discussed music in Italian, I was given a quarter to buy gelato or a cookie at Umbria's on the corner.

The day he decided to lend my mother his machine, she demurred twice, as good manners dictated, but I knew she had been subtly hinting at her need for it for several months. I helped her wrap it in a blanket. We carried it between us, as we transferred from bus to El to train. At home, she let me and one of my girlfriends record a play we'd written for school, but Boom-Boom wasn't allowed near it. Once or twice, I remember my father using it, too, although, like me, he was just goofing around. For my mother, it was a serious work tool.

I put the tapes to one side. If I could find a place that would transfer them onto CDs for me, I could listen to her again. I owed Petra a little consideration for making me open the trunk. I might have gone the next forty years without remembering I had these tapes.

All I found in my father's handwriting was a few love notes to my mother and a letter he'd written me when I graduated from college. I sat back on my heels to read it.

You know how proud I am of you, the first person in our family ever to go to college. I wish your mother was here. I wish that every day, but most of all on this day. You

211

know she saved her nickels and quarters from all those piano lessons so you could have this chance, and you've made the most of it. We're so proud.

Tori, everything you do makes me proud to be your dad. But you need to watch that hot temper of yours. I see so much of it on the streets, and even in our own family. People let their tempers get the best of them, and one bad second can change your life forever in a direction you don't want to go. I wish I could say there's nothing in my life I regret, but I've made some choices, too, that I have to live with. You're starting out now with everything clean and shiny and waiting for you. I want it always to be that way for you.

Love, Dad

I had forgotten the letter. I read it through several times, missing him, missing the love that he and my mother surrounded me with. I thought with regret, too, of the many times I let my temper get the best of me, turning difficult situations into impossible ones. Even yesterday, talking to Arnie Coleman. Or this morning, with Petra. I could get so much better a response from people if I stopped shooting first. Maybe Mr. Contreras was right. Maybe I did need to be more like Petra. I thought it over. Maybe I did. But I couldn't move myself into sanctity. I was still furious with her for raiding the trunk to begin with.

I put the letter into my briefcase so I could

take it downtown and get it framed. As I put it away, I wondered what my good-natured, peaceable father had ever done that he regretted enough to mention in this letter. I couldn't bear the notion that it had to do with Steve Sawyer.

I looked quickly through a cardboard box that held my father's memorabilia. I had kept his citation for bravery from an armed robbery he'd stopped in 1962, his wedding ring, and a few other odds and ends. There was also a baseball. I held it for a moment. Like Mr. Contreras and his wife's false teeth, I hadn't remembered putting it away. Funny, my dad's game had been Chicago slow-pitch. I didn't think he'd ever even played hardball. I realized as I turned the ball over in my hands it was autographed by Nellie Fox. That made it even stranger, because Fox had played for the Sox, and my dad had been a Cubs fan.

South Side still means White Sox. When Tony was young, you could be beaten to a pulp for showing Cubs paraphernalia south of Madison Street. Comiskey Park was a few blocks from the stockyards where my dad grew up. His high school buddies were all Sox fans. Only Tony Warshawski and his brother Bernie, sick of the stench of blood and burning carcasses, decided to risk their lives by taking the El up to Wrigley Field.

So why had Tony kept a Sox ball? It was weather-beaten, with holes in the horsehide. Maybe he'd used it for target practice, although the holes were too small for bullets.

I jumped as I heard footsteps in my entryway, and then a man's voice calling to ask if anyone was home. Petra had left my front door open on her way out, and Jake Thibaut, wandering down to check his mail, had noticed. I got to my feet, looking guiltily at my watch. I'd been mooning over family mementos far too long.

'What are those old reel-to-reels?' Thibaut pointed at the faded Scotch boxes on the floor.

'My mother's old tapes. She was a singer who was trying to reclaim her voice after twenty years of breathing iron dust. I was hoping to find a place that would put them on a CD. But, then, I don't know, my mother is dead. Maybe her voice won't sound as wonderful as I remember it. Maybe I should just let these lay.'

'Iron dust?' Thibaut asked doubtfully.

'I grew up down by the old mills.' I looked at my watch again, and bent to pick up the tapes and the Nellie Fox ball.

'Give me the tapes. I have a friend with a studio. Even if you've romanticized your mother's voice, don't you want to hear it again?'

Of course I did. He took the tapes while I stuffed the ball into my briefcase with my papers and Tony's letter. I tried to curb my impatience while Jake ambled to the hall, talking about the better quality of sound you got with some of the old eight-tracks than with digital equipment. He was helping me. I didn't need to be belligerent over a few more minutes' delay. I could curb my pit bull personality for three more minutes.

I tried to flash a Petra-type smile of thanks, with an apology for needing to run, and tore down the stairs, running to Roscoe to flag a cab.

21

Ever-More-Inquisitive Cousin

When I got home that evening, I found a massive bouquet of peonies and sunflowers on my doorstep. A handmade card showed Petra sticking her head out of Snoopy's doghouse. I couldn't help laughing at such an apology. I called to tell her all was forgiven.

'Then can we go out tomorrow and look at the old family homes?'

'I suppose so, little cousin, I suppose so.'

I felt let down, as though she'd sent the flowers to manipulate me into taking her around town, not because she had genuinely wanted to reach out to me. I hung up and went out on my little back landing with a glass of wine and the day's newspapers.

It had been another long, tiresome day. After my morning meeting downtown, I'd looked up Johnny Merton's daughter, Dayo. She proved easy to find: she was working as a reference librarian for one of the big downtown law firms.

When I called, she was understandably cautious, but she did agree to meet for coffee in the downstairs lobby of the building where her firm had its offices. Talking to a private eye about her dad didn't make her all warm and friendly, but I felt she was reasonably honest with me.

'I can't tell you anything about the people in

215

my parents' old neighborhood,' she said when I explained that I was trying to find anyone who could talk to me about Lamont Gadsden or Steve Sawyer. 'My mother left my dad when I was little. All I remember is, they had some huge fight after he locked us out of the apartment. It was that big blizzard, you know, and he wouldn't let us in. She said he was in there with his other women doing drugs and she wouldn't put up with it. So she took me to Tulsa to live with my grandmother and my aunties. All they ever did was talk about him like he was Satan in the flesh, and I got so sick of it. I came back here a few years ago to make up my own mind.'

That had been right before he was tried on the charges that sent him to Stateville. Dayo had used her training to do pro bono research for her father's defense team. She'd been unimpressed with Greg Yeoman, but he was from the old neighborhood, and Johnny could no longer afford downtown counsel.

'I don't think my father's a saint, but he's not the devil everyone wants me to believe. He did all this good for the community back in the sixties, and, if the cops and the FBI hadn't railroaded him, he might have been a community organizer instead of a gang leader. Maybe then I could have led an ordinary family life instead of suffocating with my mother and my aunties in Oklahoma.' She gave a painful smile. 'Maybe he'd be president today, starting out as a community organizer.'

When I asked how often she visited Johnny, I got the feeling that the gap between what she wanted him to be and the person he'd become was too big for her to bridge easily. She mumbled that she made the trip to Joliet for Christmas and Easter, sometimes Thanksgiving.

I brought the conversation back to Lamont and Steve Sawyer to see if she'd be willing to try to talk to Johnny about them. 'They've been missing forty years now. Your dad is the one person who might know what happened to them, but he doesn't trust me.'

She shook her head. 'I'm not doing any work for the police. Maybe my dad did some things he shouldn't have, but he's sixty-seven. I don't want him dying in prison because I helped tack another twenty-five years onto his sentence.'

'Maybe his old buddies aren't dead,' I suggested. 'Or maybe if they are, he didn't kill them but knows where their bodies are.'

She was resolute. 'Enough 'maybes' build a whole hive of bees, and I don't want to be part of it.'

We left it at that. The conversation sent me home depressed. The only helpful news I'd gotten today was a text message from Karen Lennon's friend, the nun who'd been with Harmony Newsome when she died. Sister Frances wrote that she'd be back in Chicago Sunday night and asked that I meet her at her apartment on West Lawrence after supper on Monday.

On Saturday, in response to Petra's wheedling, I got up early to take her on a tour of our family's South Side history. We started in Back of the Yards. Nowadays, nothing is left of the massive meat-packing houses that used to cover two city miles except for one small kosher shop, which provides lamb to Muslim and Jewish butchers around the Midwest.

Petra and I parked on Halsted and walked through the giant gates where drovers used to register their cattle shipments. It was hard for either of us to imagine the days when tens of thousands of cattle were unloaded every day and the drainage ditches ran with blood and offal.

'My dad used to tell me that during the Depression, when he was growing up here, the yards were the most popular tourist attraction in the city,' I told Petra. 'When the World's Fair was held along the lakefront in 1934, more people lined up here to watch cattle being killed than went to the fair.'

'Ugh! I can't imagine. All the blood and stuff might make me a vegan, and then Daddy would have six heart attacks and disown me right before keeling over.' She laughed merrily at the notion.

We walked across Exchange Place, past the remains of the International Amphitheatre, to Ashland Avenue. The Beatles had played the Amphitheatre just a few days after the Marquette Park riots. My dad had to help with crowd control. I remembered how upset he and my mother were. The riots had kept him away from home round the clock for a week, and now, because of 'hysterical teenagers,' in my mother's bitter language, he had to go straight back out.

'I begged him to take me with him. I was a bit young for full Beatlemania but was catching the fever. It was such a relief to have something fun happening on the South Side for a change. He let me and one of my girlfriends sit in the back of his squad car. We got to see the Fab Four pretty close as they went inside.'

Petra rubbed my forehead. 'I touched the eyes that saw Ringo!'

Laughing and kidding together, we meandered through the old neighborhood. Saturday is a busy time in any part of town: shopping, laundry, kids' sports, yard work, car repairs, all bring people into the streets. Ashland Avenue was crammed with women lugging children and groceries. Girls playing hopscotch and double Dutch, the staples of Chicago sidewalks, slowed progress even more.

All down the street, heads turned as we passed. Petra, towering over the crowd, her spiky blond hair shining like a Roman helmet, was startling, a freak show traveling through the neighborhood.

'When I was little, Granny Warshawski already lived over in Gage Park. My dad took me by here once just to show it to me, so I hope I remember which building he grew up in.'

This part of Ashland is still vibrant. Light industry has filled in some of the holes left by the stockyards. People tended their little gardens. The tenements were covered with fresh paint, but underneath the uninsulated siding remained. These wooden row buildings dated back over a century, to when Upton Sinclair wrote *The Jungle*.

When my dad lived here, they hadn't had

running water or central heating. He used to have to stoke the furnace on winter mornings. Running water finally arrived in the fifties. The pipes were attached to the backs of the buildings, as they had been to my childhood home on South Houston. You got just enough water into the house to supply the kitchen, so a tiny bathroom with a handheld shower was installed behind a makeshift partition near the kitchen sink. I could still remember the first time I visited a college friend in her Oak Park home. It seemed so luxurious to have a second bathroom, and a big tub to stretch out in.

A woman came up the walk with a toddler and a shopping cart in tow. Petra turned to her eagerly, asking, in competent Spanish, if we could look inside. *'Mi abuelita vivía antes en este apartamento'* (My grandmother used to live in this apartment).

The woman looked at us doubtfully but shrugged, and gestured to us to follow her in. Petra and I helped her carry the heavy cart — loaded with bottles of pop, milk, and topped with clean, folded towels — up the steep wooden steps. Inside the narrow hallway, crammed as it was with bicycles and strollers, Petra's high spirits became subdued.

'Which one did Granny Warshawski live in?' she asked me.

'Second-floor front,' I said.

'The Velázquez family,' our guide said in English. 'She's not home. But the father's mother stays with the baby. Maybe she'll let you look.'

She called to the toddler, who was staring dumbstruck at Petra. Mother and child went on down the hall, the child looking back over its shoulder at us. We climbed to the second floor and knocked on the Velázquezes' door. We could hear a baby wailing and a television blaring in Spanish. After a moment, we knocked again, and then heard a voice asking in Spanish who was there.

My cousin called back, also in Spanish, explaining our mission. Our grandmother's old home, could we have a quick look? A suspicious silence on the other side while we were inspected through a peephole and then the sound of many locks scraping back and the rickety door being pulled open.

We were instantly inside the apartment. No foyer, or other formality, stood between us and the front room, where a sofa bed stood open. The baby, who was about ten months old, lay on it, still crying. An older sibling in front of the television turned to look at us. He shrieked and ran behind his grandmother.

My cousin stooped and began playing peekaboo with him. In another minute, he was laughing, trying to grab her spikes of yellow hair. The baby, struck by her brother's laughter, stopped howling and pushed herself to a sitting position. In a second, she had scooted to the edge of the bed. I picked her up before she fell off and sat her on the floor. In the midst of the chaos the grandmother apparently decided that the easiest course was to let us take a quick look around.

I don't know what Petra thought she'd find. Sixty years, and who knows how many families, lay between our grandparents and the current tenants.

My cousin looked in the four rooms quickly, saw the arrangements made to accommodate five children and three adults: sofa bed, bunk beds, air mattresses under the dining-room table, clotheslines hung with diapers and clothes, toys stacked under beds.

Wrinkling her forehead in puzzlement, Petra asked the grandmother where the family stored their other belongings. The older woman had been reasonably friendly until then. Now she frowned, and snapped off a volley of Spanish too complex for my primitive knowledge, except for 'espías,' 'narcóticos,' and 'immigracíon,' which she kept repeating. My cousin stammered a few words. But, a moment later, we found ourselves on the far side of the door.

'What was that about?' Petra complained. 'I just wanted to see where they kept the rest of their stuff.'

'Darling, this is *all* their stuff. When you started wanting to see storage places, she assumed you were with the INS or were an undercover cop hunting for drugs.'

'My building has storage bins in the basement where we can put our bigger things. I wanted to see theirs.'

'Why on earth? What business is it of yours?' I looked at her in astonishment. 'Are you doing some kind of research for the campaign on drugs in Hispanic households?'

'Of course not! I . . . I thought maybe . . . Well, I wondered if — ' Petra stammered, her cheeks beet red.

'Wondered what?' I demanded as she broke off.

She looked around the hall, at the tricycles and skateboards. 'I thought maybe if people had more storage room they could clear out the hallways.' The last sentence came out in a rush.

'I see,' I said drily, giving her a little push toward the stairs. 'How thoughtful of you. These buildings don't have basements, at least not the way you understand basements. There's a hole underneath the kitchen end to house the furnace.'

'What if there's a tornado?'

'Fortunately, they're not as common in Chicago as in Kansas, but I suppose you could wiggle under the building in an emergency.'

When we got outside, I pointed to the outside entrance to the furnace room and to the opening under the back stairs where you could huddle if you absolutely had to.

Back in the car, as I headed over to the Ryan to go to South Chicago, I said, 'I don't know what you really wanted back there, but don't try it again on South Houston. My old house is smack in the heart of gang territory. We could get shot if anyone imagines we're dissing them. We may get hassled just for being Anglo women nosing around the block. Okay?'

'Okay,' Petra muttered, picking at a loose thread on her jeans.

22

A Scary Sidewalk

We rode the expressway south in silence. Petra kept her head studiously turned to the window, looking at the old slag heaps and collapsing bungalows without comment.

This had always been a rough part of town. But when the mills were filling the landscape with clouds of toxic dust, most people had good jobs. Now those mills are as dead and gone as the cattle that used to pour through the stockyards. Most people in South Chicago lucky enough to find work are pulling minimum wage at the fast-food joints or the big By-Smart warehouse on 103rd Street.

Unemployment rates have stood at over twenty-five percent for more than two decades down here, and street crime usually involves more than one gun. Skirting potholes big enough to swallow a flatbed truck, I pulled up in front of the house on Houston where I'd grown up.

'This is it.' I tried to sound jaunty.

I couldn't carry it off: The leaded-glass transom above the front door was still there, but two of the little glass diamond prisms were missing. The prisms had made Gabriella feel she wasn't living in just another shabby bungalow but a house with some distinction to it. She and I polished the glass every month and scrubbed the iron dust from the frame around it.

I pointed to the porthole window in the attic. 'That was my room. I used to watch the street from up there, when I wasn't driving my mother crazy being out in the middle of the action.'

Petra looked at me doubtfully. 'What did you do?'

'My cousin Boom-Boom . . . Actually, he's your cousin, too. Your dad talk about him? Boom-Boom was a hockey star, but he was murdered a dozen years or so ago. He and I used to jump off the barrier into Lake Calumet to swim in the summer or we skated on it in the winter. It's where he practiced his slap shot. I fell through a hole in the ice one winter, and the main thing we were both scared of was that Gabriella would find out. We used to climb the girders on the El to ride up to Wrigley Field if we didn't have money for carfare. Then we'd shinny up the ivy behind the bleachers and sneak into the park for nothing.'

'Gosh! Daddy's always said you were too wild, but I always thought it was because you were such a feminist. He hates libbers. I didn't know you were a street punk when you were little.'

I smiled at her. 'Why do you think I'm a PI? I couldn't take all the rules and regs in the Public Defender's Office. And they couldn't take me, either. Arnie Coleman, the judge who was hanging around Harvey Krumas at your fundraiser, he was the head of the criminal PD unit when I worked there. He gave me one bad performance review after another, mostly because I wouldn't play the county game.'

She'd started to open her door but she paused when I said that. 'What county game?'

'It's all politics over there at Twenty-sixth and California. It's not about justice or trying to get the best deal for your client, not if your client is an ordinary street criminal. As soon as there's a whiff of politics about a case — whether it's police brutality or a connected guy's kid who's been arrested or someone trying to move up the ladder — cases get decided to help careers. Arnie was probably the most skilled mover in that cesspool I ever saw and he got his reward: he's an appellate judge now and hanging with your candidate's daddy. If Brian gets into the Senate, Arnie will get a federal judgeship.'

'Vic!' Her face flushed. 'Brian isn't like that! Why do you have to be so negative and cynical?'

'I'm not,' I said. 'Just when I think about Arnie and some of his cuter tricks . . . Mind your step, we've got company.'

I'd been watching a cluster of young men in my rearview mirror. They'd been milling around the north end of the block, trading insults and cat-calling passing women while they ostensibly worked on a rusted-out Dodge pickup. A boom-box belting out rap was on the sidewalk. I shouldn't have spent so much time reminiscing. They'd started our way while I was lost in memories of my childhood.

The gang looked in the Mustang's windows, saw that we were both women and that Petra was young, and began rocking the car. 'Whachoo doing here?' the one nearest me shouted.

I put all my weight on my right side, shifted,

and flung open my door so fast that it caught him in the chin. I got out quickly. Blood was oozing from his lower lip.

'Bitch!' he screamed. 'Why you do that?'

I ignored him and looked at his friends. 'Hello, boys. Why don't you go back to your own car. I think those little kids up there are messing with your stereo.'

They looked up the street, where two small boys were darting glances between the gang and the boom-box. Two of the gang took off to deal with the kids, but the one I'd injured and his other two friends stayed near me. Petra was still inside the Mustang, but when her door was clear she uncoiled herself from the passenger's seat and hopped out to the pavement. They turned to look at her, even the one whose lip was bleeding.

'Any of you boys know Señora Andarra?' I'd done a Lexis search last night for the names of the current occupants.

'Who wants to know?' one of them, who sported Latin Kings tattoos, asked.

'Because I want to talk to her. And I'd hate to have to tell her someone in her family was acting like a punk out on the street in broad daylight.'

They started muttering among themselves, and finally backed a few steps away from us. 'We watch you. You bother her, we take care of you.' It was the Latin King again.

'You her grandson? That's good. We grannies like to know the little ones are looking out for us.' I put my arm around Petra's shoulder and pushed her onto the sidewalk and up the short walk to the front door.

It felt queer to ring a bell at a place I'd gone in and out of freely for twenty-six years. We listened to the sound die away in the house. After a time, while the Latin King moved up the walk behind us, the door opened the length of a short thick chain and a short old woman peered through the crack at us.

'Your turn,' I said to Petra.

My cousin explained in Spanish what our mission was, but Señora Andarra was adamant. We could not come in, no. Perhaps we meant well, but how could she tell? And with only Geraldo out there on the walk . . . no. If her son were home, it would be another story. But too many people wanted to rob you, and told you stories. Petra pleaded and wheedled as best she could in her classroom Spanish, but we couldn't budge the woman.

We turned around.

'Keep your head up, look confident. You own this sidewalk.'

'What do we do if they attack us?' Petra whispered.

'Say our prayers,' I said, then called out, 'Geraldo! Your *abuelita* is worried about you. She doesn't like to see you just hanging around, nothing to do with your time. She wants to see you with a good job, not ending up in the morgue like your buddies!'

Geraldo looked from the house to us. I'd been talking to his granny, we knew his name. Of course I was just guessing about what she might have said, but it wasn't hard to imagine what she might say about a kid like him. Geraldo bit his lip, backed away from us. We got into the Mustang without any other trouble from the gang, although they struck a defiant pose until we turned the corner at the end of the street and were out of sight.

'Gosh, Vic! I was so scared I thought I was going to pee back there. When you hurt that one guy, I was sure the others were going to attack us.'

'Yeah, I wondered about that, too. But in broad daylight . . . And once a bully's taken a hit, he's more uncertain of his ground. At night, in an unlit alley, I'd be rat's meat by now.'

'Could you have beaten them if they'd jumped us?'

'Nope. I could have done some serious damage, but me against five young men, not great odds — not unless you're a street fighter yourself?'

'Are you kidding? I can use my elbows in beach volleyball, but that's about it. Could you teach me some moves? If we get in a jam again, I don't want to be the helpless damsel while you do all the fun stuff.'

I laughed a little ruefully. 'I've spent my share of time in the hospital after doing the 'fun stuff,' but I'd be glad to show you some moves. Every woman needs to know what to do in a tight spot. Eighty percent of it's mental, not physical. Like just now. I was betting that Geraldo was too afraid of his granny to attack us right in front of her house.'

We drove north in a peaceful silence. I suddenly realized I hadn't heard my cousin's phone ring all day.

'I switched it off because I figured it would annoy you if I kept talking, but I've been texting here while you drive.' She paused, and then said, 'Not to piss you off about something else, but did you ever look at your dad's stuff?'

'All I found were rubies, his false teeth, and the secret plans for the invasion of Canada.'

'Canada? Why would he want to invade Canada? Why not Mexico, so we could be warm in the winter? Seriously, Vic, did you find, like, diaries or anything?'

'No, darling. Just his old softballs and a White Sox baseball. That might be worth something. It was signed by Nellie Fox.'

'Nellie? A woman played for the White Sox? Daddy never — '

'Alas, sweet P., Nellie was short for 'Nelson,' not 'Eleanor.' He was a Gold Glove second baseman for the White Sox. Anyway, the ball is so beat-up, it's full of holes. I have no idea why Tony even had it. Maybe he picked it up for your dad and forgot to give it to him. Peter's a White Sox fan, isn't he?'

'We live in KC, so it's the Royals for us. Poor us. But Daddy keeps a soft spot for the Sox.'

We talked baseball the rest of the way north. As I was dropping Petra off, she reverted to our little encounter with the punks outside my South Chicago home.

'Please don't tell Daddy about it, okay? He already thinks I'm, like, six years old, without enough sense to keep out of harm's way. And he thinks you're this mega-feminist trouble-maker. If he knew I'd waltzed right into danger at your side, he'd skin you for supper and put me in a convent.'

'He'd have to catch me first. And, fear not, you're safe from the convents: your dad and I never talk.'

23

Visit a Client . . . and Talk

I drove over to Lionsgate Manor Sunday afternoon to meet Miss Claudia. I was tired of getting the runaround from her sister, and even from Karen Lennon, on when she would be fit enough to talk to me.

The building receptionist sent me to the skilled-nursing floor, where the head nurse told me that they'd taken Miss Claudia up to the rooftop garden. The nurse warned me that Miss Claudia was noticeably weaker and vaguer. She hadn't been able to go to church this morning, and she had slept most of the day.

'On Sundays, when there's no therapy, I like our stroke and dementia patients to have a chance to be outside. Even if she doesn't seem responsive to you, she probably understands more than you'd think when you talk to her. Are you from the social welfare office?'

'No. I'm trying to find her nephew, Lamont, for her.'

The head nurse patted my hand. 'That's good of you. Real good. She talks about him all the time . . . at least as much as I can make out from what she's saying.'

The 'garden' turned out to be a dozen or so trees in pots enclosed by a low wooden fence. The manor had done what they could within their budget limits: window boxes with flowers and some vegetables hanging from the fence, big umbrellas making the space look almost gay, a place to get drinks, and, in one corner and under a canopy, a television set tuned to the White Sox game.

A couple of women were working over the tomatoes and peppers in one of the window boxes. Another group was clustered around a kitten, each trying to get the animal to come to her. The aide who was escorting me to Miss Claudia explained that they brought in different animals for therapy.

'The kitten will live here, but we have to be careful. These old ladies, they're all so lonely, they get in terrible fights over whose turn it is to have Kitty in her room at night, so we have to say Kitty lives with Pastor Karen. It's easier to bring in the therapy dogs, because they understand that the dogs have to live on the outside.'

Miss Claudia was in a shady corner, dozing in a wheelchair, with her sister knitting nearby. Even allowing for Claudia's poor health, the two women looked as unalike as two sisters could: Miss Ella, tall, narrow, pressed and ironed; the younger sister, rounder, softer. Although she was wasted by illness, Miss Claudia's face was still plump beneath her gray Afro, and you could see smile creases at her left eye, her good eye.

When the aide bent to gently shake Miss Claudia awake, Miss Ella frowned at me in awful majesty.

'My sister is very poorly today. You should

have called before coming along like this to bother her.'

'I know she's doing poorly,' I said, trying to remember not to give way to my quick temper. 'I don't want to lose the chance to talk to her altogether, that's all.'

The aide was speaking loudly and brightly to Miss Claudia, as one might offer a treat to a toddler, telling her she had a visitor, let's wake up from our nice nap. A big Bible, its red leather faded to russet along the edges where she'd held it all these years, dropped from Miss Claudia's lap to the ground. Cardboard markers, inscribed with verses, scattered around her chair.

''Ible,' Miss Claudia cried. 'Fall . . . no.'

I bent to pick it all up for her, and I tucked the markers into the front of the Bible. The covers were thick and lumpy, as if the book had suffered from the damp.

'You're always dropping that big thing,' Miss Ella said roughly. 'Why don't you leave it in the apartment and keep a small one with you that you can hang on to.'

'No.' Tears oozed out of Miss Claudia's left eye, 'Keep with me always.'

I pulled a chair up next to her left side and placed the Bible in her lap, where she could touch it. 'Miss Claudia, I'm V.I. Warshawski . . . Vic. I'm the detective who's looking for Lamont.'

''Tive?' she said, turning her head to me and getting the syllable out with difficulty.

'Yes, she's the detective,' Miss Ella said loudly. 'She's the lady that's taking our money and not finding Lamont for us. So maybe if she tells you why she can't find him, you'll let go of this idea.'

I took Claudia's left hand and held it lightly between my own two. As slowly and clearly as I could, I explained who I'd talked to and what I'd learned, or hadn't learned, about her nephew. She seemed to be following me, at least following some of it, interjecting a syllable here and there that sounded like the names I was reciting.

'I've been looking for Steve Sawyer,' I said. 'He was Lamont's friend. They were together the night Lamont left your home.'

Miss Claudia frowned. 'Not 'Teve.'

'You don't want a detective? You'd like me to stop looking?'

She shook her head. 'No, no! You look, find 'Mont. Talk bad. 'Teve . . . S-s-s-t-uh-eve . . . not name.'

Miss Ella smiled grimly at my confusion. 'She thinks his name isn't Steve. But of course it is.'

'What is it?' I asked Miss Claudia.

'No 'member. Not 'Teve.'

The aide brought over a glass of apple juice, and I held it for Miss Claudia to drink. 'Will Rose know his name?'

Miss Claudia smiled gratefully on the left side of her face. 'As' 'Ose. Love 'Mont.'

Yes, Rose Hebert had loved Lamont. 'Do you know any of Lamont's other friends?'

Claudia slowly shook her head.

I let her rest for a minute or two, then asked if she remembered Harmony Newsome. Claudia's good eye brightened, and she struggled to tell me about Harmony and the neighborhood. I couldn't make out much of her garbled syllables except that Harmony's father had been a lawyer. I think Miss Claudia was telling me he had money, he could afford to send Harmony to college, but I wasn't sure.

When I got to Harmony's death and reminded Miss Claudia that Steve Sawyer had been convicted of her murder, I brought up what George Dornick had said. 'Do you think Lamont told the police that Steve Sawyer killed Harmony Newsome?'

'Not 'Mont, no. 'Teve friend, baby, school, friend. 'Mont good boy. Not hell, good boy.' Tears leaked from her good eye again.

'See what you've done?' Miss Ella said with a kind of grim satisfaction. 'My sister can't help you. You need to leave, Miss Detective, and stop bothering us.'

Before I could voice my anger — she hired me, it wasn't my idea to ride out to Stateville or get insulted by Curtis Rivers in the last few weeks — Miss Claudia said, 'No, Ella. Find 'Mont, you.' She tapped my hand with her own good one. ''Mont 'Conda not. Friend Johnny, yes, 'Conda not. Leave, give — ' She stumbled over the word and finally picked up the Bible and showed it to me. The markers fell out again.

''Mont . . . Ella give 'Mont 'Ible, he give me. Leave, see Johnny, he say, 'Keep, keep safe, keep safe.'' She squeezed her eyes shut and struggled to speak. 'I keep. 'Mont come, I give.'

'The night he left home, he told you he was going to see Johnny?'

''Es,' she managed to say.

'Then he gave you his Bible and told you to keep it safe for him, that he would take it back from you when he came home again,' I translated.

She smiled in relief that I had understood her but didn't try to speak again. I picked up the markers and tucked them into the Bible. Before I gave it back, I turned the well-worn pages, looking to see if Lamont had left anything.

'I'll do my best for you, Miss Claudia,' I promised.

She squeezed my fingers again with her weak left hand. When she smiled, I could see what a beautiful woman she'd been before her stroke. Miss Ella was frowning more deeply than ever, but I felt better about the case when I left. Not because I had any better ideas, but because I understood now how much it meant to Miss Claudia that I find her nephew.

I felt a little less optimistic after talking to Rose Hebert that night. She didn't know what Miss Claudia meant, that Steve Sawyer wasn't Lamont's friend's name. 'Of course his name was Steve. Maybe he called himself Steven to be formal, but I don't know what else Miss Claudia had in mind.'

24

Fire in the Nunnery

At six Monday evening, I rang the bell to Sister Frankie's apartment on the fringes of Uptown. She lived in a square box, the kind of characterless building that went up in the sixties, with metal-framed windows set level against the tan brick walls so that you didn't even have a ledge to hold a window box. The Mighty Waters Freedom Center had offices on the ground floor. The rest of the building seemed to be private apartments, some with nuns; F. Kerrigan, OP, and C. Zabinska, BVM, for instance. From the other names, and the discarded toys I could see in the entryway, it seemed that a number of families lived here, too.

The building sat flush with the walk, without even a token patch of grass in front. No one looking at the cracks in the bricks or the open windows where fans tried to stir an evening breeze to life would accuse the sisters of violating any vows of poverty.

After a minute, I rang the bell again. The lock would have been easy to undo with a credit card, but I leaned against the door and watched the street while I waited. Someone had opened a hydrant on the far corner, and kids, mostly boys, were racing in and out of the jet of water. Couples embraced, at bus stops or in alcoves. A woman whose matchstick legs stuck out in front of her like Raggedy Ann's was sitting on the bus stop bench beating her thigh with a shaky fist, muttering, 'You can't tell me that, you can't tell me that.' In the alley, kids were lighting firecrackers: the Fourth was only a week away.

It had been a full day, and if I hadn't been so impatient to hear what Sister Frances could remember of her day in Marquette Park forty years ago I would have gone home for an early supper and bed.

Karen Lennon had called around noon to thank me for visiting Miss Claudia. 'Miss Ella is angry, but I'm glad you didn't wait for me to give the green light. Miss Claudia feels much more at peace now. I think she's ready to die, knowing that you are committed to finding her nephew.'

That statement had alarmed me: I realized Miss Claudia was frail when I saw her, but I hadn't been imagining her as close to death.

Lennon tried to reassure me. 'The doctor says she's stable, but, with strokes, that can change rapidly, too. But after meeting you, and feeling reassured that you're taking her seriously, that could make her feel less stress, so it could help her get stronger.'

When we hung up, I felt a renewed stab of urgency in the search for Lamont, but I didn't know what I could be doing. With a sort of helplessness, I put in a second request to see Johnny Merton out in Stateville. Perhaps by the time the visit came through, I could think of some quid pro quo that would make the head

239

snake speak to me. 'Parseltongue, that's what I need,' I murmured out loud as I brushed my teeth. A language for communicating with snakes.

The door suddenly opened behind me. 'Detective? I'm Frankie Kerrigan. Sorry to keep you waiting. We were having a short meeting on our Iowa refugees.'

Frankie Kerrigan was a thin, wiry woman, around seventy, with curly gray hair that had once been red. Her face and arms were freckled and sunburned. She wore a T-shirt and jeans. Her only badge of office was a plain wooden cross on a thin chain.

She seemed to realize I was searching her for signs of nun-ness, because she flashed a smile, and said, 'When I have to talk to a judge, I put on a veil and a skirt, but, here at home, I get to wear jeans. Come on up, Detective.'

I followed her into the hall. 'You know I'm a private investigator, right, not a cop?'

'Yes, I remember that. I didn't know how you like to be addressed.'

'Most people call me Vic.'

The hallway was a jumble of strollers and bicycles, like any urban building. Unlike most, the halls and stairwell were scrubbed clean; I could smell the disinfectant as I trotted up the stairs after her. The Virgin of Guadalupe sat in a niche at the turn in the landing. At the top of the first flight, a weeping Jesus looked at me from a foot-high cross.

'How was Iowa?' I asked while she unlocked her own front door.

'Depressing. Five hundred families broken up by these ridiculous raids, women and children left homeless, the business that employed them shut down for loss of workers. We're doing our best. But the judicial atmosphere these days is so punitive, our best is pretty futile.'

She ushered me into a front room that was furnished simply but with warmth: bright throws on the daybed and two chairs, bookcases built of a light wood and filled floor to ceiling. A small fan sat in one open window. In the other window, she'd built a shelf to hold a planterful of red and orange flowers.

She brought tea — 'Hot tea is the best thing to drink in hot weather, I've always believed' — but didn't waste time with other preliminaries.

'I can't tell you how happy I am that someone is revisiting Harmony's murder. She was an amazing young woman. I met her when I went to Atlanta to work with Ella Baker, and Harmony was one of the SNCC volunteers there. She was a student at Spelman. But she was from Chicago and came back here at the end of the spring semester to do organizing. She'd already been arrested three times in the South, during sit-ins and trying to register voters. That gave her a kind of glamour and credibility with young people in her neighborhood.'

She picked up a photograph from a small desk. 'I found this after you called last week. Harmony's mother gave it to me after the funeral. And when we started the Freedom Center, we named it in Harmony's honor, after her favorite Bible verse.'

The old eight-by-ten showed the young woman whose face I'd seen in the *Herald-Star* story, but more alert, more attractive, than in the old file photo. She was standing next to SNCC founder Ella Baker. Both women were smiling, but with a kind of fundamental seriousness that made you feel the importance of their mission. The picture had been inscribed, 'Let justice pour down like waters.'

I handed back the picture. 'I hope you realize that I'm not revisiting her death but trying to find Steve Sawyer, the man who was convicted of killing her. You said on the phone you hadn't been happy with the verdict.'

'No, I wasn't, and I did try to go to the police when I learned about the arrest.' Sister Frankie frowned over her teacup. 'You see, Harmony and I were marching next to each other when she suddenly collapsed. I thought at first it was the heat. You have to understand, the noise was so intense, and the heat, and the hate ... We couldn't hear each other, let alone any individual voices from the mob. But all the young men from the neighborhood, all those gangbangers, they were clustered around the leadership — Dr. King, Al Raby, and so on — near the front of the march.'

She flashed a wry smile. 'We women were at the back . . . Women and children last, you know, when it comes to public action or recognition . . . Harmony got hit from the side. At the moment, it was so shocking, I couldn't think at all, let alone analyze what happened or even think about looking for a killer.

'Later, though, after the funeral, after the horror of the march and Harmony's death subsided a little, I started thinking it over. The missile had to have come out of the mob, out of the crowd surging around us. All the gang members were up front, you see, around Dr. King and Al Raby. The person who killed her was at the side, and that meant it couldn't have been a black person. The mob would have murdered any black man if he'd been in their midst.'

I felt let down. I'd been pinning my hopes on something substantial, an explicit identification. 'So you didn't see who hit her?'

She shook her head. 'I offered to testify at the trial, but Steve Sawyer's attorney wouldn't put me on the witness list. I tried to insist, but my bishop called me and told me I was out of line. The cardinal was trying to calm passions in the city, and, there I was, stirring them up.' She smiled sadly. 'Nowadays, that wouldn't stop me. But then, I was only twenty-six, and I didn't know how far I could go before the hierarchy would stop me.'

'What was it you thought you could add, your opinion about where the gang members were standing relative to you and Harmony?'

'No. It was something else. One of the boys had a camera. He was taking pictures of us, and I hoped — '

A loud bang cut her off midsentence. A rifle report . . . an M-80? Glass splintered and jangled, a large starfish-shaped break now in the window over the flowers. Sister Frankie sprang to her feet as a bottle filled with liquid sailed through the break, the telltale rag in its mouth.

'Get down! Get down!' I screamed.

She was bending down to pick up the bottle when a second bottle flew in. It hit her in the head and burst into flames. I grabbed the throw from the daybed and flung it and myself on her, wrapping her up, rolling her along the floor. I heard a third bottle land, and then screams from the street, car tires screeching, and, above it all, the hissing of fire, the snapping of flames, as fire grabbed books, bookcases, my own jacket. Choking on smoke and gasoline fumes, I rolled myself on top of Sister Frankie, trying to put out the fire licking at the arms of my jacket. Nun, throw, detective — an ungainly bundle — rolling to the door. I stuck up a quickly blistering arm, fumbled for the knob, tumbled into the hall.

25

Alphabet Visitors — FBI, OEM, HS, CPD

It was the dead of night, and my father was still out on patrol, still facing rioters someplace in the midnight city. People were throwing Molotov cocktails at him. I could see the bottles flying at his head, and I cried out, trying to warn him, which was stupid because he was miles away and couldn't hear me. My mother mustn't know I was frightened. It only made her worries harder when she had to comfort me as well as herself.

Our house was never truly dark. Flares from the mills created a ghostly light even at two in the morning, and the sky, always yellow from the sulfur vapors, gleamed dully all night long. Light seeped through the curtains and made my eyes hurt. My arms ached and my throat was sore. I had the flu. And, somewhere in the background, my mother was talking. A doctor had come to the house and was asking me how I felt.

'I'm fine.' I couldn't complain about being sick, not with Papa out fighting a riot.

'What's your name?' the doctor wanted to know.

'Victoria,' I croaked obediently.

'Who is the president?' the doctor asked.

I couldn't remember who the president was and I started to panic. 'Is this school? Is this a test?'

'You're in the hospital, Victoria. Do you remember coming to the hospital?'

It was a woman's voice, not my mother, but someone I knew. I struggled to come up with her name. 'Lotty?'

'Yes, *Liebchen*.' Relief flooded her voice. 'Lotty. You're in my hospital.'

'Beth Israel,' I whispered. 'I can't see.'

'We've bandaged your eyes to protect them from light for a few days. You got a bit scorched.'

Fire. The Molotov cocktails hadn't been flung at my dad but at Sister Frankie.

'The nun . . . Is she . . . How is she?'

'She's in intensive care right now. You saved her life.' Lotty's voice quavered.

'My arms hurt.'

'They were burned. But you got medical help fast, and there are only a few patches where the underlayer of skin was compromised. You'll be fine in a few days. Now I want you to rest.'

A man was speaking in the background, loud, demanding that I answer questions. Lotty answered in the voice that made Max bow and call her *Eure Hoheit*, 'Your Highness' in German. The surgeon, as Princess of Austria, telling the man that I would answer no official questions until she was sure I wasn't still in shock.

Lotty was protecting me, I could rest, I could relax and be safe. I drifted off to sleep, riding on a field of violets. A saber-toothed tiger prowled through the violets. I crouched low, but it smelled me. My flesh was burned. I smelled like steak on Mr. Contreras's grill. I tried to scream, but my throat was swollen, and no sound came out.

I struggled back to consciousness and lay panting in the dark. I felt my hands. They were wrapped in gauze, and the pressure was painful because they were still swollen. I tentatively felt my blistered eyelids. They, too, were padded in gauze.

A nurse came in and asked me to rate my pain on a scale of one to ten. 'I've hurt worse, I think,' I whispered. 'Maybe a nine. Is it day or night?'

'It's afternoon. You've slept for five hours, and I can give you some more pain medication now.'

'How is the nun? How is Sister Frankie?'

I could feel her moving near me. 'I don't know. I just came on shift. The doctor will be able to tell you.'

'Dr. Herschel?' I asked. But I was already drifting back to the fractured lines and colors of morphic sleep.

A baseball sat on the kitchen table, rocking back and forth from a passing freight train that shook the house. It was Christmas, and Papa had gone to the ballpark without telling me. He and Mama and a strange man had been arguing in the middle of the night, their loud voices waking me up.

'I can't do it!' Papa shouted.

And then Mama heard me on the stairs and called to me in Italian to go back to bed. The men's voices dropped to whispers, until the man shouted, 'I'm tired of you preaching to me, Warshawski! You're not the cardinal, let alone a saint, so get off your plastic crucifix.'

The front door slammed, and the baseball started to roll off the table. It was a cannonball now and rolling toward my head, its fuse blowing sparks, and I woke again to darkness, drenched in sweat. I fumbled on the nightstand for water. There was a pitcher and a cup, and as I poured I spilled water on myself, but that felt good.

Someone came in with a cup of broth. It was strangely hard to find my mouth with my eyes bandaged, as if loss of sight meant loss of balance, loss of feeling. A nurse arrived to take my temperature and ask me my pain level.

'I'm crappy,' I rasped, 'but no more morphine. I can't take the dreams.'

I wanted to wash my hair, but that was out of the question until the bandages came off. The nurse sent in someone to sponge me off, and I dozed fitfully until Lotty arrived.

'The police want to question you, Victoria. I see you've discontinued your morphine. How much pain are you in?'

'Enough to make me know I was in a fire, but not so much I want to scream about it. How is Sister Frankie?'

Lotty put a hand on my shoulder. 'That's why they want to talk you, Vic. She didn't make it.'

'No!' I whispered. 'No!'

Sister Frankie had marched with Ella Baker at Selma. She stood with King in Marquette Park. She sat with men on death row. She housed Guatemalan asylum seekers and testified for immigrants. No harm came to her until she talked to me.

Lotty offered me Vicodin or Percocet to help

me through the interview, but I welcomed the pain in my arms and the burning in my eyes where my useless tears leaked out. By some fluke, I was alive when I should also be dead. V. I. Warshawski, death dealer. The least that should happen was that I feel a little pain.

I could sense bodies filling the room. Two men from Bomb and Arson identified themselves, but I could tell there were others, and I demanded to know who was with them. There was a shuffling of feet and muttering, and then they went around the room, giving their names.

I didn't recognize any of them: a man and a woman from the Office of Emergency Management, our local branch of Homeland Security, tagged along; a field agent from the FBI.

Lotty had cranked up the bed so that I was more or less sitting. I had my arms in front of me on the sheet. The IV tube going up to the bag that was giving me antibiotics and fluids swung against my shoulder. My little plastic friend and Lotty: my team against the police, the Bureau, and Homeland Security.

The Bomb and Arson men announced that they were taping the session. One of them asked if I was ready to make a statement.

'I'm ready to answer questions but not to make a formal statement, not until I can see well enough to read any document you ask me to sign.'

One of the group, I think the man from OEM, was wearing a kind of musky aftershave that made me feel sick to my stomach. The CPD's Bomb and Arson team was leading the inquiry. It was one of them who had me state my name for the record.

'V. I. Warshawski.' As I spelled Warshawski, I remembered Petra's a warrior in a rickshaw on a ski and had that horrible impulse to laugh that seizes us at moments of grief and fear.

'What were you doing at Sister Frances's apartment?' a member of the Bomb team asked.

'We were meeting to discuss a forty-year-old murder.'

A murmur went through the room, and the woman from OEM asked whose murder.

'Harmony Newsome. Sister Frankie — Sister Frances — had been with Ms. Newsome when she died.'

'Why are you interested in this old murder . . . Vicki, is it?'

'Vicki, it isn't,' I said. 'You may call me Ms. Warshawski.'

There was a shifting and more muttering, and the temperature in the room went up a few degrees. Good. Why should I be the only one feeling burned?

'Why are you interested in this old murder?' the FBI's Lyle Torgeson asked.

'I'm not . . . very.' I started to explain my search for Lamont Gadsden and suddenly felt so tired that I thought I might go to sleep midsentence. It seemed to me that I had been looking for Lamont Gadsden and Steve Sawyer my whole life.

'Why did you go to Sister Frances's apartment?' Torgeson again.

'That was where she asked to meet me,' I said.

'She wanted to talk to me. She said she'd been troubled for forty years by the verdict against Steve Sawyer.'

'And why was that?' said one of the detectives, truculent: *We in the Chicago Police Department do not bring innocent people into court.*

'I don't know. We got three sentences out before the bombs fell.'

'What did she say?' Torgeson asked.

'She said Iowa was depressing.'

'We were warned that you think you're funny,' the man from OEM said, 'but this isn't the time or place.'

'Do I look to you like someone in the throes of merriment?' I said. 'I'm in pain, I'm in shock, and I would love to think you've got a really active crime scene unit going over every square inch of the Freedom Center and the sisters' building. I'm also mildly curious about why the OEM and the FBI are here. Do you think a terrorist was after Sister Frankie?'

A sucking in of breath and another buzz around the interrogation circle. 'Anytime someone starts throwing bombs around, we're curious,' Torgeson finally said. 'As a citizen, you have an obligation to help us in our investigation.'

'As a human being, I am deeply grieved that Sister Frankie died and that I couldn't do anything to keep that from happening.'

'So tell us, as a human being, what Sister Frankie said.' Torgeson's voice was heavy with sarcasm.

'Sister Frankie said Iowa was depressing.

She'd just come back from trying to help the families of the people your buddies in INS scooped up and arrested for the crime of working in a meat-packing plant. She said it was . . . Oh, I get it.' I leaned back against the egg-carton hospital mattress. 'Sister Frankie was helping people who were in this country illegally. That's why you're all here, panting like badly trained bloodhounds.'

Lotty's fingers gripped my shoulder: *Steady there, Vic. Keep your temper under control.*

'Do you think her death is connected to her work in Iowa?' I said.

'We're asking the questions this afternoon, Warshawski.' That was the woman from OEM, determined to be as tough as the men around her.

I smiled tightly. 'So you do think her death is connected to her work in Iowa.'

'We don't know,' Torgeson said. 'We don't know if Sister Frances was the target or another member of the Freedom Center. It might even have been you. You've made yourself plenty unpopular with some people in this town.'

The accusation was so ruthless, so unsettling, that I almost missed the woman from OEM saying, 'We thought the target could also be one of the families who live in the building. Some are illegals. Some are dealing drugs.'

'You know a lot about them,' I said. 'Fast work.'

It's an amazing thing about lack of sight: you feel people's emotions more than when you can see them. I could feel Torgeson withdraw into

252

himself, as if a glass wall had slipped between him and the room.

'You know about them because you've had the Freedom Center women under surveillance,' I said. 'You've been watching them, tapping their phones. America is facing international terror threats, and you're following a bunch of nuns.'

'We are not at liberty to discuss our actions, nor are we required to do so,' the OEM woman snapped.

I ignored her. 'You're dogging the sisters and you couldn't stop a fire bombing.'

'We moved as fast as we could,' Torgeson protested. 'We were undercover. It didn't look like a serious attack at first, not until we saw the flames in the windows.'

'What in the name of sweet Fanny Adams did you think it was?' I cried.

The room became completely quiet. I could hear the hospital noises, the pages, the squeaking of rubber soles on worn linoleum.

One of the Bomb men cleared his throat. 'Tell us what happened inside the apartment.'

I shook my head, exhausted. 'We heard the window break. For five seconds, I thought it was street noise. Kids had been setting off firecrackers in the alley. I thought it was an M-80 that had misfired.'

Behind my bandages, I shut my eyes, trying to remember the few minutes I'd spent with Sister Frankie. 'Then I saw a bottle come in through the window. I saw the rag, I knew it was a fire bomb. I screamed at Sister Frances to get down, but she went to pick it up. And then another one came through and . . . and . . . '

She was on fire. With my eyes shut, I could see the flames engulf her wiry hair, her skin turn white beneath the yellow flames. I was shaking and heaving, and Lotty was telling everyone they had to leave.

'We need to know what Sister Frances told Warshawski here about Harmony Newsome.'

'You are in my hospital by my sufferance only,' Lotty said coldly. 'I have told you the time has come for you to leave and you will leave.'

'Doctor, you may mean well,' the woman from OEM said, 'but we have powers here from the Department of Homeland Security. That means we talk to Warshawski until we're ready to leave.'

I could smell Lotty's fury. I felt my plastic tube move, and suddenly I had slid out of the room, down the waterslide at Wolf Lake, with Boom-Boom yelling my name. He was trying to dunk me in the lake, but Gabriella pulled him away from me, and I started to breathe again.

26

And Now Murray

Thanks to whatever Lotty injected into my IV, I slept the clock around. When I woke, the pain in my arms and eyes had subsided to a manageable throb. When a volunteer came in to help me with some kind of liquid goop that I'd been cleared to consume, I asked if she'd also help me with the phone.

I called Mr. Contreras first. He had seen the story on the news, but the hospital was blocking my calls, he said. He had called Lotty, who reassured him, but it was still a relief to him to hear from me in person.

'Don't worry about the dogs none, doll, on account of I got that service you used when you was in Italy to come around. And Peewee' — his nickname for my cousin — 'she's been rallying around. She took Mitch into work with her this morning, and, last night, she went up to your place to get the sheets changed and everything, and even bought you yogurt, so you'll be comfy when they let you out.'

That was reassuring, sort of. After the business with my trunk, it made me tense to think of my cousin wandering around my apartment. Maybe she'd collected the Nellie Fox ball and hoped, with her usual optimism, that I wouldn't notice it was gone.

'Then there's that nice fella who just moved in, the musician: he's been helping with the dogs, too,' Mr. Contreras added. 'But Murray Ryerson, he's been around, him and some other reporters. I told him he should be ashamed, acting like a hyena following after the lions, picking up the food they did all the work finding.'

Mr. Contreras has never been crazy about any of the men in my life, but for some reason he actively dislikes Murray. I deflected the complaint as best I could and patiently answered his questions. I even took his rough words of comfort in stride: I wasn't to blame myself. Nuns who went around working for terrorists knew they were taking risks. It wasn't my fault someone had fire-bombed her the night I chose to visit.

After he and I finished, I got the volunteer to dial my office so that I could speak with Marilyn, the temp. She was overwhelmed by phone calls. It hadn't occurred to me, but of course I was a media sensation.

'If it bleeds, it leads' is the old news bromide. And, if a nun bleeds, it leads for days. Julian Bond had called, as had Willie Barrow and other prominent civil rights veterans. Immigrant rights activists had held a vigil outside the hospital, and two men Sister Frankie had helped free from death row were staging a hunger strike outside police headquarters, demanding action in finding her killers. Since I'd been with her when she was murdered, I was understandably a person of interest to the TV crews.

'They keep calling, and some have been here,

256

thinking you were hiding out. What should I tell them?'

'That it will be a week before I'm well enough to talk to anyone, and they should go away and find blood someplace else.'

We went through the more manageable part of my incoming calls. The subcontractor doing surveillance for me in Mokena. Some outstanding reports to clients, which I managed to dictate to her. And messages to various other clients, to tell them I'd be back in my office within the week and would talk to them then.

In the afternoon, I was wheeled to the ophthalmology department, and my eyes were unbandaged. Although the doctor had the blinds pulled and the overhead lights turned off, even the murky gray light made me wince. At first, I could see nothing but spark-filled spirals. After a few minutes, though, shapes swam into focus.

The doctor examined me closely. 'You are very lucky, Ms. Warshawski. The burns on the lids were not severe and are already healing. For the next few weeks, you'll need to wear dark glasses with photochromic lenses whenever you are outside, whether the sun is shining or not, and anytime you're in a brightly lit room. If you wear glasses, you need to get prescription sunglasses to use in front of a computer for the next month or two. And stay away from TV and computers altogether for two more days. That's a serious order, okay?'

He gave me an antibiotic salve to put on and under the lids twice a day, and told me it was safe to wash my hair.

When they brought me back to my room, with a pair of those outsize plastic sunglasses they give people after cataract surgery, the resident came around to inspect the rest of my body. My arms were rough and red. I'd been wearing a linen jacket, since I'd dressed professionally for my meeting, and while the fabric had charred it had spared my skin from more severe burns.

My hands had suffered the worst damage. When the dressings came off next week, I'd need to wear cotton gloves anytime I went outside.

When I finally crept into the bathroom and looked in the mirror, I looked sunburned, but my face only had a few blisters along the hairline. I'd apparently buried my face in the throw while I tumbled Sister Frances out of her room, which also had saved me from serious burns. What made me look bizarre wasn't my shiny red cheeks but the clumps of hair missing from my head. I looked like a dog with mange.

Even so, I had been staggeringly lucky to escape the full force of the fire. If only I'd pulled Sister Frankie down instead of screaming at her . . . I could see the bottle hitting her head over and over again every time I closed my eyes.

The resident had said they would discharge me tomorrow if I continued to hold my own. In the meantime, they were removing my IVs. I could switch to oral antibiotics and actual food.

'You know you've created a kind of media circus at the hospital?' The resident was a young man, and a media circus was clearly a welcome change of pace for him.

Apparently, the hospital security staff had

found one reporter trying to get into my room while I was asleep that morning. They had gotten the city to arrest another man they'd discovered at one of the nursing-station computers calling up Sister Frankie's and my charts.

'We put a block on incoming calls to your room. The switchboard says they've clocked a hundred seventeen calls.'

I hadn't thought there could be a plus to a hospital stay, but missing a hundred seventeen media calls proved me wrong.

When the doctor finally remembered he had other beds to visit, I put on plastic mitts to protect my hands and took a shower in the little bathroom. I felt better physically, but exhaustion, medication, and depression made me go back to the bed in a sort of numb lethargy.

I put on my heavy glasses and lay half dozing. Someone brought a species of lunch. I begged for coffee, thinking caffeine might lift some of the fog in my brain. The attendant said it wasn't on my diet, and I lay back down, nauseated by the wobbly red Jell-O on the tray.

By and by, I thought of my clothes. My wallet had been in my handbag and that was probably melted into the remains of Sister Frances's home, but I often stuff loose bills into my pockets. I found eleven dollars and thirteen cents in my smoky clothes. My cellphone was there, too, but the battery was dead.

I pulled my Lario boots onto my bare feet and put on my torn and charred linen jacket. I looked in the little mirror in the bathroom. Between the costume, my clumpy hair, and the outsize glasses, I looked like I belonged on the Uptown streets outside the hospital, collecting cigarette butts. I made it down the hall on wobbly legs; two days in bed, with no food and a lot of shock, had atrophied my muscles. A hospital security guard at the nursing station looked at me curiously but didn't try to stop me. I rode down to the first-floor lobby.

Hospitals have realized that the cash register chings louder if they install an espresso machine. They don't study how to make it good, figuring a clientele under stress will drink anything. I wasn't in a position to be picky, either. I ordered a triple espresso from an attendant who, taking in my costume and my mangy head, asked to be paid first.

While he pulled my shots, I looked across the lobby to the front of the building. The media circus had shut down most of its rings, with only one camera truck still there. As I squinted through my glasses, I could just make out a couple of people with picket signs — the immigrant rights activists, perhaps, or maybe a striking local or even abortion protestors. The lenses were too opaque for me to be able to read the signs themselves.

My hands were so thickly wrapped that I had to hold the cup with my fingertips, and I had trouble opening the sugar packets. I finally tore them with my teeth, spraying sugar over myself and the floor before managing to get some in my coffee. I was heading for the elevators when I spotted my old pal Murray Ryerson from the *Herald-Star* at the reception desk. He was collecting a visitor's pass and grinning with satisfaction at the clerk. So much for the lockdown on reporters.

I felt vulnerable and exposed, with no underwear under a shabby hospital gown, only my smoky jacket keeping my breasts and buttocks from public view. I retreated into a chair behind a potted plant and watched until Murray was inside an elevator.

As I waited, Beth Blacksin from Global Entertainment went up to the reception desk and started gesticulating in indignation, pointing at the elevator. So Murray had scammed his way in. A hospital security guard joined Beth.

Hospitals have a million exits and stairwells. I left the coffee shop by the far end and went into the first stairwell I came to. One flight, and I felt as though I'd been sandbagged, my legs wobbling, my head dizzy. I leaned against the wall and drank some of my coffee. It was bitter — they hadn't cleaned the machine heads anytime recently — but the caffeine steadied me.

A doctor came running down the stairs but paused when he saw me. 'Do you belong here?'

I held out my wrist with my plastic patient tag looped above my gauze hands. 'I got turned around when I went downstairs for coffee.'

He read my tag. 'Your room is on the fifth floor. You'd better take an elevator. I'm not sure you should be up and about at all . . . Definitely not climbing five flights of stairs.'

He opened the door to the first floor and held it while I walked past him. 'I can call for a wheelchair.'

'No, the nurses told me I needed to start walking. I'll be okay.'

He was in a hurry and didn't stay to argue with me. I looked at my tag. Sure enough, it had my room number on it. That was a mercy: I hadn't bothered to check it when I left.

I found a secondary elevator bank and saw a sign for the hospital library. Carrying my coffee in my fingertips, I walked past the Orthopedic Outpatient Clinic and Respiratory Diseases and came to the library. To my relief, this was merely a room filled with donated books, mostly unread review copies with publicists' letters still inside the front covers. No staff were present to question whether a person in heavy dark glasses and no underwear ought to be there.

I turned out the overhead lights and curled up in an armchair. Time to stop feeling sorry for myself and guilty about Sister Frankie. Time to think, to work.

The feds had been watching Sister Frances's apartment and hadn't intervened in the attack on her. Did that mean they wanted her dead or had they been out getting pizza and not noticed whoever threw the Molotov cocktails?

The coffee helped, but not enough to get my muzzy brain fully functioning. I uncoiled myself from the armchair and took some of the publicity letters out of the books. Scrabbling in the drawers of a little desk, I found an old pencil stub. It would have to do. I couldn't see well enough to write, and the pencil stub was too blunt for cursive, so I used block letters.

1. FEDS WATCHING FRANKIE: WHY?
2. LAMONT GADSDEN = SNITCH: TRUE?
3. WHAT IN BOTTLES — PRO OR STREET-GRADE ACCELERANT?

Who would tell me any of these things? There was something else, too, another important question, nagging the back of my mind. I took off my boots, tucked my legs under me, and let my mind drift. I dozed and woke and dozed, but it was Lotty's anger that kept coming to the surface. It couldn't be about Lotty. It must be the law enforcement people she sent about their business yesterday. They had asked something odd.

I stuffed the paper into my jacket pocket and bent to pull my boots on. When I stood, I had to clutch the chair to keep from falling over. It was infuriating to be so weak. I needed to be out on the streets, talking to people, not so shaky that a walk down a hospital corridor did me in. I made my unsteady way back to my room.

I had just sunk down on my egg-carton mattress when a nurse looked in. 'Where have you been? We've been looking all over the hospital for you! Didn't you hear us page you?'

'Sorry. I was testing my legs and got so tired I fell asleep in a chair. I didn't hear anything.'

She took my temperature and felt my pulse and disappeared to spread the good news that I was back. As soon as she was gone, the bathroom door opened, and Murray came out.

'Well, well, Warshawski. They were telling the truth. You're not dead yet.'

'Ryerson, get the *fuck* out of my hospital room.' I was startled into fury.

'Oh, those sweet words.' He grinned and peered at me. 'You know, you do look pretty strange, if you don't mind my saying so.'

'I do mind. I survived a fire. It was extremely unpleasant. Now leave.'

'After you talk to me, my fire-eating private eye.'

'I'll talk to you if you do something for me.'

He bowed low over his tape recorder. 'As you command, O Queen, so shall it be done.'

'I need some clothes. I can't wear these. And my wallet and credit cards and whatnot are all at the sister's apartment.'

Murray sat up. 'I'm not going to your place. You know the old guy hates me. He'd sic that hellhound of yours on me, and I'd be fish food before I could explain why I was rummaging in your closet.'

'Buy me something, then. Jeans, a long-sleeved white shirt, and a bra. That's all I need.'

'A bra? You mean, like brassiere? Ix-nay.'

'Murray, you were wearing a twenty-something blonde at Krumas's fundraiser. You can't tell me you blush and get prickly heat in a lingerie department. Size 36-C. And size 12 shirt, 31 long jeans. You record all that for posterity?'

'Okay,' Murray scowled. 'I got it. Now, what were you doing at Sister Frances Kerrigan's home to get her killed?'

I sat up in bed and looked at my arms. 'Somehow, I don't seem to have a shirt on.'

'Before we talk? Do you know what it took to

get in here? I had to find the name of a patient and pretend to be visiting her. And then I had to skulk around until I could get at a computer and hack in to find your room number. They won't let me back in. I'm not leaving until you talk.'

'Yeah, I figured you'd welsh on your end of the deal, but don't worry your perfectly groomed head. Mr. Contreras will be glad to bring me some clothes. He loves me most when I'm on the DL.' I closed my eyes behind my dark lenses and leaned back against the pillows.

'Oh, damn you, you manipulative bitch, Warshawski!'

'I'm going to call the nurse in ten seconds, Ryerson. I'm not the bottom-feeder who hacked into a hospital computer system.'

'You're the bottom-feeder who got a nun fried.'

I sat up and pulled off my shades. 'You put that out anywhere — in print, on a blog, in a text message — and you will spend the rest of your life defending a libel action, do you hear me?'

There was an uneasy silence between us, before Murray said, 'You were there when she was attacked.'

I ignored him. 'And to speak in such language about Sister Frances's death . . . She worked her whole life for social justice and civil liberties, and you think you can talk about her death like a Chris Matthews gag line! Do you know what it's like to hold someone whose head is on fire, burning on top her body like the wick on a candle? Get out of here!'

'I'm sorry, V.I., okay? We all spend too much

time trying to think of the next clever, cynical thing to say. That was tasteless and thoughtless. I apologize.' He pulled out his cellphone, in contravention of all the posted signs, and called someone to buy me clothes. He even gave his gofer a credit-card number and told her to deliver them to the hospital.

I put my shades back on. The dim light in the room was making my eyes hurt. And, besides, I'd started crying, which I didn't want Murray to see.

'What are your sources saying?' I asked after a moment. 'Do they think she was attacked because of her immigrant work?'

'We're not getting anything off the street about that,' Murray admitted. 'The nun in charge of the Freedom Center, a Sister Carolyn Zabinska, says they got death threats back when the Iraq war started — the nuns were opposed to it and started these weekly vigils against it — but no one's ever threatened them because of their prison or immigrant-aid work.'

He paused. 'People are wondering why she was attacked the very night you visited her.'

I lay very still in the bed, eyes closed. 'What people? Besides you, of course.'

'Just what I hear around,' Murray said.

'Ever since Global bought the *Star*, you've been more on the entertainment side than the crime beat,' I said, still angry, wanting to prick him as he had me. 'So who you hear from doesn't carry the punch it used to.'

'When have I *ever* skimped on a story, Warshawski?' Murray was furious now, too. 'You on your pedestal, it's easy to work solo as an investigator, but I have to work for a company if I want to write for a newspaper. And my sources trust me.'

I looked at my wrapped hands and wished I worked for a big company where someone would pick up the slack when I was on the disabled list. 'So what are your sources telling you about the perps? Lawrence Avenue was hopping when I rang Sister Frankie's bell. They all suffer from witness-phobic amnesia?'

I couldn't see his face through my lenses in the darkened room, but Murray was still breathing hard. He didn't speak for a long moment, but, despite my nasty accusation, he was a reporter through and through. He wanted my story and knew he had to answer some questions if I was going to talk.

'There are a ton of witnesses to the perps. A Ford Expedition drove up at high speed, honking. Everyone jumped out of the way, and the Expedition pulled up onto the sidewalk. A guy — or maybe a gal, but they're pretty sure a guy — with a stocking pulled over his head got out, threw the bottles, jumped back in, and the Expedition took off before anyone really realized what was happening.'

'License plate?'

'No one bothered. Or they know and aren't telling. I've heard both stories,' Murray said. 'One of my sources says the boys in the alley recognized the SUV and are afraid to admit it for fear of being targeted next. Someone who will fire bomb a nun will pretty much do anything.'

I was quiet for a moment, digesting that. 'The FBI and OEM had a stakeout going. Any news out of them?'

'Yeah, the news that the First Amendment is DOA. We have to clear anything we print through them. Turds! And so's my editor. Bitch just nodded and blinked, and said the rules have changed and we need to follow them if we're going to bring people the news.'

His words brought my own police interrogation back to me. That was the question nagging at me, the woman from Emergency Management wanting to know what Sister Frances had told me about Harmony Newsome. I lay back against the mattress, feeling sick again. OEM already knew about Harmony Newsome when they talked to me.

In halting words, I explained why I'd been at the Freedom Center: the old murder, the search for Lamont. And the fact that OEM already knew about my interest in Harmony Newsome before their investigator talked to me.

'Is that because they were monitoring Sister Frankie's calls?' I finished. 'Or mine? Or both? Murray, if she died because I was there — '

'Hey, hey, Wonder Woman, don't get all weepy now,' Murray protested.

I couldn't help it. The doubts that had nagged me all summer about my personality, why I couldn't keep a relationship alive. Did I bring destruction to everyone around me?

27

In the Fired House

Lotty sailed into my room just then, followed by two of the residents and a medical student. Lotty sent Murray out of the room with a comment that stung like the snap of a whip.

I fumbled for tissues on the cart next to me. Lotty found the box but warned me not to rub my eyes.

'How did Ryerson get in here at all?' she demanded. 'What is going on in this hospital, that I give a specific order only to have it overridden? I have expressly forbidden any visitors in your room to make sure neither reporters nor police harass you. You didn't invite Murray in, did you?'

She had two fingers on the pulse in my neck. 'This is why you can't have visitors. You're vulnerable. You shouldn't be crying like this. And they tell me you disappeared this afternoon while I was in surgery. Was that to organize this rendezvous?'

'I went down to the coffee shop for an espresso, and the trip did me in. I fell asleep in a chair and didn't know people were paging me.'

I didn't like lying to Lotty, but it was sort of the truth. I wondered if she was right, though. I wondered if I'd wanted to see Murray. I could have reported him to hospital security when I

269

spotted him in the lobby, but I didn't. Maybe my unconscious brain was hoping he'd track me down.

Lotty grunted, and asked the residents to update her on my progress. While the medical student stood respectfully to one side, the two residents reviewed the damage to my corneas and optic nerves. I felt a stab of frustration, followed by a bigger stab of guilt. I was alive, I would recover. Maybe while I was on the DL, I could train myself to sleep days and work nights.

'I'm thinking of bringing you home with me when they discharge you tomorrow.' Lotty sounded like she was adopting a dog that had been returned to the pound too many times by people it bit. 'I'm worried about your health. And I'm worried about your safety.'

'My safety? Murray was saying that some sources think the bombers were after me, not Sister Frances. Have you heard the same thing?'

Lotty dismissed the residents and the student, and sat on the edge of the bed, frowning. 'I was thinking more about your recklessness. Does he have any proof?'

'I don't know. You booted him out before I could get him to come clean. I wouldn't even be worrying about it if the woman from Homeland Security hadn't pressed me on what Sister Frances told me about the Newsome inquiry.' I looked at Lotty's dim outline. 'Lotty, I can't go home with you if I'm a target of fire bombers. I can't risk you being hurt.'

'You'd be safer at my place than in your own home. We have a doorman, we have security.

You're completely exposed in your building. And if someone threw another fire bomb, those children on the second floor would be hurt.'

'I'm so helpless!' I burst out. 'To save my eyes and skin I have to sit in the dark. I need to be out talking to people, I need to be at my computer looking up data. What am I going to do?'

Lotty put an arm around me. 'Does everything have to happen today? In a few days, you'll be able to get around, as long as you're careful about the sun. You know how it is when you're in the hospital: you feel more helpless there than after you get out.'

She stayed until a supper tray arrived at six and insisted on my eating something that might once have been a chicken. When she left, I tried to sleep, since I couldn't read or watch TV. Instead, I kept thrashing around in the narrow bed, worrying about my role in Sister Frankie's death.

A little before eight, a volunteer came in with a shopping bag that had been left at the front desk for me. Murray's gofer had come through with my clothes. The bra was a plain white that I wouldn't have chosen for myself, but it didn't matter. With my bandaged hands, I couldn't fasten it, anyway. I managed the buttons on the shirt and pulled on the jeans. The gofer had dutifully brought me a size 31. After two days of living on IVs, I could have gotten away with a 30.

Just being dressed made me feel better. I pulled on my soft brown boots again and looked

271

in the bathroom mirror. Something would have to be done about that hair: I looked like a freak show.

The by-product of hospitalization is plastic. The room was full of bags and trays and specimen cups and banana-shaped things for throwing up in. I filled a bag with cups, made a hump in the bed that might look like a sleeping V.I., turned out the lights, and looked into the hall.

Eight o'clock. Visitors were leaving, nurses were handing out meds. A crowd to mingle with. Auspicious.

You know the old movie where Humphrey Bogart has been sandbagged and pumped full of drugs and, even though his head is spinning, he gets up and goes after serious bad guys? I've always thought it was really stupid and unrealistic.

I was right. I tried to stride confidently, despite my freaky hair and the big plastic glasses, but, like Bogie in *The Long Goodbye*, I saw the hall spin around me. I had to clutch the wall to keep from falling over. Not so auspicious.

When I reached the front lobby, I was sweating and light-headed. The hospital was a bit over two miles from the building where Sister Frankie had lived. Normally, I could have walked it, but I was nowhere near normal. I still had eight dollars. Not enough for a taxi, but it would get me there and back on the bus.

I wobbled my way two blocks north to a Lawrence Avenue bus stop. Murray had unsettled me. I kept stopping, not just because I was unsteady but to see if I had company, whether cops or robbers. If I really had been the fire bombers' target, I was hoping they were monitoring me so closely that they knew I was still in the hospital. Tonight might be my one chance to go back to the Freedom Center apartments without anyone knowing.

One thing about the Uptown neighborhood: women with weird hair who have trouble staying upright are a dime a dozen. Two women just like me, stooping to scoop up cigarette butts in the midst of a ferocious shouting match, passed while I waited for the bus. No one gave any of us a second glance.

A bus lumbered up to the stop. I fed two of my crumpled bills into the money maw, awkwardly because of my gauzy mitts, and slumped back onto one of the seats set aside for the disabled and elderly. I felt disconnected from the world around me, and when we got to the Kedzie stop I had to coach myself on how to walk down the steps.

My car was parked on Kedzie, but my keys had been in the handbag I'd dropped in Sister Frankie's apartment. I walked up Kedzie to see if I could get into my Mustang — I have picklocks in the glove compartment — but of course I'd locked all the doors. However, the city hadn't forgotten me: three tickets for meter violations were stuffed under the wipers. I ground my teeth but left the tickets. I couldn't do anything about them tonight.

It was easy to spot Sister Frankie's apartment from the street: the windows were boarded over and the brick and concrete around the frames were charred black. Lights showed through open windows on some of the upper floors, though, meaning the fire had been contained quickly enough for the building's wiring and plumbing to be usable. That was one mercy, that others hadn't been injured in or made homeless by the blast. It also meant the federal morons watching the building hadn't stopped the fire department from doing their job.

The street was full, as it had been three nights ago, with kids and shoppers and lovers and drunks. People stared at me: the building was a stage and I was a new actor on it, but I couldn't help that.

I took off my plastic dark glasses. The sun had set, the streetlamps were on, and the city was bathed in the haze of midsummer twilight. Surely that wouldn't hurt my eyes. I pushed the gauze back on my right hand, exposing my thumb and my forefinger, and used the edge of the glasses to push in the tongue on the front door. As I'd thought the other night, it was a simple lock to undo. I hoped if OEM was watching, they wouldn't come after me.

The stairwell smelled like a lab sink, a musty, sour chemical stench mingled with charred wood and damp. I wished for a flashlight, the only light coming from a single bulb two stories up. I worried about missing steps or tripping on debris, but my flashlight was also in my glove compartment. The things you can do so easily with money: walk to the nearest drugstore, buy a flashlight. Hop a cab, buy a new outfit. No wonder women who look like me walk down the street shouting their heads off.

I stopped at the landing in front of the Virgin of Guadalupe. She was barely visible in the dim light. I stroked her rough-carved wooden cheeks. It would be so wonderful to think she could protect me, to believe Sister Frances was even now clasped to her bosom. I crept on up to the second floor and turned right toward Sister Frances's apartment.

The hall was even darker here because the windows facing the street were boarded over. Each step was a gamble, like walking on a rocky beach in the dark. I couldn't tell what I was stumbling across: wall-board, wires, parts of light fixtures. I ran my fingertips along the wall to steady myself but lost my footing when the wall disappeared. I grabbed at open air and found myself on my knees in the rubble.

Even to my damaged eyes, the yellow crime scene tape across Sister Frances's door gleamed dully in the dark. I found the knob and turned it. Unlocked. The door was sealed, but it gave way to a firm shoulder push.

Inside the apartment, the air was so acrid that my eyes started to tear. I put my plastic glasses on to protect my eyes, then took them off. The thick lenses meant I couldn't see anything at all.

I stepped backward, catlike, from the heart of the damage. Sister Frances had brought tea in from the kitchen, and I was hoping I might find a flashlight in there. In the dark, there is no sense of distance or space. I kept banging into furniture until I found a wall that I could follow step by cautious step.

I finally found the swinging door that opened into the kitchen. It seemed like the gate between normalcy and hell. On one side were the charred, sodden remains of Sister Frankie's life, on the other was an *Ozzie and Harriet* set, everything clean and tidy. The windows weren't boarded over, and, in the lights from the back stairs and the alley streetlamps, I could make out the shapes of stove, refrigerator, cabinets. The nun's breakfast cup and bowl were on the counter with a box of cornflakes, set out for the morning meal she wouldn't be eating. I tried the lights, but the power had been turned off to this part of the building.

I couldn't find a flashlight, but I took a spatula and a ladle from a jar by the stove. I saw matches and a candle, but as my hand hovered over them my whole body shuddered at the idea of more fire.

Moving cautiously back to the front room, I could see enough in the ghostly light sifting in from the kitchen doorway to start picking through the debris. I wanted to find my handbag. But what I really wanted was glass from the Molotov cocktail bottles.

I'd been in a chair near the door when the barrage had started. I'd put my bag on the floor next to me. I squatted on my haunches and shuffled forward. My fingers pressed against a damp, matted mess. It felt like a clump of rotting lettuce, but when I forced myself to delve more deeply I realized it was a book. The floor was thick with dead books, and I shuffled past them on legs that shook with grief as much as fatigue.

I found a damp, revolting mass of Styrofoam that might have been the chair cushions, and bits of the frame of the chair, but I didn't come across my bag. However, in the middle of the room one of my clumsy hands closed on a piece of glass. It took several tries with the spatula to lift the shard from the floor and into the ladle and then into one of the plastic cups in my bag. Feeling around the area, I found bigger pieces: the neck of a bottle and a chunk that might have been part of the base. I collected these in my makeshift containers as well.

I had no way of photographing the spot where I'd found this evidence or labeling the evidence bags, which, anyway, weren't certifiable as free from contamination. And while this evidence could never be used in court, it might tell me something helpful about the assailants.

I pushed myself to my feet. I was spasming up and down my body with fatigue. I longed to lie down where I was, on the pile of soggy books, and give way to exhaustion. I groped for a wall to steady myself. My mother's face came to me, the day she came home from the doctor to tell me there was no hope, no treatment, no help, her dark eyes large against skin turned transparent and luminous with mortality.

'Victoria, my darling one. Grief and loss and death, they're part of life on this planet. We all mourn, but it is selfish to turn mourning into a religion. You must promise me that you will embrace life, never turn your back on the world because of your private sorrow.'

277

My grief had come in the loud sobs of adolescence, and then in shouting matches with my dazed, helpless father.

'Your *papà is not as strong as you and me, carissima. He needs your help, not your anger. Don't turn against him now.*'

The words had brought no comfort then and brought no comfort now. They were a burden, a load I had to carry, that of needing to be stronger than the strongest person near me. Sister Frances had died. I had to be strong enough to look after her in death since I'd been unable to look after her in life.

I picked my way backward, slogging through books and boards and cushions like an Arctic explorer who'd never reach the Pole. I was nearly at the door when I saw a light dance underneath it and dance away. I held my breath. A phantasm of fatigue? It came again, a flashlight poking along the jamb. OEM? FBI? Punks? I had nothing to defend myself with except a kitchen spatula and no strength to use it.

The door opened. A tall figure stood there hesitantly, playing the flashlight around the room, and then turned to look over the shoulder. The movement swept the light upward so that it played on the figure, revealing spiky hair.

'Petra Warshawski!' I said. 'What are you doing here?'

28

And Fire in the Old Homestead

The flashlight clattered to the floor, and my cousin screamed. As I stooped to pick up the light, I thought I heard retreating footfalls. I pushed past Petra and looked down the hall but didn't see anyone.

'Who was that?' I demanded.

'Vic ... It's you!' She was breathless and frightened. 'I thought you were in the hospital.'

'I am. What are you doing here, and who came with you?'

'No one. I'm on my — '

'You're not a very convincing liar, Petra. You don't have the guts or experience to come into a burned-out building on your own. Who was with you?'

'One of the guys who works on the campaign with me,' she muttered. 'He took off when I screamed, and I don't want him to get in trouble, so don't ask me his name, I won't tell you. Anyway, you shouldn't be yelling at me. I came here for you.'

'Did you, now?' I was so weak that I had to lean against the charred wall. 'What noble deed were you doing on my behalf?'

'Uncle Sal told me you'd left your wallet and everything here. I thought I could find it. He said neighborhood punks would break in and help themselves to anything that wasn't nailed down.'

'That has the ring of authenticity,' I said applaudingly. 'I can believe Mr. Contreras would use exactly those words. You're doing better.'

'Why do you have to act like a bully?' Petra demanded. 'Why can't you believe me?'

I retrieved her flashlight and swept its beam around the room. 'I believe you. Go look for my handbag. I'm too exhausted to move, but I'll hold the light for you.'

She glowered at me but moved gingerly into the room. She was wearing her high-heeled boots and wobbled on the uneven surface. I pointed the light toward the place where I thought I'd been sitting.

'If it's here, that's where it should be. Try each step before you put your full weight on your leg. You don't want to go through a burned floorboard.'

She tiptoed over to the remains of the chair and knelt, as I had done, to feel around its sides. 'This is gross. It's, like, Dumpster diving.'

'What is going on in here?' A second flashlight suddenly brightened the room.

I was so tired, and so focused on Petra, I hadn't heard the newcomer in the hall. My heart pounded. I could hear it in my ears like the ocean roaring. This was a recipe for early death, personal inattention on this scale.

'Who are you and why are you in this apartment? You can answer me quickly or talk to the police.'

'I'm V.I. Warshawski,' I said quietly. 'I was here with Sister Frances when she was killed. And you are . . . ?'

'Sister Carolyn Zabinska.'

I had heard the name, but I was swaying badly and couldn't make sense of anything. Murray had said . . . He'd said I was the real target. I blinked, trying to clear my head. I turned to look at Zabinska. Her flashlight blinded me. My knees buckled, and I was suddenly on the floor, Petra's flashlight falling from my useless hands.

I never really lost consciousness, but I couldn't summon the strength to speak. I heard the nun ask Petra who she was. I heard Petra say I was supposed to be in the hospital but had insisted on coming to the apartment. She didn't know why but thought I was hoping my handbag would still be here.

I struggled to speak. I was baffled by my cousin's lies. Was she instinctively trying to save her own skin? More footfalls sounded. 'No police,' I finally gasped. But it wasn't police, it was two more nuns. And, between them and my cousin, I was half carried, half dragged up the stairs to the fourth floor.

'We can't use the elevator until the wiring has been completely tested,' one of the nuns apologized.

We went into a clean living room, a copy of Sister Frankie's, with books and bright throws and a statue of the Virgin, and I was put in an armchair. Someone forced hot, sweet tea into me, and I thought maybe it really was Wednesday night again, that I was back at Sister Frankie's, that the fire, my eyes, my hands, all that had been a nightmare, and now . . . I sat up . . . And now I would pull myself together and stop being a tragedy queen.

'I don't have my bag,' I said.

'I picked up your bag after the fire.' That was Sister Carolyn's voice. It was cold. I was a selfish bitch, worrying about my private possessions in the middle of a disaster.

'Not my handbag, my evidence bag.' I tried to stand, but the sisters kept me in the chair.

Sister Carolyn squatted so I could see her face. 'Evidence?'

I drank down the rest of the tea. It made me feel marginally better, but it was still hard to be coherent. 'Evidence about the fire. Hard to explain. Bottle fragments, the police should have taken them. Test . . . for assel . . . acc . . . ' I was close to tears with frustration at not being able to speak, and I remembered Sister Claudia, her tears, her garbled English.

'What was in bottles?' I finally managed to say.

'What difference does it make? Frankie is dead whether it was gasoline or scotch!' one of the other nuns cried out.

'Matters. Matters. Ordinary fuel. Anyone, but I think pros.'

There was silence for a moment. Then Sister Carolyn said, 'I know you're exhausted, but I need you to explain what you're saying. Are you saying this was the work of a professional arsonist?'

Another sister handed me a second cup of tea, laced this time with brandy. I choked as I swallowed the alcohol, but it did its job, giving me the fleeting illusion of clarity. 'The accelerant. I think it was some kind of jet fuel, something that burned fast and very hot, or the books wouldn't have gone so fast, and neither would — ' I broke off. 'Her head . . . I tried to catch her, to wrap her, but her head — '

Hands were all around me holding me, and, after another swallow, I managed to say, 'I wanted to know two things. Did the police take the fragments in for analysis? I don't think they did or I wouldn't have found such big chunks of broken bottle. And, if not, I want a private lab I use to do an analysis, tell me what was used.'

Sister Carolyn Zabinska nodded in understanding, and added that she wanted to talk to me about the attack itself, she needed to know what happened. 'I was planning on calling on you. As I said, I found your handbag. I tried to see you in the hospital, but they have a lockdown on your visitors, even nuns. But if you've been released — '

'She hasn't been!' Petra said. 'She broke out just to come here tonight.'

'That's reassuring,' one of the other sisters said. 'Not to be rude, but you look like death on a mop handle, and I thought this was another sign of our execrable health care system, that they'd released you before you were fit.'

'Yes, she needs to be back in bed,' Zabinska said. 'I'll collect your evidence bag from Frankie's. If you tell me where to take it, I'll make sure it gets to your forensics lab. But it's time your niece — oh, cousin, is it? — drove you to the hospital.'

'Of course I will,' Petra said. 'But how am I going to get her past the front desk into her bed?'

'Which hospital?' one of the sisters asked.

'Beth Israel,' I said.

'I have a pass,' the sister said. 'I work there with the HIV/AIDS moms.'

She murmured something to the other two, who gave a ripple of laughter. I dozed and then came to with a start as I felt them fastening a scarf around my head.

'Okay, Sister V.I.,' Zabinska said. 'On your feet. We're going to bring a little succor to the ill and bed-ridden.'

The three nuns were laughing. They'd donned habits. I remembered Sister Frankie saying she wore hers whenever she had to go in front of a judge. The nuns helped me to my feet and showed me my face in the bathroom mirror. They'd pinned a veil around my face, hiding my chopped hair.

It was startling to see my eyes emerge from a nun's face, as if the piece of cloth had changed who I was. Too wild-eyed and drawn to be Audrey Hepburn in *The Nun's Story*. Maybe Kathleen Byron in *Black Narcissus*.

Zabinska and the sister who worked with the HIV moms each took one of my arms and guided me out the door and down the stairs, with Petra and the third sister following. We were moving slowly because of me and had reached only the top of the third flight when we heard a crash from the floor below us.

Sister Carolyn dropped my arm. 'That came from Frankie's place.'

Feet pounded down the hall below us. Sister Carolyn ran down the stairs. The HIV sister stayed with me, but the other nun ran after Sister Carolyn and my cousin pelted after her. I wanted to lead the charge, but I had to grab the banister and move one slow step at a time.

We reached the turn in the landing in time to see a man running down the stairs, followed by the nuns and Petra. We heard Sister Carolyn demanding that the man stop, and then the front door opened, tires squealed. A moment later, Petra and the nuns reappeared.

'Someone went into the apartment and made off with your bag,' Zabinska announced. 'How did they know to look for it?'

'Don't know.' I shook my head wearily. It was hard for me to think. 'Feds been watching building, you know that? Maybe them. Should've remembered. Maybe followed me from hospital . . . Thought I was clear, but not too clever right now.'

'The feds have been watching us?' the HIV nun echoed. 'How do you know that?'

'In hospital . . . Told me . . . ' I was starting to drift.

'We almost had him,' Sister Carolyn said. 'He was wearing a stocking cap, and I grabbed it instead of his shoulder. Then he opened the door so hard he hit Mary Lou in the nose, and we got tangled up with each other. Now I'm really angry. If he was a federal agent, he'll have some real explaining to do, beating up a nun in her own home.'

Mary Lou's nose was bleeding. The HIV nun sat her on the stairs and tilted her head back, stanching the blood with her own veil. Other tenants came into the stairwell: more nuns, families with small children. The noise grew to a clamor that I couldn't take in my current state. I collapsed on the stair next to Mary Lou with my plastic dark glasses back over my eyes.

'I need to lie down.' I was panting. 'Sisters . . . Go to Sister Frankie's . . . Look for bottle fragments . . . Bring flashlights . . . Bring camera, bring clean bag . . . Take pictures where you find . . . Pick up with glove . . . something clean . . . Put in bag . . . Seal . . . label . . . Now!'

Again the sisters murmured among themselves. The HIV nun, who had the hospital pass, would go with me to Beth Israel. Sister Carolyn and Sister Mary Lou would take care of hunting for more glass fragments.

Petra ran ahead to get her Pathfinder while the three nuns got me down the stairs. As they helped me into the backseat of the SUV, Sister Carolyn handed me my purse.

'You're not what I was expecting when I looked in your billfold and saw that you were a detective.'

'That's okay. You and your pals weren't what I expected when I learned you were nuns.'

She smiled and cupped her hands on my forehead, a caress that was a blessing. 'We'll pray for your speedy recovery.'

When the resident made rounds the next morning, he was dismayed to see that I'd had a setback. He ordered me to stay in the hospital an extra day. Lotty saw that I had fresher bruises on my arms and legs than could have come from the fire, but she didn't ask, and I didn't tell.

I walked up and down the hall a dozen times, trying to build my stamina, but I had to go back to bed afterward, which was infuriating. That was basically how I spent the day, walking and sleeping, Mid-afternoon, I went downstairs for another espresso.

When I returned to my room, I found Conrad Rawlings in the visitor's chair. Conrad is a cop. We've been friends, enemies, lovers, collaborators, off and on for over a decade.

I was happier to see him than I would have thought possible a few days earlier. 'Have you been transferred up here?'

'Nope. Still down in your old 'hood. You and fire: you can't leave it alone, can you?' The words were harsh, but his tone was sympathetic enough to take the sting out of them. 'Your eyes going to be okay?'

'They tell me,' I said gruffly.

'I read the report. Nasty fire, that, killing a nun and all.'

'Was there any word about the accelerant?' I demanded. 'It looked like it had to be rocket or jet fuel, it burned so fiercely and so fast.'

He shook his head. 'Early days for forensic results. But fires are tricky. Gasoline could get the job done if the perp was lucky, you know that. So don't go starting a conspiracy theory, trying to put cops or the FBI in your sights just because some woman from OEM rubbed you the wrong way.'

'Is that why you came up here?' I demanded. 'To tell me to pull back from holding the feds accountable? Damn it, Conrad, they've been watching the Freedom Center. They could have done something besides watching it all unfold for them on their — '

'Whoa, there, Ms. W.! I'm not here on anybody's business but my own.'

I looked at him, puzzled. Nothing I'd been working on lately involved South Chicago, but I waited for him to speak. Make the interrogation come to you, don't race out to meet it. That was advice I'd always given my clients in my public defender days, and it's the hardest advice to follow.

'You and fire, Ms. W.,' he repeated. 'I don't know if it follows you around or you bring it with you.'

He waited for a while. But when I still didn't respond, he said, 'You were in South Chicago last Saturday.'

In the trauma and drama of the last few days, I'd forgotten taking my cousin around the South Side. 'How nice of you to come all the way up here to tell me.'

He smiled briefly, not warmly. 'You stopped at a house on Ninety-second and Houston. You wanted to get inside.'

I watched him through my dark glasses.

'Any particular reason?' Conrad asked.

'I am *damned* tired of cops and feds asking me to justify every step I take. Is this Iran or America? Or isn't there any difference anymore?'

'They had a fire Sunday night. When we got there, the lady, a Señora Andarra, told us two women had been there, and they said they had grown up in the house and wanted to look around. She was afraid they were from a rival gang to her grandson's. She was afraid they set the fire to punish her for not letting them into the house.'

'That sounds like me, all right, gangbanger torching an old lady's house.'

Conrad leaned forward. 'You showed me the house once, the place where you grew up, your ma's tree and everything.'

That was true. In the spring, before I left for Italy, I'd been coaching a basketball team in my old high school, and Conrad and I had occasionally had a drink together after the games. One evening, in a fit of nostalgia, I'd shown him my home, along with the place on the breakwater where Boom-Boom and I used to jump into Lake Calumet, and various other high points of my childhood.

I sat up. 'I have a young cousin who's spending the summer in Chicago. She wanted a tour of historic Warshawski family sites. If you go to Back of the Yards and Gage Park, you'll find we've been there, too. If those two places have been torched, I'll start to get seriously interested in your questions. Was anyone hurt at the Houston Street fire?'

'Nope. Old lady got herself, her daughter, her grandkids out. And, not only that, in a rare moment of civic cooperation the fire department came before things got out of hand. Anyway, there never really was a fire, so the structure is okay.'

'That's a mercy.' I lay back down again.

'You going to ask me how it started?'

'Faulty wiring? Geraldo doing reefer in bed?'

'Smoke bomb. Someone broke a window and threw it into the living room while they were eating supper. Everyone ran out the back door, and a couple of lowlifes came in through the broken window and helped themselves while the family was waiting for the fire department.'

'Scum,' I agreed. 'I'm very sorry to know this, of course, especially if they broke one of those windows with the prisms across the top. Those prisms were what made my mother feel she could tolerate living in South Chicago.'

'You don't know anything about this, Ms. W.?'

I knew I was furious, but I was still so tired, and lethargic from the residue of morphine in my system, that I couldn't feel the anger. 'Conrad, I'm tired, I'm in pain, I held a burning woman in my arms a few nights ago and couldn't save her life. Don't make me play twenty questions. And don't accuse me of things you know are simply beyond me. One more innuendo about this, about how I might be implicated in an attack on the people who live in my childhood home, and you will never speak to me again. Even if you want to buy me World Series tickets, you'll funnel your invitation through my attorney.'

He sucked in a breath. 'The lady says she saw you. She says she went around to the front of the house to wait for us and the fire department and saw you across the street watching it all.'

I made a face. 'Oh, please. It was dark, right? And she'd seen me once through an inch-wide chain bolt. She saw someone else and is confused. Or she knows who really did it and is so frightened of that person that she wants to finger a stranger.'

Conrad stood up and looked down at me. 'I believe in you, Vic. I really do. I'm the only person in the Fourth District who knows you grew up in that house, and I'm keeping it that way. For now. But I'd like to put you in a lineup for Señora Andarra . . . for my own peace of mind, if nothing else.'

29

All Those Friendly Government Agents

The next few days were a time of frustrating inaction while I let my eyes heal enough that I could get to work. Lotty took me home with her, and I continued to build up my strength, using the gym in her building's basement, making phone calls during the day while she was at her clinic or the hospital.

My first day at Lotty's, Mr. Contreras came over in the morning before Lotty left for work. He brought a small suitcase with clothes that Petra had packed; he would have been embarrassed to rummage in my underwear drawer himself. He also brought the dogs, which annoyed Lotty because her apartment is full of glass tables and museum-quality artwork, including a small statue of Andromache salvaged from the ruins of her grandparents' art collection. Mitch's exuberant energy made her so tense that she terminated the visit quickly, on grounds that I didn't have the stamina for it.

'You mean *you* don't,' I said. But I took the dogs out to the hall behind the kitchen, where we waited for the service elevator.

'Peewee wants to visit,' Mr. Contreras said. 'I told her I was sure you'd want to see her.'

'Absolutely. The sooner, the better. Can you

go up to my place and collect my phone charger so she can bring it with her?' I couldn't tie up Lotty's phone but I needed to start connecting myself to the land of the living. 'And here are my car keys. Get her to drive you over to pick up my car on Kedzie before I get a hundred meter violations and twenty boots.'

I didn't think I could stand to use my old handbag again. When I had stuck my hand in to fish out my keys, it came out covered in ash. Sister Carolyn had known I was a PI only because my license had been the plastic on top when she looked at my wallet. The credit cards underneath it had fused together with my driver's license. I called my card companies for replacements, but I'd have to go in person to the Secretary of State's Office for a new PI license.

After Mr. Contreras left, Lotty went to her clinic on Damen. I resisted the impulse to go back to bed and phoned Sister Carolyn instead. I wanted to know if she'd been able to find any more bottle fragments in Sister Frankie's apartment.

'The police came almost as soon as you'd left. They wanted to know who broke the seal on Frankie's door. I told them it must have been the intruder we chased down the stairs. They put a padlock on the door, so we can't get in.'

'Bolt cutters,' I said absently, flexing my fingers inside their gauze wrappers, imagining working a pick into the padlock.

'We'll think about that,' the nun said drily. 'But I want to know who's watching our building. When you were here, you said it was

293

the federal government.'

'The feds came to see me in the hospital: someone from Homeland Security, someone from the FBI, and local guys from the Bomb and Arson squad. It was the day after the fire, so I don't remember it clearly. They know who lives in your building, all the families. Come to think of it, they're probably listening to this conversation, so forget the bolt cutters.'

'Eavesdropping!' Zabinska was almost speechless with fury.

I suggested she come see me at Lotty's so we could talk about it privately. I wanted to speak to her anyway, now that I was more alert mentally, to learn anything Sister Frankie might have said to her about Steve Sawyer's involvement in Harmony Newsome's murder.

Before Lotty left, she had made me promise to stay inside. But I wanted to be in motion. After doing as much of a workout as I could handle, and having a phone meeting with Marilyn Klimpton at my office, I wandered restlessly around Lotty's apartment. In the side room where she keeps her television (off-limits) and her library overflow (off-limits), I found a sewing basket with a pair of shears in it. I went into the bathroom and started chopping my hair.

When I was five, my father gave me a doll for Christmas that had a huge halo of dark hair. It was JFK's first year in office, and dolls all had the Jackie do. Boom-Boom and I took a pair of scissors to that doll, and, by the time we'd finished, she looked much as I did now. Dentists shouldn't drill their own teeth and detectives shouldn't cut their own hair. At least, not when their hands were wrapped up in boxer's tape.

A little after one, when I thought I might go mad from inaction, the cops showed up. They knew I'd been sprung; they probably knew Lotty wasn't home. It was time to talk.

I put on my heavy dark glasses to underline my invalid status. Just to be prudent, I rode the elevator to the lobby to make sure they were really cops, not robbers. I hadn't actually seen any of their faces in the hospital, but their voices told me these were essentially the same players who'd interrogated me last week.

The FBI had sent Lyle Torgeson again, but the feds had beefed up their presence with someone from Homeland Security. The city had sent only the woman from the Office of Emergency Management instead of the duo who'd come to my hospital room. The CPD sent the same two guys from the Bomb and Arson squad, a young white man with a crew cut who was already developing a paunch and a Latino about my own age who was balding and had big fatigue circles around his eyes.

'I don't have Dr. Herschel's permission to bring all these strangers into her home,' I told the doorman. 'Is there a conference room we could use?'

'There's a room in the building manager's office,' the doorman said doubtfully. 'It's kind of small, though.'

'We can take you down to Thirty-fifth and Michigan,' the Latino Bomb and Arson guy suggested.

'You have a warrant? . . . Then we'll meet here. There are only six of us, after all.'

The doorman called up to the building manager to see if the room was free and to send someone down to escort us so that he wouldn't have to abandon his post at the entrance.

It was a small room, and getting six chairs around the round table meant we all had to be careful to keep our knees to ourselves. I was sorry in a way that I'd kept them out of Lotty's place, but if they were uncomfortable inhaling one another's bad breath, which the woman from OEM had to a remarkable degree, they wouldn't stay long.

I kept my big plastic glasses on mostly to annoy them. They would want to try to read my facial tics, how I moved my eyes and so on, and now they couldn't.

'You look like the bad end of a catfight,' Torgeson said. 'You get your hair caught in a wringer over at the nun's place when you went back there?'

'Everyone's taping this, right? So the FBI and OEM and CPD are all going to get the same useful transcript. The real question here is' — I paused long enough to see that they were all leaning forward, hoping for some gem of self-revelation — 'why is a woman always characterized as being in a catfight after an altercation? I'm sure with the research you've done on me, you know I have two dogs, so it's a good bet I'd be more responsive to a dogfight metaphor. And yet your underlying sexism made you — '

'Enough,' Torgeson barked. 'You know damned well what I was talking about.'

I shook my head. 'Mind reading isn't one of my skills. And I haven't been tapping your phone, so I can't rely on your conversations to tell me what you're thinking or talking about.'

'Ms. Warshawski, we know you left Beth Israel to return to the nun's apartment four nights ago.' It was the white guy from Bomb and Arson.

When I didn't say anything, he said, 'Well?'

'Is there a question?' I said.

'What were you doing at the nun's building four nights ago?' he said, his voice tight from the effort not to lose his temper.

'I was in the hospital four nights ago,' I said.

When the HIV nun had escorted me back inside, she'd flashed her hospital ID at the security guard and stopped to chat briefly with one of the nurses. No one looked at me, a rookie nun, new to the HIV/AIDS service, head lowered. No one on the fifth floor had commented on my absence, either, when I slipped back into my room or the next morning, so I didn't think it had been noticed.

'You were seen entering the Freedom Center building,' the woman from OEM said. 'What were you doing there?'

'I was seen?' I echoed. 'That's an old, old ploy. I need more than that to persuade me I was at Kedzie and Lawrence instead of in my hospital bed.'

The OEM woman pulled a set of stills from her briefcase and laid them on the small round table in the middle of the room. We all took turns looking at them. They were time-stamped, and they showed a woman whose dark hair held a few white streaks wearing jeans and a white shirt. They were shot from behind, so you couldn't see where her hair had been shaved back from her temples. Nor could you see that she was using the edge of her plastic lenses to snap the tongue back in the front-door lock.

'I don't know,' I said. 'It's not like this person is wearing a jacket marked 'V.I. Warshawski.' And I think I'd remember if I'd been there. You have some shots showing me leaving, some where I could see my face? I don't recognize myself from behind.'

There was a momentary silence. I'd left wearing a nun's veil, my face down, two other sisters and my cousin holding me close. They had the shots, but they probably didn't know what to make of them.

'Look, Warshawski, this isn't supposed to be an antagonistic meeting,' the Latino guy from Bomb and Arson said. 'We assume you're on the same team we are.'

'And what team would that be, Detective?'

'That you want to catch Sister Frances's killer,' he said.

'Oh, I definitely want to do that,' I agreed.

'Then why don't you tell us what you were doing at her apartment?' That was the FBI's Lyle Torgeson.

I yawned. 'I wasn't at her apartment.'

'Let's forget four nights ago,' Torgeson said. 'The night of the fire . . . You agree you were there that night? . . . Tell us why.'

'Right. I went to talk to Sister Frances about Steve Sawyer.'

'We know about that,' the man from Homeland Security said.

'You have bugs planted in her room?' I asked. 'They're good quality, I guess, if they survived the fire and you retrieved them. Not like the crap weapons you buy from China and sell to Afghanistan.'

'You were bugging the room?' the white Bomb and Arson detective said, turning to the feds. 'Why the fuck were you doing that?'

'National security,' the Homeland Security man said. 'I can't say any more.'

'Beautiful umbrella,' I murmured. 'From now on, whenever I do anything particularly embarrassing, I'll just cry 'National security!' and refuse to say anything else.'

'That's enough,' Torgeson snapped. 'What were you doing in Sister Frances's apartment?'

'National security,' I said.

The two Bomb and Arson squad detectives swallowed smiles. Harmony did not reign supreme between the federal and local law enforcers. I let them bicker with one another for a few minutes.

'I have a question for you,' I said. 'You know why I went to see Sister Frances, to discuss the case of the man who'd been convicted of killing Harmony Newsome in Marquette Park forty years ago. Sister Frances was marching with Ms. Newsome that hot summer day and said she didn't think it was possible that Steve Sawyer killed Ms. Newsome. Are you reopening the case?'

'He was tried, convicted, did his time. We're not interested.' That was the Latino cop.

'Then why was that the last question OEM asked me in the hospital, why did I care what Sister Frances had to say about that old murder?'

'I think you misheard. You were drugged, in a lot of pain,' Torgeson said.

'You're the ones with the tape recorders.' I looked at my fingertips. 'Go listen to the conversation. I don't have anything else for you.'

The crowded room was momentarily quiet. Then the Bomb and Arson team started asking me questions that I could answer, to lead them step-by-step through my brief time with Sister Frances. It wasn't meaningful or helpful, but I was the only witness.

The more times I recounted the Molotov cocktails sailing in on us, the less real they became. It was easy to describe them glibly, as if they were a plot detail in a thriller and not a death-dealing event.

When I finished, I asked what residue they'd found in the bottles: gasoline? rocket fuel? jellied bomb accelerant?

'We can't answer questions like that,' the Homeland Security man said. 'They're in connection with an investigation linked to our national security.'

It was my turn to remember I needed to keep a leash on my temper. 'What about the perps? You must have pictures of them, time-stamped and everything, right? Anything you can show on the street for an ID?'

'We can't comment. It's an investigation linked to our national security.'

'But these pictures aren't?' I picked up the stills of me at the entrance to the Freedom Center building. 'That's good. I'll show them to Sister Carolyn, see if she knows who this might be. Given that someone was in Sister Frances's apartment that night, she might recognize who.'

'If you weren't there, how do you know someone was in the dead nun's apartment?' Torgeson pounced.

'You just told me.' I got to my feet, holding the stills. The woman from OEM leaned over, spraying me with her fetid breath, and grabbed the pictures.

'These are government property and are highly classified.'

'I know,' I said. ' "An investigation linked to our national security." '

She glared at me. 'I'd strongly advise you not to suggest to a nun that she take a bolt cutter to a room that's been secured by the police.'

I smiled at her. We were playing a game where the person who keeps her temper longest wins. 'You know, we live in a county where patronage workers get paid a hundred thousand dollars a year not to work. So it cheers me no end to see that you really are earning the salary my tax dollars pay for. You've been hard at it, and I'll see you get a note stuck in your personnel file.'

30

Line Spinners

Even though I'd walked away triumphant from that skirmish, there was no way I could win a larger battle with the law. The real question, if I could get my tired brain to return to duty, was why they cared so much. Their questions, their whole attitude, seemed more about Sister Frances's and my conversation than her murder.

I had to be honest enough to admit my arrival at the murder scene two days later warranted investigation. But why did they have such an elaborate stakeout on the building in the first place?

The interrogation had worn me out. I tried to make some notes, in big block capitals with a felt-tipped marker, but the effort put me to sleep. When I woke, it was because the doorman was calling on the house phone: Sister Carolyn Zabinska had arrived.

'You don't look well. Are you up to talking?' she greeted me.

Her own face was pinched and gray with grief. She was tall and sturdily built, but her shoulders were bent forward with pain.

'It's just my hair,' I said, steering myself away from self-pity. 'I tried to trim it with sewing shears and was singularly inept. The FBI was ruder. They said I looked like the losing end of a catfight.'

'Yes, the FBI. That's what I want to talk about . . . One of the things, anyway.'

She followed me onto the balcony off the living room, where Lotty has a little table and chairs in the summer. I offered refreshments, and left her standing there, looking out over Lake Michigan, while I burrowed in Lotty's kitchen. She practically survives on Viennese coffee, but I found some German herbal infusions in the back of a drawer. When I returned to the balcony with a tray, precariously balanced between my bandaged palms, Sister Carolyn sat down and asked how I knew the FBI was watching the Freedom Center building.

'I don't know if the FBI is involved. Homeland Security took the pictures.' I explained what I'd learned from today's interview, including the news that the feds photographed everyone entering and leaving.

'That's so outrageous. Why on earth?'

'I don't know. When they questioned me in the hospital, they were dancing like rhinos around the subject. They implied it could be because of your tenants. You're the one who knows if you're treading on their toes.'

'Treading on their toes? It's true we protest at the School of the Americas. We work with poor immigrants, with refugees, with people on death row. We're involved in affordable housing. And peace. But we don't do anything clandestine or immoral. We don't sell drugs or weapons or spy on people.'

'You know darned well you're rocking the whole aircraft carrier with those issues. America as armed camp is the status quo. Peace, letting in immigrants, ending torture, ending the death penalty: no wonder they think you're a threat. There must be a whole floor of that building on the Potomac dedicated to your Freedom Center.'

'But that means we're endangering the other tenants,' Zabinska said, worried. 'We don't own the building, but the management company that does has been pretty generous. They let us run the Freedom Center out of the ground-floor apartments. Five of us sisters attached to the center rent there, and we've ended up working with a lot of the other tenants because so many are either refugees or are trying to figure out how to get health care or housing vouchers. Maybe we should see about moving the ones who're most at risk for deportation. Everyone's pretty scared as it is because of the fire bombs.'

'You'd better be very careful where and how you talk about it,' I warned her. 'They probably are listening to all your conversations, not just your phones.'

She was outraged, of course, especially when I explained how hard it is to detect or block a sophisticated eavesdropper, which the feds certainly are. We talked over her options. Technological solutions were outside her budget, and playing cloak-and-dagger, with codes and meetings off premises, was too time-consuming.

'Besides, that kind of secretiveness would drive us mad. It's so counter to our vows and our mission. But maybe we should start leaving through the alley when we want to be private.'

I made a face. 'It would be easy to mount tiny

surveillance cameras on the light poles in the alley. It depends on how much they care about you.'

Sister Carolyn pushed the heels of her hands against her eyes. 'I know these are important matters, but it's hard to pay attention to them right now. We're all still in shock at losing Frankie. The violence of the attack, that's very hard to absorb. But losing her . . . I wasn't ready for that. I'm the head of the Freedom Center, but she was our real leader, spiritually, psychologically, in all the ways that count most. I need to understand why she was killed.'

I bit my lower lip. 'I wish I knew, but I don't.'

'When I looked in your wallet and saw your PI license, I thought maybe you'd come to spy on her. I didn't realize then that the government was already spying on us. I thought maybe an anti-immigrant group had hired you.'

I went through my tired story about hunting for Lamont Gadsden and Steve Sawyer. When I mentioned Karen Lennon's name, Sister Carolyn's heavy expression lightened for a moment.

'Karen . . . Of course I know her. She's on our Death Penalty committee, and we've done some work together on affordable health care. How did she find you?'

'By chance. She was in a hospital ER when I came in with a homeless man who'd collapsed on my sidewalk.'

'And Dr. Herschel — this is her apartment, I realized — I was surprised to learn you were staying with her.'

I've known Lotty half my life now, ever since I

was an undergraduate and she was advising an abortion underground. Sister Carolyn took that in without blinking. Some of her immigrant clients got medical care at Lotty's storefront clinic, and Lotty had saved the life of one of their pregnant women when she was shot in the abdomen. It clearly made me a better citizen in Zabinska's eyes that Lotty was my friend and that I was working with Karen Lennon.

I finally brought the conversation back to my own inquiry. 'Did Sister Frances ever talk about Steve Sawyer's trial or the march in Marquette Park where Harmony Newsome died?'

'I was a child when that happened, a middle schooler at Justin Martyr. Frankie came to speak to us as part of the cardinal's outreach program. A lot of the children booed and called her names, but she made me see the world in a different way. I came to my vocation because of Frankie.'

She shook her head, trying to shake tears away. 'She wouldn't have talked to me about the murder at the time because I was a child. And by the time I went through my novitiate, and ended up back in Chicago with her, it was twelve years later. So many other things started happening that we needed to tackle — the School of the Americas and the Guatemalan asylum seekers, and then the loss of jobs and health care — that we didn't dwell much on that past. Did she think this Steve Sawyer was wrongly convicted?'

'He may have been. All I can say, with any certainty, is that he was very badly represented in a trial that was a travesty, at least as far as I can tell from the transcript. Sister Frances said she wanted to testify at the trial but the defense wouldn't call her.'

I stopped, my throat was so dry I could hardly get the next words out. 'A reporter suggested I was the real target, but he wouldn't tell me who he'd heard that from.'

'Killing a nun to keep her from talking to you or you from talking to her, these things have happened in Nicaragua or Liberia, but here? We think we're so safe here, and yet my own government is spying on me. The government are the people who would have known she was talking to you.' Her eyes widened in horror, and she choked out, 'You don't think they . . . that they . . . '

I grimaced. 'What? That the Contras might kill a nun but not Homeland Security? I don't think they did. But I can't swear to anything right now, except that I feel pretty vulnerable.'

Zabinska pleated Lotty's linen tea napkin over and over in her fingers. 'The work that you're doing for Karen, for these two old women in Lionsgate Manor, how much are you charging them?'

'My standard fee is a hundred fifty an hour plus expenses.'

'We can't afford that. Is there any chance you could work out an arrangement with us? I want you to find out why Frankie died. We'll all feel better if we know why.'

I could feel the request coming before she said it, but I didn't try to fight it. I owed Sister Frances the effort of an investigation.

'Yes,' I said quietly. 'I'll feel better, too.'

We talked through the various issues the Freedom Center worked on that might have brought someone to the boiling point. We talked about people who might have harbored a personal resentment against Sister Frances. Even saints make enemies. It's how they become martyrs.

At the end, I said, 'The best thing you can do is get back into that sealed apartment and bring me some bottle fragments.'

'You suggested bolt cutters,' she said doubtfully.

'Or a hammer. That door isn't too sturdy. A few good whacks on the panel would take care of it. I'd do it myself, but I'm a bit out of action right now.' My padded hands would be unwrapped in two more days. If they'd healed sufficiently, Lotty would let me go home.

Sister Carolyn got up to leave, but she took the tea things to the kitchen and washed them for me first. In the hall, as she waited for the elevator, she said, 'You know, taking a hammer to that door would cheer me up. Some kind of fierce action, for a change. If we find any bits of bottle, one of us will bring them over tomorrow.'

Later that evening, Petra arrived, bubbling with so much energetic goodwill that I felt exhausted almost from the moment she got off the elevator. When Lotty let her in, Petra danced down the hall to the guest room, where I was dictating notes to send to Marilyn.

Petra had remembered the charger to my phone, amazingly enough, and also brought my mail, which she dumped on the bureau before settling in a wing chair by the window. 'Shall I open it and read it to you? There must be a hundred letters here!'

'No, most of them are bills. They'll keep another day. How are the dogs? What's happening with the campaign? You still the golden-haired girl?'

She laughed. 'I don't take any of it too seriously. I think that's why I'm so popular. Everyone else is, like, totally ambitious, you know, hoping for big jobs when Brian gets to the Senate so that they can have *really* big jobs when he's president.'

'And what are you hoping for?' I asked idly.

'Just to get through the summer without making a mistake that'll get everyone else in trouble.'

She spoke with such unexpected seriousness that I took off my heavy dark glasses to look at her. 'What's going on, Petra? Is someone suggesting you've done something wrong?'

'No, no. I don't want to think about it tonight. You know that baseball you said you found in Uncle Tony's trunk, the one signed by someone in the White Sox?'

'Nellie Fox, you mean? Yeah, what about it?'

'I mentioned it to Daddy, and he'd love to have it. Did you keep it? I mean, you said it would be worth something if you auctioned it on eBay.'

She was floundering, and I stared at her with even more surprise. 'Petra, what is the matter with you tonight? I kept the baseball, but I don't know what I want to do with it. It meant something to my dad or he wouldn't have kept it with his Good Conduct citation. I'll think about it.'

'Where is it?' she persisted. 'Could I take a picture and send it to Daddy?'

'Petra, you are up to something. I don't know what, but . . . '

She flushed, and played with her array of rubber bracelets. 'Oh, he's turning seventy next year, and Mom and I were trying to think of something really special to do. I thought of the baseball, and — '

'I thought you just said you'd talked to him about it and that he'd love to have it.'

'Why are you biting on me like I was some steak bone? I'm just making conversation!' She nearly tilted the wing chair over in her agitation.

'Then let's make some more conversation. What really brought you to Sister Frances's apartment the other night? And who came with you?'

'I told you — '

'Baby, I've been listening to line spinners since I was six, and you are not in the majors. Not even double A.'

She scowled at me. 'If I tell you now, you'll make even more fun of me.'

'Try me.'

'I thought, it's not like you have an assistant or anything. And when we went to South Chicago, I loved how you dealt with those gang-bangers. I thought if I went in and found something — a clue or something — maybe you'd take me on as

310

an apprentice when the campaign winds down. But if you're just going to laugh at me . . . '

Her face was so red that it almost glowed in the soft light of the guest room. I slid off the bed and knelt next to her, patting her shoulder.

'You want to be a detective? You know the 'fun stuff' you said I got to do, after I tangled with that gangbanger on Houston Street? Your folks would eat me for lunch if you were working for me and got your eyes burned. Not to mention that you could have gone through the floor in that apartment.'

I sat back on the daybed as another thought occurred to me. 'Petra, someone threw a smoke bomb into my old house on Houston last Sunday. Señora Andarra said she saw one of us watching from across the street. That wasn't you, was it?'

'Vic! You told me not to go down there alone.'

'Does that mean no?' I asked. 'You weren't trying to play detective and get into that house?'

'I wasn't playing detective at your old house, okay?' Her face turned red again in her agitation. 'Now I'm sorry I ever said anything to you about it. Daddy says your mom spoiled you something rotten, so you never learned how to let anyone else be in the limelight.'

'That a fact? Is that what you were doing at the Freedom Center the other night? Showing me how to let you be in the limelight?'

'Oh, you twist everything I say the wrong way.' She strode from the room, her rubber bracelets bobbing up and down on her arms.

Her exit was a little anticlimactic: one of her

311

bracelets flew off as she reached Lotty's front door. I bent to pick it up; it was white and labeled ONE. It was supposed to make us want to get together as one planet to solve AIDS and poverty.

I shut my eyes. I was supposed to be the grown-up in this situation. I handed her the bracelet, and said, 'If I try to learn how to share the limelight, will you try to learn how to listen to directions?'

Her flush faded. 'You mean you would let me study detecting with you?'

'Most of what I do is truly tedious, like all those bills on the bureau there,' I warned her. 'But if you want to work for me for six months, see how you like it . . . Sure, we can give it a try when you're through with Brian's campaign.'

She flung her arms around me, pressing into the raw new skin on my chest, then ran into the waiting elevator. I stopped in the living room to say good night to Lotty. I was puzzling over Petra's words, and her behavior, with Lotty — Could Petra be serious about trying to emulate me? Could she be lying about being in South Chicago last Sunday? — when Lotty's phone rang.

It was Carolyn Zabinska for me. 'Vic, we went to Frankie's place as soon as we got in tonight,' she said without preamble. 'A demolition team had come in from nowhere and stripped the room. The building manager said it was an anonymous benefactor who wanted to do something good for the church and that builders would be arriving tomorrow.'

31

Home in Tatters

A few days later, I left Lotty's for home. My gauze had come off, revealing puckered red skin underneath. I was to wear special gloves day and night, a kind of lacy mitt. There was to be no swimming for now, and no sun for some months to come. I graduated from my special plastic-lensed dark glasses to ordinary dark glasses. I was cleared for viewing television and computer screens and for driving a car.

I spoke with the doorman several times during my stay with Lotty. He hadn't seen anyone lurking around, waiting for an injured private eye to emerge. No strangers had come calling for me except the law, my first day there. I was beginning to believe the attack on Sister Frances had been connected to her work at the Freedom Center. The thought didn't stop my wanting to find her killers, but it eased my nightmares. I hadn't killed her. I'd only been the helpless witness to her death.

While I was recuperating at Lotty's, I wasn't idle. I returned all the calls from the media that had piled up. Sad but true, part of being a successful PI is for people to see your name on the Web.

This was especially important because my temporary agency phoned to say that Marilyn

313

Klimpton was quitting. 'She didn't expect to be there on her own with so many angry clients and all the reporters and so on trying to reach you. Also, you being attacked in that bombing, she's afraid for her safety, being alone in your office. We don't think we can send anyone to replace her right now.'

'Then I don't think you and I will be working together again in the future, either,' I said grandly.

This was just great. Not only was I out of commission but the backlog waiting for me would be growing to Himalayan proportions again. I called my answering service to tell them to handle the phone during normal business hours, and then I started phoning my clients to see what business I could subcontract out and what could wait a few more days for me to get to it personally.

Some people had already moved their inquiries to bigger firms with more detectives. Prudent. If your lead investigator is singed, go where you know there's backup. I thought of my bills and tried not to panic. I thought of George Dornick's Mountain Hawk Security and his offer to hire 'Tony's daughter.' I hoped it wouldn't come to that.

And I worried, too, about my cousin. Something wasn't right with her story about why she'd shown up at the Freedom Center the night I'd gone back there. It was flattering to think she wanted to emulate me, but I was having a hard time believing it. And the smoke bomb at my old home on Houston . . . Señora Andarra had told

314

the cops she saw the woman who grew up in the house watching from across the street. Conrad thought that had to be me because he associated only me with growing up in the house. But Señora Andarra probably thought of Petra and me as a family unit . . . It had been Petra who spoke to her in Spanish.

Although Petra had sworn angrily she hadn't been playing detective in South Chicago, she hadn't categorically denied being there last Sunday night. But why would she have been down there? I couldn't begin to imagine a reason.

I finally put the idea aside and called the management company that handled the Freedom Center building, hoping they could tell me who had sent over a demolition team to gut Sister Frankie's apartment and prepare it for the builders. They couldn't or they wouldn't tell me.

I left a message on Sister Carolyn's cellphone to see if she could get any information out of the contractors. She was in a meeting with an INS attorney, but she called back several hours later to say she'd talked to someone from both the wrecking crew and the builder. Both contractors insisted they didn't know who hired them. They had been promised cash, almost double their usual fees, if they would drop everything and take care of the building.

'They didn't want to tell me even that much, I guess because they were afraid I might report them to the IRS, but I put on my costume and assured them that all I wanted was information.'

Her costume. Oh, the veil, right. I asked who

315

had given them the money, but she said they claimed it was a middle-aged white man, someone they had never seen before.

'Don't tell me,' I said drily. 'He was wearing a trench coat and a felt fedora.'

'I don't know,' she said. 'Would it make a difference?'

'Yeah. It would be a giveaway that they were lying instead of just a probability.'

'You think they really know who sent them?'

I was sitting at Lotty's kitchen table, my frustration at my inaction just about at the boiling point. 'I don't know, of course, but my best guess is that they owe someone important a favor or they're gofers for someone important. Maybe they're a minority-contracting front, I don't know. But to drop everything like that, they have to have a pretty good idea who sent them. And then your place being under surveillance, and that police seal on Sister Frankie's door, didn't stop them for five seconds.'

When we hung up, I called the detectives from the Bomb and Arson squad who had been over to interrogate me. The Latino cop was in.

'You know your crime scene doesn't exist anymore?' I said.

'What are you talking about?'

'I just got off the phone with one of the nuns who lives there. A building crew showed up, not anyone the sisters hired, and took down the door, stripped the room. I hope you secured any samples you took. Someone's going to a lot of trouble to keep that fire from being investigated.'

316

He didn't exactly thank me. It was more of a snarl, a demand for Sister Carolyn's phone number, and a warning that I'd better not be behind any destruction of evidence.

I missed Amy Blount badly. I could have sicced her on the contractors, gotten her to track down the ownership trail. I wondered if I could turn it over to my cousin, see how she would handle a routine search through incorporation records. If she failed, I was no worse off than I was when I started.

I tried Petra on her cellphone. She was at the campaign office, and we were interrupted several times by people who came by to see her. Each time, she announced that she was on the phone with 'my cousin, you know, the one who got burned in that fire last week? So I'll get back to you right away, but she needs my help.'

When I finally got her full attention, she was enthusiastic and bubbled over with questions. I gave her the URLs of a couple of websites I subscribe to, and told her I'd e-mail her the passwords so she didn't have to try to write them down in midconversation.

'If the subcontractors haven't made it into the database, you'll have to go to the State of Illinois Building to check their incorporation filings.'

'But what if they incorporated in some other state? Don't they usually do it in Delaware?'

'If they're big enough to incorporate in Delaware, you should find them online, but good catch. If you find them, please, little cousin, do not go tracking them down by yourself. Contractors have short fuses and big hammers.'

317

'Oh, Vic, so do meatpackers. I grew up around them. I know how to talk to people without getting their undies in a bundle. Anyway, I can outrun a guy who's weighed down by a big hammer. You'll see.'

I would see. I frowned at the phone, wishing I understood what was really on Petra's mind, and hoping I hadn't started her on a quest where she'd get in over her head.

Lotty took the afternoon off to drive me around, first to the hospital, where her presence let me jump to the front of the line.

From the hospital, we drove to the bank. Until I got all my plastic replaced, I didn't have a way of getting cash, so I brought my passport and cashed a check for a thousand dollars, hoping that would see me through until a new ATM card arrived.

Our last stop was my hairdresser's, so I could get my weird clumps of hair shorn to a uniform length. Something between baldness and a Marine buzz cut was how it looked at the end, but certainly way more attractive than the Mangy Dog'd do I'd been sporting.

It was a pleasant day, a sort of mini-vacation after the trauma of the past ten days, and we finished it by eating supper with Max at a little bistro on Damen. He and Lotty drove me to my apartment, where Mr. Contreras and the dogs tumbled out to greet me. The dogs showed such ecstasy that the medical resident across the hall threatened to call the cops if Mr. Contreras and I didn't silence them at once. Even that didn't dampen my pleasure at coming back to my own home. Lotty gave me a long hug and relinquished me to Mr. Contreras, who insisted on carrying my bag up the stairs.

My pleasure died as soon as I opened the door. I was so shocked that I couldn't take it in at first. My home had been ripped to shreds. Books lay on the floor, my stereo was dismantled, music had been dumped so the inside of the piano could be inspected, my trunk stood in the living room with my mother's evening gown wadded up on the floor next to it.

My first reaction was a kind of despair, a desire to get on a plane for Milan and spend the rest of my life in the little hill town where my mother grew up. My second response was fury with my cousin.

'Come on, Vic,' my neighbor protested. 'Cut the kid some slack. How could she be behind this?'

'There are no signs of forced entry,' I said. 'You let her in with my keys, right? She's been obsessed with this baseball I found with my dad's stuff, and this has all the earmarks of a spoiled kid wanting what she wants when she wants it.'

'I let her in, yeah, but that was two days ago when she stopped in for your phone charger. She didn't stay long enough to do this kind of damage. And, anyway, you got her all wrong. I don't know what's wrong with you, cookie, but it's like you're jealous of her for being young and pretty and lively. I thought you was better than that. Really, doll, I thought you was.'

'How can you talk like that when my

apartment has been trashed! Look at this!' I held up my mother's gown. 'She knows how much this matters to me and she just wads it up and dumps it like it's an old dish towel.'

'I'm just saying, Petra couldn't a done this no matter what you think. And I didn't let anyone else in, so this was a professional, someone who could bypass all your locks and gates and stuff and get in anyway. They had to've done this late at night, when me and the dogs was sound asleep. Your cousin wasn't here in the middle of the night.'

I called Petra's cellphone, but there wasn't any answer. I left a message telling her to call me the instant she picked up her voice mail. With the dogs and Mr. Contreras accompanying me, I walked through my apartment, looking at wreckage. The old man was right: Petra wouldn't have been so wanton. But neither would a professional. Unless it was a professional deliberately trying to terrify me. In which case, they had done a great job.

'But what could they be looking for?' I asked Mr. Contreras. 'Except for that Nellie Fox ball, there's nothing here that anyone would want. Besides, as I keep saying, there's no sign of forced entry.'

'Maybe Petra forgot to lock up behind her,' my neighbor suggested.

'Then why was it locked when we came up the stairs just now?' I was teetering on the brink of meltdown and kept hysteria out of my voice by effort of will alone.

Mr. Contreras wanted me to call the police,

320

but I'd had my fill of the law. Although the more chaos I saw, the less I thought my cousin had caused it, I didn't want a crime unit to find some trace of Petra there. If she'd done this, I'd tackle her myself.

I spent the rest of the night cleaning. Mr. Contreras stayed to help, picking up books, helping fold clothes, cleaning the kitchen with me. In my dining room, dishes had been pulled from the shelves with the same recklessness apparent everywhere else. The old man knelt, grunting, to pick up cups and plates and wipe them before putting them back on the shelves.

My mother's red Venetian wineglasses, which she had wrapped in her underwear and carried in her one small suitcase when she fled Italy, were piled on the floor. I picked them up, my hands shaking so badly I was afraid I would break them, and held each up to the light. I had lost two over the years and cracked a third. Now a fourth had a chip in the base.

I held on to the fourth glass, unable to keep from crying. When Bobby and Eileen Mallory had their first baby, Gabriella had brought these glasses out to drink a toast after the christening. That was the first time I remembered seeing them, and my mother had told me their history. The wineglasses had been a present to her grandmother in 1894 on her wedding day. They had been carried by Gabriella into hiding as a memento, even though they were an unwieldy and fragile burden. She had managed to carry them from Pitigliano to Siena, where she hid in her music teacher's attic, and then, hours before the Fascists arrived, smuggled them to the hills, where she hid with her father until bribes and luck got her passage on a ship to Cuba. Not one glass had broken. But me? I'd now damaged half of them. Victoria Iphigenia, the ox.

I don't know how long I sat there, while Mr. Contreras tiptoed around sympathetically putting away books and papers. Peppy came to lay her head in my lap. I put the glass down to stroke her, then finally got to my knees on my way to return the glasses to my breakfront.

I was getting to my feet when I saw that my photo album had been flung under the table. I got down on my knees again and crawled between the legs after it.

My eyes were aching from overuse and my hands were throbbing, but I turned the pages, trying to figure out if any of the pictures were missing. A number had come loose from their little corner mounts. I doggedly went through the album, slipping in the loose ones, including one of my parents toasting each other with the Venetian wine-glasses. I winced and turned the page. The picture of my father with his slow-pitch team was missing.

I looked under the table, then sifted through the album a second time, but the picture had disappeared.

32

Vanishing Cousin

We finished a little after one. Mr. Contreras left the dogs with me for protection, and I made sure all my door and window bolts were shot home on the inside, but, even so, I slept badly. Every time Mitch scratched or a car honked too loudly, I jumped awake, heart pounding, sure the next minute would bring a home invasion or a Molotov cocktail through a window. Finally, around five, the lightening sky made me feel safe enough that I dropped off.

The dogs woke me at nine, whining to get down to the back garden. I slumped out after them, sitting on the back porch with my head on my knees, until the hot sun burning my neck reminded me that I couldn't be outside without protection.

Back inside, I tried my cousin again. She answered just as I thought the call was going to roll over again to her voice mail.

'Uh, Vic, uh, I can't do that thing for you that you asked me.'

'Petra! I can barely hear you. What's going on?'

'I can't talk to you now.'

She was still speaking in almost a whisper. I answered sharply that I needed some answers from her at once about what she'd been doing in my apartment.

'I wasn't there,' she said. 'Except when I went

to make your bed and stuff.'

'You didn't look around for that baseball you wanted?'

'I did look in the trunk, but I put everything back again. So don't get too mad at me, please, Vic. I can't talk right now, I've got to go. And I can't find those guys for you.'

She whispered so fast before hanging up that I couldn't squeeze in another word. I walked to the front window and frowned down at the street. I'd told my cousin the other night that I was an expert at detecting line spinners, but I'm not sure how true that boast was. Someone very skillful was spinning me around, but whether they were using Petra or she was a willing participant or even just a bystander I couldn't make up my mind.

I flicked the cord on the blinds and realized I was standing in such a way that anyone on the street could see me if they wanted to aim a gun or a bottle at me. Whatever Petra might or mightn't have done, it was impossible to picture her throwing a Molotov cocktail at anyone. Or even the smoke bomb that had driven the family out of my childhood home last weekend. Mr. Contreras was right. She was exuberant and careless, not mean-spirited or cruel. That was how I would write her up at her performance review.

I heard the dogs whining and scratching at the back door and went to let them in. I knelt to talk to them. 'I'll take you guys for a good walk tonight after the sun goes down, but this is it for now.'

I dressed carefully, in a high-necked T-shirt and loose-fitting linen trousers and jacket that covered my arms and chest. I put on the white cotton gloves I needed to protect my hands and found a wide-brimmed straw hat that I sometimes wore at the beach. When I was finished, I looked like Scarlett O'Hara protecting her fragile skin, but it couldn't be helped.

To complete my protective gear, I went to the safe in the back of my bedroom closet. My intruders had shaken out my wardrobe, but they'd missed the safe, which is built in behind my shoe bag. Occasionally, I have a document so sensitive, I don't want to leave it in my office overnight. Otherwise, all that I keep in it is my mother's diamond drop earrings and pendant and my Smith & Wesson.

I made sure the gun was still clean — I hadn't been to the range for several months — and checked the clip. I didn't know for sure that I was in someone else's sights, but it made me feel a little better when I snapped my tuck holster over my belt loops.

I went door-to-door, in the best detective tradition, to find out if anyone had seen the person who'd gone into my apartment. And how they'd made it past all my locks without forcing them. Of course, some people were out at work, but the older Norwegian woman, who's lived on the second floor for a decade, had been home, as had the grandmother of the Korean family. Neither of them had seen or heard anything unusual.

Jake Thibaut came blear-eyed to the door in a

T-shirt and shorts. I'd woken him, but I couldn't help it. And how was I to know what time he got in at night? He didn't recognize me at first.

'It's the hair,' he finally decided. 'You cut off all your curls.'

I ran my fingers through the buzz cut and winced as I touched the bruises. I kept forgetting about my hair when I don't look in the mirror.

'Did you hear anything in my apartment two nights ago? Someone came through with something like a forklift and knocked the place apart.'

'Two nights ago?' He rubbed his eyes. 'I was playing out in Elgin. I didn't get home until two or so, but maybe I saw your forklifters leaving. I was getting my bass out of the back of my car when I saw two strange men coming down the walk.'

I sucked in a breath. 'Black? White? Young?'

He shook his head. 'I thought maybe they were clients of yours, paying a secret visit, so I didn't get close. They had that kind of Edward G. Robinson look that makes you think that you should keep your distance.'

'Were they driving or on foot?'

'I'm pretty sure they got into a big dark SUV up the street, but I'm not good with cars. I can't tell you what the make was.'

'You didn't see a tall woman with spiky hair lurking about, did you?'

He laughed. 'You mean that girl who comes to visit you — what, your cousin, is she? No, she came around a few times while you were away, visiting the old guy, but she wasn't part of that team. These guys were bulky, not skinny and spiky.'

I left with a measure of both relief and worry: relief at the reassurance that Petra hadn't been involved in this break-in and worry about who had sent people to search my apartment.

I picked up my car from the alley, where Mr. Contreras had put it when he rescued it. I'd left my briefcase in the trunk some million or so years ago when I'd gone to visit Sister Frankie. When I opened it to stick in a new set of papers for some meetings I'd scheduled that afternoon, the first thing I saw was the Nellie Fox baseball. I'd completely forgotten about stashing it in there.

I laughed softly to myself. Poor Petra. She could have boosted the ball without my knowing the difference if she'd only thought to look in the trunk. I held it up to the sun, squinting at it through my dark glasses. It was stained and worn. Someone had played with it, maybe Grandpa Warshawski. He died when I was little, but he'd been a Sox fan.

The ball also had holes in it, and that was mystifying. A couple of them went all the way through the ball, so I wondered if my dad and his brother Bernie had run fishing line through it to hang it up for batting practice. I tucked the ball back into my briefcase and drove to my office.

Until she sank under the weight of my media calls, Marilyn Klimpton had done a good job of sorting files and papers. Even though messages had built up, and some incoming documents needed sorting, the office looked in pretty good shape, especially compared to the mounds of papers I'd found on my return from Italy.

I booted up my computer and looked at the message page from my answering service. Among the nuisance calls from media outlets were a pointless threat not to tamper with evidence from the Emergency Management woman and some client queries. There also was a message from Greg Yeoman, Johnny Merton's lawyer. I was on the list of confirmed visitors to Stateville for tomorrow afternoon, could I please call to confirm.

I suddenly felt so tired, I went to the cot in my back room to lie down. I'd forgotten about putting in the call to Yeoman. I had done it after I saw Miss Claudia at Lionsgate Manor, I remembered now. The murder of Sister Frances, my own injuries, the invasion of my apartment had all pushed Ella Gadsden and her sister completely out of my mind. I lay there in the dark for close to an hour. I finally got back on my feet and called Greg Yeoman to confirm that I would make the drive out to Stateville the following afternoon.

Thinking about Sister Frances reminded me that I wanted some background on the demolition and building contractors who were taking care of her apartment. Petra was going to find out about them for me, but she couldn't do it. And it really wasn't that big of a job.

Sister Carolyn had given me the contractors' names: Little Big-Man Wreckers and Rebound Construction. Both were owned by a man named Ernie Rodenko, at 300 West Roscoe. His seemed to be a midsize company, doing about ten million in business every year, and specializing in fire and flood rehab. The address would put him at the intersection of Roscoe and Lake Shore Drive, which wasn't zoned for business, so his office must be in his home. Which meant I might drop in on him, in the evening, when I could go out without all my unguents and hats and so on.

I entered the address in my PDA and continued working through my messages. In the afternoon, an appointment took me to a building in the east Loop, across a wide plaza from the skyscraper where Krumas for Illinois had its headquarters. After my meeting, I wondered if I should drop in on Petra, to see if she might tell me something face-to-face that she couldn't say over the phone.

It could be, of course, that she'd been chewed out by her boss for too many personal calls. Maybe her old boss didn't care much about in-office discipline, but Petra was on Les Strangwell's staff now. From what I knew of Strangwell, you belonged to him body and soul. You didn't fritter away time on your cousin's projects when you had to get Brian Krumas into the Senate. In case Strangwell was keeping a close watch on my cousin, I decided to leave her alone.

Before returning to the hot summer afternoon, I turned into the coffee bar in my client's building lobby for an iced cappuccino. As I waited for them to make my drink, I stared idly around the way one does and caught sight of a familiar face at one of the spindly tables tucked into the corner of the bar. The thinning dark hair combed sharply back from a jowly red face, I'd seen him, two weeks ago in Lake Catherine.

What had brought Larry Alito into downtown Chicago on a hot July day and into a coffee bar instead of a beer joint? I was going to slide back into the shadows when I realized my outsize hat, dark glasses, and gloves made a pretty good disguise. I collected my drink and went to sit on one of the high stools by the window near Alito's table.

The man he was talking to looked like many other middle-aged middle managers with spreading middles. He had fine sandy hair that had receded to the middle of his head, which he wisely had trimmed short instead of trying for a comb-over. With his turned-up nose and pursed mouth, he had the expression of a perpetually surprised baby. Only his small gray eyes, cold and shrewd, made it clear that it was he, not Alito, who was running the meeting.

I couldn't hear any of their conversation because the coffee bar had a sound track with a loud bass thumping. The two men were going over a set of papers in a manila folder, and the man running the meeting was tapping the papers with his thumb. He wasn't happy with the work Alito had given him. I pulled out my cellphone and took a quick shot of the two of them while pretending to be texting. When they got up, I waited until they were almost to the building lobby before I followed them.

As they reached the lobby, they separated without looking or speaking to each other. The meeting commander headed for the exit, while Alito studied the door to a FedEx shop near the coffee bar. I knelt on one knee to adjust my socks. Alito may have been a crappy cop, but he'd spent three decades studying wanted posters and he might recognize me close up despite my disguise. From my kneeling position on the floor, I looked out at the plaza and saw that the commander was going into the building where the Krumas campaign had its offices.

Alito's phone rang, and I stood, moving behind him to a newsstand where I picked up a pack of gum. 'Yeah,' he said into the phone, 'Les already told me, and I know what he wants. You think I'm some kind of retard, you have to double-check everything I do? . . . Oh, the same to the horse you rode in on!'

He snapped his cellphone shut and stormed through the revolving door. 'Les' had told him, had he? That man with the sandy hair and cold eyes: that was Les Strangwell.

I took my coffee out onto the plaza and sat in the shade. What line connected Strangwell to Alito? Of course, ex-cops do freelance work all the time, but what kind of security work did the Krumas campaign . . . George Dornick. Dornick was advising Brian on terrorism and Homeland Security issues. He was Alito's ex-partner. Maybe Dornick was throwing some crumbs his way.

But what crumbs? I thought of my apartment. Someone who knew how to pick locks in a sophisticated way had gotten in there. A cop would have access to all kinds of tools. And George Dornick, with his special security services, had access to even more. But what could I have that Dornick, let alone Les Strangwell, might want? The picture of my dad's softball team? Larry Alito had been in it, as had Dornick, Bobby Mallory, and a lot of other guys.

Alito was proud of his police service. It defined him. I couldn't imagine any reason why he would want the picture unless it was pure spite against me. But there wasn't any reason for that, either.

I didn't have enough data to make up a believable story. I gave up trying, and took the El back to my office. Elton Grainger was out front, hawking *Streetwise*. He didn't recognize me at first. But when he realized I'd been in a fire, he was all sympathy.

'And a nun got killed, you say? Oh, Vic, I don't have a TV, I don't see the news. That's terrible. No wonder you haven't been around. How's that cute cousin of yours?'

'Cute as ever.' I tried not to grind my teeth. 'Anyone been coming around looking for me while I've been away?'

'I haven't been looking. But I'll put out a guest book. Anyone comes up to the door, they got to sign in with me.'

He parodied a hotel doorman, and I had to laugh. Of course it was idiotic to think Elton would pay attention to anyone scouting out my office. I typed in the code on the door lock and went inside, keeping a hand on the handle of my gun in its tuck holster.

When I was inside, I searched the office, from the cot to the bathroom I shared with my sculpting lease-mate, but no one was there. I answered a few e-mails. But I had reached the end of my stamina, and set out for home.

When I got there, I found Petra out in the backyard with the dogs. Mr. Contreras had his barbecue going. She was sitting on the grass with her arms around Mitch, who acknowledged my arrival by lifting his head to look at me. Peppy, at least, came over to meet me.

'Poor Peewee is beat. They got her working too hard,' Mr. Contreras announced. 'We're doing burgers and corn. You want some?'

I accepted gratefully, and went upstairs for wine and a salad, leaving my hat and gloves. I brought some cushions down with me and stretched out on the grass, where I could see my cousin's face. She looked pinched and anxious. But when she saw me studying her, she tried to grin in her usual enthusiastic fashion.

'I'm pretty beat myself, first day back on the job. I had to go to the Prudential Plaza this afternoon, and I finally got a look at Les Strangwell.'

'You didn't talk to him, did you?' Petra asked, a little breathless.

'Not about you, not about anything. Guy has freaky eyes, don't you think?'

She shivered but didn't say anything.

'Petra, are you in trouble at work?'

Mr. Contreras frowned and started to protest, but he caught my little headshake and was silent.

'No, no! Why should I be in trouble? I do

333

whatever they tell me to, and faster than a speeding bullet.'

'You just seemed jumpy on the phone today. And you're definitely not your usual high-voltage self tonight.'

She played with her stack of rubber bracelets. 'It's like Uncle Sal said: they're working me too hard. I even have to go back in tonight, as soon as I scarf down some of Uncle Sal's home cooking. What took you downtown? Are you still looking for that missing gangbanger? Did you think you'd find him in the Prudential building?'

'Yep. Selling bonds out of the fiftieth-floor office. Actually, I'm going back out to Joliet tomorrow afternoon. Johnny Merton, the head snake charmer, has agreed to see me again, and I'm hoping the murder of Sister Frances may jolt him into telling me something.'

'You're going out to the prison tomorrow?' she repeated, looking at me anxiously.

'Why not?'

She bit her lips. 'Just . . . uh . . . I don't know . . . you're still hurting, I mean.'

'I'm a renewable resource.' I took a hamburger from Mr. Contreras and sat up to keep it out of Peppy's mouth. 'I'm like Hercules, except I regenerate my spleen, my skin, and my brain every morning.'

She laughed in a distracted, forced way and changed the subject, also in a distracted, forced way. She fed most of her hamburger to Mitch, then got up to leave.

I followed her to the side gate. 'Petra! What is wrong here?'

334

Her large eyes filled with tears, and she stared at me for a long pause, then said, 'Leave me alone, can't you? Do you have to pry into everybody's business?'

'No,' I said slowly. 'No, of course not. But you're acting — '

'I know what I'm doing. Leave me alone!' She slammed the gate.

'You haven't been riding her over your place being torn apart, have you?' Mr. Contreras and the dogs had bustled over to join us.

I shook my head. 'I wish now I had gone to her office today. Maybe I will after I get done with Johnny tomorrow.'

But the next day was when I came back from Stateville to find that intruders had been in my office and wrecked it with the force of an F5 tornado. That was when I found Petra's white rubber ONE bracelet on the cement apron outside my back door. That was the night I spent with Bobby Mallory and the FBI trying to find any trace of my cousin.

After that sleepless night, my uncle Peter and aunt Rachel arrived. My uncle unleashed his own F5 on me, blaming me, at high volume, for anything that might have gone wrong with Petra. I tried to ride out the storm without fighting back because I knew raw rage was the only way he was able to express his fear. I was afraid, too, and so was my aunt. Finally, after several hours of his useless screaming, Rachel took Peter downtown to meet with the FBI's Special Agent in Charge.

33

Losing a Follower

After Peter and Rachel left, I had a long talk with
Mr. Contreras, which included a promise to
involve him in any action necessary to rescue
Petra. I even shared with him the list I'd made of
all the odd questions I had about my cousin
during the past few weeks: the Nellie Fox
baseball, her relentless interest in the contents of
my trunk, her wish to see any storage places in
the old family home in Back of the Yards, her
effort to tour my own childhood home in South
Chicago, her arrival at Sister Frankie's gutted
apartment last week, the smoke bomb that
forced the Andarra family to vacate the house
the night before Sister Frankie's murder.

At first he put up a spirited defense of her
youth and impulsiveness, but by the time I got to
her late-night trip to the Freedom Center even
Mr. Contreras was uneasy. 'But, doll, if she was
doing something she shouldn'ta been, it was
because she was pushed into it. You listen to me.
She's as good as gold, little Peewee, and don't
you go thinking otherwise. When you get to the
end of this story, you're going to find Johnny
Merton was behind it. Mark my words.'

'Let's find her first and argue over who got her
in over her head later, right?'

He agreed gruffly, and watched while I printed

out a couple of shots I'd taken of Petra on my cellphone. I also printed random pictures off the Web of young blond women: some celebrities, some pictures that people had posted on their blogs, finishing with a few shots of myself.

I uploaded the photo I'd snapped of Alito and Strangwell at the Prudential Plaza the other day. It wasn't a very clear shot, but it was the only one I could find of Alito. Strangwell was highly visible. His website showed him with various Illinois politicos, with U.S. presidents and a Supreme Court justice, and with entertainers like Michael Jordan. I guess if you were coming to Strangwell for help, the portraits showed you what kind of access a thousand dollars an hour bought you. I printed a couple of those images, and pulled one of Dornick from the Mountain Hawk Security website as well.

The old man finally left when I went into the bathroom to get ready for my day outside. As I covered my face and arms with protective creams, it seemed somehow wrong to be tending to my body when my cousin's life might be in danger. I put on my hat, my gloves, checked the clip in my gun and put it in its tuck holster, and went out the back door.

Jake Thibaut was on his little porch with a cup of coffee. 'That's a fetching costume. You going undercover on a Civil War plantation?'

I tried to smile but found my voice cracking instead. 'It's because of the fire. Because of . . . Sorry, my cousin has vanished in a way that has me pretty freaked. I've got to go, see what I can find out.'

He walked down the five steps to our common landing. 'You need any kind of help from me? You know, anything that doesn't involve a handgun or some kind of physical heroism?'

I started to say no, then remembered that Thibaut had seen the people who broke into my apartment as they left early Tuesday morning. I pulled my folder of photographs from my briefcase and showed them to him.

'I know it was dark, and these aren't great shots, but could any of these guys be the ones you saw?'

'It's impossible to say.' He tapped the picture of Alito and Strangwell. 'They're sitting, so I can't tell how tall they are. This one' — he was touching Alito — 'he's broad enough, but . . . I'd have to see them walking. I measure people's height against Bessie. My bass,' he added when he saw my puzzled look.

I put the pictures back in the folder. As I started down the stairs, Thibaut said, 'They looked menacing. Remember that.'

I nodded soberly. Menacing didn't even begin to cover the way these people had acted.

I went out the back gate and picked up my car in the alley. In the frenzy we'd all been in since last night, no one had talked about seeing if Petra were at home, doped or . . . or not dead. I was going to make her apartment my first port of call, then head to South Chicago.

I hadn't had time to replace the lump of melted plastic in my wallet with a new driver's license, and I didn't want to waste an hour explaining that to a traffic cop, so for the few miles that lay between me and Petra's loft I stayed within the thirty-mile-per-hour limit, stopped at all stop signs, and even braked when the light turned yellow.

My picklocks were still in my glove compartment. I rang Petra's bell, but there was no answer, even though I leaned on it for a good thirty seconds. I didn't want to be seen using my picks in broad daylight, so I got inside on the tried-and-true method of ringing every bell in the building. There is usually someone careless enough to buzz you in, and I was lucky with the third bell I pushed.

I took the stairs up to the fourth floor two at a time. By the time I reached Petra's door, I had a stitch in my side where my gun was poking me. The woman who'd buzzed me in was shouting up the stairwell. I tried to steady my voice when I called down an apology, I'd rung the wrong door. The voice of an educated white woman was reassuring to her, and she called back an acknowledgment. I heard her door close, and I knelt to work Petra's lock.

My hands were shaking. I was slow, exhaustingly slow, and my cotton gloves kept slipping on the picks. I took off the stupid gloves but still felt like I was stirring molasses with my fingers.

When I finally got inside, the apartment had a churchlike quiet. A tap was dripping somewhere. That ping of water on enamel was all I could hear. I found myself tiptoeing through the big room that made up the bulk of the loft, looking for any signs of my cousin or anything that would give me a hint about where she'd gone.

Petra hadn't bothered much with furnishing the place. She had an overstuffed sofa, one of those big, sacklike things, covered in a kind of taupe denim. An outsize teddy bear was sitting in the middle of it, staring at the windows, with a sad smile on its face. Its wide plastic eyes unnerved me. I finally turned it facedown.

She had a television on a rolling stand, a rolling computer table, and an armchair that matched the sofa. She had no curtains for the long row of windows, just the blinds that came with the apartment.

I hadn't been here, except the night I unlocked the door for her, so I had no idea what might be missing if she'd left under her own steam. No drugs in the bathroom, but her electric toothbrush and Waterpik were still in their stands. Her tube of Tom's Toothpaste was carefully rolled from the bottom up.

In the area where she slept, she had a futon and a dresser. A change of clothes was tossed carelessly across the futon, trailing onto the floor, and more clothes were half on hangers or had been allowed to fall to the closet floor.

A stack of wicker baskets by the bed held books, magazines, and a box of condoms. I wished I knew who she was dating or whether the box was simply there for insurance. I flipped through *The Lost Diary of Don Juan*, hoping that the lost diary of Petra Warshawski might fall out, but I didn't see anything in her handwriting, not even a checkbook. With someone in the Millennium Gen, you couldn't tell if that meant she had run away, taking her checkbook with her, or that she did all her banking online.

The one thing I had hoped to find was her laptop, so I could see who she'd been e-mailing what to. Although she seemed to do most of her communicating by texting, a computer might have longer documents, more of a key to what she was doing. At a minimum, I could have seen what websites she'd been visiting lately.

The big room flowed into a kitchen with a tiled work island and a big cooktop, with a grill and a restaurant-sized exhaust fan. The fancy appliances seemed wasted on my cousin. Her refrigerator held wine and blueberry yogurt and not much else. In the morning, she'd grab a carton and eat it on the bus. At lunch, she'd pick up a sandwich and eat it at her desk. And at night, the group of friends she'd made would all go out for Thai or Mexican. Or so I pictured it.

A door by the refrigerator led to a small deck and back stairs. When I pulled the door open, it swung crazily on its hinges and then fell off. I jumped out of the way just in time to avoid a smash on the head.

The noise, the shock of the door collapsing under my hand ... I leaned against the work island, shaking. When my heart was more or less normal, I saw my gun was in my right hand. I hadn't noticed drawing it.

Whoever had come in through the back hadn't bothered with the finesse of picklocks; they'd simply crowbarred the hinges out of the doorjamb and then propped the door up when they left.

What had they taken? The computer? My

cousin at gunpoint? I moved the door and went down the back stairs. There were cigarette butts on one landing, but they looked old, the residue of a smoker sent outside to indulge, not a recent watcher. The stairs ended in an asphalt areaway that was separated from the alley by a high fence and a gate. I opened the gate. Its lock was still in place. But a row of parking spaces lay behind the gate, and the intruder could have waited out there for someone to park and simply followed that person in.

I propped the gate open and walked the length of the alley. My cousin's shiny Pathfinder was sitting there, all locked up. I opened it and looked through the receipts and empty drink containers. I got down on my knees and looked under the seats, in the glove compartment, in the spare-tire compartment, under the hood, under the fenders. I detected that Petra drank a lot of smoothies and bottled water, didn't go in for soft drinks, ate at El Gato Loco, and wasn't careful with her credit-card chits. After searching the alley, the only other clue I found was that a lot of people drink at night and can't be bothered to find a trash can for their empties.

I returned to Petra's place through the back. I needed to do something about the broken kitchen door. On my way out through the front. I saw the building-management company name on a plaque. I called them to report the broken door. And called Bobby Mallory to tell him that someone had broken into Petra's apartment.

'That 'someone' wasn't you, was it, Vicki?'

'They broke the back door getting in. I was

there just now, trying to see what was missing, and I'm wondering if they stole her computer. Or maybe forced her at gunpoint to go into my office.'

Bobby catechized me on what my aunt and uncle were up to. When I told them they were meeting with the FBI this morning, he was skeptical. The Bureau was stretched too thin with terror watching, he claimed. He didn't think they could find Petra even if she'd been kidnapped.

Bobby's comments only increased my own high level of terror. I wished I knew whether my next step was a waste of time or not. Fear paralyzes you, makes it hard to act creatively.

It wasn't until I'd driven three blocks that I realized I had company. After the fire bombs, after the trashing of my home and office, after Petra's disappearance, I should be taking triple precautions, making sure no one had planted bugs or bombs in my car before climbing into it, riding around the block two or three times to make sure I was clean before I went anywhere. It was only this sixth sense I'd gotten from all my years in the business that made me note that the bike messenger, the same one who'd been riding behind me on my way over to Petra's, was in my side mirror again.

A bike was a great way to do a tail within the city. Any maneuver I made, he could react faster to than a car. Of course, he couldn't follow me onto Lake Shore Drive. But anyone smart enough to use a messenger as a tail had a car or two as backup.

I pretended I hadn't noticed him and got onto the drive. I didn't bother to check for tails. If they wanted me to know, they'd reveal themselves. If they didn't, my best strategy was not to try to flush them out now.

I pulled off at the first downtown exit, and stopped at the second hotel I came to. I turned my car over to the valet, explained I was going to a meeting and that I wasn't a guest, and went inside.

There's a network of underground passages that connect the hotels and high-rises on the east side of the Loop. I took the lobby escalator down, slipped behind a pillar, and knelt down. I didn't see anyone behind me, but I still took off my Scarlett O'Hara hat and left it behind a potted palm. It just made me too damned easy to track.

I waited until a group of women all came down together, laughing and talking, and moved just in front of them so that we all seemed to be walking along the underground corridor together. They peeled off at one of the subterranean take-out joints.

I darted into a neighboring gift shop, where I bought a Cubs cap. Going up and down escalators, buying a frozen yogurt, I didn't see the same face twice. I bought a red CHICAGO sweatshirt at another gift shop and pulled it on over my linen jacket. Although the weight of the sweatshirt on a hot day made me feel as though I were encased in a burka, I wasn't instantly recognizable.

Still underground, I finally headed to my

344

original destination: the Illinois Central station. There was a twenty-minute wait for the next train to South Chicago. I bought a ticket and stood near the door leading to the tracks. When they called my train, I waited until the last possible moment before sliding through the doors and down the stairs. I thought I was clean, but you never know.

The slow ride to South Chicago was like a backward journey through my life, the ride I'd taken with my mother so many times as a child, past the University of Chicago, where my mother had wanted me to study. 'The best, Victoria. You need to have the best,' she would say when the train stopped there to let off students.

Ninety-first Street. End of the line. A certain desolation attached to the conductor's announcement. *Life ends here.* I walked the four blocks from the station to my old home.

At least Señora Andarra's grandson and his friends weren't visible this morning, but a couple of helpless-looking men were sitting on a curb with a bottle in a brown paper bag. Somewhere, a car stereo was pouring out a bass so loudly that the air was vibrating from it.

At my old home, I saw the boarded-over window that had been broken to throw in the smoke bomb. The prisms across the top were splintered, too. I concentrated instead on the decorative-glass fanlight over the front door, which was still intact.

I rang the bell. After a few minutes, when I wondered if she'd gone out, Señora Andarra opened it the length of its stubby chain. '*Esta ventana,*' I stumbled in my bad Spanish, pointing at the fan. '*Mi madre amó esta ventana también.*'

The fact that my mother also loved that window didn't make Señora Andarra smile, but it did keep her from slamming the door in my face. Using painful pidgin Spanish interlaced with English and Italian, I tried to explain that I was a detective, that I had photographs. Could she look at them, let me know if any of the people in them had been at her house when the bomb came through the window?

The whole time I spoke, she stared at me through the crack in the door, her dark eyes frowning in her nut-colored face. When I finally stumbled to an end of my story, she took the folder from me. As I'd feared, she singled Petra out with no trouble.

'*¿Su hija?*' she asked.

I was tired of everyone thinking Petra was my daughter, so I dutifully explained she was my cousin. '*Mi prima. ¿Y los hombres?*'

I thought she lingered on the shot of Alito with Strangwell, but I couldn't be sure. She finally shook her head, and said she didn't know any of them, hadn't seen any of them. I walked back to the station and waited for the northbound train to whisk me back to civilization, or whatever it was.

34

The Boys in the Back Room

On the train north, I called Conrad Rawlings at the Fourth District. Of course, I should have gone to see him before visiting Señora Andarra, but I didn't feel I had spare time for getting police permission to talk to people in my cousin's orbit.

Conrad was predictably annoyed, but he'd seen the news about Petra; he was more interested in finding out why she'd been at a crime scene in his bailiwick than yainching at me for not calling him first.

'Is there anyone else you can place at the crime scene that you might care to mention? Not that we cops can compel testimony. The laws keep us from getting answers to questions that might help solve crimes. But if you're in the mood . . . '

I ignored the savagery in his tone. 'I showed Ms. Andarra a shot of Larry Alito with Les Strangwell, but they didn't look familiar to her.'

'Spell the names.'

I could hear him tapping at his computer.

'Any special reason you think a cop and a politico — a big Gorgonzola politico, from what Google is telling me — would be involved in a two-bit home invasion?'

'Alito's an ex-cop, and he's sniffing around

this story somewhere, somehow. Strangwell is my cousin's boss at the Krumas campaign.'

'And that's reason enough to suspect he's a villain, because anyone who tries to boss the Warshawski women around must be a criminal?'

'I can't talk about this now. Not with you hostile and me out of my head with worry.' I pressed the OFF button.

A detective who's out of her head with worry is useless. I slipped off my shoes and pulled my feet up to sit cross-legged on the seat. Took deep, low breaths, tried to empty my mind of fear, to fill it with a useful to-do list.

The police and FBI had both canvassed the street where I have my office, to see if anyone could describe the men who'd been with Petra, or at least the car they'd driven — if they'd come by car. Naturally, they wouldn't share the results with me. I didn't want to retrace all those steps, not on my own: there must be several hundred people in that section of Milwaukee, between the businesses and the apartments. But I could talk to Elton Grainger. I couldn't remember whether I'd seen him yesterday or not. He was usually at the coffee bar across the street during the day. If he hadn't been too drunk, he might remember seeing Petra with her entourage.

Petra's college roommate, Kelsey Ingalls. My aunt wouldn't give me her phone number, but Kelsey was the person Petra might have confided in. I could surely find her in one of my subscription databases.

Those two tasks meant I should go to my office, but when the train pulled into the

Randolph Street station I realized I was underneath the building where the Krumas campaign had its headquarters. Maybe Petra had confided in one of her coworkers. Maybe Les Strangwell would tell me what she'd been working on. What was it Johnny's daughter had said? *Enough 'maybes' make a hive.*

I went through the maze of underground corridors and found my hat where I'd left it, stuffed behind the potted palm: not a good mark for the cleaning staff but easier for me. I put the Cubs hat and CHICAGO sweatshirt in my briefcase. I kept forgetting the Nellie Fox baseball. It was in there, too. My case now bulged so much with discarded clothes that I couldn't zip it shut.

I checked in with the lobby guard, who phoned up to the campaign. She did a creditable job with my name, Petra having probably accustomed her to it. The guard looked at my passport, printed out a pass, and directed me to the elevators that would carry me to 41.

When I got off the elevator, I barely had time to admire the giant red-white-and-blue posters with Brian's bright smile and keen eyes. A thirty-something woman, with a mass of reddish curls, hurried through the double glass doors to greet me. She was carelessly dressed in a yellow shirt whose tails partly hung out over a floral-print skirt, and she started speaking almost before she was through the doors.

'Where have ... Oh! Who are you?' Her hands, which she'd been brandishing in annoyance, fell loosely at her sides.

349

'V. I. Warshawski . . . Who are you?'

'Oh! Petra's cousin, the detective. Petra forgets her ID about once a week, and the front desk has to call for permission to let her in. I was hoping this meant she'd shown up. Where is she?'

'I wish I knew. I want to find out what she's been working on to see if it'll give me any hint about where she might have gone.'

The woman glanced uncertainly at the double glass doors. 'Maybe I'd better ask Mr. Strangwell. She's been doing more for him lately than for me.'

'You're . . . ' I squeezed my eyes shut, trying to remember if Petra had ever called her boss by name.

'Tania Crandon. I run the NetSquad, which is where Petra started. Before she got so important that she only takes orders from Mr. Strangwell.' When she realized how resentful she sounded, the skin at her throat and chest flushed in the blotchy way that afflicts very fair people.

She was wearing an ID around her neck, which she swiped against a pad on the doors. When they clicked open, I followed her into the campaign hive. Her cellphone tweeted to let her know she had messages coming in. She glanced at these and thumbed responses as we walked past campaign workers. They were gathered in knots over computer screens, arguing in corners, answering cellphones and landlines, shrieking news at each other across the tops of cubicles.

Ms. Crandon looked like a senior citizen in here. Most of the staff was Petra's age. Regardless of race or sex, they all seemed to share my cousin's exuberant energy. Maybe Krumas really did signal a change in politics as usual in Illinois.

Various youths scurried up to Tania with questions. One asked for Petra. They couldn't respond to some rumor on drilling for oil in the Shawnee National Forest without her input, she'd been doing the research.

'See me after lunch,' Tania said. 'I'll have something for you by then.'

Our destination was the southwest corner of the floor. This part of the operation was quieter, with a row of offices banked along the south wall. The corner suite included a secretary, who was handling a phone console with the panache of Solti on the podium. Tania bent to murmur in the secretary's ear. The woman looked at me in surprise, made a call of her own, hit a key on the computer on the desk, and unlocked the inner-office door.

Tania followed close behind her. They shut the door too fast for me to see inside, but not too fast for me to hear my uncle's voice raised in a hoarse shout. So Peter, too, wanted to know what Strangwell had his daughter doing. That was a help. The politico might share more with her father than with her PI cousin.

A few armchairs were arranged to give visitors a view of the Bean, the big sculpture in Millennium Park in which you can see sky, city, and self reflected in its stainless steel curves. I stood for a few moments at the window, watching tourists photograph themselves, but the light was so bright that I had to put my dark glasses on, and then I couldn't see much.

As the minutes stretched on, I left the window. I tried the office door, but it was locked. I scowled at it, then left the area looking for the NetSquad. I had a feeling that if I didn't find Petra's coworkers now, I'd be hustled off the floor before I could talk to them.

The campaigners were deep in conferences or text messages and cellphones. A youth who finally responded to me told me the NetSquad was in Sector 8.

'Sector 8 is which way?'

'We're in pods. Communications is Pod 1, nearest the elevators. Pod 2 is R and D. Sector 8, the NetSquad, straddles the two.' He went back to his computer, finished with me.

Pods, sectors: they'd clearly grown up playing too many sci-fi games on their handhelds. The energy and self-absorption of the campaigners, which had seemed entertaining at first, began to grate on me.

When I finally found Sector 8, I saw the young woman who'd wanted Petra's input on oil drilling in the Shawnee Forest. About five kids were at their computers. It was hard to get a real count because they never sat still for long. Someone would type furiously for a bit, yell, 'I'm sending you this, read it before it goes live,' and then take off, while another two or three staffers would emerge from other pods, look at what was on-screen, sit down to type a comment, then drift away again.

I finally managed to get a young man with a shock of black hair falling into his eyes to pay attention to me. 'Petra Warshawski.'

'Petra? She's not here. She disappeared. They think she's been kidnapped.'

The magic words brought the whole pod to his desk, where they started arguing about whether Petra had been kidnapped or had disappeared on a secret assignment for Strangwell.

'Petra could be doing an undercover assignment for the Chicago Strangler,' a young woman with a number of piercings said. 'She never says what the Strangler has her doing.'

'Running a hit squad,' the sole African-American youth on the team suggested.

'The Strangler feels free to machine-gun the whole opposition in broad daylight,' the pierced woman said. 'You wouldn't have to be undercover for that.'

'Who would Petra talk to if she had a tough problem to unknot?' I asked.

That quieted the group for a minute, but a young woman in jeans and layered tank tops said, 'We don't work like that. It's more, like, how do I do this, and we all, like, brainstorm and come up with different ideas. Brian's campaign, it's about change. It's not about personal glory. So we, like, all work together.'

'What if Petra had a personal problem?' I asked.

The African-American kid said, 'She didn't have personal problems that I could see . . . I mean, before the Strangler pulled her off the team. Then, I don't know if working for him went to her head or he had her doing something she didn't like, but she stopped eating with us after work. We don't know what she's doing or who she's talking to.'

'Guy's a fucking organizing genius,' the first kid I'd spoken to said.

'Granted,' the African-American youth said. 'But would you want to go to El Gato Loco with him?'

The pierced woman laughed. Another young woman came along and asked who was going where for lunch. Before they all took off, I handed cards around.

'I'm her cousin. She disappeared in a way that's got me seriously worried. And the Chicago police and the FBI are on it, too, so I'm surprised they haven't been around to talk to you. If you can think of anyone she might confide in, or anything she's said that would tell me why she took off, call me please.'

They were e-mailing with excitement before I even left the pod. Police, FBI: way too cool to keep to yourself. I walked slowly back to Strangwell — the Strangler's — corner of the floor. The kids admired him, but he frightened them. And, at the same time, they had been jealous of Petra for being singled out to work for him.

Strangwell's door stood open now. Tania Crandon was next to it, working her cellphone. The secretary was standing next to her desk, talking on the landline. Strangwell, frowning, watched from the doorway.

'We didn't know what happened to you!' Tania pocketed her phone.

'I know. It's a big operation, easy to get lost

in.' I smiled amiably. 'I wanted to talk to Petra's coworkers, to see if she'd been in touch with any of them.'

'And had she?' Strangwell asked.

'I don't think so. They say that she turned standoffish when she started working for you. Was that one of your conditions?'

His cold eyes turned fractionally chillier. 'I expect everyone who works for me to protect the confidentiality of our clients. The fact that NetSquad talked to you without permission makes me think I haven't been clear in communicating that rule.'

Tania Crandon flushed again. It was clearly supposed to be her fault that her team had chatted with me. She started to apologize, but I cut her short.

'You have a young and energetic team. And I'm guessing that if you tamp down their exuberance, you'll lose the best qualities of their work. I'm V. I. War — '

'I know who you are. Your uncle is here. We'd all like to talk to you, to make sure you don't do something that might jeopardize our ability to find Petra.'

I didn't know if he was being an SOB because I'd spoken to the NetSquad, or because I was Petra's cousin and she'd disappeared on him — or because it was his nature — but I followed him into his office. I knew Peter was there, of course, and it wasn't surprising to see George Dornick, since he was advising the campaign on security, but I was startled to see Harvey Krumas as well.

Of the four men, only Strangwell looked at ease, his cold, shrewd eyes surveying me to see how I was reacting to the group. Harvey and Peter were both flushed — whether from anger, fear, or some other emotion — I couldn't decipher their expressions. Even Dornick, a vision in pearl-gray shantung and pink shirting, looked ill at ease.

I moved forward before Strangwell could take complete control of the encounter. 'Mr. Krumas, we met at your son's fundraiser on Navy Pier. George, have you come in to augment police efforts to find Petra? Mr. Strangwell, can you tell us what Petra's been working on the last ten days or so? She's been seen in some odd places, and it would help if I knew whether you'd sent her to them or she'd been going on her own.'

'Odd places?' Dornick said. 'Like what?'

'Like the Mighty Waters Freedom Center a few nights after it was fire-bombed.' I touched my face inadvertently. 'Like my childhood home the night someone threw a smoke bomb through the window.'

'Petra wouldn't go to South Chicago, not unless you took her there. Damn it, Vic, if you put her in front of a crew of gangbangers — ' My uncle's outburst lacked conviction, apparently even to himself, since he let Dornick cut him off midsentence.

'Les says Petra was playing at detective for you, Vicki.'

'Vic,' I corrected.

Strangwell ignored me. 'I had to read Petra the riot act when I found she was looking up

356

information for Vicki here on campaign time. I'm sorry, Peter. Now I can't help wondering if I wounded her pride, and she ran away.'

'It's not like Petra to be hypersensitive,' my uncle said, 'but you're such a ruthless SOB, Strangwell, maybe you were crueler than you realized at the moment.'

'This is a very strange chorus.' I was trying not to lose my temper because that would cost me judgment. 'Is that what you did while I was waiting? Agree on the song and the harmony? Petra ran away because big, mean Les was too tough for her? I chewed her out good and hard for rummaging through my private possessions, and she bounced back like the proverbial Pillsbury Doughboy. But now you want me to think she might have run off because Les hurt her feelings?'

'George is putting a team together for us,' Harvey Krumas said. 'We know you love your cousin. But someone like you will hurt us more than help us.'

'Someone like me being what?'

'A pretty ineffectual solo op,' Strangwell said crisply. 'You haven't found a person you've been hunting for over a month. But you did get a wonderful nun killed.'

I felt it where he intended it, right below the diaphragm, that place where your insides collapse in on you when you think of all the terrible mistakes you've made.

'I'm impressed that you've gone to so much trouble to uncover my workload.' I tried to keep my voice steady. 'Still, I don't think you should discount what I can do.'

'I don't want you to do *anything*.' My uncle was close to tears. 'Rachel has left town to be with the girls, and I'm turning everything over to George. He's in charge.'

'What did Derek Hatfield tell you when you met with the FBI?' I asked. 'Is he comfortable, too, with letting George's team run the search?'

'They're overworked, Vicki,' Dornick said. 'Of course they'll put some agents in play. But Hatfield knows what I can do, and he knows he can trust my operatives to behave sensibly if it turns out we have a ransom or hostage situation on our hands.'

I looked at my uncle. 'Petra usually calls Rachel at least once a day. Hasn't she been in touch at all?'

My uncle made a rough, meaningless gesture. 'We kept calling and getting her voice mail. Why she can't answer — '

'Her battery seems to be dead,' Dornick said.

I raised my eyebrows. 'You've been using your GPS monitors to track her, then. Where did you last pick up a trace?'

Dornick pressed his lips together. He hadn't meant to tell me he was tracking Petra, but he didn't compound the blunder by trying to deny it. 'We didn't get on it until early this morning, so we don't know where she went after she ran out your back door.'

'Now that you have Hatfield's acquiescence in letting the private sector handle the search, what are your plans?'

Dornick smiled thinly. 'The first thing we'll

do, of course, is to sweat Merton.'

I was astonished. 'You really think the Anacondas are involved in this, Georgie?'

He flushed at the nickname. 'Don't be naïve, Vicki . . . Vic. You know that even doing life at Stateville, Merton runs a big chunk of the South and West sides of this city. Drugs, whores, ID theft. We can squeeze him where it hurts.'

'And that would be where?' I asked politely. 'He can't do more time than he's already doing.'

'He's proud of his daughter. We can put pressure on her.'

'I didn't think they were close,' I objected.

'That doesn't mean he wouldn't be upset as hell if her law firm decided she was a security risk,' Dornick said.

'And if it turns out Merton had nothing to do with Petra's disappearance, will you restore Dayo Merton's reputation and make sure she gets another job as good as the one she has now?' I asked, adding to my uncle, 'Is that how you'd want Petra treated?'

'If he's behind her disappearance, he's already treating her — '

'Okay. So you'll start by sitting on the Hammer. And, at the same time, just in case . . . '

'We'll pull in some of the Anacondas who hold a grudge against . . . well, let's say, against your dad. People like this Steve Sawyer you've been looking for.'

'You know where he is?'

A little smile played around Dornick's mouth, condescension mostly. 'I feel pretty confident I can track him down.'

'And we'll talk to you, Vic,' Strangwell said. 'We need to know what Petra was doing for you.'

Peter was looking at Harvey Krumas with an odd, almost pleading expression. It seemed to me that the two men were holding their breath, waiting for my answer.

'Nothing, really.' I spoke slowly, studying their faces, trying to guess what they were hoping to hear. 'When I was injured in the fire that killed Sister Frances, my eyes were damaged. They told me not to look at a computer for a few days, and Petra offered to look up an address in one of my databases. Then she told me Les here had sat on her and that she couldn't do the search.'

'Are you telling the truth?' Harvey Krumas demanded.

'That's a useless question, Mr. Krumas. If I say yes, would you believe me? And why on earth would I say no? Besides, why do you care? It's data that's readily available to the public at large. What difference does it make if Petra saw it or not?'

Before any of the men could speak, we heard a muffled shout outside the door, a scrabbling sound as the lock was pushed back. The door opened, and the candidate himself walked in.

35

In the Hall of the Titans

Harvey Krumas gaped at his son. Dornick got to his feet, but, for once, he seemed at a loss, looking from Peter to Harvey and then to Les Strangwell, who picked up the cue and spoke first.

'Brian, you have a full schedule with donors in L.A. today. Why did you cancel that? We're going to have to do some serious damage control out there now.'

'Chrissake, Les, the damage control isn't about me and some B-movie starlets but about finding Petra Warshawski. I need to be here.' Brian's tie was unknotted, and his dark hair hadn't seen a comb for some time.

'We have the situation under control,' Les said. 'George is putting his best people into finding Petra.'

'How about just once, Les, Dad, George — and whoever you two are' — Brian looked at my uncle and me without recognition — 'just once, we pretend this is my campaign, my life, my staffers, that we aren't all pawns in your big power game. I want to know what the cops have said about Petra and what we know about her disappearance. And why is George here, at damage-control central, instead of meeting with his best people to get them moving?'

'We want to minimize media attention on Petra's disappearance,' Strangwell said. 'You coming back here like this sends a message that we think it's more serious than it is.'

Brian's face turned white. 'Are you saying it isn't serious when a young woman on my staff vanishes into thin air? The Web is saying the FBI suspects kidnapping. And you're nuts if you don't think the media isn't already on it like flies on a dead cow. When I got to LAX this morning, I had a dozen mikes under my nose wanting to know where I was when the kid disappeared and what did I think about it, and on and on and on. Tell me what's happened. Not the sound bite you think I should chew on but what the cops and the FBI have said and done.'

'Of course,' Dornick said. 'I'll tell Derek Hatfield he should give Brian a full briefing on what the Bureau knows. And I'll go to my office and get my team organized. Warshawski, you want to come with me?'

I started to get up, surprised at the invitation, then realized Dornick was talking to my uncle. As soon as Brian heard the Warshawski name, he realized who my uncle was and crossed the room to his side.

'I'm sorry, Pete. With all this crisis, I didn't recognize you. I'm sorry as hell about Petra. I can't believe her work with the campaign had anything to do with her disappearance. But George will find her, I'm sure, whatever she was doing. Is Rachel here? Do you need anything? A place to stay? Anything at all?'

'That's right,' Harvey Krumas put in. 'Come

on out to the house, Pete. Jolenta will be glad to have you to look after. We all feel helpless, and she needs to be doing something.'

'Helpless? Not you, Harve.' My uncle gave a bitter smile. 'Besides, I want to be where I can get to the FBI or — or anyone — fast. I'm fine at the Drake.'

'The Roscoe Street apartment, then,' Brian urged. 'I can go out to Barrington Hills with Dad. Why should you run up a hotel bill?'

'No, you need to stay in the city, where you're accessible,' Strangwell told Brian. 'Now that you're back here, we can schedule some events and some press. This is a good opportunity to build support with women, showing how sensitive you are to their needs . . . violence against women, that kind of thing. Art and Melanie are standing by with some ideas on how to craft — '

'Les, you are a fucking machine! I don't want you to craft a statement on how to talk about a missing kid. I want a rundown on what we're doing to find her. And Pete, I want to make sure you and Rachel are getting all the support you need. You're sure you don't want the apartment?'

'Thanks, Brian, let's leave it lie. Vic, you can ride up to the Drake with me.'

That was an announcement, a command, that the meeting was over. Harvey Krumas and George Dornick lingered to talk to Strangwell, but Brian left the office with Peter and me.

'You're Petra's cousin? Aren't you the person I talked to last night? Am I right that she was in your office yesterday and that's the last place she was seen?'

'Vic doesn't know anything about Petra,' Peter growled. 'She thinks Petra was in her office, but she can't prove it.'

'It was her bracelet I found outside my back door,' I said to the candidate.

'A million kids wear those rubber bracelets,' Peter said.

'And Rachel identified her from the video footage. I went to Petra's apartment today. Someone broke down her back door. She had something somebody wants or knew something. Ever since Strangwell moved her onto his personal team, she's behaved oddly. What did he have her doing, Mr. Krumas?'

'You don't need to know that,' my uncle said quickly. 'It won't help find her.'

'Petra got into something over her head. Her laptop is missing, so we can't check the websites she visited. But either she got in with a dangerous crowd on her own or something she was doing for the campaign got her in trouble. Does she have a drug habit I didn't recognize?'

'No, damn you to hell!'

'Gambling?'

'Get your mind out of the gutter you live in. My girls were brought up to live decent lives. I don't tolerate the crap that Tony let you get away with. If Petra was kidnapped, it's because you introduced her to those fucking Anacondas!'

My uncle's roar brought people out of their cubicles to stare at us. They did a double take at the sight of Brian and began moving their thumbs madly over their handhelds. A small crowd gathered fast, some staffers demanding autographs, others just cheering their boy.

'I'd better say a few words,' Brian muttered to us.

To his team, he flashed his Bobbyesque smile, holding up a hand to acknowledge the applause like a modest major leaguer acknowledging a home run. He gave a quick thank-you to the group for their hard work, a mention of Petra's disappearance and how worried he knew they all were, an assurance that if a sparrow fell, Brian Krumas would rescue it.

'That's it, guys. These are a couple of people who are going to help us find Petra.' He ushered Peter and me into a nearby conference room. 'I'll talk to the FBI, of course, but — Vic, is it? — better fill me in on what you know.'

'I think she ran out the back door of my building,' I said. 'I'm hoping she ran clean away from the two people she was with, but I can't imagine where she's gone. I need to talk to her college roommate — '

'No, you don't!' Peter screamed. 'You need to stay the fuck away from this — far, far away from this — and let George handle it.'

'Peter, we're all upset, but — '

'You're not just useless, you're dangerous!' my uncle shouted. 'George knows more than any detective I've ever heard of, private or public, including the FBI. He'll find Petra without letting it get messy. If you look for her, chances are she'll burn to death in front of your eyes.'

I turned very cold, but I said levelly, 'Petra was looking for something the last few weeks. She organized an outing to your old place in Back of the Yards. She was on Houston Street ten days ago when someone forced an evacuation from my old home. She went to the Freedom Center three days after Sister Frances died. What was Petra looking for? Something for you, Mr. Krumas? Or was it for you, Peter? Is that why she was claiming an interest in the Warshawski past?'

My uncle shook his head like a cornered bull. 'My girl wants to look at her family roots, and you want it to be some filthy story involving the Anacondas or whatever mud you wallow in.'

I thought of Petra's fixation with the Nellie Fox baseball. I dumped the red sweatshirt and Scarlett O'Hara hat on the conference room table and pulled the ball from my case.

'Why did Petra want this so badly, Peter?'

Peter and Brian both bent over my hand, looking at the ball with the same puzzlement, and then my uncle's face turned the color of putty. Sweat covered his face so fast it was as if he had sunk in a pool of water.

'What is it?' Brian asked.

'It's nothing. It's an old baseball,' Peter muttered. But he was clutching a chair back for support.

I began to worry about his heart, but when I said I'd get water and call Rachel he brushed my hand away with a violent gesture. 'Leave Rachel out of this.'

'My apartment was ransacked two nights before Petra disappeared. Is this what they were looking for?'

'How should I know?' my uncle said. His voice

had lost its belligerence. 'You're the one who's so friendly with the blacks in this city, not me.'

'The people in my apartment weren't black. Someone saw them.' Of course my witness said he couldn't make out their race, but my patience was wearing thin. 'Did Petra mention the ball in one of her daily chats home? Did you tell her to come back to my place to get it?'

'Nellie Fox. She knew I was a Nellie Fox fan, so she — '

'Peter, who are you protecting? Petra had never heard of Fox. When I mentioned his name, she thought the Sox had put a woman at second. Why won't you tell me what the story is with this ball?'

'There is no story. There's nothing to know about it.'

I rolled the ball in my hand while my uncle watched uneasily. The door opened, and Strangwell and Dornick came in with Harvey Krumas, who looked in surprise at my uncle and me. Once again, though, it was Strangwell who spoke first.

'Brian, the kids said you'd popped in here. We've got Global Entertainment in the situation room. Gina's here to do your makeup.'

The candidate let Strangwell lead him away, but Harvey Krumas and Dornick demanded to know why Peter wasn't back at the Drake lying down. 'You look like crap, Pete. What's going on here?'

'Brian wanted to talk to me,' I said. 'Peter wanted to stay close to me. We were talking about what Petra might have been looking for in my childhood home. Any hunches?'

Dornick said, 'I don't know Petra, so I don't know what might have struck her fancy. Girls her age get romantic ideas about family history sometimes. Maybe she thought there were Warshawski heirlooms.'

'Mr. Krumas? You know her better than I do. You're her 'Uncle Harvey,' after all. Peter says she wasn't looking for a baseball.'

'This is outrageous,' Harvey fumed. 'Pete's sick with worry — we all are — and you're treating this like some video game.'

I tossed the baseball in the air, caught it, and put it into my briefcase. 'You're right. I'll get this to a lab, see what they can tell me about it, and start searching for Petra.'

'No!' Peter said. 'How many times do I have to repeat it? Stay the fuck out of this!'

Dornick said, 'Out of curiosity, Vicki — Vic — if you were going to look for her, where would you start?'

'I started at her apartment, but someone had been there ahead of me. Since Peter doesn't want me looking, I'm not going to hunt elsewhere. But I would probably talk to Larry Alito.'

'Alito?' Krumas and Dornick spoke his name in unison. Then Dornick said, 'I wouldn't trust much that an alkie like Larry would have to say.'

'He met with Les Strangwell a couple of days ago. I'd like to know what Strang — '

'How do you know that?' Krumas demanded.

'I'm an investigator, Mr. Krumas. It's my job to find out stuff. I'm not sure what it would take to get Alito to tell me about that conversation, or some of the other things he knows, but — '

'Guy would sell his wife for a six-pack, probably turn in his own kid for a keg. Stay away from him, Vic, he's bad news.' Dornick was giving me an indulgent smile, as if I were a toddler who needed extra coaching.

'He's short-tempered and he drinks, but he's an experienced cop. And Strangwell wanted him for an urgent, confidential assignment the day before Petra disappeared.'

Dornick laughed. 'You think Larry has something to do with Petra's disappearance? I'm surprised you've made it in this field as long as you have, Vic. An imagination like yours belongs on TV. Speaking of which, what are you imagining about that Nellie Fox baseball?'

'And you know it's a Nellie Fox baseball because . . . '

The words hung in the air. For a moment, Harvey looked like a stuffed bear on a mantelpiece. And then Dornick laughed, and said, 'Lucky guess. Fox was the household god in your grandfather's family for everyone except your renegade father. Pete, let me give you a lift up to the Drake. Vic, listen to your uncle and stay the hell away from searching for Petra.'

36

What on Earth Is Going On?

I left the men hailing cabs on Michigan Avenue, I wanted to see all three of them out of sight before reclaiming my car, but even then I took a roundabout route, catching a bus down Michigan to the south end of Grant Park, where only a handful of tourists passed the homeless guys lying on the grass, and it would be easier to see if I had company.

Everything in the meeting I'd just left was setting off warning bells. When Peter should have been with his wife, or talking to cops, or even talking to me, why was he huddled with Harvey Krumas and George Dornick in a meeting in the office of Chicago's most feared political op? And then there were the repeated injunctions for me to stay away from Petra, as if they knew where she was or maybe had received some kind of threat or even a ransom note.

It wasn't until I sat at the foot of a statue on a shallow flight of stairs that I realized how tired I was. Using the red sweatshirt from my briefcase as a pillow, I leaned back against the crumbling concrete steps and shut my eyes.

The Nellie Fox baseball meant something important, even devastating, to Peter. Harvey Krumas and Dornick both knew about the ball; that was clear from their reactions. Petra had

370

been ordered to get it from me. That was why she had behaved so oddly about it, with her clumsy story about wanting it for a surprise present for her father. Dornick or Krumas, or even Les Strangwell, had learned that I had the ball probably because Petra had burbled away about it at the office.

I could almost hear her gusty laugh as she informed her pod mates in the NetSquad: 'Can you believe I thought the White Sox had played a woman at second? Daddy would disown me if he learned I didn't know about Nellie Fox! My cousin says he was, like, a big star a hundred years ago.'

All the Millen Gen interns texted or Twittered constantly. Nellie Fox, transgender ballplayer, would become part of Twitter that day. That part was easy to imagine. Word filtered up to . . . Whom? The candidate? The Chicago Strangler? The candidate's father? One of them told Petra she had to get the baseball from me.

That much I could believe, but I wasn't sure that the ball was what the thugs who'd torn apart my house and office had been hunting for. Why had they taken the picture of the slow-pitch team if all they wanted was the ball?

'It doesn't make sense,' I said, so lost in thought I spoke out loud.

'That's what I be saying all along. It don't make no sense. Those rockets they send up, they messing with the weather. Then they use their cellphones to watch you, see if you know what they up to.'

The speaker had been around the corner of

371

the statue's plinth from me, on another short flight of steps. When he realized I was actually listening to him, he asked for a donation so he could get something to eat. I stared at him without seeing him. *They use their cellphones to watch you.*

They were watching me. They'd tailed me this morning. Were they watching Petra as well? *'Damn it, little cousin, who are you working for?'* Not Dornick, or he'd know where she was. Maybe he did know where she was. Maybe that was why he didn't want me looking for her. I thought about flipping a coin. Heads, he doesn't know where Petra is. Tails, he does.

Was that what they were all talking about in Strangwell's office? How will it play out for Brian Krumas's campaign if we produce Petra versus us leaving her in hiding? Was that why my aunt had gone back to Overland Park, because Dornick assured her he knew where the kid was and would produce her safe and sound? But that really made no sense, Petra helping thugs break into my office and then they put her on ice. Well, maybe I could see it. They didn't want their thugs ID'd, so they wanted to keep Petra away from the cops.

On an impulse, I tried Rachel's cellphone. It rolled over to her voice mail. I tried her home number in Overland Park. The phone was answered by a man, who refused to say who he was or where Rachel was, only that he would take a message for Rachel.

I couldn't tell a complete stranger to ask Rachel whether Dornick knew where Petra was hiding. The man answering the phone could be anywhere in the world intercepting Rachel's and Peter's calls, and he could be working for anyone.

I gave him my name and number, but no other details, then demanded to know who he was.

'Someone who's answering the phone.' He hung up.

I hugged my knees to my chest. After the Navy Pier fundraiser, Les Strangwell had pulled Petra onto his personal staff. It was then that she'd suddenly announced an interest in my childhood home and the house in Back of the Yards. And in my dad's possessions in the trunk. She knew I had the baseball. So there was something else that Strangwell wanted her to find. A photograph, since intruders had stolen the picture of my dad's team? Something involving baseballs or baseball teams? What did I have that could matter to Les Strangwell and George Dornick? Nothing. Nothing at all, except obviously the Nellie Fox ball, which brought me back to where I started, spinning like a globe. No, nothing as grand as a globe. Spinning like water spiraling down the drain.

Peter and George Dornick wouldn't care about Brian's campaign, only Les Strangwell and the candidate's father would put that first. But when I showed up unannounced, they kept on talking behind closed doors for half an hour. They were deciding on how to handle me. But what were they deciding to do about Petra? And why had my aunt gone home?

'Was it a game to you, little cousin? Or did

they utter those mystic, magic words, 'national security,' and get you to believe them? They told you under no circumstances to confide in me. What about your Uncle Sal?'

'Not Uncle Sal, Uncle *Sam*, Uncle *Sam* be watching you. He know when you be sleeping, / He know when you awake, / He say it all be for national security's sake.'

My partner on the other side of the statue's plinth was still in full throttle on the people he said were watching him. Since I myself kept talking out loud, it was hard for me to feel that I was a more stable girder on the bridge than him. When was it paranoia and when were they really watching you?

I got up and pulled a five from my pocket for my companion. One thing about our outbursts: they'd driven everyone else away from us. Although, these days, with so many people spouting their secrets into the ether, it was hard to know who had real friends and who had invisible ones.

I crossed Lake Shore Drive at Roosevelt Road and waited for a northbound bus at the natural history museum. My cousin was queen of the texters. When we were riding back from South Chicago together and I mentioned I hadn't heard her on her phone, she'd confessed she'd been texting. Had she sent a message to Strangwell, telling him we hadn't been able to get into the Houston Street house? Did he send a team down then to throw a smoke bomb into my old house so they could search for . . . what?

Petra texting. She'd been texting at the

Freedom Center. Petra leaning in the doorway to Caroline Zabinska's apartment, her hands busy in front of her. I'd been ninety percent unconscious, and she hadn't thought I'd notice, but maybe she'd summoned the person who collected the bag of evidence I'd been gathering, those pieces of the Molotov cocktail bottles I wanted to send to the Cheviot Labs to test what kind of accelerant had been used.

The FBI and Homeland Security had both been watching the Freedom Center building, but they'd claimed they didn't have any record of the person who'd broken in to get my evidence bag. So they knew who'd gone in and didn't care. Or someone who had very big clout persuaded the feds to look the other way. They had photographed me going in that night, but not Petra. And not the person who'd stolen the evidence bag. And then, the very next day, the apartment was taken apart by some tame construction company, paid for by a man who wanted to make a donation to the sisters for the Freedom Center. Very cute.

Brian Krumas had said something critical during the meeting. It had only registered at the time as a faint puzzler, and now, playing back what I could remember of the conversation, I couldn't put my finger on it. It was something about his relationship with my uncle, something that connected my uncle to Sister Frankie, but the more I pushed on it, the further it retreated from my mind.

Petra wasn't a drug user, I was sure of that despite putting the question to Peter. As for gambling or some other expensive vice, I couldn't picture it. But I wouldn't have pictured her breaking into my office, either.

I was tangling myself up like a bowl of cold spaghetti. Assume, for sanity's sake, that Petra was an unwitting or unwilling partner in Strangwell's machinations. She was an overgrown puppy, not a malicious schemer. If she was in over her head, I needed to help her out. If she was trying to hide out in this big, bad city, or if she was hitchhiking to her friend Kelsey's, Homeland Security, or even George Dornick's Mountain Hawk Security team, could track her easily. I needed to warn her. They know when you're sleeping, they know when you're awake, and, if you're texting, they can find you so fast it will take you completely by surprise.

I pulled out my phone. I didn't have the nimble thumbs of a twenty-year-old, but I tapped out:

Petra: wherever u r, stop texting, calling. Take battery out of phone: disconnect. U can b traced by GPS. Lay low until I send all clear. Trust me. Vic.

Please trust me, little cousin, I begged in my head. *I promise if you are in the hands of baddies, I will not jeopardize your safety. But if you are hiding and scared, let me clear this up. I'm putting my best person on it.*

Of course, I, too, could be traced through my cellphone. Piece of cake, for a sophisticated crew. I called my voice mail and left a message that I would be off cellphone for a while and gave the number of my answering service for people to call. I took out the battery and stuck it in my briefcase.

Five buses had stopped while I'd been churning over what I knew or didn't know. I boarded the next one, a Number 6, that lumbered over to Michigan and slowly took me up to the hotel where I'd left my car this morning. When I handed my ticket through the cashier's window, I was told someone had already paid for my parking. I asked to see the receipt, sure there was some mistake, but when the attendant found it it was for cash. No one could remember what the man looked like who paid the bill, but he'd described the car, told them the ticket number, even paid a lost-ticket premium.

Strangwell, or Homeland Security, wanted me to know they could find me and deal with me whenever it suited them. I drove home slowly, meandering along the side streets, not because I wanted to check for the tail that was surely behind me but because I was too tired for speed. They could find me and stomp me out. Why hadn't they done so already? Maybe because they thought I had whatever it was they were looking for. As soon as I produced whatever it was, they would dispose of me. Sister Frankie's head, full of flames, appeared in front of me, and I shuddered so violently that I had to pull over to the curb until it passed.

The hunt, with a full pack of hounds closing in on a lame and limping fox and her brash and ignorant cub, that was my cousin and me just now. I went back to my burrow because I didn't know where else to go. But I didn't feel safe, reaching home.

I took my neighbor and the dogs into the backyard, away from any possible surveillance, and explained the situation as best I could, given how little I understood of it myself.

'You don't think Peewee's pa is really in on this!' Mr. Contreras was horrified.

'I think he knows what his pals are looking for, and he's a frightened man indeed, but I don't believe he knowingly put his kid in harm's way.'

'So where is she?' the old man fretted.

I shook my head. 'I'm too tired to think clearly. I'm hoping she's run away, hoping they don't know where she is. If she calls you, tell her to lay low. Then tell her to hang up at once before they can trace her. These guys have me totally off balance. If only I had the faintest idea what they want!'

37

A Bass Ride . . . or Was It Vile?

The old man and the dogs helped me search my apartment for any obvious intruders or bombs. Mr. Contreras offered to feed me, but I was too tired to eat. As soon as they left, I went to bed and fell deeply asleep. I was so tired, none of my anxieties had the power to disturb me. But when my phone rang at one in the morning, I was instantly awake.

'Petra?' I cried into the mouthpiece.

'Ms. Warshawski, is that you?' The voice on the other end was diffident.

'Who is this?' I choked out.

'I woke you again. I'm sorry. It seems like it's only in the middle of the night that I have the courage to talk to you.'

I'd been so sure the call would be from Petra, or a ransom demand, that I couldn't think of anyone else, any other context. I lay back in the bed, trying to calm my pounding heart enough that I could think.

'I saw about your cousin on the news. It's a terrible worry, when someone you love disappears on you.' The hesitant voice was flat.

Behind the speaker came the sound of hospital pages. *Rose Hebert!* My skin crawled. *She had snatched Petra so that I could understand how bereft she'd been at losing Lamont Gadsden.*

'Knowing how you must be suffering, I've been feeling guilty that I haven't been wholly truthful with you.' She took a breath, the way she had the last time she called in the middle of the night, when she launched into the painful admission of her love for Lamont Gadsden.

'When you asked if I knew another name Steve Sawyer might be using, I said no. But back in the sixties, the Anacondas, they all took African names. Lamont, his code name in the gang was Lumumba.'

There was a long silence, during which I thought I might break into hysterical laughter. Petra had disappeared, perhaps been kidnapped, and the only thing Rose could think of was her long-vanished lover. It was hard to think of a response, but, in the end, I asked what Steve Sawyer's gang name had been.

'I don't know, but it was probably African. Like I told you, Johnny Merton, he gave his girl an African name. Johnny was big on all those African independence movements. He made Lamont study up on Lumumba, and Lamont talked to me about Lumumba and the Congo that summer, the summer before he disappeared, when he was trying to persuade me to be liberated with him . . . '

Her voice trailed off, into the confusion of memories of adolescence, where liberation meant sex as well as politics. I wondered why Rose hadn't told me earlier; what about me would have made her think I would find African nationalism shocking.

She answered in her half-dead voice, 'I guess I

380

was afraid if I told you about Lamont and Lumumba, you might be, well, like some folks, like my daddy even, who thought if you called yourself after an African national hero you were next door to being a Communist. And then you'd stop looking for Lamont.'

I managed to thank her, and to tell her not to worry, that I'd see whether I could find Lamont under his nom de guerre. 'Is there anything else it would be good for me to know? Something we could cover tonight? It may be hard to reach me for the next week or so.'

She thought about it seriously but decided she didn't have any more secrets to reveal, at least not this morning. After she hung up, I lay back down, but I couldn't get back to sleep. My brain started jumping around again among all the confused ideas I'd had yesterday afternoon. *Lumumba.* I tried to think about Patrice Lumumba, but it wasn't a good meditation. Instead, visions of his torture and death blended with my images of Sister Frankie's death, my fears about Petra, my fears for my own safety.

I sat up. I'd heard the name Lumumba recently. It was connected in my mind to my father, which didn't make any sense at all. It was my mother, not my father, who cared about international politics. She would have talked about Lumumba's murder. But I would have been too young at the time for the name to stay with me.

I went into the living room and plugged in my laptop. Sitting cross-legged on the couch, I looked up Lumumba. He had died in 1961. I couldn't possibly be remembering a conversation about him that went that far back into my childhood. Since I was awake and alert, I searched for Lumumba in the databases I use for background checks. I found a singer with the name and a doctor in New York, but deeper looks at them showed that both were too young to be Lamont Gadsden under a new name.

It was two in the morning, the heart of darkness, the time of deepest loneliness. I thought of Morrell, in Mazär-i-Sharif and wondered if he, too, was awake and lonely or if his old friend Marcie Love was keeping him company. Or perhaps a new friend more in tune with his mind than I had been.

These were such strange times we were living through, the Age of Fear, with endless war around the world, never knowing who we could trust, with our bank accounts and our e-mails an open book to any garden-variety hacker. Even though I use the Web constantly, I'm an old-fashioned detective. I do better on foot and in person than through the ether.

Someone had gone after Petra the old-fashioned way, breaking into her apartment. Had they made off with her laptop, or had she taken it with her? I looked again at the rudimentary surveillance footage from my office camera that I'd e-mailed myself. It didn't look to me as though any of the office breakers — Petra or her two companions — were carrying a backpack or anything big enough to be holding her laptop. So someone had gone after that, looking for . . . her e-mails, I supposed . . . or to see whether she'd been looking up African national heroes.

Spy software. Of course, Petra had used my office computer, my big Mac Pro, one night at the beginning of the summer. That was how she'd known my keypad code. I wasn't a high-tech wizard, but I knew enough to see which websites she'd been looking at. They might tell me something. And it was better, anyway, than sitting in the dark, feeling the Age of Fear close in on me.

I started to get dressed again, but I paused while zipping my jeans. I had to assume from now on that whatever I did, wherever I went, I'd have some shadow from Homeland Security, or Mountain Hawk, or maybe both, and I'd just as soon not be caught alone on the streets in the middle of the night. Even if I could sneak out to my car, it was possible — perhaps probable — that they'd installed some kind of GPS tracker in it, some little gizmo I wouldn't be able to find easily. They wouldn't have to stay with me on the streets to keep tabs on me. They could use their hotshot triangulation software to watch me online.

A thump on the back stairs made my heart jump again. I took the Smith & Wesson and slipped into the kitchen, tiptoeing on the tile. I laid my head against the door and squinted out through the glass. And felt another bubble of hysteria rise in me. The sound was Jake Thibaut, hauling his double bass up the back stairs to the third floor.

I put the gun down and unlocked the kitchen door. When Thibaut reached the upper landing, he jumped almost as much as I had on hearing him.

'V. I. Warshawski! Don't sneak up on me like that! I don't have insurance that covers dropping bass down stairs when surprised by detectives.'

'Sorry,' I said. 'I'm so edgy these days that, when I heard you, I thought it was my housewreckers on their way back. Where were you playing?'

'Ravinia. And then we went out for a drink or three. What are you doing up at this hour? Any word on your cousin?' He drew the bass up next to him.

'If anyone has heard about my cousin, they're not telling me.' I measured myself against the bass's case, an idea coming to me. 'How drunk are you?'

'Bass players don't get drunk. It's one of our hallmarks. Long, tall instruments give their players hollow legs. Why, you want me to bow a perfect fourth for you?'

'I want you to smuggle me in your case out to someplace where I can catch a cab and not be seen.'

He was quiet for a minute, and then said, 'How drunk are you?'

'Not drunk. Terrified.'

He rested the bass against his back door. 'You don't seem like the *terrifiable* type.'

'No, of course not. We PI's thrive on death and danger. We don't have the feelings ordinary people do. I'm a disgrace to the club, letting trifles like a missing cousin and a murdered nun rattle me.'

384

In the dim light coming from my kitchen window, I saw him give me a speculative look. 'Anyone going to shoot at me or set me on fire if I wheel you out to Belmont Avenue?'

'Anything is possible. You ever been held up by a junkie who thinks he can sell your fiddle for a fix?'

Thibaut laughed softly. 'One advantage of playing a really big instrument: people know they can't race off down the street with it. Let me put Bessie to rest, and I'll be with you. I hope you're clean. I don't want sweat and grease or anything on the inside of the case.'

I went back into my place and carefully wiped all the protective cream from my face and arms. I realized I was hungry; I hadn't eaten since breakfast yesterday morning. Fatigue and anxiety had kept me from thinking about food, but I was suddenly ravenous. Thibaut came into my kitchen as I was hastily putting together a cheese sandwich.

'You can't eat inside the case,' he said. 'Probably you won't be able to breathe in it, either. The old guy downstairs is going to sue me if you suffocate?'

'Nah. He'll just let the dogs chew on your bass.'

Thibaut helped himself to a chunk of the pecorino I was eating. 'I can't carry you down the stairs. I'm not sure the case would hold your weight, but I'm sure I can't.'

'I'll come down the front stairs and get out to the garden through the basement door. When you're at the bottom of the back stairs, I'll try to creep along in your shadow. I'll wait to climb into the case until you're at the back gate. You can wheel me down the alley to your car.'

I went into my bathroom to rub mascara on my cheekbones so they wouldn't reflect light back from the streetlamps; I hoped it wouldn't come off in Thibaut's case. I put on a navy windbreaker and stuck my keys and my new wallet, with cash and passport inside, in my hip pocket. I checked that the safety on the Smith & Wesson was on, pulled a Cubs cap low over my forehead, and ran as lightly as I could down the front stairs.

The only difficult moment came as I passed Mr. Contreras's front door. Mitch let out a sharp bark and a whine, demanding to join me. Once I went past him and into the basement, he quieted down.

When I slid back the bolt on the basement exit, Thibaut was just bumping his case down the last flight of back-porch steps. I waited for him to reach the walk, then slipped into his shadow. He worked the move like a pro, not looking over his shoulder for me but pulling out his phone and complaining to someone he addressed as Lily, 'You must be stoned as well as drunk to want to practice the Schulhoff piece this hour of the night. But, my little chickadee, to hear is to obey. I'm on my way.'

At the back gate, I managed to stuff my sixty-eight-inch frame into the fifty-six-inch case. As Thibaut had warned. I could barely breathe. The few minutes where he bumped along the broken concrete into the alley and, panting and wheezing, laid the case across the flattened-out entrance to the backseat were an agony for my spine and neck. Once I was on the seat, he unhooked the case's hinges. I pushed the lid up a few inches with my knees so that I could straighten out my spine.

Again without looking over his shoulder, Thibaut asked for my office address. I told him he could drop me on Belmont, where I'd flag a cab.

'V. I. Warshawski, I didn't seriously risk the life of this twenty-two-hundred-dollar case to drive you four blocks. Tell me where you're going.'

I didn't put up a serious fight. I was glad of the offer. I sent him on a route up past Wrigley Field, turning onto side streets until he was sure no one was following him. Finally we drove to an intersection a block north and east of my office. If the office was under surveillance, I didn't want anyone registering Thibaut's car in a database.

I flexed my spine and did a few neck stretches before leaning into the driver's window to thank him. 'Who's Lily?'

'The fox terrier we had when I was a kid. When all this is over, I'll play a concert for you. The Schulhoff concertino, to commemorate my most exciting performance since my Marlborough Festival debut.'

He squeezed my fingers where they rested on his open window. The warmth of his hand stayed with me as I slipped into the shadow of the buildings on Oakley.

38

Confession in Myspace

I didn't know any unobtrusive way to get into my office. The alley exit opens only from the inside, and the windows are twelve feet from the ground. It would have to be through the front door.

At this hour of the morning, all the trendy bars and cafés in the area are closed. The coffee shop across the street would open in a few hours, but right now its glass front gleamed black under the streetlamps like a pond.

I moved cautiously down the street, gun in hand. No one was out that I could see. But if pros were conducting surveillance, it could be done by remote camera. They wouldn't have to be on the street.

A rat leaped from a garbage can at my approach, and I came close to screaming. I had to stop and gulp down the wave of panic that swept over me, as it ran out onto the sidewalk. Still, I couldn't hold back a little cry. A car drove up the street and turned left onto Cortlandt. It was missing a taillight. Dornick looked like the buttoned-down type who wouldn't let you work for him if your car was missing a light. Or would he use a car like this to make me think he wasn't watching me?

Or he could be . . . Enough! The Age of Fear

makes you crazy. I took a breath, crossed the street, and tapped in the new door code to my building. The lock wheezed as it always did, a loud sound in the still night, but I was tired of fear. I boldly opened the door, stopping long enough to tap each of the numbers on the pad so that anyone using a UV spray wouldn't be able to tell which ones unlocked the door. I flicked on the lights, not caring that they would spill out onto the street and advertise my presence.

My office suite still had a crime scene seal across the door, but I broke it and went into the chaos. For a moment, my spirits flagged again on seeing the mess. I made a feeble stab at straightening things out, putting drawers back in the desk, returning ordnance maps to their shelves, but the chaos was overwhelming. I wondered who I could hire to help since the temporary agency had backed away from me at warp speed.

I tried to remember the date that Petra had been in my office to use my computer, but I could only guess. It had been around two weeks before the Navy Pier fundraiser. I set up a program to find all the Internet sites visited during those weeks.

While the program ran, I knelt to collect papers from the floor, gathering them in a big bundle and laying them on the couch. One of the documents was the transcript of the Steve Sawyer trial. I flipped through the pages, looking again for my father's name, but instead 'Lumumba' jumped out at me.

'Lumumba has my picture,' Steve Sawyer had said on the stand.

Lumumba: Lamont, in the Anaconda's secret code. Lamont had Sawyer's picture. What did that mean? Was it some cryptic way of saying that Lamont had fingered him? Or did it mean he was expecting Lamont to testify for him. As in, Lamont has my picture, Lamont has my back.

I wondered if Curtis Rivers would interpret ... Curtis Rivers! I smacked my forehead. African names. Kimathi, that was what Rivers called the man who swept the sidewalk in front of his store. While my Internet-search program was running. I pulled up a separate browser window and looked up Kimathi.

Dedan Kimathi, a rebel leader in Kenya in the 1950s. Feeling a sort of nervous dread, I put the name into the Illinois Department of Corrections database. There he was: January 1967, convicted of murdering Harmony Newsome, served forty years, released a year ago January. No time off for good behavior, often in isolation for unspecified, violent outbreaks. Living since his release on Seventieth Place, at the same address as Fit for Your Hoof.

I stared at the screen for a long time, remembering Rivers's fury when I'd asked where to find Steve Sawyers, of Hammer Merton's scorn when I asked him the same question.

My brain was frozen. I couldn't concentrate on those old Anacondas or Miss Claudia's dying needs. If Petra hadn't gone missing, I'd have driven straight to Curtis Rivers's shop and camped out until he and Kimathi-Sawyers emerged. And then I'd have energetically convinced them to tell me what had happened to Lamont-Lumumba. But Petra was fragmenting my mind and sapping my energy.

I closed the browser window. The search program had finished, turning up over a thousand URLs for the ten days I'd bracketed. I started scrolling through them, startled to see the amount of time I spent on the Internet. It took about twenty minutes for me to find where Petra had been, but, once I got there, it was dead easy to follow her in. She'd been updating her MySpace pages. She hadn't logged in as Petra Warshawski. Instead, her page was called 'Campaign Girl.'

I had to create my own MySpace page to look at Petra's. I signed up under Peppy's full name, Princess Scheherazade of DuPage, and even created an e-mail address for her. I began to see why people liked using the site. The process of making up Peppy's biography and interests, the music she listened to — currently, 'You Ain't Nothin' But a Hound Dog' — took me away from my dark, disaster-filled office and my fears for my cousin's safety. For twenty minutes, I was in a fantasyland of my own creation.

Campaign Girl loved Natalie Walker's *Urban Angel*. She had five hundred friends. To read the messages they sent her, I needed Petra's password. Trying to figure that out would require either better computer tracking skills or more inside knowledge of Petra than I had. I concentrated on the posts she'd made on her profile page.

She started by explaining that she had to post anonymously because she was working on an important Senate campaign and if she said anything under her own name, or her candidate's name, she could get both of them in trouble.

'So I'm just Campaign Girl for now. And all of you homeys out there, *PLEASE* don't screw up and call me by my real name. Not unless you want me to lose my job. And that goes quintuple for you, Hank Albrecht, wanting stuffy old Janowic to win. My boy is going to beat yours with one hand behind his back. And I have a bottle of beer riding on it.'

I looked up Hank Albrecht, one of Petra's 'friends.' He had gone to college with my cousin and was in Chicago working for the incumbent.

A few days later, Petra was writing about the work she was doing for Brian, whom she scrupulously only called 'My Candidate.'

I know all you vegans out there think I'm the wickedest person on the planet, but I love being the meat queen, showing up at a Sunday barbecue loaded down with ribs and sausages. Mostly, it's for my teammates on the campaign. Whoever thought work would be this much fun?? I'm, like, doing blog searches to see who has bad stuff to put out against My Candidate, like anyone could, and the whole world wouldn't know it was the biggest crock ever. But everyone who meets My Candidate thinks Mr. President four years down the road, so we have tons of media and money and everything. And I'm, like, Saint Joan on a charger, going out and looking for dragons who want to attack us.

392

It wouldn't take a sophisticated code breaker to realize who Petra was, or who her candidate was, based on her posts. In fact, as I skimmed the comments, it was clear that many of her MySpace friends knew that the candidate was Brian. There was competitive ribbing from Hank Albrecht, the guy working for the incumbent. There were passionate pro-Brian posts. And then there were quite a few people who wrote about altogether unconnected stuff: dogs, clothes, favorite restaurants.

Petra wrote about Mr. Contreras and me. I was code-named DC, for 'Detecting Cousin.'

Every now and then I go over to see Uncle Sal, not that we're really related, and DC, who really is my cousin. She's, like, almost my mom's age, isn't that weird? Uncle Sal, who my detecting cousin only calls 'Mr. C.,' he can't get enough of my dad's company's ribs or of me. My cousin is jealous of me, isn't that fun? Uncle Sal likes to flirt with me, and it used to be her, you know. Sometimes they seem like an old married couple having the same kind of squabbles everyone's parents do. Oh my God, we all may end up like our parents, isn't that freaky?

I went over yesterday, and Uncle Sal was scolding DC for wanting to go talk to this old gang leader who's doing a hundred years for murder or whatever. And she's, like, it bugs me that people are too pissed off at me to answer the simplest questions, and I'm, like, so put on your big-girl underpants and move on. And Uncle Sal thought that was hysterical and laughed his head off. So DC got really huffy but was trying not to show it. I mean, I thought being a detective was more dramatic, like solving murders, collecting clues, not going out to prison to talk to some kind of ignorant black gangbanger.

I remembered that episode, and it made me angry that Petra had put it out for the whole world to read about. I made a face at the computer screen. 'Put on your big-girl underpants now, V.I.,' I muttered, and read on.

I focused on her posts about the work she'd done for Brian, wondering if any of the dragons she'd been sent to slay would turn out to be biting back, but they seemed innocuous enough. She had tracked down a rumor that Brian had been seen in a Rush Street leather bar. She'd handled a post that he'd taken money from someone who'd been arrested for selling kiddie porn.

She'd written about DC breaking into her apartment the night she dropped her keys by the front door. And then we came to the Navy Pier fundraiser.

We had this huge fundraiser, and I am, like, a superstar because My Candidate chose one of my guests for his big photo op. My guest was a World War II hero, and he wore all his battle medals and everything, and was on the front page of a bunch of papers, including the *Washington Post*, which my dad always says is a liberal rag, but it's so important. Anyway, I'm, like, a star at the campaign, even though it was a total fluke, but the head of the campaign, who we all call the Chicago Strangler, was superimpressed and pulled me out of the NetSquad to do special assignments directly for him. Some of my coworkers are a little huffy, 'cause some of them have been with My Candidate from Day 1, and I'm a Joanie-come-lately. But, well, that's life.

Up through that post, Petra's tone had been like her speaking voice, breezy, confident. A few days later, she wrote more soberly.

I thought they promoted me because I did such a great job. Turns out it was because I can't keep my big mouth shut. I said some stuff about something that the Strangler wants to know more about, something that happened a million years ago that could come back to bite my candidate. It's so confusing. It's something I said, but I have no idea what, but now the Strangler says I have to dig it up, even though I don't know anything about what happened or even what I'm really looking for.

It's like *Spy vs. Spy*, and I have to spy on my DC, which in some ways is fun, seeing if I can outsmart a person who's been a detective for twenty years. But mostly I hate it, because the Strangler says I can't trust anyone. He says if I tell a single soul what I'm looking for, it could get people killed, especially if I tell my detecting cousin. The Strangler says she'll go out of her way to hurt people I care about, and I know that when she's angry she goes off the deep end. She saved this homeless guy's life, but she almost killed me because I didn't respect her mother's dress. So watch Campaign Girl morph into Undercover Girl.

A week went by, and Petra made her final post.

If you say something that puts everyone you care about in danger only you don't know that it's a big secret, are you really to blame? And then how do you know who is your friend and who is your enemy? I can't tell anymore. I wish I'd never come to Chicago, but it's too late. I can't go home.

I sat back in my chair and rubbed my eyes. Petra, with her perpetual cheerful broadcasting of everything she knew, had said something that put the powerful people around her on alert. DEFCON 3 and dropping. I could hear the alarms ringing in Les Strangwell's office.

I didn't know the things that Petra might have talked over in the office — these clearly ranged from my breaking into her apartment for her, since one of her Web posts dealt with that, to my visiting Johnny Merton — because she'd even blurted that out at the Navy Pier fundraiser.

Certainly, anyone reading the posts on her MySpace profile would know what she was doing. I imagined the Strangler coldly reading over her shoulder. He could be any one of those five hundred 'friends,' invisible, like a shark floating under her toes.

I had an uncomfortable memory of the morning in my apartment when I'd blown up over her pawing through my trunk. My anger had frightened her, and it had created a gulf between us. I thought again of all the times my dad had told me my temper would get me into serious trouble. My God, he'd been right, but I'd never taken his words seriously to heart.

I had to find Petra. I didn't even know where to begin my search. I felt like something large and clumsy, a rhinoceros, easy to spot as it crashed through the underbrush and about as effectual an ally in times of trouble.

I made a list of things I'd said or done and things Petra seemed interested in:

1. Johnny Merton and the Anacondas.
2. The house in South Chicago, where Petra had stood watching when the thugs threw their smoke bomb through the window.
3. The Nellie Fox baseball.
4. Her obsession with whether my dad had left a diary.
5. Her arrival at the Freedom Center the night I went to collect evidence.
6. Her nervous whisper that she couldn't look for the contractors who'd been hustled into Sister Frankie's apartment.

It was four in the morning. I'd slept for seven hours, until Rose Hebert's phone call woke me. But fatigue, born of stress, my still-healing body, and my recent sleepless nights, was overwhelming me. I went into the little back area and reassembled my cot and air mattress. Oblivious to the threat of another break-in, I sank back into sleep.

39

A Different Car, a New Crib

In my dream, Miss Claudia was standing over me. 'Lamont will come back,' she said in clear, plain speech. 'My Bible tells me so.' She was waving her red leather Bible under my nose. She shook loose the dozens of cardboard page markers. When I put my hands out to catch them, they turned into photographs and floated to the floor before I could reach them.

If I could only study them, they would tell me exactly where Petra was and why she'd run away. But when I gathered up the pictures, they burst into flames in my hands. And suddenly I was holding Sister Frankie, her skin yellow-white beneath the burning candle of her hair. Behind her, Larry Alito and George Dornick were laughing with Harvey Krumas and my uncle. And Strangwell was there, pointing to my uncle and saying, 'You know why she had to die.'

I woke sweating and weeping. For a moment, I was disoriented in the black space. I thought I was back in Beth Israel, with bandages over my eyes, and I flailed around my cot trying to find the call button for the nurse. Awareness gradually returned. I swung my legs over the edge of the cot and fumbled my way to a light switch, moving slowly to keep from tripping over the drawers that had been dumped on the floor.

It was eight in the morning, long past time for me to get going. My lease-mate has a shower at the back of her studio because she welds big pieces of steel and polishes them with caustic substances and needs to be able to wash off in a hurry. I stood under a cold spray of water, trying to wake myself up, and returned, shivering, to my own office to put my clothes back on.

I picked up the list I'd made in the middle of the night of the things that Petra seemed to be trying to track and took it with me to the coffee shop across the street. While I waited in line for my espresso, I saw Elton Grainger out front hawking *Streetwise* and accepting donations with his usual unsteady bow and flourish. I took my drink, along with a bag of fruit, yogurt, juice, and some rolls, and went out to the street.

'Elton! I've been hoping for a word with you.' I held out the bag. 'Help yourself. Juice? Muffin?'

'Hey, Vic.' His bloodshot blue eyes shifted uneasily from me to the sidewalk. 'I'm okay. Don't need no food today.'

'You always need food, Elton. You know what the doc said at the VA when you passed out in June: you have to stop drinking and start eating so it doesn't happen again.'

'You leave me to sort that out. I don't need you hovering over me.'

'Okay. No hovering. You know my place was seriously busted two days ago. I wonder if you saw who went in?'

'Vic, I told you before, I ain't your doorman.'

I pulled a twenty from my wallet. 'Early Christmas tip for the non-doorman. My cousin was there. I want to know if you can ID the two people she was with. They were all wearing coats, even though it was September and hot.'

He eyed the twenty but shook his head. 'Don't know any cousin of yours, and that's a fact.'

'My cousin, Elton — the tall, cute blonde — you met her with me a couple of times, right after you got out of the hospital. *Petra*.'

'Sorry, Vic. I know you saved my life and all, but I never heard of her.' He turned away from me to greet a couple who were heading into the shop. '*Streetwise*. New edition today. *Streetwise*.'

I couldn't get him to look at me again. Finally, I pushed the twenty into his hand, along with a blueberry muffin, and walked up the street toward Armitage.

I was fuming. Someone had gotten to Elton, scared him into silence. I should have swung by my office yesterday before starting my journey to South Chicago, should have talked to Elton then. If me saving his life, let alone the twenty — the price of a bed for a night or a week in the tank — couldn't budge him, someone was putting heavy pressure on him.

Strangwell wouldn't shake down a homeless guy personally, that was way beneath him. But he knew people who would. Larry Alito, for one. I'd seen him with Les Strangwell the day before Petra disappeared. Strangwell gave him an assignment: 'I know what Les wants,' he'd snapped at someone who called to check up on him. Could it have been Dornick?

I turned around and went back to my office, where I once again called up the images from my video camera. It was impossible to tell who was who. If not for my aunt Rachel's insistence, I wouldn't have known the figure in the middle was Petra. Today, magnifying details as much as I could, it seemed to me that the man on her left was gripping her arm. His cap was pulled low over his face, his coat collar was pulled high around his chin, but the general shape could have been Alito's.

I tried to imagine what it would take to get him to tell me the truth about whether he'd been there. Certainly not my girlish charm. Would a threat that the FBI was involved worry him? Not if it came from me. He would have too many contacts from his years in the force to worry about veiled and vague threats from me. Only the possibility that Strangwell and his pals would leave him to take the fall might persuade Alito to start talking.

I looked up his phone number and called the house up in Lake Catherine. When Hazel answered, I asked for her husband.

'Larry doesn't want to talk to you,' she said in her gravelly South Side voice.

'I don't want to talk to him, either,' I said, 'but there's something he needs to know. I figure I owe him a tiny favor, since he used to work with my dad. He's been identified as one of the men who forced my cousin Petra to break into my office two days ago.'

She was silent.

'I'm going to call Bobby Mallory, but I'll wait four hours before I do. You be sure to let Larry know, okay, Ms. Alito? Larry is one of the guys who — '

'I heard you the first time!'

The connection went, and I stared at the phone. I'd promised to wait four hours to call Bobby, but I hadn't mentioned the press. I called Murray Ryerson's cellphone and gave him the same message. Unlike Hazel Alito, Murray had a bucketful of questions, starting with who had made the identification.

'Murray, there's a good possibility that every call I make is monitored, either by Homeland Security's Chicago office or by Mountain Hawk Security, or both, so I'm not giving away confidential information over the airwaves. Anyway, it's not a rock-solid ID. I'd double-check with Les Strangwell at the Krumas campaign — '

'Strangwell?' Murray's normal baritone rose an octave. 'What were you sitting on that the Krumas campaign cares about? Why would they hire — '

'Murray, darling, I'm spreading rumors right now. I don't have any facts. I don't think I have anything that the Krumas campaign cares about. All I can tell you for sure is that Strangwell did meet with Alito last week. And he asked Alito to do something for him.'

'Where are you? In your office? I'll be there in twenty — '

'I can't set up meeting times and places. I'm going to be on the move for the next few days. So, that's all for now.'

I hung up on a barrage of questions. The phone rang again, as I checked that I had my wallet, keys, and gun. I pulled my Cubs hat low

403

on my head. No moisturizers or unguents to protect my healing skin today. The Cubs, those frail reeds, would have to look after me.

My phone was still ringing as I locked my office door behind me. If anyone was monitoring my calls, I had only a few minutes to get out of the area before they had a watcher in place. I didn't run up the street, but I walked fast, and I turned left at the first intersection.

As soon as I left Oakley, I was on a quiet residential street where it was easy to see whether anyone was with me. I moved north and west in a random way until I reached Armitage.

I needed to find a car that couldn't be traced to me. I couldn't rent one, I didn't have my driver's license. Even if I did, Homeland Security, if they were paying attention to me, they'd know the minute I rented a car or bought a plane ticket. While I was talking to Murray, I had suddenly thought of not only where I could get a car but also a bolt hole, assuming I could cover my tracks coming and going.

I walked to the El stop, not bothering to look around, and rode the train into the Loop. I got off at Washington Street and walked through the underground tunnel into the basement of the Daley Center, where traffic court and a bunch of other civil courts sit. Since I had my gun on me, I couldn't do the safest thing, go through security and watch who came in after me, so I followed the maze of corridors and came on the underground entrance to a trendy Loop restaurant.

The staff were just gathering for the day, the

Hispanic stockmakers and cleaning crew. They looked at me narrowly but didn't try to stop me. I went through the doors into the kitchen and found an exit that took me into a parking garage. I walked up the ramp and out onto the street and made my way back to the El, where I rode the red line north to Howard Street.

It was a long ride, and I could watch all the changing characters who got on and off. By the time we reached the Evanston border, I was reasonably confident that I was clear. I changed to the Evanston train and rode it three stops. No one was with me when I got off. No bicycles circled around me, no cars passed and then repassed me.

Morrell and I had broken up in Italy, but I still had the keys to his condo. And I knew where he had hung the spare key to his Honda Civic. I couldn't afford to use the phone to call anyone I knew, but I could spend the night, drive the city, even change my underwear. When I let myself in, I found my favorite rose-stenciled bra still hanging in his bathroom. I thought I'd lost it in Italy.

40

The Shoemaker's Tale

Morrell's Honda started on the first try, which was a relief. I'd worried that the battery might have run down after sitting in the garage for three months.

Going to Morrell's place had left me melancholy. Little traces of my life surfaced wherever I looked — a pot of my moisturizer in the bathroom; *Sleeping Arrangements*, which I'd read aloud to him when he was recuperating from his bullet wounds, next to the bed. When I put away the juice I'd bought, I found a container of Mr. Contreras's homemade tomato sauce in the freezer.

Morrell and I had spent two years together. He had put me back together when I'd been tortured and left for dead on the Kennedy Expressway, I'd helped him when he'd been left for dead in Afghanistan. Maybe that was the only time we could really help each other, when we were near death. When we were near life, we couldn't sustain the relationship.

The tomato sauce made me realize I needed to notify Mr. Contreras, as well as Lotty and Max, about where I'd vanished to. The easiest person to tell would be Max because I could slip into Beth Israel through a side door and get to his office. If anyone was tracking me, they'd be keeping an eye on Lotty's clinic, on Damen Avenue, as well as her condo on Lake Shore Drive. Since Max lived in Evanston, if my friends wanted to reach me Max could slip a note under Morrell's door on his way home.

It felt queer to be alone in an apartment and to know I couldn't use the phone. It was like being in an isolation tank. I quickly wrote a note to Max, telling him where I was, how to reach me in this age of the Internet, and asking him to get word to Lotty and Mr. Contreras.

I picked Morrell's car keys from the top dresser drawer in his bedroom. Morrell's extreme tidiness, which had been a source of friction between us — or maybe it was my extreme messiness that bothered him — was useful when it came to finding anything in a hurry. In my apartment, a team of skilled searchers had torn the place apart without finding what they wanted.

As soon as I pulled out of Morrell's garage, I felt nervous and exposed. Morrell had been out of my life all summer. I didn't think anyone hunting me would know about him, but I could be wrong. When all this was over and I had found Petra safe and sound, I would have to invest in a GPS jammer. That would force anyone tracking me to follow me physically instead of doing it the lazy electronic way.

Situations like this usually key me up. I get just nervous enough to be sharp while remaining confident about my ability to deal with whatever comes along. It was Petra's disappearance, coupled with Sister Frankie's death, that made me so skittish.

Deep breaths, V. I., I admonished myself, *deep yoga/singer breaths. You and the breath are one.* After a near miss with a *Herald-Star* delivery van, I decided meditation and driving weren't an ideal mix and returned to skittishness. I forced myself to believe I was in the clear, got off the side streets and took the main ones to Beth Israel. When I got there, I circled until I found street parking. At the emergency-room entrance, I went in, head up, a confident walk; security didn't try to stop me even though I didn't have a badge on.

I've known Max's secretary, Cynthia Dowling, for years. She had stopped by my room when I'd been laid up the previous week. Today, she congratulated me on my quick recovery. Max was in a meeting, she said. Naturally. Executive directors are always in meetings.

I gave her the note I'd written. 'You haven't seen me since I was released from the hospital, have you, Cynthia?'

She smiled, but her eyes were worried. 'I don't even know your name, so I can't say that I've seen you today. I'll see that Max gets this when he's alone. Do you know anything about your cousin?'

I shook my head. 'Not enough of a whisper to even have a direction to follow. But I'm talking to people who can talk to people, and maybe one of them will finally start giving me real news.'

I left by a side door and jogged back to Morrell's car. I drove down Damen Avenue as the closest route to the expressway. The light at Addison turned yellow just as I got to the intersection. Without a driver's license, without an insurance card for the Honda — Morrell kept his in his wallet — I was being very law-abiding. I came to a virtuous halt. The car behind me honked in annoyance.

'Roscoe, Belmont, Wellington.' I counted off the streets out loud, nervous about needing to get to the South Side ahead of Dornick. 'Roscoe!' I shouted.

The car behind me honked again, this time because the light was green, and then zoomed around me, almost colliding with the northbound traffic. Roscoe. Brian Krumas had told Peter he could stay in the Roscoe Street apartment. The contractors who had shown up at the Freedom Center were owned by a guy with offices on West Roscoe. I made a U-turn just as the light was turning yellow again, forgetting my need to be utterly obedient to traffic signals and having my own near miss with an oncoming bus. Stupid, stupid. What had been his name? The exact address? The nuns at the Freedom Center could tell me.

I'd almost reached Irving Park Road when I realized that if I drove to the Freedom Center, I'd show up on Homeland Security cameras. I needed a phone or a computer. Therefore, I needed to find an Internet café. I drove along Addison toward the lake. Just before Wrigley Field, I found what I needed.

I paid cash for a card that I could stick into one of their machines. Compared to my Mac Pro, the Windows machine they had was painfully cumbersome to use, but I logged on to one of my search engines and hunted contractors

409

on Roscoe Street. Rodenko, that was it, 300 West Roscoe. Harvey Krumas had an unlisted phone number, but I found him, too, through my best search engine, Lifestory. The house in Barrington Hills, a place in Palm Springs, a flat in London. And the pied-à-terre in Chicago. At 300 West Roscoe.

Three hundred West Roscoe? I stared at the address. Harvey Krumas was Ernie Rodenko? He owned Ernie Rodenko? Either way, he had quickly mustered a couple of small-time contractors to clean up Sister Frankie's apartment and used his home address for the holding company. However it had been worked, when Petra looked up the subcontractors, broadcasting the news all over the office in her loud, cheerful voice, Les Strangwell heard her. Les was protecting Harvey. Or was it Brian? Did it matter?

I felt odd: cold, hot, queasy, remote. I wasn't fit to drive, not the fifteen miles to Curtis Rivers's shop, but it was all I could think of. I had to find Steve Sawyer before Harvey and Strangwell and George Dornick turned him into a fall guy for Petra.

I have no memory of leaving the Internet café to go to my car or of driving to the South Side. I don't remember if I stayed on Damen or went to the Ryan. I didn't look for tails. I was an automaton moving through space. It wasn't until I was walking away from the car that I came back to earth. I leaned against a light pole and sang a few vocal exercises, forcing myself to breathe, to get some semblance of calm for the hard interview ahead.

When I reached Fit for Your Hoof, Kimathi-Sawyer wasn't on the street. I opened the door to the shop and parted the ropes to the interior. I'd forgotten the whistle and the recorded 'Welcome to Chicago' announcement and flinched as they sounded.

The chess players were sitting at their board. The balding man with the paunch was still wearing his Machinists T-shirt; the skinny, darker one had on an outsize lumberjack's shirt. Curtis Rivers stood behind the counter watching them play, a toothpick jutting at a jaunty angle from his mouth.

The *Sun-Times* was on the counter. My cousin's picture had made the front page. HAVE YOU SEEN ME? the screamer headline read. The radio was still tuned to NPR. It was *Worldview* time in Chicago. The men had been talking, but when they looked up and saw me, the room became so quiet that even Jerome MacDonald seemed to sink to a whisper.

'You're not welcome here,' Rivers said.

'Gosh, and you've been so subtle up to now I never would have guessed. Tell me about Steve Sawyer.'

'I'll tell you all I've said before, which is you've got a hell of a nerve to come here and ask about him.'

'He changed his name legally to Kimathi, didn't he, before the trial? But Lamont never went that far. He was Lumumba only to the inner Anaconda circle.'

Rivers shifted the toothpick from one side of his mouth to the other but didn't speak. I saw a red handbag on one of the ropes made of the kind of leather that I love, a soft, supple calfskin.

'At his trial, Kimathi-Steve was expecting Lamont to show up with some pictures, wasn't he? And Lamont never arrived.' I stuck up an arm and unclipped the bag.

'Ask your daddy about that, Ms. Detective. Oh, right, your daddy is dead. Pretty convenient, isn't it?'

I looked inside the handbag. There was a zip compartment where you could put your wallet and a pocket that would just hold your cell-phone. I was not going to lose my temper. And I wasn't going to start yelling about my father.

'You remember George Dornick, of course, since you remember Tony Warshawski,' I said, still peering into the bag.

The cold eyes on the far side of the counter didn't give anything away.

'And you've seen the news that my cousin is missing.' I paused again but still got no response.

Rivers picked up the *Sun-Times*. 'Cute blond white girl, of course it's big news. I'm sure the cops can find some black man to implicate before the day is done.'

The chess players were watching me as if I were some complicated move on their board. I looked up from the handbag at Rivers.

'They already have.'

Rivers turned off the radio. The quiet became absolute. I found a price tag tucked into an outside compartment: five hundred thirty dollars. A bag like this would be triple that at a downtown store. I put it over my shoulder and

412

went to inspect myself in a narrow strip of mirror behind the ropes.

'Johnny.' I continued to study my silhouette.

'Man's in Stateville. Hard to see how he could be out grabbing white chicks off the street.'

'They figure he still has a lot of friends around town who'd do a favor for him. They're going to try to pressure him through his daughter.' I turned around, not in a hurry, and leaned against the mirror.

'His daughter?' Rivers frowned. 'What can they do to her? What I hear, she may not be proud of him. But she doesn't pretend she doesn't know him.'

'I don't know what they *will* do, but I'll tell you what they *can* do. Plant evidence that she's trafficking drugs for him. Plant computer files that show she's dipping into private funds at the law firm where she works.' I fiddled with the opening on the bag, a clever little tongue in hard leather that slipped into a catch.

When the whistle sounded and the loud-speaker announced 'Welcome to Chicago,' we all jumped. I had my hand inside my tuck holster; Rivers had his under the counter. A woman parted the ropes, bringing in a pair of high heels that needed new soles. Rivers bantered with her but kept an eye on me.

When the whistle blew as she left, he said, 'They hurt Dayo, Johnny will get revenge one way or another. That won't make him confess to snatching your cousin.'

'Here's how I see it. Either my cousin is dead or she's bolted, and they don't know where she's

413

run. If she's dead, if they killed her, first they make Johnny crazy by screwing with his kid and then they get a Stateville snitch to claim he heard Johnny confess to putting a contract out on Petra — on my cousin — because he's still mad at me for various reasons.'

It was painful to talk casually about Petra in such a way, clinical, detached, as if she were a movie script I was reading. The really hard sentence came next.

'They say they'll put the rap on Kimathi. They'll say he killed Petra as payback.' I braced myself in case Rivers or his friends came after me.

'And, by God, he would be in his rights to.' Curtis Rivers's voice was soft with a menace that chilled my bones.

'Why?'

'Why?' Rivers spat at me. 'What, is he supposed to be just one more Jesus-loving nigger, getting tortured but saying 'I forgive them all because hate curdles the soul'? He doesn't forgive you, and I don't forgive you.'

'I'm not asking you to forgive me, but I would very much like to know what I did to earn this anger.' I had dug my fingers into the soft calfskin of the bag I was still holding in an effort to keep the trembling in my legs out of my voice and hands.

'You would like to know! As if you don't — '

'Mr. Rivers, we had this conversation two months ago. I was ten years old when Harmony Newsome was murdered. All I know about the story is from reading newspapers, reading the trial

414

transcript, and from a brief conversation with Sister Frances, which was cut short by her murder.'

'And you were conveniently at her side when she died.'

'I held her in my arms as her hair burned.' My voice did tremble at that. 'I have raw wounds on my scalp and arms and chest and nightmares that don't go away.'

'And so does Kimathi have those nightmares.'

'Tell me what happened, Mr. Rivers.'

The chess players had been silent, almost motionless, during our interchange, but the machinist said, 'You got to tell her, Curtis. You were out of bounds just now over Sister Frankie. Ms. Detective here never caused Frankie's death, and you know it.'

The lumberjack nodded in agreement. Rivers scowled at his friends but went into the back of the shop. I heard the deep rumble of his voice and frightened cries from Kimathi. More rumbling, fewer cries, and Rivers came back out with Kimathi clutching his arm.

'This woman here, her daddy was Officer Warshawski. Tell her what happened when they came for you.'

'She's going to take away my nature,' Kimathi whispered.

'There's three of us here, we're bigger than she is, she can't cut you or hurt you. And you are safe at night, she can't break in through all my gates.'

I held out my hands, empty hands. 'I can't hurt you, Mr. Kimathi.'

'It was all on account of Harmony's death, the

way the police reacted to Harmony's death, I mean,' the machinist said softly. 'The city didn't care about Harmony. But Harmony's brother did. Saul was sixteen; he was proud of his sister, and her death was almost a mortal blow to him. Until Sister Frankie persuaded him that they could use the lessons of the movement as a call for justice in Harmony's death. Saul and Frankie, they started holding a vigil outside the police station every Sunday. They got TV crews down, they got the papers to write it up. Cops knew they had to pick up someone or the South Side would blow up all over again. So they picked on Kimathi here.'

Kimathi was trembling, looking at his feet.

'Tell her what happened. 'Officer Warshawski came and picked me up in his squad car,'' Rivers prompted.

'He pick me up, he take me to the station,' Kimathi whispered, his eyes large, flicking a glance up at me.

I kept my hands open in front of me. My heart was pounding so hard that the pulses in my neck were choking me.

'I was surprised. I didn't know I killed Harmony. She so sweet, so pretty, so special. Too special for me. I tell that to the officer, and he say, 'Save your story for the detectives and the lawyers, son, I'm just the man with the warrant for your arrest.' And then he say, like they do, 'You have the right to remain silent,' and all that stuff.'

'And then?' My mouth was dry, and the words came out in a harsh squawk.

416

'The detectives come in. They laugh. I'm the party . . . I'm the *death* of the party to them, a big joke. They tell me I kill Harmony. They tell me confess, make it all easy, only I didn't remember killing her. Now I can't remember, one way or another. The demons, they come and claw at me day and night . . . Maybe the demons kill Harmony. Maybe the demons say, 'Kimathi, you a devil, too. You in the gang. Just like pastor always said, you a child of the devil, you bound for hell. Go ahead, kill that sweet girl for all us demons.''

'You never killed a soul in your life, Kimathi,' Rivers said. 'Those detectives messed up your body and messed up your mind. You tell this white girl how they did.'

'They chain me up.' He was so ashamed at the memory that he looked at the floor. Tears seeped from the corners of his eyes. 'They chain me, they call me nigger. They say I the song-and-dance man, dance for them. They put me on the radiator. They burn the skin off my butt, it bleed. They laugh. They say I singing for them. Then they put electricity on my manhood, they run a current. They say, 'This nigger boy a good dancer.' They laugh. They tell me next they gon' cut off my manhood. So I tell them the words they want to hear, that I kill Harmony, that blessed child of Jesus.'

I felt tears spilling from my own eyes and a revulsion so strong it doubled me over.

'Yes, a pretty story, white girl, isn't it?' Rivers said.

'And Tony Warshawski?' I managed to whisper.

'He come in the room, two times, maybe more . . . I'm hurting too bad to count.'

'And what did he do?'

'He tell them to stop. But they tell him, 'Don't act like Jesus Christ on the dashboard, Warshawski. This for your brother.''

41

Rousting an Uncle

My legs gave way, and I found myself sitting on the floor. Curtis Rivers looked down at me without pity, but I didn't want any. *'This for your brother'* . . . *'This for Peter.'* Tony watched Alito and Dornick chain a man to a boiling radiator, watched them run a current through his genitals. My daddy — my wise and good and loving father . . . My hands were wet. I thought I would see blood when I looked at them, Steve Sawyer's blood, the blood of every prisoner my father had watched in Dornick's or Alito's custody, but it was only tears and snot.

I don't know how long I sat looking at the dust on the cracked linoleum, watching a spider crawl along the baseboard. I wanted to lie down on that floor and sleep away the rest of my time on the planet. After I'd found Petra, after I'd found Lamont, maybe I could curl up and die.

'This for Peter.' The Christmas Eve conversation I had remembered after seeing Alito came back to me again, my father saying, *'You got your promotion. That's enough, isn't it?'* and Alito replying, *'You want to see him in prison?'*

At last, I pushed myself up to a standing position again. My shoulders ached.

My father had been tense all fall after the summer of riots. I didn't remember anything

419

about the demonstrations that Harmony's brother had organized with Sister Frankie, but they would have been outside my dad's station. I could picture the tension inside the station, the Mayor's Office putting heat on them, demanding an immediate arrest.

So the State's Attorney's Office organized a frame: get one of the Anacondas; they're all guilty of something. Who knows why they picked on Sawyer or who put his name in play. Larry Alito? My mind flinched at the idea of naming my father. Arnie Coleman played along as the public defender conveniently assigned to the case. You choose the guy most eager for favors, most likely to play your game.

In Cook County, it didn't take a genius, or even very much money, to persuade the head of the criminal defenders unit to give you a weak link. After all, by the time I was with the PD, and Coleman had moved into the number one chair, I saw him do it over and over. My coworkers and I knew money was changing hands. We just never knew how much.

I took a shuddering breath and looked at the four men. I needed to be a professional in this situation, which meant I had to pull myself together. I might not have another chance to talk to Kimathi.

'Mr. Kimathi . . . If I can, I'll find the person who really did kill Harmony Newsome. But I'm afraid that means I need to ask you a few more questions.'

Kimathi swallowed convulsively and edged behind Curtis.

'At the trial, Mr. Kimathi, what did you mean when you said Lumumba had your picture?'

'That's right, Lumumba has my picture.'

'But what picture?' I asked.

'He told Johnny. Johnny promised, and then no one came, they all left me. They all afraid the demons coming for them. I covered with demons.' He suddenly thrust his head under my face, bending over and skewing his body so that he looked at me sideways, his tongue sticking out like a Mayan mask. 'See my demons? See how they crawling on me?'

I willed myself not to back away. 'Those aren't your demons, Mr. Kimathi. They belong to the detectives who tortured you. You tell those demons to go away, to go home where they belong.'

'Oh, they mine, they been living with me a long time. Pastor Hebert, he told me . . . he told me I'm bound for hell, hanging out with Johnny and Lumumba instead of coming to church. The demons, Pastor sent them to remind me every day.'

It was close to unbearable, talking to him, but I managed to keep my voice from cracking. 'What about the pictures? What pictures did Lumumba have?'

Kimathi pulled his head upright and looked at Curtis, his brow wrinkled in worry. 'Lumumba said he had a picture of who killed Harmony, but did I kill her? Did he have my picture?'

'You never killed her, Kimathi,' the machinist said. 'And the white girl is right about the demons. They're not yours. Send them to the person who owns them.'

As Kimathi spoke, I realized that was what my house-and-office wreckers had been hunting: the picture that showed who killed Harmony Newsome. That's why Petra wanted to see my childhood homes, to see if Tony had taken that vital piece of evidence away, a picture that proved who killed Harmony. Would it be his brother in the frame? Would Tony go that far, out of loyalty to his family, and steal evidence and hide it at home?

'What happened to Lumumba?' I felt as though I were splitting in two, between the emotions pounding inside me and my calm investigator's voice asking questions.

Curtis shook his head. 'Johnny knows. It happened during the blizzard, that much I can tell you.'

'You were at the Waltz Right Inn the night before the storm,' I said.

Rivers nodded fractionally. 'Lamont came in with Johnny, like Sister Rose said. They went off into the back room, talked between themselves, then came out, joined the party. Lamont took off about two a.m. And that was the last time we saw him.'

'Johnny went with him?'

'No. And they weren't fighting. Believe me, if Johnny had wanted to put a hit out on Lamont, we all would have known. But we were scared about what was happening to Steve ... to Kimathi. I think Johnny and Lamont were talking about that, talking about whatever pictures Lamont said he had.'

'You think Lamont is dead?'

'I'm sure Lamont is dead,' Curtis said. 'Brother didn't have anyplace to hide that we didn't know about. Miss Ella, she had family in Louisiana. They would have taken him. But we still would have heard. If anyone knows what happened to Lamont, it's Johnny. I thought Johnny had seen a demon himself, when the snow cleared and we all crawled out again. After that storm, he would never let anyone mention Lamont's name on the street around him.'

I squeezed my forehead with my hand. 'What can I possibly offer Johnny Merton that would get him to talk to me? He wants the Innocence Project working for him, but frankly — '

'He's not innocent of what they sent him down for, but he never killed Lamont Gadsden.'

I fished in the handbag, looking for a tissue, before remembering the bag belonged to the shop. The machinist chess player pulled a handkerchief out of his pocket and let me wipe my face and hands. All four of us knew what I could offer Johnny Merton: proof of who really killed Harmony, proof of who killed Lamont and where his body rested.

Kimathi telling his story, me collapsing in the face of it, that had shifted the relationships in the room. Rivers and his friends weren't on my side, exactly, but I was no longer an enemy. I guess you could say I was on probation.

I looked at the soiled handkerchief. 'I'll wash this and get it back to you, but I have a lot to do first. A lot of ground to cover and not much time. You need to get Kimathi out of here. George Dornick knows where he is, and it would be pathetically easy for them to break in here. Kimathi has to go someplace where no one would think to look. And you have to make double and triple sure that no one is on your back when you move him. They're sophisticated, and they have a lot of money to throw around.'

Rivers said, 'I have a shotgun, and I was in Vietnam. I can look after — '

'No, you can't. Dornick has firepower that makes Hamburger Hill look like a pie-throwing contest.'

'Listen to her, Curtis,' the lumberjack said softly. 'She's telling you for Kimathi's sake. No time for ego-tripping here, brother.'

The machinist nodded. 'We'll take him away right now. You want him, Ms. Detective, you ask Curtis. Less you know, the better.'

He turned to Kimathi and began talking to him, cajoling him. Kimathi didn't want to leave without Curtis. I thought I might start screaming. I wanted him out — now! — before Dornick or anyone else showed up here.

I parted the ropes to leave and realized I was still holding the red handbag. I returned and put it on the counter. 'This bag has attached itself to me, Mr. Rivers . . . And I see, anyway, that I've stained it . . . I lost all my cards and whatnot in the fire, but, if you put it away for me, I'll pay for it when I get the cash together.'

Rivers studied me up and down with somber eyes, then handed the bag to me. 'I'm going to take a chance on you, Ms. Detective. You've extended yourself here today. And if you don't come through with the money, heck, I can leave

424

your body in George Dornick's office, claim he was responsible.'

It was a feeble joke, but we had all been so tense that we burst out laughing. All but Kimathi, who jerked away when he saw me laugh. '*They say I the song-and-dance man . . . They laugh.*' That sobered me up in a hurry.

I asked Rivers to let me out through the back, into the alley, just to give myself a little comfort zone. On my way out, I again urged the chess players to follow with Kimathi as fast as possible.

Once I reached Morrell's car, I moved quickly, pushed by a nervous energy so frantic that I found myself flooring the accelerator and taking terrible risks in the traffic on the Ryan. At least I wasn't texting, or playing the tuba, at the same time.

I pulled off the expressway, got out of the car, and tried to take some deep breaths, tried to regain some kind of center, but all I could see was my dad, the face I loved and trusted, looking through a one-way window into an interrogation room.

'You all right, there?' A police car had pulled up behind me without my noticing.

I felt the blood drain into my legs, but I clutched the car door and managed a smile. 'Thanks. I had a cramp in my foot and thought I'd better get off to work it out.'

The officer tipped a wave but waited until I got into the car and slowly merged onto the Ryan. He followed me, as I studied traffic in my side mirrors, kept to the speed limit, signaled my lane changes. A bubble of hysteria kept threatening to overwhelm me. *We serve and protect:* the Chicago police motto. Was he protecting me? Was he making sure I hadn't pulled over for a drug deal? Was he bored? What did he do in the station when he brought in a suspect?

I left the Ryan again at the main downtown exit and put the car in the underground garage near Millennium Park. I locked the red bag in the trunk. If I got to a point where I had to run, a bag like that would slow me down. It would also be easy for some tracker to follow.

Out on the street, the late August sun was blistering, and all that I had in the way of protection was my Cubs cap. No jacket, no lotions to protect my skin. I felt such a surge of self-loathing, anyway, that it seemed to me it would be good if the sun peeled the skin off my arms.

I was in too much of a hurry for public transportation and hailed a cab to take me to the top of Michigan Avenue. There's a vertical shopping mall across the street from the Drake Hotel, where my uncle was staying. I went into the mall and found a stationer, where I picked up a pad of paper, an envelope, and a pen.

The Four Seasons Hotel was attached to the mall at the sixth floor. I walked through the connecting door into the subdued colors and calm of wealth, smiled at a concierge, and found an alcove where I could do some writing. I chewed on the capped end of the pen, trying to figure out what I wanted to say.

426

Dear Peter

Your big brother Tony covered your ass all those years ago, but I know now that you killed Harmony Newsome. There is no statute of limitations on murder, and I don't feel Tony's protective attachment to you, I won't try to save you. What I'm wondering, though, is why you would sacrifice Petra. I thought at least you had a father's normal love for his children.

If you want to talk to me, I will be in the gazebo across from the Drake for ten minutes. If you don't show, I'll be on my way. Will Bobby Mallory sit on the truth for you?

V.I.

I sealed up my note in the envelope and addressed it to my uncle. Across the street, I entered the lower lobby of the Drake, where there's an arcade of shops. A bellman was standing near the stairs leading to the Drake's main lobby. I gave him a five and asked him to deliver the envelope at once. Then I walked quickly through the arcade to the hotel's north entrance.

It was 1:23 when I handed the letter to the bellman. Assume Peter was in his room. Assume the bellman delivered the envelope right away. Peter would call Dornick . . . or Alito . . . or Les Strangwell. Something should happen within twenty minutes.

Just across the street from the Drake is a little park, a triangle made by the hotel, Michigan Avenue on the left, and Lake Shore Drive as the hypotenuse. Beyond the drive lie some of the city's most beautiful sand beaches. This time of year, the Oak Street Beach was packed with tourists, tanners, swimmers, and volleyballers, but the triangular park was essentially empty. A homeless man was asleep on a patch of grass outside its gazebo.

I walked along the row of cars parked on the south side of the triangle. Only one had someone sitting inside. There was a service van in front of one of the condos, and it could have held a surveillance team, but I didn't think Dornick or Strangwell would feel the need to keep that sophisticated of a watch on Peter.

I walked back to Michigan Avenue, which was filled with shoppers and tourists. A trio of black youths banged homemade drums on the corner.

A tunnel goes under the avenue, but I crossed at street level. I was in the company of a woman who had a leash with a dog at the end of it in one hand and a cellphone in the other that was glued to her ear. A nanny with a baby buggy, also on a cellphone, was behind me. I felt reassuringly anonymous, just one more person in a ball cap enjoying the end of summer.

I sat on a bench in a bus stop on the far corner and watched the park. An elderly man with a toy poodle shuffled over from one of the condos near the hotel. The dog sniffed at late-blooming orange flowers while the man stared vacantly into the distance. A hard-muscled young woman jogged past the gazebo, down a ramp leading under Lake Shore Drive and to the beach. A few bicyclists emerged on the return route.

Seventeen minutes after I'd handed the envelope to the bellman, my uncle appeared. His hair was uncombed, his shirttails hung half out of his trousers. He certainly wasn't resting easily these days. While he looked in and around the gazebo, I checked the opposite side of the street. No one was lingering on the sidewalks. No new cars hovered in the area. I climbed down the stairs to the tunnel under Michigan Avenue and emerged on the path to the beach.

'Peter!' I called sharply. 'Over here!'

42

Roughing Up the Uncle

'What the hell are you up to?' Close up, my uncle looked worse than I'd thought. His eyes were bloodshot, he was unshaven, and he smelled of stale alcohol.

'What the hell are you up to, Peter, letting Petra take the fall so that you don't have to face the — '

'Goddamn you, you ignorant bitch, I am protecting my daughter.' For a moment, we both thought he was going to hit me.

My mouth creased in a sour smile. 'Sending her out to find police evidence that Tony squirreled away for you? Involving her in arson and criminal trespass at my old South Chicago house and at my current house and office?'

'You don't know anything!' His roar brought the cyclists and joggers around us to a brief halt: *Did I need help?*

I smiled and waved at the concerned citizens, who were happy to leave us to our quarrel. I kept the smile on my lips and my voice light, conversational. We didn't need to draw a crowd.

'I know that in 1967 Steve Sawyer was brutally tortured into confessing to a murder he never committed. I know he served forty years, doing *very* hard time, in your stead. And I know he thought there were some photographs proving who really killed Harmony Newsome in Marquette Park during that 1966 riot. I know that Larry Alito brought evidence of the murder over to our South Chicago house back around Christmas 1967 and that Tony took it to keep your sorry ass out of prison.'

'I didn't kill Harmony Newsome,' Peter hissed.

'Then who did?'

Peter looked around, wondering who was listening. 'I don't know.'

'Brilliant,' I said. 'It wasn't me, I wasn't there, I didn't do it. Every cop and every criminal lawyer hears that line a hundred times their first week on the job. You weren't in Marquette Park, Tony didn't take evidence, Larry Alito — '

'Shut up! I was in Marquette Park, okay? Is that a crime? It was my neighborhood park, my friends were all there.'

'What, you guys went there to play ball, and then suddenly, in the third inning, this huge riot broke out? And then what? You got lost in the crowd and started throwing bricks and rocks and stuff in the hopes they'd point you to your way home?'

'You're just like your tight-assed bitch of a mother, acting like she was the Madonna and all the saints poured into one — '

'Call me any name you like, you two-bit bully, but do not insult Gabriella.' My hands on my hips, my face close to his. He backed away.

The silence lingered between us. Peter was fidgeting, worried about what I knew, what I might say. But I was weary, of him, of fighting, of myself. And when I finally spoke again, it took an effort to go through the motions.

'You went to Marquette Park in 1966, but you didn't kill Harmony Newsome and you don't know who did. But you sent Petra out looking for the evidence just in case it came back to bite you. Only it's bitten Petra instead. Take it from there . . . Tell me how you're protecting her.'

His face was white underneath the stubble. 'Don't preach at me. You're the one who got Petey in trouble in the first place, introducing her to gangbangers and taking her to slums.'

'No, no, no.' My hands were over my ears, trying to stop the barrage of lies. 'She wheedled me until I took her to see all the different houses you and Grandma Warshawski and Tony had lived in. I thought at the time Petra was behaving strangely, especially her wanting to see where everyone stored their stuff. I tried to get her to tell me why, and she wouldn't. But of course she wanted to see if, by any chance, Tony had left behind that photograph!'

'You're making this shit up to cover your own butt,' my uncle said.

'Peter, someone ID'd Petra, ID'd her standing on Houston Avenue while thugs threw a smoke bomb into the house and ransacked it. What did you have her doing?'

'People make mistakes all the time when they're asked to ID someone. Petra wasn't there. You might have bought off a witness — '

'To get my own cousin in trouble? Or for any reason whatsoever?' I wanted to pick him up and bang his head against the concrete barricade above us.

432

'Do you understand, I am crazy with worry. I will say or do anything to see Petra doesn't get hurt. And if that means accusing you — of *anything* — I'll do it.'

'You know they'll never let Petra walk away from this,' I said. 'When they find her, they'll dump her body someplace where they can implicate one of Johnny Merton's boys. They'd like it to be Steve Sawyer, of course, as Dornick suggested in Strangwell's office yesterday. Dude's already gone down once instead of you, why not twice?'

'Dornick told me back then that Sawyer was a killer, he and Merton both,' Peter burst out. 'Sawyer was just going to prison for a different murder than the one he actually did.'

'Have you ever watched someone put electrodes on a man's balls and run a current through them?' I asked.

He squirmed, and his hand went reflexively to his crotch.

'After a time — and not a very long time — he'll say anything to get it to stop. Tony watched Larry Alito and George Dornick do this to Steve Sawyer. He tried to get them to stop, and they told him they were doing it for you.'

'I didn't kill the girl, damn it!' Sweat poured from Peter's face, although it could have been the hot sun of course. My own face was aching from the sun hitting my burns through the Cubs cap.

'Why did you send Petra out to look for the photos?'

'I didn't.' He was hoarse. 'I didn't know what

433

she was up to. Rachel was worried about Petey, said she sounded strange, subdued, not like herself, and she stopped calling every day the way she usually did. I thought it was the work on the campaign. Strangwell's a hard boss. Petey isn't used to that much discipline or responsibility.'

'Was Strangwell at Marquette Park with you in 1966?'

He shook his head. 'Les is a friend of Harvey's, helped him on the PR side, taught him how to handle congressional hearings, that kind of thing. Harvey was Les's most important client before the Strangler became a political op, so of course Les moved in to run the kid's campaign.'

'Dornick?' I prodded. 'Was he at Marquette Park with you?'

'Dornick was a cop. He was in the park, but he was holding the line around King. We razzed him about it at — ' He stopped, realizing how bad that sounded in today's context.

'We?' I prodded.

'All of us from the neighborhood,' he muttered.

'Harvey Krumas was there, too?'

'I said all of us from the neighborhood, and that's all I'm saying.'

'If you didn't kill Ms. Newsome, why did Tony cave and take evidence when Dornick and Alito threatened to send you to prison?'

'They could manipulate the evidence, Tony knew that.'

'And that Nellie Fox baseball . . . What was it evidence of?'

434

'I don't know what you're talking about,' he muttered unconvincingly.

'That's what Alito dropped off at my dad's, isn't it? The night he said you'd go to prison if Tony didn't hide it?'

'That baseball didn't prove one damned thing. George thought he was being so cute — ' He cut himself short when he realized how much he was revealing, then continued. 'Tony believed me when I swore to him that I never hurt that black girl. Why can't you cut me the same slack?'

'Because, my dear uncle, you are willing to let George Dornick put a bullet through my head to protect yourself all over again. And despite your protestations that you'd do anything for Petra, I don't see you going to Bobby Mallory, spilling your guts, so that your kid can come out of wherever she's hiding and stop fearing for her own life! I'd love to know what they're giving you that's wonderful enough for you to let everyone around you — your brother, me, but, most of all, your daughter — take the fall for you.'

I waited a moment, hoping he'd say something, anything, to give me a handle to turn. When he remained silent, I started down the stairs that led to the tunnel under Michigan Avenue. Peter called after me; I waited for him at the bottom.

'Leave town, Vic.' He pulled out his wallet and tried to shove a fistful of twenties at me. 'Leave town until all this blows over.'

'Peter, it's not going to blow over. Bobby Mallory is already pulling a thread out of this ball of yarn. Don't tell me your friends can force him to drop the investigation.'

He looked around again. 'If Homeland Security tells Mallory to stop, he'll stop.'

The interrogation I'd undergone after Sister Frankie's death — Homeland Security had been there and wanted to know what the nun had told me before she died — had that been at Dornick's behest? Did he, or Strangwell, have so much clout they could shut down a Chicago Police investigation?

'So they're waiting for me to produce the photographs before they kill me,' I said slowly. 'Once they have the pictures and I'm dead, they'll feel safe.'

My uncle shifted uneasily. Maybe no one had said it out loud to him, but they'd made it clear that he'd get Petra in exchange for me and whatever evidence was still floating around from Marquette Park all those years ago. 'Where are you going? What are you doing now? If you talk to Bobby — '

'I'm not telling you what I'm doing because I don't want to be an easier target for your pal George than I already am. If you have anything to say to me, put it out on the Web. I'll try to find a safe place to check my e-mails now and then.'

He grabbed my arm, trying to hector me into making a public declaration that I would drop the investigation, but I was angry, scared, and short of time. I shoved him away and sprinted through the tunnel and up the other side. I jumped into the first cab that came along and rode south to Millennium Park.

The skin on my arms and scalp was throbbing from where the sun had burned the raw patches. There are a couple of big fountains in the park, slabs of glass where water falls from the top and children dance and slide in it as it hits the ground. I held my burning arms and head under the water, not minding that my clothes were getting wet, keeping myself just turned away enough that the water didn't hit my back hip and my gun sitting in its tuck holster.

I don't know how long I stood, soothed by the water, oblivious to the exuberant children around me. I finally trudged on leaden feet to the garage entrance. A man was selling *Streetwise*.

'Come on, beautiful, let's have a smile on that gorgeous face of yours. Nothing is this bad. Not if you have a roof over your head and a family that loves you.'

'I don't.' I walked past him into the garage.

In Morrell's Honda, I leaned back in the seat, my wet clothes squelching against the vinyl upholstery. I could picture Morrell's expression — annoyance quickly suppressed — at my dripping in his car. Suppressed, because he'd see how distraught I was, my confidence in my father's essential rightness undermined. Morrell was so kind — and, well, moral — he would always put his need for order behind another person's need for compassion.

'*This for your brother.*' That's what Steve Sawyer-Kimathi said Dornick and Alito had told Tony. *We're torturing Kimathi for your brother's sake.* And Tony had turned around and left them to it.

'Nothing *is this bad. Not if you have a roof over your head and a family that loves you.*' What kind of love had Tony given me — all that wise, patient advice — what had it been grounded in? And my mother: how much had she known about Steve Sawyer and her husband's brother and her husband?

I thought of some of the men I'd known over the years: my ex-husband, Murray, Conrad. My ex-husband and Murray Ryerson were ordinary, ambitious men, but Morrell at least was decent, even heroic. Maybe I carried some taint I'd never been aware of, something I'd been unwilling to face. Melodrama. The trouble was, I'd never imagined any taint could be attached to my father.

I was unexpectedly wracked again by sobs, so violent that they banged me against the steering wheel. I tried not to howl out loud, the last vestige of reason warning me not to attract attention.

43

Death of Not Such a Good Guy

I finally returned to Morrell's place, too worn by my emotional storm to do anything but sleep. When I woke again, it was after six. I went into the kitchen to make a cup of tea and found that Max had slid a note through the back door on his way home.

> *Karen Lennon was looking for you this afternoon. She says your client, Miss Claudia, is slipping out of this life but has asked for you off and on all day. Captain Mallory called on Lotty at her clinic this afternoon. He needs to see you urgently but wouldn't tell Lotty why. I got the news that you're safe to Mr. Contreras and Lotty, but felt I shouldn't let them know where you are.*
> *Max*

I drank tea, slowly. I felt like someone convalescing from a devastating illness, that if I moved too quickly the fever would return and carry me away for good.

Bobby wanted to see me. He had gone to the clinic in person, hadn't sent a minion. He knows Lotty, knows that the sight of a police badge stirs such terrible memories in her that even the best cop in the world receives a hostile reception, but, even so, for a routine inquiry he would have sent Terry Finchley. So he needed me badly and he needed me privately.

But Miss Claudia was slipping out of this life. She might have died while I was weeping in Millennium Park. I finished the tea and carefully washed the mug. Morrell would be quite cross if he came home from Afghanistan to find it dirty in his sink.

I looked wistfully at the phone. The trouble with the Age of Fear is that you don't know who is listening in on your conversations. You don't know if you can talk safely or not. Probably I could talk to Karen Lennon without anyone else catching the call, but the possibility that I'd jeopardize my safe house meant I couldn't work on probabilities.

It was too late in the day to expect to find Karen at Lionsgate Manor. I drove down to Howard Street, the honky-tonk dividing line between Chicago's Mexican-Pakistani-Russian north border and the very much more staid Evanston, and found a pay phone at the El stop there. Even more amazing, the phone's cord and handset were both attached, and the phone asked me to deposit a dollar when I listened to it. I put my battery in my cellphone just long enough to look up Karen Lennon's contact information, then called her cell from the pay phone.

'Vic, thank goodness! I've been trying to reach you since last night. I finally called Max this morning, and he told me you're having to stay underground, so thank you for coming up for air and getting back to me. I'm sorry about your cousin, but Miss Claudia's been asking for you. I've been afraid she'd pass while you were hiding.'

'If I go to Lionsgate Manor now, will I be able to see her?'

'If I'm with you, it should be okay. I'm home, but I can be there in twenty-five minutes. I'll meet you at the main entrance, okay?'

'*Not* okay. I don't know how long I can stay undercover, but I can't have anyone know where I am. I'll meet you outside Miss Claudia's room.'

Karen wanted to know how I'd get into the building; you had to go past the guard station at night. I told her not to worry about that, just to give me the room number. She started to object, but I cut her off.

'Please, I don't have enough time to do the things I have to do. Let's not waste the last hours of Miss Claudia's life arguing about this.'

I drove along Howard until I came to a shop that sold uniforms and business apparel. There are several ways to be invisible in a large institution. The best, in a nursing home, is to be a janitor. If you show up in a nurse's uniform, all the other nurses think they know you and study your face too closely. A janitor, however, at the low end of the food chain, gets only a cursory look. I found a jumpsuit in gray, which I put on over my jeans, and a square-cut cap. I bought a big mop to complete the outfit. I stuck my gun into a side pocket — not the safest way to carry a firearm, but I wanted it close to hand.

When I reached Lionsgate, I parked on a side

street so I could get away fast if I had to. Mop in hand, cap low on my forehead, I walked down the ramp at the manor's parking garage and entered the building using one of those elevators. On the ground floor, I had to pass the guard station to get to the main elevators. The massive woman behind the counter, wearing a Lionsgate pale blue security blazer, was watching television. But she looked up as I passed and called out to me: Who was I? Where was my security ID?

My Polish is limited to a few stilted phrases garnered unwillingly as a child from Boom-Boom's mother. Tonight, I didn't stop walking but shouted over my shoulder in Polish instead that dinner was ready, it was getting cold, come to the table at once, something I'd heard Aunt Marie say four or five hundred times. The guard shook her head with the kind of annoyed incredulity accorded ignorant immigrants, but she returned to the small TV on the counter in front of her.

I rode up in an elevator with a real member of the cleaning crew. She was collecting dirty laundry and rolled her cart off at the eighth floor. When I reached Miss Claudia's room, Miss Ella was sitting with her sister on the room's one chair. Karen was on the lookout for me. She hurried over and greeted me in a low voice, taking my arm and escorting me to Miss Claudia's bed.

Another woman lay in an adjacent bed, her breath coming in short, puffy bursts, a machine next to her beeping every now and then. I pulled a curtain between the two women to create the illusion of privacy.

My client frowned at me. 'Our affairs haven't been very important to you, have they? You took our money, but you didn't find Lamont. And it seems you've stopped looking for him the last month.'

'I think your sister wants to see me,' I said as gently as I could. 'How is she?'

'Maybe a little stronger,' Karen said. 'She ate some ice cream, Miss Ella says.'

Miss Claudia was sleeping, too, her breath sounding much the same as her neighbor's, shallow, ragged. I sat on the bed, ignoring the client's outraged snort, and massaged Miss Claudia's left hand, her good hand.

'It's V. I. Warshawski, Miss Claudia,' I said in a deep, clear voice. 'I'm the detective. I'm looking for Lamont. You told Pastor Karen you wanted to see me.'

She stirred but didn't wake. I repeated the information several times, and, after a bit, her eyes fluttered open.

''Tive,' she asked.

'I found Steve,' I said.

'She's asking, are you the detective,' Miss Ella corrected me.

'I'm the detective, Miss Claudia. I found Steve Sawyer. He's very ill. He was in prison for forty years.'

'Sad. Hard. 'Mont?'

I clasped her hand more tightly. 'Curtis . . . You remember Curtis Rivers? Curtis says Lamont is dead. But he doesn't know where he's resting. He says Johnny knows.'

Her fingers gave mine a weak response. Miss Ella said, 'The Anacondas! I knew it was their doing.'

'I don't think Johnny killed Lamont, but he knows what happened to him. I'll try my best to get him to tell me.' I was speaking slowly to Miss Claudia, wondering how much sense she could make of my words.

Miss Ella huffed. 'You'll try and you'll get the same results you've come up with all summer. Nothing.'

I didn't try to answer or even look at her but kept my attention on her sister. Miss Claudia lay silent for a moment, taking conscious, deeper breaths, preparing herself for a major effort. 'Bible.' She pronounced both consonants clearly. 'Lamont Bible . . . You take.'

She turned her head on the pillow so I could see what she intended. The red leather Bible was on the nightstand by her head. 'Find 'Mont. He dead, bury with him. He 'live, give him.' Another deep breath, another effort. 'Promise?'

'I promise, Miss Claudia.'

'Lamont's Bible?' Miss Ella was outraged. 'That's a family Bible, Claudia. You can't — '

'Quiet yourself, Ellie.' But the effort in making clear speech was too hard for Miss Claudia, and she sank back into half-intelligible syllables: ''Hite girl, 'hite 'tive, I want give.'

Miss Claudia watched me until she was sure I had the Bible, sure I was tucking it into the big side pocket of my overalls, not handing it to her sister. She closed her eyes and gasped for air.

Miss Ella favored her sister and me both with bitter words. Especially her sister, who had always traded on her looks, never cared how much Ella worked and did, and spoiled Lamont when Ella told her time and again that she had ruined him by sparing the rod. If Miss Claudia heard, she didn't respond. She had worn herself out speaking to me. I knew she wasn't asleep because, as she lay there, her eyes fluttered open from time to time, looking from my face to my pocket where the end of the big red Bible was sticking out.

Holding her hand, I sang to her the song of the butterfly, the favorite of the lullabies of my childhood. '*Gira qua e gira là, poi si resta supra un fiore; / Gira qua e gira là, poi si resta supra spalla di Papà*' (Turning here, turning there, until she rests upon a flower; / Turning here, turning there, until she rests on Papà's shoulder).

Miss Ella sniffed loudly, but I sang it through several times, calming myself along with Miss Claudia, until she was deeply asleep. When I got up to go, Miss Ella stayed in the chair, I suppose not wanting to dignify her sister's bequest to me by acknowledging me, but Pastor Karen followed me into the hall.

'I know you're under a lot of stress right now, and I'm sure your cousin is your biggest worry, so it was a really good thing you did, coming over here to see Miss Claudia.' She put a hand on my arm. 'This man you mentioned, Curtis . . . Do you think he's telling the truth about Lamont?'

'Oh, I think so. He doesn't know what

445

happened to Lamont, but it involved Johnny Merton, and it was so terrible that it shocked Merton into silence. And Merton . . . You'd have to know him to understand that a death he'd find shocking might turn you or me as mad as . . . as poor Steve Sawyer.'

I gently dislodged Lennon's hand. 'Something about Lamont, or Johnny and Steve Sawyer and the Anacondas, is connected to my cousin. The man who's running security for the Krumas campaign, where my cousin worked, he was the cop who interrogated Sawyer forty years ago and tortured him into confessing.'

Karen gasped. 'Torture? Are you sure?'

Sawyer-Kimathi's mangled, burned body flashed in my head: *They say I the song-and-dance man . . . They laugh.* Would I ever be able to forget that? 'Yes, oh yes. I wish I wasn't, but . . . I know it happened. I don't understand it, not all of it, but my uncle, and Harvey Krumas, the candidate's father, they grew up together, and they still watch each other's backs. The murder that happened in Marquette Park all those years ago, they're both implicated in it, and that means — '

I couldn't bear to go on, couldn't bear to add that that meant my own uncle was implicated in Sister Frankie's murder because his old buddy Harvey rushed a contracting crew over to her place to bury any evidence I might be able to dig up. I pressed my hands against my temples as if that would push all that knowledge out of my head.

'This is terrible, Vic. Why aren't you going to the police?'

My smile was twisted. 'Because Dornick is an ex-cop with lots of pals on the force, and I don't know who there I can trust anymore.'

Karen started to ask me how Lamont was tied to Dornick, but my own words reminded me that Bobby Mallory had been trying to reach me. I interrupted her to ask if I could use her office phone to make a few calls.

We rode down to the second floor in silence, Karen shaking her head as if mourning all the sorry souls I'd told her about. While she unlocked her office door, I once again connected my cellphone long enough to look up Bobby's unlisted home number.

Eileen Mallory answered. 'Oh, Vicki, I'm so sorry about Petra. This is a terrible week. We never knew Peter at all well, but please tell him and Rachel that if there's anything we can do, anything at all — a place to stay, extra help from Bobby's team — they must let us know.'

I thanked her awkwardly and said Bobby had been trying to reach me. He hadn't come home yet. She gave me his cellphone number. And another message, a personal one for me, so warm and loving it made my eyelids prick.

Bobby's response wasn't nearly so tender. 'Where are you?' he demanded as soon as I answered.

'Wandering around the city like a demented ghost,' I said. 'I understand you wanted to talk to me.'

'I want to see you at once.'

I looked at Karen Lennon's scarred desktop. 'You know, Bobby, that is not going to happen. I am hiding from George Dornick, hoping I find Petra before he does.'

'If Dornick's on your ass, I'll give him a medal for bringing you in.'

'That would be one you would hand him at my funeral, then, and you could congratulate each other on laying me and a lot of ugly department history to rest.'

I wasn't sure how much time I would have before Bobby's tech team figured out where I was calling from. I decided I could stay on the phone for three more minutes.

'Victoria, you have crossed an acceptable line. You've always imagined that you could do my job and that of thirteen thousand other good, decent cops better than we can. You've always imagined when we chew you out, it's because we're stupider or more corrupt than you. But now you have gone further than I will allow.'

'By criticizing George Dornick?' I asked.

'By fingering, if not murdering, Larry Alito.'

I had been watching the second hand go round on the institutional clock on Karen Lennon's wall, but that news jolted me.

'Alito is dead?' I repeated stupidly.

'Get your head out of your butt.' Bobby was truly furious to use such coarse language talking to me. Even though he disapproves of me, he usually sticks to his no-swearing-at-women-and-children code when we're speaking. 'His body was found down by the river near Cortlandt this afternoon. And Hazel says you'd called up there this morning, threatening him.'

44

Escape in Contaminated Laundry

While I'd been speaking to Bobby, Karen had been standing at her window, aimlessly twitching the blind pull. She turned to me as I hung up. 'There are a lot of police cars out front. We don't usually get so many here. Do you think — ?'

'I think I don't want to find out.' I looked wildly around, hoping a hiding place would open up, but all I saw was my mop. The cops wouldn't be fooled by a generic jumpsuit and an unused mop. They'd be inspecting all the janitors, even the one I'd seen in the elevator.

'Linen carts . . . They're taking dirty linen someplace. Where?'

Karen thought a minute, then pressed a speed-dial number on her phone. 'It's Pastor Karen. I've been with one of our critically ill patients and have some soiled linens. Where can I find the nearest bin? . . . I stupidly carried them down to my office . . . No, I'll come back up. I want to get them out of here, and I'm going to have to scrub after handling them, anyway . . . Number eleven, right.'

Her mouth set in a thin, firm line, she opened her door, looked around, and beckoned me. 'Elevator eleven. Let's go.'

I followed her through the maze of corridors, muscles tensing, to a rear service elevator. We

449

could hear the scratchy echoes of police radios, the frightened shouts of Lionsgate residents wanting to know if there was a killer running loose in the halls, but we didn't actually see any cops. Karen pushed the button on elevator 11. There was a stairwell nearby, and I could hear the pounding of feet. Our elevator arrived, but I stood frozen, watching the stairwell door until Karen shoved me into the elevator and pressed the button to close the doors.

I let out a loud breath. 'Thanks. I'm losing my nerve.'

She put a finger over my mouth, jerking her head toward a camera in the ceiling, and began talking excitedly about the need for the janitor staff to do more for the AIDS cases in the hospital. 'I have to scrub now because I've been handling infected linens and syringes. Can't the cleaning crew do more?'

'It's what happens when you outsource cleaning,' I said, switching on the harsh nasal of the South Side. 'They're paid by the room, not by the hour, and they don't do the job an in-house service does.'

The elevator was hydraulic, and it seemed to me that in the time it took us to go from the second floor to the sub-basement a crew could have disinfected all fifteen floors of the manor. Karen and I babbled about AIDS and cleaning until my mouth felt like a bell with a very dry clapper hanging in the middle. The hydraulics finally hissed to a halt.

The doors opened onto a holding bay. Two dozen linen-filled carts stood there. Karen muttered that the laundry service would be by at midnight for pickup. The shower rooms for staff stood beyond the bay, and, next to them, a locked dressing room. Karen found a master key on her chain and unlocked the door. Uniforms were inside, hazmat suits, booties, all those things. She tossed me hat, gloves, mask, and a white jumpsuit and told me to get into a cart and get covered. I grabbed my gun and Miss Claudia's Bible, then stripped out of my gray suit, burying it in the middle of one of the other carts, and pulled on the white jumpsuit. I put on the hat, the gloves, and the mask, and burrowed into the cart. A few minutes later, Karen appeared, and when I peeked at her she looked ominous in her own jumpsuit, hat, gloves, and mask. She flashed a bright red placard at me that read DANGER! HIGHLY INFECTIOUS, then covered me up. She whispered that she was tying the placard over the top of the cart. We'd hope for the best.

She pushed the cart onto the elevator. I lay there as it wheezed up a story to the entrance of the parking garage. The police had placed a guard there. I lay sweating in the linens while he demanded to know who Karen was and what she was doing.

'I'm getting these AIDS-infected linens to our cleaning service as fast as possible.'

'I'm checking all hospital IDs,' he said. A brief silence, and then he said, 'You're the pastor? And you're handling linens? I don't think — '

'Officer, it is my job to certify every death in this hospital. It's my job to go through

451

possessions and make a list for the next of kin. It's my job to take bloody linens off a bed and cart them off when one of our patients passes and the cleaning crew has finished for the day. I can't have foul matter in a room overnight. Another lady shares that room, and I won't have her waking up and seeing the dreadful aftermath of someone else's death. But if you want to carry these out for me, I would be very grateful. My day started at six this morning, and I am weary. I would love to get to my own home.'

I wanted to applaud and cheer. The pastor might have been pushing wanted detectives out of hospitals for years, she was so smooth, so natural, in her mix of admonition and arrogance. The officer apologized, and said hastily he'd leave her to handle the cart.

We bumped quickly through the parking lot. I heard the chirp as she unlocked her car and the thump as she opened the trunk.

'I'm lifting sheets. They'll block the view to the elevator. Then get into the trunk. You'll be able to breathe, I think. At least enough until we're in the clear.'

She was in charge, and I meekly followed her instructions. In another moment, the trunk closed. I heard the rattle of the cart as she rolled it a short distance away. And then we moved smoothly out of the garage. Apparently the cop at the inside entrance had called over to the cops guarding the exit, and there was only a brief halt, before we were in motion again.

Between the bass viol's case and the Corolla trunk, I would choose the Corolla, but only because I was cushioned by the sheets and could put my knees up. Air was in short supply in both. I was thankful when Karen finally decided it was safe to let me out. She had driven up to a side street next to the campus that housed the University of Illinois's sprawling medical facilities.

I climbed out and scrabbled through the soiled laundry for my gun and Miss Claudia's Bible. All of the burrowing and dumping had shaken Miss Claudia's page markers out of it and damaged the spine and creased some pages. I smoothed the pages out that had gotten creased and put in as many of the page markers as I could find.

'What do you want to do now?' Karen asked.

'I'd like to give you a big smooch. And then I'd like to take a shower. You ever get tired of pastoral work, you could open an agency easy.'

The pastor laughed. 'I don't want to go through that again, ever. When I had to get that cart past that cop, I thought my pressure was going to start pushing blood straight out of my head and all over the garage . . . Where do you want to go from here?'

Morrell's car was still down near Lionsgate Manor. We agreed it might not be smart for me to show up there again tonight. Everything I wanted to do involved making phone calls, from talking to Murray Ryerson to finding Petra's college roommate.

'You can make those calls from my house,' Karen offered. 'I have an early meeting tomorrow, and it'd be easier on me if you spent the night with me than driving you up to Evanston.'

She rented the second floor of an old workman's cottage on the Northwest Side. It was on a quiet street, a few blocks from the river, with a little balcony where she sat in the mornings to drink coffee. She showed me to the bathroom and gave me towels and soap. I was a good four inches taller than Karen, but I could wear her T-shirts. She gave me one to sleep in.

When I got out of the shower, Karen had opened a bottle of wine and set out a plate of cheese and crackers. A big orange cat she called Bernardo materialized and wrapped himself around her legs. Somehow, despite the traumas of the day, just being able to sit and talk naturally, even to laugh without worrying about who was eavesdropping, raised my spirits.

After a glass of wine, I felt able to call Murray for details about Alito's murder. Karen had one of those phone services that lets you mask the number you're calling from, so I didn't need to worry about it showing up on Murray's caller ID. Of course, as soon as Murray heard my voice he wanted to know where I was. And a lot of other tedious stuff.

'Murray, darling, as I said earlier, I'm on the move. The more time you waste asking frivolous questions, the less we have for a heart-to-heart. I haven't heard the news, except a report that Alito's body fetched up on the riverbank down by one of those big scrap-metal yards. Tell me what happened.'

'Warshawski, it's all take with you and no give. I bought you a shirt, I bought you jeans, I let Dr. Herschel take a piece off me, and now this?'

'I know, Murray. Every time I see you in that sky-blue Mercedes convertible, I'm thinking, *There he goes, the people's reporter, never thinking of himself, always giving.* So give.'

'Oh, damn you, Warshawski! Alito was shot at close range, very close range, by someone who probably had an arm around him, very pally, and then dumped him over the bridge. What I'm hearing, whoever killed him must've thought Alito would go into the river or get buried in scrap. Instead, he landed in a pile that was due to be brought up for remelting. The guy operating the forklift fainted, almost fell onto a molten rebar belt.'

Murray paused a beat, then said, 'A lot of people think it's quite a coincidence, you calling me this morning to tell me you'd spotted Alito breaking into your office and him showing up dead this afternoon.'

I drank some more wine. 'Murray, does anyone at the *Star* feel attached to facts these days? Say, just in the interest of protecting the paper from a libel suit? I told you I'd found a witness who ID'd Alito. I couldn't have spotted him at my office myself because I wasn't there. I was in Stateville with the Hammer at the time Alito was breaking in.'

Murray brushed that off. 'I talked to the widow . . . What's her name? Hazel? Right . . . She said you'd threatened him.'

'Yep, I been hearing that. I told her exactly what I told you. I have a witness who ID'd him. Period, end of story.' I twirled the wineglass around, watching the light change the colors on

455

the surface. I had changed Alito's life, too, twirling a story around him as if he were wine in a glass.

'Of course I threatened him,' I said roughly. 'I didn't know my words would get him killed. I hoped they'd goad him into doing something that would betray himself or his handlers to me. But when I spoke, I pushed him and his handlers to the brink.

'Alito wasn't going to take the fall alone, not if Mallory or the FBI were coming after him, so he called . . . whoever hired him. Let's say, oh, George Dornick, his old partner when they were both with the force. Or one of Dornick's clients . . . Call him Les, just to give him a name. Alito's a drunk. He has a pension and a little boat and nothing else. Les and George are afraid he'll crack. He can do heavy lifting for them, but not if he's going to lead someone like Bobby Mallory straight to them.'

'Les?' Murray exploded. 'Like Les Strangwell?'

'Good night, Murray. Sweet dreams.'

I hung up, and grimaced at Karen. 'I think I really did send Larry Alito to his death. I think . . . I don't like myself very much today.'

'Did someone really identify him going into your building?'

I shook my head. 'It was a hunch, and apparently an accurate one, since it must have sent him scrambling to Dornick, or even Strangwell.'

I repeated Murray's description of the murder. 'It must have been Dornick . . . I can't see Strangwell embracing Alito, either . . . But his old partner? The man who gave him odd jobs to help him run his boat and his little retirement bungalow on the water? Yes, Alito would feel he had to trust him.'

'Maybe you did set in motion the events that got him murdered today. But you can't be greedy over guilt, you know. If he hadn't been the kind of person who would break into your office, your phone call wouldn't have made any difference in his life.' Karen looked at me earnestly, her round young face flushed.

''Greedy over guilt.' I like that. I have been greedily guilty all day.' My distress over my father swept through me again, a wave that made me shut my eyes in pain.

I changed the subject. We ended up drinking the whole bottle of wine and laughing over family stories, like the one about her grandmother whose father wouldn't let her learn to drive so she took the family car and drove it into the horse pond and then calmly went in the house, packed a suitcase, and took off for Chicago.

It was close to midnight when I finally helped my hostess pull the sofa apart and turn it into a guest bed. For the first time in a week, I slept eight hours. Like a tranquil baby.

45

The Good Book . . . and the Bad Ball

Karen had already left for her early meeting when I woke up. She'd made coffee and put a note next to the carafe, asking me to call her on her cellphone before I took off. 'Someone needs to know where you are. I'm your pastor. They can't compel my testimony.'

I smiled a little at the thought of Karen as my personal pastor. She didn't get a morning paper, so I took a cup of coffee back to the sofa bed to watch the television news. After the daily economic horror story, Alito's death dominated the morning shows.

Only Beth Blacksin, on Global Entertainment's Channel 13, suggested a sinister falling-out among friends as the motive behind his murder. And while she didn't name any names, she did say that Alito had been doing freelance security work for an important Illinois political campaign. I blew Murray a silent kiss. He must have talked to Beth, since the *Star* was also owned by Global.

Beth's story would force Dornick and Les Strangwell to spend some energy on damage control, which would take a little heat away from their searches for me and Petra. On the other hand, two of the networks mentioned the

'Chicago private eye, whom police badly want to question, after hearing of threats she made against the dead man.' One of them even had put my photograph on the screen, fortunately an old one copied from a newspaper. It had been taken when I had a head full of curls, not my current Marine cut.

'And I want to question you, too, Bobby,' I muttered. 'Who are you covering for? How much did you know back in 1967? You, too, were in Marquette Park during those riots.'

I got dressed, in my jeans and Karen's T-shirt. I'd rinsed my underwear out in her bathroom last night, but my socks were kind of funky. I decided to borrow some from Karen, although I felt a few qualms going through her chest of drawers looking for a pair. Her underwear was severely utilitarian, but her socks were fanciful, almost kiddish. I skipped Hello Kitty and some bright red devils and angels and settled on a pair showing Lisa Simpson jumping rope.

I hoped I wasn't pushing my luck, assuming that my pastor's landline was open. After all, she was connected to some of the Freedom Center's programs and might be getting the same federal scrutiny the nuns got. But I called my answering service, anyway, and found it had been deluged again with media calls, everyone wanting to interview the private eye whom the police badly wanted to question.

My clients were more squeamish. I spent almost an hour persuading two law firms to stay with me. A third wouldn't return my calls, and I didn't blame them. Until I could come out of hiding, I was a pretty sorry excuse for an investigator.

Bernardo, the big orange cat, appeared and decided I was better than no company at all. He began following me, winding in between my legs, so that I had to be careful not to trip over him. He jumped up onto the table next to the sofa bed while I was stripping the sheets off it and converting it back to a sofa and started sniffing my Smith & Wesson.

When I snatched the gun out of the way, he began exploring Miss Claudia's Bible. My attention was on the gun, checking the safety and putting it in my tuck holster, so I didn't see his leap, just Miss Claudia's Bible flying off the table.

'Bernardo!' I cried. 'That book took a beating last night. It doesn't need you throwing it around. We're holding it in trust.'

The spine, which had cracked during the flight through the laundry, split completely with the fall. I didn't want to try to tape it together, which would damage the fragile leather, but I could put a rubber band around it and leave it at Karen's until I had time to glue it properly.

The fall had opened the binding along the spine and pulled the leather away from the front cover. It was when I started to press the leather around the edges of the buckram cover boards underneath to hold the leather in place, that I saw the negatives poking out from beneath the endpaper. I sucked in a breath and sat down slowly, as if I were balancing a crate of eggs on my head.

I carefully peeled the endpaper back completely. There, between the buckram and the paper, were two strips of negatives inside a folded sheet of onionskin. I risked putting my battery back in my cellphone long enough to use the camera, shooting the strips the way I found them in the Bible under the endpaper, then shooting my own fingertips pulling them out. Each strip had twelve exposures on it. On the onionskin wrapping, in faded block letters, Lamont Gadsden had printed PICTURES TAKEN IN MARQUETTE PARK, AUGUST 6, 1966.

I held the negatives up to the table lamp, but it wasn't possible to make them out. I'd have to find someone with dependable skills and a real darkroom, not an ordinary photo shop. The Cheviot Labs, a forensic engineering lab I use, was the only place I could think of. They were in the northwest suburbs, which meant risking a trip down near Lionsgate to pick up my car. It was better for me to gamble on being spotted than for me to entrust the negatives to a messenger.

I called Karen, who was just finishing her meeting, and told her I was going to pick up Morrell's car. 'I've found something that I need to get to a lab. I'm going to leave it at your place while I fetch the car because I can't afford to be found with it on me. I'll write down what you should do with it in case I don't make it back here.'

'Vic, is this about Lamont? If it is, it was me who started you on this journey. I'm going with you to the end. I'll be home in fifteen minutes.

Wait for me in the alley.'

I didn't put up even a token argument. I was glad to have my personal pastor take charge. I wrapped the negatives back in their onionskin, then slipped them between the pages of a copy of *Harper's*.

I watched for Karen through the kitchen window, and, as soon as her turquoise Corolla appeared, I ran down the back stairs. While she drove, I told her about the pictures that Steve Sawyer-Kimathi had thought would clear him in court forty years ago.

She nodded and pushed harder on the accelerator. We reached the Cheviot Labs industrial park a little before eleven. I had called my contact in the company, Sanford Rieff, from Karen's cell while we were en route. Sanford brought Cheviot's photography expert out to the lobby with him, introduced him as Theo, and hurried back to a meeting of his own.

Theo, dressed in black as behooved a would-be auteur, spoke in a rumbly Slavic accent. He had crooked teeth, and a silver pentacle in his left ear, but he handled the negatives carefully, slipping them out of the brittle onionskin Lamont had wrapped around them and into a plastic sleeve.

'These pictures may provide evidence of a murder,' I said. 'One that took place forty years ago. And they're going to be needed as part of a trial, so do your best. They're all that remains in the way of evidence, so please — '

'Don't screw up? I understand.' Theo smiled reassuringly. 'These come from Instamatic camera, my own first camera, a used one I found on black market in Odessa. I treat as my own.'

He had me watch as he logged the negatives into a database: the number of strips, the number of frames, my name with the date and time I'd brought them in. 'Okay? We have cafeteria, we have park, make yourselves comfortable. Maybe one hour, maybe two.'

I was too restless to sit in their lunchroom. Karen came outside with me but stopped at a bench to make calls of her own while I walked around the perimeter of a little lake. The Canada geese, who've become the scourge of the northern United States, were out in force, drilling peg holes in the ground and leaving unappetizing deposits behind them. I skirted the soiled path and went into a small wood. I kept trying not to look at my watch, but I couldn't bear walking too far from the Cheviot building.

Finally, a little after one, Theo came to find us, beaming like an obstetrician who's about to announce a normal delivery. 'You can come now. I have made many shots, cropped, shaded. You see what you can see.'

There had been twenty-four black-and-white negatives in the Bible, but Theo had multiplied them into over a hundred prints, each with several different exposures, some cropped to focus on individual faces. Theo had clipped most to light tables around a conference table. Some were blown up and attached to the walls.

'That's Lamont, with Johnny Merton,' I murmured to Karen, as we started with the first picture on the first negative, which showed three black youths, arms linked across one another's shoulders, wearing the berets that wannabe revolutionaries used to sport. 'You can see Johnny's tattoos. I'm guessing Steve Sawyer is the third man. I've never seen a picture of him when he was young.'

Their faces were solemn but joyful, getting ready for a big adventure. Lamont didn't appear in any of the other pictures. It had been his camera, after all. He had several shots from the beginning of the march, including one of Martin Luther King, Jr., at the front and Johnny nearby.

'That might be a collector's item,' I whispered to Karen. 'When this is all over, Miss Ella might sell it, get a little comfort for herself.'

We moved on to look at Harmony Newsome's ardent young face. She was arm in arm with a solemn-eyed nun.

'Frankie,' Karen murmured.

Lamont had also photographed rictuses of hate in the crowd. He'd gotten one of the vilest of the racist signs — BURN THEM LIKE THEY DID THE JEWS — that littered the park, and he'd caught a can of pop just as it exploded in a cop's face. Onlookers, their faces indistinct, seemed to be cheering.

As the violence increased, the pictures began to get blurry — there had been too much crowd motion for an unsteady hand with a little Kodak — but almost every frame told some recognizable piece of the story. We looked at a man throwing something, both the missile and the man indistinct. In separate prints, Theo had done as good a close-up of both as he could. The

464

missile remained a blur, but the man's face might be identifiable.

'I think that must have been the Hammer,' I said, looking at a snake-covered forearm pushing Dr. King's head down. 'Dr. King was hit by a brick that day. Maybe Johnny was trying to get him out of the way.'

Harmony Newsome appeared in the next shot, clutching the side of her head. Her hand was covering something round and whitish that seemed to be stuck there. In the next frame, she had crumpled to the ground, the round whitish thing having fallen from her hand. Theo had focused on it and blown it up so we could see it was a ball with spikes of some kind in it.

Following that close-up, we saw a cop in riot gear, squatting to retrieve the spiked ball. In the next frame, he was standing and stuffing the ball into his trouser pocket. Both shots were blurry, but you could still tell what he was doing.

At the next light table, I cried out loud. My uncle Peter, his face in clear focus, was pointing a finger — in congratulation? in admonition? — at the man who'd thrown the missile and who seemed to be clasping his hands over his head in a kind of victory dance. His features were indistinct, but Theo had done his best with different exposures, different croppings. The square jaw and shock of thick, curly hair made me think it was a young Harvey Krumas, but I couldn't be sure.

'That ball.' I walked back to the light table with shots of Harmony Newsome lying on the ground. 'I want to see it as clearly as possible.

And the cop. We'll never see his face, but his badge is turned to the camera. Can you get the badge number?'

Theo had loaded all his different exposures and prints into a computer program. 'Always is best to start with negatives,' he said, 'but maybe here is enough information to tell us this story.'

Karen and I stood behind him while he fiddled with the images. On the ball, underneath the nails, you could just make out the big swooping *F* followed by the *o*. *Nellie Fox*.

I sucked in my breath. I'd been sure without the picture, but it was still hard to have it confirmed. Those holes that I thought my father and my uncle Bernie might have punched so they could hang up the ball and use it for batting practice, those came from nails. Someone had pounded nails into a baseball. Somehow had thrown it at the marchers and gotten Harmony Newsome in the temple. And then someone had retrieved the ball and removed the nails.

I felt a sick apprehension as Theo focused on the four-digit badge number of the cop in riot gear. When we finally could read it, I let out a little sigh. I didn't know whose it was, but I still could reel off my father's by heart. At least it hadn't been him pocketing a murder weapon at a crime scene.

46

Discovery

I made up a storyboard out of a selection of pictures: Sister Frankie with Harmony New-some, Harmony with her hand over the ball after it struck her in the temple, Peter with the man who might have been Harvey Krumas, the close-up of the ball, the cop pocketing the ball, the close-up of his badge. Theo let me use a computer to type captions for the pictures and a letter to Bobby Mallory. I addressed him formally by his title, not just because he'd pissed me off believing Hazel Alito's wild accusation against me but because I didn't know what he'd been doing in Marquette Park all those years ago. He'd been a nineteen-year-old rookie getting baptized by fire under the protective arm of veteran officer Tony Warshawski.

What had any of them done in the park that day?

Dear Captain Mallory:
These pictures were taken by Lamont Gadsden in Marquette Park on August 6, 1966. I found the negatives this morning, and they are now in a secure location. I believe the people who broke into my home and office this past week were looking for these negatives.

As you perhaps recall, in January 1967 Steve Sawyer was arrested and convicted for the 1966 murder of Harmony Newsome (photograph 4). No murder weapon was ever produced. Sawyer's conviction was based solely on an uncorroborated confession that was extorted under torture by George Dornick and Larry Alito.

At his trial, Mr. Sawyer tried to insist that Lamont Gadsden had pictures which proved his innocence. The photographs attached to this letter raise serious questions, at minimum, about the chain of custody of evidence at his trial.

Before you ask the State's Attorney's Office to file charges against me in Larry Alito's death, I suggest you revisit this 1966 murder, the 1967 trial of Steve Sawyer, and, in particular, that you discover the identity of the officer wearing badge number 8396.

For my protection, I am sending a copy of this letter to my lawyer. I am notifying Judge Arnold Coleman, who served as Steve Sawyer's public defender during his trial, and Steve Sawyer. I am also notifying Greg Yeoman, who is John Merton's current counsel.

You may leave a message with my attorney about what next steps you wish to take in resolving both the 1966 murder and your baseless accusations against me in the death of Larry Alito.

While Theo made up a dozen copies of my storyboard, I called Freeman Carter, my lawyer, and told him I had evidence so hot that it needed to be in a vault.

'I wondered when I would hear from you, Warshawski. The cops have been to my office already demanding that I produce your body, so I knew it was only a matter of time before you remembered you had a right to counsel.'

'I'm hoping it won't come to that, Freeman. But let me give you a quick thumbnail of what's happening.'

I explained as much as I knew, about Lamont and Steve-Kimathi and Dornick, Krumas and my uncle. I even reported finding the Nellie Fox baseball in the trunk of my family's possessions.

'So what do you want me to do with all this?' Freeman asked.

'Hold on to the pictures and the baseball. Hold off the cops. I need to find Petra now if I can, and then I'll worry about everything else.'

Theo, who'd heard my end of the conversation, said Cheviot could store the negatives and the extra prints for me, but I explained that the state could compel Cheviot to produce them. My lawyer had certain privileges that could keep the government at bay, at least for a few days. I did ask Theo to use their messenger service to deliver my storyboards to Bobby, Judge Coleman, and Greg Yeoman. I would drop a copy off at Fit for Your Hoof myself, if I could do so without a tail, but I wanted to watch Freeman Carter put my originals and the hundred prints Theo had produced in his office safe.

By the time Karen and I got back on the tollway, we were in the middle of the oozing

Chicago rush hour. *Slow hour*, it should be called. While we drove, Karen reported on the repairs to Sister Frankie's apartment at the Freedom Center.

'The men doing the work are doing a terrible job. After tearing the place apart, all they've done is put up some studs. They started to work on the wiring and blew the circuits for the whole building. And the sisters couldn't even get the building management to restore power until they offered to send pickets to the owner's home.'

'Yes, I think those are phantom builders, sent by Harvey Krumas to make sure any evidence of the fire bombing got destroyed.' It was one of my nagging worries about Petra. Had she really texted Dornick or Alito or Harvey himself to come get the bag of bottle fragments I'd collected from the fire bombing?

Karen moved on to a piece of encouraging news: Miss Claudia was a little stronger today. Karen had sent a pastoral intern to check on her and other high-needs patients, and she'd heard from the intern while we were waiting for Theo to develop the pictures.

'It's as if turning over the Bible to you took enough of a load off her spirit that she had some strength left for her own life,' Karen said. 'It makes me wonder if she knew all along that those pictures were in there.'

'Don't you think if Miss Claudia knew about the pictures, she would have pulled them out and had prints made?' I objected. 'What I imagine happened is that Lamont went to consult Johnny about what to do with the pictures, whether he should risk trying to testify at Sawyer's trial.

'Maybe Lamont had prints made, prints that disappeared when he did, but he was smart enough to stash the negatives with the one person who really believed in him: his auntie. He couldn't count on Rose Hebert. She was too much under her angry father's control. And he couldn't count on Johnny, who might barter them to save his own skin in some plea bargain down the road. But Claudia adored him and stood by him. So he peeled open the endpaper, inserted the negatives, and gave the Bible to Claudia. She must have noticed the cover was lumpy. And, at some level, she might have suspected he had something hidden in there. But she probably was afraid to find out what it was.'

'Why?' Karen inched forward toward the Deerfield Toll Plaza. I fished in my wallet for exact change.

'She didn't know about the pictures, but Ella kept claiming Lamont sold drugs. Claudia might have thought she was holding a packet of heroin or some acid or something.'

We were both quiet for a few car lengths, but Karen kept glancing at me, biting her lips. She finally blurted out, 'There's something you need to know, but I've been worrying about how to tell you. When I talked to my intern, she said some men had been around looking for me. They heard from the head nurse that you and I were both visiting Miss Claudia last night, and they thought I would know where you were.'

'Cops?' I demanded.

Karen shook her head. 'My intern wouldn't

know something like that. She assumed they were, but she didn't think to ask for any ID. And, after everything you've said today, I do wonder if they could be with George Dornick's company.'

I rubbed my forehead. 'That means they could be at your home. After we go to my lawyer's, you'd better let me come back with you to check for an ambush. If it was Dornick's people, he may also have dug up your cellphone number, which means they could be tracking us.'

I smiled bleakly. 'No one is safe if they are around me. Dornick is doing an excellent job of driving that point home. Perhaps you and Bernardo could move into an empty room at Lionsgate Manor until this mess gets cleaned up.'

'I'll be okay, Vic. They'll believe me when I explain I'm just the pastor who's been too naïve to see through you.' She made a soft O of surprise with her rosebud lips, and I laughed.

'It's my Victorian face,' she added. 'No one ever thinks I understand the big bad world. It's you who's in trouble and in danger.'

The traffic began moving marginally faster. I kept checking the road, using the makeup mirror in the sun visor and peering into the right wing mirror. The same cars crawled around us. I couldn't tell if any of them were paying us special attention. It was when we oozed off the Kennedy into the Loop that I began to wonder about a certain gray BMW. It had an impressive collection of antennas, and for the last few miles on the expressway it had seemed to be trading places with a black Ford Expedition. Karen's turquoise Corolla was easy to pick out in a crowd, and they hadn't needed to stay close to us until we exited. But then the BMW swooped around two cabs and a bus and landed in front of us. The Expedition was moving in from the side.

'We have company,' I said. 'I'm jumping out before they pin us. I'll try to send a cop your way.'

Before Karen could react or speak or even slow the car down, I had stuffed the envelope of negatives and prints into the back of my jeans and opened the passenger door. I held on to it tightly, got my feet and myself out and running alongside the car, then slammed the door and tore off down LaSalle Street toward Freeman's office. I heard whistles, screams, the screech of tires, and then a messenger bike was on the sidewalk, doing wheelies around me, while another one came at me from the south.

I pushed through the first revolving doors I came to and sprinted through the arcade. I heard steps behind me, shouts of outrage as my pursuer collided with someone, but I didn't waste time looking back.

The envelope was digging into my rear as I ran, but the pain reassured me that I still had my precious cargo. I should have left it at Cheviot. *Regrets, save them for later*, I panted to myself, and sprinted around a trio of slow-moving women to the building's rear revolving door.

Wells Street seemed to be full of messenger bikes. Real messengers? Pursuers? Impossible to tell the difference. A bike jumped the curb and headed straight at me, another was approaching from the side. I could see the glint of a pistol in the first man's hand. As he lifted it, I pulled off my Cubs cap and rolled on the ground. When he reached me, pointing the pistol at me, I stuffed the cap into the spokes of his bike. The bike wobbled, toppled. The pistol went off. The crowd screamed and scattered, and I sprinted up the stairs to the El.

A train was rumbling into the station. I shoved past a line of commuters sliding their cards through turnstile slots. They yelled at me angrily, and the stationmaster hollered in his microphone, but I jumped over the turnstile and ran up the final flight of stairs. I managed to squeeze through the train's doors just as they were closing.

The car was packed. I collapsed, standing against the doors, sobbing for air, while the mass of commuters pressed into me. My gun was cutting into my side, the envelope into my back. My legs were trembling from my run and from my fear. I thought of Karen back on Monroe Street. I hoped that when they saw I'd gone, they'd left her alone. Please, please don't let her be one more person injured in my wake.

For several stops, I rode without being conscious of where I was, moving away from the doors as we pulled into a station, leaning back against them when they closed again. We were heading north on the Brown Line, I finally realized. And, wherever it dropped me, there might be watchers waiting for me. How big an operation could Dornick afford to mount against me? How many El stops could he stake out? Was I making him more powerful than he possibly could be?

I couldn't ride the train forever. I got off at the next stop, Armitage Avenue. It's in the heart of Yuppieville, and there was a good crowd to cover me leaving the station.

Because it was Yuppieville, it was filled with a million little boutiques. I longed for a wig, something that would really transform me, but the best I could come up with was another hat, a white golfing cap. The thousand dollars I'd cashed last week was dwindling, but I bought a new shirt, too, replacing Karen's navy T-shirt with a white one that proclaimed G-R-R-L POWER. Maybe it would rub off on me. It had been days since I'd had dark glasses on, and my eyes were aching from the glare. I went into a drugstore and found a cheap pair. And lipstick. In a coffee shop, I picked up an extra-large herbal tea and went into their restroom to wash off and plan my next move.

When I was clean, and rehydrated, I felt marginally better. But I couldn't imagine any course of action, no way to get out of the area, no useful destination that would help me find Petra, no way to get my photos to Freeman Carter. By now, Dornick might have scoped out Morrell's Honda. I couldn't take a chance on doubling back to Lionsgate for the car. I couldn't go home or to my office, although I was halfway between the two.

Outside the store, a homeless man was hawking *Streetwise*. '*As long as you have a roof over your head and a family that loves you,*' the guy in Millennium Park had intoned yesterday. A roof that you can't get to, a family that's trying to gun you down. I gave the man a dollar. And thought of Elton Grainger.

He, too, was near here. When Elton wouldn't give me a straight answer or look in me in the face, I'd been sure he'd seen Petra running from my office. Months ago, he had told me how to find his crib. I would find it. I would threaten to camp out there until he told me what I wanted to know about my cousin.

I'd been heading gradually west from the station while making my purchases. I waited at a bus stop and got on the westbound bus. I fished some singles out of my pocket for the fare, then watched through the back window as we trundled along. It was a tiresomely slow ride, but I was too spent to walk. And at least this way, I could see if anyone had spotted me.

At Damen Avenue, I got off the bus and set out on foot. Chicago streets are tangled here because of the way the river snakes through the Northwest Side. I needed to get under the Kennedy Expressway and then follow Honore to the river. A shack under the railway embankment, Elton had said.

Rush hour was over. People were beginning to fill up the restaurants that lined the streets. I felt overwhelmed with envy for the diners I could see through the windows, eating and laughing together. This was what it was like to be Elton, trudging back each night from his station outside the coffee bar on my street, a Vietnam veteran

476

with no home and only the price of a bottle or a sandwich in his pocket.

On leaden feet, I walked under the expressway and turned east and then north again. The railway embankment was surrounded by razor wire, but there was a gap hidden by the Kennedy's shadow. I slipped through it and crawled up the embankment. Decades of Chicagoans had tossed their garbage from their cars, and, in places along the embankment, it was waist high. I could see the path Elton had carved through the refuse and followed it up to the tracks and down the other side, where the embankment ended at the river's edge.

I didn't spot Elton's shack at first, and wondered if in his paranoia he had misdirected me. However, a faint trail led through the under-brush and refuse, and I followed it to the river. The water here was a thick brownish green. Ducks bobbed in it, along with plastic bottles and sticks. There wasn't a visible current, and mosquitoes rose in clouds from the thicket of shrubs that lined the bank.

From the river's edge, I looked back and finally saw the shack, almost invisible against the underbrush and discarded tires. It had a faded logo from the C&NW railroad on it; I suppose they'd once used it for storage. As I got closer, I saw Elton had put a rain barrel on the roof and fixed up a showerhead. There weren't any windows in the shack, and the boards it was built with were gray-black with damp, but he had covered any holes with a variety of metal, Styrofoam, and plastic sheeting.

I clambered up the embankment and made my way around to the side where the door was. 'Elton? You home? It's V. I. Warshawski. We need to talk.'

I rapped smartly on the panel and heard a movement from inside the shack, an intake of a sob. I pulled open the ramshackle door. My cousin Petra blinked at me from a nest of sleeping bags.

'Vic! How did you know? Who told you? Who's with you?'

I couldn't speak. I was so overcome with relief at the sight of Petra that I just stood there, shaking my head in wonder.

47

A River Runs Through It

I was on the floor, holding Petra, while she sobbed against my shoulder. 'Vic, I'm so scared, it's so awful, don't yell at me. I didn't mean . . . I didn't want — '

'I'm not going to yell at you, little cousin,' I said softly, stroking her dirty hair, 'when it's my hot temper that made you too scared to trust me.'

'They told me if I talked to anyone, they'd shoot Mom and the girls and Daddy would go to prison, I didn't know what to do. They said you wanted Daddy to go to prison, you were just using me, and if I didn't help them, if I talked to you about what I was doing, you'd punish me and him and Mom and everyone.'

'Who are *they* Les Strangwell? Dornick?'

She swallowed a sob and nodded.

Mosquitoes were swarming into the shack, biting us through our clothes. I had to close the door, although there wasn't much air in the small space. With the door shut, it smelled of damp river mud and stale sweat. The only light came from a couple of makeshift skylights Elton had created by cutting squares in the roof and filling them with discarded windowpanes. Outside, the sun was starting to set. I could just make out my cousin's bleached, frightened face.

'It started with the Nellie Fox baseball, didn't it?' I said. 'The day you found it in my trunk, you talked about it in the office.'

'Me and my ultra-big mouth! It was only partly the ball. Everything started at the fundraiser when I talked about Johnny Merton in front of that creepy Judge Coleman. I heard him tell Uncle Harvey that you'd better not be screwing around in the Harmony case, which at first I thought was funny. I thought he was saying something about you and music, or your mom, or something. And Uncle Harvey said they'd nailed the Anacondas for that, and he didn't want this to be some snake coming back to life after its head got chopped off. And then, the day after the fundraiser, when Mr. Strangwell brought me in to work for him, he told me it was top secret because you wanted to sabotage Brian's campaign.'

'I see. So he told you I had some kind of evidence that would destroy the campaign and you had to find it?'

A train thundered overhead, shaking the shack. We had to wait for it to pass before we could talk. When the noise finally died away, we could hear the ordinary sweet sounds of a summer's evening, the birds' last songs, the little insects chirruping.

'The evidence?' I prodded my cousin when she remained silent.

'At first, it seemed like a game, going around to all those places where Daddy and his folks used to live, and then it turned scary. When that nun got killed and you were in the hospital, they

480

told me there would be something in her apartment, and they sent this horrible, horrible man to take me there. That was when I started to get really afraid and I almost told you, but then I thought of what they said about you being, like, an old lover of Johnny Merton's and — '

'What!' I was jolted into sitting up. 'Petra! Jesus, no! I represented him when I was a public defender, but he was one of the scariest people I ever met, at least until I got to know Les Strangwell. And you don't sleep with your clients even if you want to. Please, tell me you believe me on this!'

'Don't get mad at me, Vic, I can't take it!' Her voice held an undercurrent of hysteria. She'd been alone with her fears too long.

'No, baby, I'm not mad at you. But it upsets me that they would tell such a big lie about me. I like you enough that I don't want you to believe it, that's all.'

'Okay,' she muttered.

I waited a tick, hoping for more, something like 'Of course I don't believe it,' but when she said nothing I pushed her to finish her story. 'So you came along to Sister Frankie's apartment with the horrible man . . . Was that Larry Alito? . . . And when you found me there, you signaled to him to leave. And then you texted him and told him to come get the bag of evidence.'

'It sounds awful,' she whispered, 'hearing you say it out loud, but it got worse. They told me you had these old pictures, that was what they wanted to find, but they wanted the baseball, too. See, every morning Mr. Strangwell would

481

ask for a report from me on what you were doing and what you were looking for, and when I told him you wanted me to do a little work for you, then he was really excited and said to do everything you asked and report back to him. But when I looked up those contractors, I saw their address was the same as Uncle Harvey's Chicago apartment, and that was weird. So I asked Mr. Strangwell, and then he said . . . he said . . . ' For a moment, she couldn't go on, but then she managed to pull herself together. 'That was when the Strangler said if I didn't do exactly what he said, Mom and the girls would die and Daddy would go to prison.'

I kept petting her and crooning to her, trying to assure her that we could fix it all so that no one got killed or sent to prison, although I wasn't sure about either of those things. Finally, when she seemed a bit calmer, I asked how she'd ended up here in Elton's shack.

'That was after they made me open your office for them.'

'Yeah, babe, I know that much. I saw you on my video camera.'

'They said you had a picture that might send Daddy to jail,' she whispered. 'When I told them you and I hadn't been able to get into your old South Chicago house, they made me go down there with them to show them which house it was. Then when Uncle Sal gave me your apartment keys so I could make up your bed and bring you some yogurt — you know, while you were staying at Dr. Herschel's — Mr. Strangwell made me give him the keys to make copies.

'I guess then they tore your house apart. I wasn't there. This one man, the one they called Larry, he found an old picture of Uncle Tony and all of them playing ball together, and the Strangler was just totally pissed, because he said only a drunk idiot would think that proved anything about anyone. So they decided they had to go through your office.

'I had to go with them. They wouldn't let me just tell them your keypad code because the Strangler said if you were there — like, maybe you didn't get in to see the snake man — you'd let me in. Then they went just totally crazy inside your office, and I was terrified they would kill me because I'd seen too much. And Mr. Dornick kept phoning the Strangler and saying how could he be so sure a big-mouth like me wouldn't end up babbling it all to you. So I pretended I was having my period, that I was bleeding and needed the bathroom, and went down the hall.

'This horrible man, the one they called Larry, he was standing there, holding his gun, and I saw the back door and just bolted outside and ran like fury. And Elton was there, out on the street, so I remembered how he talked about his crib. And I begged him to save my life. So the bus was just coming, and we jumped on. And he brought me here. And I've been too scared to leave.'

While I cradled her, I tried to think of a safe house, someplace where Petra at least could sleep while I tried to get the police to listen to my side of the story. I was imagining and discarding ideas when Petra suddenly asked about the pictures.

'What are they?'

'It's an old story and an ugly one. Your father was at a riot in Marquette Park in 1966 — '

'A race riot, you mean. When blacks were tearing down the neighborhood.'

'Those came later. This was a white riot, your father and your uncle Harvey and about eight thousand other people screaming and yelling at Martin Luther King. The pictures show your father and your uncle Harvey in the vicinity of the murder of a black woman. They show a police officer — I'm guessing it was either George Dornick or Larry Alito — pocketing the murder weapon. Later, Dornick and Alito tortured a black man into confessing to the murder.'

'No, you're lying! Daddy couldn't . . . Uncle Harvey wouldn't — '

I cut her off. 'I know how you feel, because my father was involved, too. He watched the torture, and when he tried to stop it they threatened to send Peter to prison. So my father — my father, the best man I've ever known — he turned his back on the torturers to save Peter. And later he took the baseball — that Nellie Fox baseball, the murder weapon — to save your father from prison.'

'That's not true!' Petra screamed, getting to her feet. 'You're making this up!'

'I wish I was.' I got to my feet, too, and reached under my shirt for the photo album. The light was too dim for her to make out much, but she pretended to study the pages.

'Sister Frankie was at the march with the

484

murdered woman. She was killed to keep her from talking to me. Why do you think they sent you to her apartment to collect evidence? It was to keep someone like me from turning it over to the cops. That building is under Homeland Security surveillance because the nuns provide assistance to immigrants, but they didn't take your picture, or Larry Alito's, the night you two showed up, because George Dornick has good connections to Homeland Security.'

'I can't let you publish these,' she whispered. 'You mustn't, you mustn't.'

'Petra, forty years of wrong are sitting on us. On you and me, I mean. Forty years of wrong our own fathers did. I can't even guess how many other men Dornick and Alito tortured. I can't keep quiet, not to save Peter, not even to save Tony.'

'Oh, *damn* you,' she choked. 'It's like Uncle Sal says, you're the only one who gets to be right. The rest of us don't count in your universe.'

'Damn you, too, Petra Warshawski. You've put my life in danger along with your own. If you'd told me all this a month ago, Sister Frankie might still be alive. How many people have to die to protect Peter?'

We were glaring at each other, our noses almost touching in the cramped space, both panting with fury and fear, when we heard footfalls crashing down the side of the embankment. The noise of many people, not Elton. Flashlights played around the embankment. The summer evening was ending, and the pale light coming in through Elton's skylights had turned purple while we quarreled. I squeezed Petra's arm and put my hand over her mouth.

The envelope of pictures . . . They had to survive, whatever happened to me. I looked wildly around and grabbed a black garbage bag from the pile of bags and blankets on the floor. I rolled the envelope up in it. I didn't have time to get the bag or Petra out of the shack. I stuffed it into a crack and pushed my cousin against the sliver of wall next to the door. I stood in front of her. When the door opened, we wouldn't be instantly visible.

I pulled the Smith & Wesson from the tuck holster, flipped off the safety, and spoke directly into my cousin's ear. 'When I say go, you stoop down, run out of there, and jump in that water. Swim across, get to Uncle Sal.'

It wasn't a great plan, but it was all I had. Even in the purple light, I could see her eyes large and terrified in her pale face. The muscles in her throat moved, but she only nodded.

'This is the place?' The voice was George Dornick's.

'Yes, yessir, it is,' Elton, quavering, barely audible.

'What a dump. You are a worthless piece of shit, you know that?' Dornick, amused, contemptuous. 'Open the door. I want to see the girl myself.'

'You said you wasn't going to hurt her none,' Elton was anxious. 'You told me you just wanted to talk to her.'

'That's right, dirtbag, no one's going to get

486

hurt. The girl needs to go home, that's all.' That was a third man, a stranger, and when he laughed a couple of other men joined in: Dornick and two, perhaps three, subordinates.

Petra's heart was jumping against my shoulder blades. I reached behind me and squeezed her hand. The shack door swung open. A flashlight played around the tiny space, found my feet. I dropped, rolled, and crashed into the figure behind the light, knocking him to the ground.

'Go!' I yelled, and kept rolling, away from the shack so that the second flashlight followed me. I heard Petra behind me. I fired at random to cover her dash out the door, down to the river, the moment's hesitation, the splash as she dropped into the water. *Good girl!* I started down the slope after her, but the lights followed me, and someone fired. I dropped into the brush, landing on something large and sharp, rolled away again, and fired blindly toward the light.

'That's Warshawski. Goddamn it, where's the girl?'

'Someone jumped in the water.'

The person I'd knocked over had recovered, and I saw the flashlight beam going down to the water. A shot sang out over the river, and ducks began honking and squawking. Wings flapped, and the man shot again. Shouts sounded from the far side.

I tried working my way to the bank. An old tire and a shrub tripped me. I moved backward on my knees and one hand, keeping my gun in front of me. More shots, and then Dornick was spreading his troops in a triangle around me. Dornick shouted a command, and two guns fired in succession, one on either side.

I edged backward while he issued his orders, but the men in the triangle around me were all shining their lights into the brush where I'd landed. I was a fox in the hunt. They had light-finding, heat-seeking missiles, or some crap, that would take care of me.

'Where are the negatives, Vic?' Dornick called.

'My lawyer has them, George.'

'You never made it to your lawyer. We were there ahead of you.'

'I messengered them into town . . . The same time I sent Bobby Mallory his copies.'

Bobby's name stopped him briefly, but Dornick only said, 'We know you were on your way to Carter's office. We were listening to that girl's cellphone.'

'Girl's cellphone? You mean the Reverend Karen Lennon? I bet you were fun as a little boy, Georgie. Bet you were the one who crawled under the jungle gym to look at your classmates' panties. Did you start with that and then move on to torturing mice and cats? Captain Mallory isn't going to watch your back anymore, Georgie. Not when he reads my report.'

'Without the negatives, your report doesn't mean shit,' Dornick said. 'You tell me where they are, and I'll let the drunk go.'

'It's okay, Vic,' Elton quavered. 'You don't have to do nothing on my account.'

'What happened, Elton?' I called. 'How'd they know you had Petra here?'

'Someone in the coffee place across from your office,' Dornick said. 'They told us a homeless guy had gone off with the girl, and we started shaking all the winos and weirdos in Bucktown. And a guy like Elton doesn't take a lot of shaking before he falls off the tree, isn't that right, dirtbag?'

'I'm sorry, Vic. I know you saved my life and all and I wish you hadn't, that's the God's truth. If you'da let me die, my little girl wouldn't be in so much trouble. *Your* little girl, I mean. She's a real nice gal, Vic. You can be proud of her. So don't worry about me no more now, you hear? You don't need to look after me no more, okay?'

Dornick ignored Elton's quavery apology. 'I want those negatives, Vic.'

He ordered his crew to come into the brambles after me. 'Alive: I want to search her. I don't want her dead . . . yet.'

The men crashed down the bank and into the thicket. I fired and hit one of them but missed the other two. And then they had me by the arms, and I was kicking, shooting, but the end was ordained at the beginning. They held me while Dornick ran his hands inside my clothes, squeezed my nipples.

I stomped hard on his instep and kicked back at the kneecap of the man behind me. Both men cried out. They weren't used to pain. I broke free, but Dornick grabbed me before I could start running. He wrenched my gun away and tossed it into the underbrush. An underling held me while Dornick slapped my face. Left side, right side, left side.

'You watch too many old Nazi flicks, George.' I said. 'That's always what Erich von Stroheim does.'

He hit me again. 'You're not as smart as Tony always claimed you were. Where are the pictures?'

'Freeman has them.'

'No, he doesn't.' *Slap*.

'I put them in a FedEx box on Armitage,' I said.

'Take the shack apart,' Dornick ordered. 'She wouldn't even leave them with a messenger from Cheviot. She sure didn't put them in a box.'

I had shot one man; the second man was holding me. Dornick held a gun on Elton while the fourth man dismantled his home. Elton gave little cries of misery as the walls were peeled apart, plastic bags torn open, his nest of sleeping bags ripped apart. It took a good twenty minutes, but the black garbage bag was gone. Petra must have grabbed it on her way out, determined to save Peter's hide.

Dornick was angry now. He held his gun on me, and I could see the red triangle of the laser sight in the dark toying with my chest, my head, figuring where best to shoot so as not to hit his lackey.

I went limp in the man's arms, took a breath — the kind Gabriella always wanted, down, down to my tailbone, shutting my eyes: '*Breathe, don't think. Breathe, don't think*' — and began my mother's signature aria, '*Non mi dir, bell'idol mio*' (Say not, my beloved).

Dornick's gun sounded, and I flinched. I

490

couldn't help it, ruining Mozart's fluid line, thinking instead of breathing. He'd missed.

'You goddammed asshole, you — '

The grip on my arms loosened. I broke free. I kicked hard against the kneecap, rolled to the ground, rolled toward Dornick. Elton had seized his legs. Dornick was flailing about, trying to get an angle where he could shoot Elton and not hit himself. He was stronger than the homeless man, but all that meant was that as he thrashed about he dragged Elton with him.

I gave a primitive yell, smashed my hand into his forearm, and seized the gun. A moment later, the embankment was awash in blue.

48

Up Against the Wall . . . All of You!

A police launch had arrived, but it took us all a few minutes to realize that. Two of Dornick's banditti tried to run off, but the launch turned its spotlight on the shore. A couple of cops pulled out rifles and ordered the men to stop where they were. Dornick was doubled over on the ground, but he shouted for help:

'Officer down! Officer down!' he cried. 'Get that bitch before she escapes. She grabbed my weapon.'

'He's a liar,' Elton cried in a high-pitched gabble. 'Vic, she was here with her girl. They were hiding from this man here. He's a psycho. We seen plenty like him in Vietnam, rogue soldiers who start shooting their own men. He'da killed Vic if I hadn't tackled him. And he broke my house in little pieces, just for nothing but to make me feel bad.'

'You look her up,' Dornick said. 'She already murdered one cop this week. She's out for revenge on the whole police force.'

Men in Kevlar vests jumped ashore. They covered all of us with their assault rifles and herded us onto the launch. I was shaking so badly, I almost fell into the river. The cops hoisted me over the side of the launch, and left me under guard while they went back for

Dornick's wounded thug.

Petra was sitting in the stern, wrapped in a gray police blanket. In some dim part of my exhausted mind, I felt relief at knowing she was safe. But mostly I wanted to lie down on the deck and sleep.

Once we were all on board, Dornick had the gall to try to pretend I had held him hostage — him and his three banditti — and forced them to the river, where I proposed shooting them, just as I had shot Larry Alito.

'That's not true, Mr. Dornick.' Petra called out from the stern. 'You know you tried to kill me and Vic. I don't even know how she escaped, except I guess she's more resourceful than you.'

That made me smile. The cops wouldn't let me go over to Petra, so I blew her a kiss.

In the meantime, though, the river police had looked me up and found Bobby's outstanding warrant on me. They cuffed me, and told me I had the right to remain silent, but as we rode downriver I kept repeating Bobby's cellphone number and telling them to call Bobby before they booked me and left Dornick free to flee their jurisdiction. Petra's insistence that it was Dornick who'd been threatening us made them decide to give me at least enough of the benefit of the doubt to call Bobby, who ordered them to bring all of us in.

At the Grand Avenue Landing station, they transferred us from the launch to a paddy wagon. It was one of the old beat-up ones, without springs or shocks. Dornick was beside himself with rage. Him, the head of Mountain

Hawk Security, a twenty-year veteran, in the wagon with common criminals.

'I'm not a common criminal, Mr. Dornick,' Petra said. 'And neither is Vic. And Elton sure isn't. So please be quiet.'

Elton was having the toughest time of all of us, being crammed in with so many people. He was sweating, and his teeth chattered. And each time we hit a pothole, he seemed to think it was a grenade, and he'd try to hit the floor but was held to the seat by his handcuffs. 'That one was close. Charlie's closing in. Move your big feet,' he muttered.

'Elton. We're in Chicago. It's Vic. You saved my life.' I leaned as close to him as I could in my handcuffs. 'Mine and Petra's. We'll get your house repaired. Hold on for another hour. We're going to make it.'

'That's right, Elton. You're the best. It's Petra — your girl Petra — remember?' my cousin chimed in.

Elton stopped mumbling to himself long enough to say, 'You're a good girl, Petra. We'll get out of here alive, you trust me for that one.'

Dornick said, 'Trust you, you drunken rat? Shut up! I'll deal with you later.'

'George, you're the rat in this van, and you are finally going to go into that big old rattrap where you belong. You know how much fun they're going to have with you in Stateville when they learn you're the man who tortured Johnny Merton's boys? I do hope your will is up-to-date.'

Dornick lunged across the seat at me, but the

494

cops riding with us held him back.

Petra huddled next to me on the narrow seat. Under her police blanket, she was still wet from the river. I clasped her hands with my own cuffed ones.

'So how did you get all these boys in blue to show up in time to save my life?' I asked.

She'd swum the river, she said, but she hadn't been able to climb up the slick logs that lined the far bank. 'There was some kind of iron ring. I got hold of that and screamed my head off. There're these town houses up above, and someone heard me and came outside. She'd heard the shots and was feeling pretty nervous.'

The woman who responded to her screams called the police. When a squad car arrived, Petra cried out that muggers were shooting at me across the river. The cops in the squad car summoned the boat.

'Oh, Petra, little cousin, you've been scared, but you showed real courage and real resourcefulness. When all this is over, you keep remembering that. Put all those bad faces away in a drawer and put your own courage out in the living room.'

Petra gave a little sigh and curled against me. The cops didn't try to pull her away.

The night wore on interminably from there. The paddy wagon unloaded us at headquarters. When we'd all been placed in a big interrogation room at Thirty-fifth and Michigan and left to glower at one another for an hour or so, Bobby made an entrance in his shirtsleeves. Terry Finchley followed, in a suit and tie, carrying a briefcase bulging with manila folders.

'Bobby! Good to see you.' Dornick switched on his hail-fellow voice, a hearty baritone. 'Congratulations on the promotion. Well deserved.'

Bobby ignored him. And he didn't look at me, either. When he spoke, it was to the air above our heads. 'I'm trying to get Harvey Krumas down here. Peter Warshawski is on his way over from the Drake. We'll wait to get started.'

Finchley unloaded his briefcase. We could all read the label on the top folder: HARMONY NEWSOME. At that point, Dornick demanded that he be allowed to call his lawyer.

Bobby, still not looking at him, nodded at Terry, who handed Dornick a cellphone.

When Dornick demanded privacy, Finchley gave his thinnest smile. 'You were a cop for a lot of years, Mr. Dornick. You know the drill.'

Dornick's eyes glittered with fury. If he managed to walk away from any charges tonight, none of us would be safe in our beds. He called his lawyer. He was short and to the point. Then I took the phone to call Freeman Carter's cellphone.

Freeman was at dinner at the Trefoil. He first talked to Bobby, then came back on the phone with me. 'You're going to be there awhile, Vic. Don't say anything stupid. I'll see you by ten.'

I was astonished, looking at the clock, to see it was only a little before nine. I thought I'd been on the river fighting George Dornick my whole life. Another twenty minutes had dragged by before Peter came in, flanked by two cops.

'Petra! Oh my God, you're safe, Petey . . . Petey . . . '

496

He was at her side, clinging to her, but she pushed him away.

'Daddy, don't touch me, don't come near me . . . not until you explain what you did.'

'Don't talk, Warshawski,' Dornick growled.

'No, you don't need to talk, Mr. Warshawski,' Bobby agreed. 'I'm going to do that. You just take one of those empty seats.'

He laid a slim file on the table: the photo book I'd sent him this afternoon. 'We're going to start at the beginning: Marquette Park, 1966. I was a rookie, and that was a hell of a time to join the police force. Another rookie in my class was Larry Alito. He had the great good luck to be partnered with Tony Warshawski . . . the best cop who ever wore this uniform.'

Bobby looked directly at me for the first time when he said that. I bit my lips together.

'Alito's badge number was 8963. You can see it here, on the chest of the man picking up a baseball. That ball was a murder weapon used to kill a black girl in the park that day. Harmony Newsome, pride of her family, marching next to a nun. A black kid named Steve Sawyer confessed to the murder, we all know that.'

'Good police work,' Dornick said. 'Case closed.'

'Bad police work,' Bobby snapped. 'Case reopened. No proper forensic evidence was presented at the trial. We didn't have the murder weapon then, but it should have been possible to tell from the bruising and contusions and so on that she'd been struck by a projectile, not by someone stabbing her in the eye at close range.'

497

He tossed the photo book across the table at my uncle. 'You and someone else are in these pictures. He throw that ball or you?'

Peter licked his lips, but he looked at the pictures. 'Harvey. He told me Dornick said that someone at the march had taken pictures. Damn it, did Tony have them all along?'

Petra was looking at her father, her face strained, very white underneath its layer of grime. When he saw her expression, he winced and looked away.

'Harvey Krumas?' Bobby said.

Dornick interrupted Peter to warn him again not to talk. 'They're recording all this, Warshawski, so shut the fuck up.'

'Lamont Gadsden had the negatives all along,' I said quietly. 'He took the pictures with his Instamatic. He's been missing since the night of the big snow of 'sixty-seven. Three months ago, his auntie hired me to find him. She filed a missing persons report all those years ago, but George and Larry or their friends treated her like scum and didn't try to find Mr. Gadsden. Now his aunt is dying, and she wants to see him, or know where he's lying, before she can rest.'

Dornick was fidgeting in his seat, trying to interrupt, but Terry Finchley shut him up. 'Did you find him, Vic?'

I shook my head. 'No, but I found these pictures. Mr. Gadsden had put the negatives inside his Bible, and he left it with his aunt the last night he was seen alive. She gave it to me last night, not knowing it held dynamite, just wanting me to return it to her nephew when I found him.

498

It was a pure fluke that I found them . . . thanks, really, to you, George. If you hadn't tried one fancy touch too many — fingering me for Alito's death — I wouldn't have been on the run. I wouldn't have dropped the Bible. But that cracked the spine open, and the negatives fell out.'

Bobby flicked a glance in my direction. 'Some time you're going to tell me how you got out of that Lionsgate Manor without my people finding you.'

I smiled bleakly. 'Magic, Bobby. It's the only way a solo op like me can function against high-tech crap like George here has.'

'Those negatives,' Dornick said, contemptuous, 'they don't exist. You manufactured these prints . . . and not by magic. Anyone could create these out of stock shots of the riot.'

'Yes,' Bobby said. 'Where are the negatives, Vicki?'

Vicki. So we were friends again. I looked at my hands.

'Here.' Petra spoke into the silence around the table. 'I took them with me into the river.' She pulled the black plastic bag from under her blanket.

49

Guilt All Around

Dornick lunged for the bag, but one of the uniformed men put a hand on his shoulder. Another picked up the bag and handed it to Bobby.

'Let the record show that these negatives, which had been in Claudia Ardenne's Bible and came into my possession last night, are being given to Captain Robert Mallory. There are two dozen negatives, in two strips of twelve each, from film Lamont Gadsden shot in Marquette Park on August 6, 1966.' Nothing in my voice betrayed my overwhelming relief or surprise that Petra had saved the negatives.

Bobby sent for an evidence technician. While we waited, the black trash bag sat next to him on the table. A pool of brackish water spread around it. Dornick couldn't take his eyes off the water or the bag.

When the tech arrived, Bobby told her that there was valuable evidence in the bag, that he wanted to see the negatives after they'd been saved and logged in. She put the trash bag in a bigger bag, saluted, and left.

There was a commotion in the hall about then, and Harvey Krumas came into the room, trailing lawyers, like a peacock spreading his tail feathers. Freeman arrived at the same time. He was impeccable in black tie, his white-blond hair trimmed within an inch of its life. Les Strangwell was at Harvey's side.

Freeman inserted a chair next to mine. 'Vic, why is it that when you're in extremis, you stink from mud wrestling? Why can't you ever call me when you've had a shower and are wearing that red thing?'

'I want to be sure you love me for myself, not for the outer trappings of frilly femininity. There are a couple of waifs at the table who need help . . . Elton Grainger' — I gestured toward Elton, who'd shrunk deep inside himself while we had been talking — 'and my cousin, Petra Warshawski.'

'Petra doesn't need your help!' Peter said. 'She's got me here.'

'You're a suspect in a murder case, Peter. And your shenanigans put her life in danger. So I think it would be best if you let Freeman represent her for the time being.'

'Peter, George, Bobby,' Harvey interrupted, 'this is shocking. Let's get it all sorted out fast so we can go home to bed.' Harvey, the big man, very much in charge.

'In a moment, Mr. Krumas,' Bobby said. 'Let's just finish with these pictures. I think you'll recognize them.'

He nodded at a uniformed cop, who took the photo book from the table in front of Peter and opened it at the page that showed a young Harvey doing a victory dance while Peter pointed a finger at him.

'That's you in Marquette Park in 1966, Mr.

Krumas,' I said helpfully, 'seconds after you threw the nail-studded baseball that killed Harmony Newsome.'

Krumas stared at the photo. One of his lawyers kept a firm grip on his shoulder.

'Just before you got here, Captain Mallory was explaining that Larry Alito picked up the baseball,' I added. 'Why did he do that?'

'George . . . ' Peter said hoarsely. 'George told him to do it.'

'Goddamn it, Peter, I can sue you for slander if you say one more word,' Dornick said.

'You threatened my daughter, you threatened my wife and little girls, you want me to watch your back now?' Peter said. 'Jesus! It was a riot, we were young, we were hotheads. Harve and I, we went over to the park to see what was happening. We wanted to see the famous Dr. King who all the hoopla was about. Harvey brought his Nellie Fox ball. He showed it to me, it was packed full of nails. 'If I get a shot at King Nigger, I'll take it.' That's what he said.'

'Warshawski, after all we did for you, for you to turn on me like this, it's really hard,' Harvey said, more in sorrow than anger.

'Yes, your father gave me a job, he got me my big start in life. But did that give you the right to try to kill my girl?'

'Don't get so emotional, Pete,' Dornick said. 'No one wanted to kill your girl. We just were getting her to help us with Harve's boy's Senate campaign.'

I stared at him, rocked, the way one always is at such monumental lies. Freeman shook his

502

head warningly: *Don't attack him in here. Leave that to me.*

'So Harvey had a shot at Dr. King,' I went back to the main story. 'He threw the ball. Only Johnny Merton, standing next to King, pushed King's head out of the way.'

I reached for the photo book and flipped through it to show the Hammer's arm pushing King's head out of the way. 'Your ball hit Harmony Newsome and killed her, Mr. Krumas. And George helped you out . . . because you all grew up together on Fifty-sixth Place.'

'George had to put on his riot gear and be Mr. Cop, turn against his own, but he knew where his loyalties lay,' Peter said. 'With us, with the neighborhood we were fighting to preserve. Have you been down there? Have you seen what those people did to our house? Ma looked after that place — '

'It's very hard, Mr. Warshawski,' Detective Finchley said smoothly. 'Very hard for everyone who lived through that time.'

It hadn't even registered with Peter that there were black police officers in the room — not just Terry Finchley but three uniformed officers as well. My uncle's face turned the dull mahogany of embarrassment, and Petra's pale skin blazed crimson under its caking of mud. I felt pretty shame-filled myself.

'And George knew where his true loyalties lay,' I prompted. 'Not with the city he'd sworn to serve and protect but with his homeys, with Harvey, whose daddy owned Ashland Meats, and with you, Peter. His high school buddies. George wasn't far away when Harvey threw that baseball. He *saw* what happened.'

Bobby was still looking at a place over my head, but he nodded in my direction. So I went on.

'George sent Larry Alito into the middle of the marchers to pick up the ball. Alito turned himself inside out with excitement, a rookie getting to play with the big boys. He did what he was told, and George saw he got a promotion right away. Rookie to junior detective, no questions asked. Alito took to the job like the proverbial duck.

'When the heat came down from the Mayor's Office to arrest someone for Ms. Newsome's murder and George decided one of the Anacondas could carry the can for Harvey, Larry was the eager boy who attached electrodes to the suspect's testicles and ran a current through them until he fell apart and confessed to anything the detectives wanted him to say.'

Petra gasped in shock and turned to stare at Peter. Peter looked at the table in front of him. Detective Finchley was making an effort to control himself. I saw the pulse throbbing in his left temple.

'You're making that up.' Dornick broke the silence. 'There's no evidence, no nothing, except a conviction in a court of law of one Anaconda scumbag who was guilty of murder three times over in other cases where we couldn't make it stick. He was the Hammer's go-to boy. And the Hammer, he was too slick for us. But we nailed that bastard for the Newsome murder.'

Bobby looked at Finchley, who opened the

bulky folder in front of him. 'Officer Warshawski filed a protest after your interrogation, Mr. Dornick. Warshawski put a written statement in the case file saying he had witnessed the suspect being subjected to extreme interrogation measures and that he believed the conviction was tainted.'

'And Tony was sent to Lawndale and Larry got a promotion,' I said softly. 'And Peter got a big job with Ashland Meats. And then, a month before the big snow, Larry Alito brought the baseball over to our house. I don't understand why Alito didn't hang on to it himself, but he gave it to Tony. He said Tony should keep it because he, Larry, had kept Peter out of prison.'

There was another silence around the table, until Bobby asked, 'Where's the baseball, Vicki?'

'In the trunk of my car. I think. Unless George here broke in and swiped it.'

Dornick made a gesture, a man who can't believe he let the big one get away, but he didn't say anything.

'But what happened to Lamont?' I asked. 'Lamont Gadsden? He had the pictures and he disappeared.'

'Merton must've killed him,' Dornick said. 'Another useless gangbanger whose ma cries that her little boy never did anything wrong in his life. Oh no, it was his auntie, you say?'

'Lamont Gadsden came into the Racine Avenue station early in the morning of January twenty-sixth,' Detective Finchley read from the bulky file in front of him. 'The desk sergeant logged him in, with a note that he had evidence in the Newsome case. The sergeant paged detectives Dornick and Alito, who took him away with them. There is no record of him leaving the station.'

The night wore on from there endlessly. Peter and Harvey and George seemed to be fighting over who had done what, and I knew, in a detached way, that that was a good thing because one of them would be forced to admit something pretty soon. I wondered what little world Elton was inhabiting right now and if it was possible to join him there rather than continue at the table with these men.

Around two in the morning, Freeman said he didn't think I could be of any further assistance. He assumed Bobby was dropping the notion that I had anything to do with Larry Alito's death.

'Karen Lennon . . . ' I said. 'Before I go, I need to know that she's all right. She dropped me downtown a hundred hours ago when I saw George's team closing in on us.'

Finchley gave me one of his rare smiles. 'She a pastor? About as big as a minute? She's okay. She's been on the phone to the captain all night.'

I felt myself smiling in relief and turned to Dornick as I got to my feet. 'You just can't kill everyone, Georgie. There's always going to be someone left behind who lets the truth creep in.'

Petra rose to join me. She looked small and frail despite her height. The two of us roused Elton, who was murmuring something only he could understand. Freeman then drove us to my place, where we woke Mr. Contreras and the dogs.

Mr. Contreras had a fine time fussing around us. He even let Elton use his shower and a razor while Petra and I cleaned up in my place.

When we came back down, we found that Elton had drifted off into the night. Mr. Contreras said, 'He thanked me for the razor and the clean clothes, but he said to tell you two gals that he needed to be by himself for a while, said you'd understand. Now, you come in here, I been frying eggs and bacon. Peewee here, she ain't nothing but a walking bone right now. And V. I. Warshawski, you don't look much better.'

I helped Mr. Contreras make up his spare bed for my cousin. She was asleep within seconds of lying down, with Mitch curled up alongside her. I took Peppy up to the third floor, and didn't even remember locking my door.

50

The Rats Attack . . . Each Other

Miss Claudia went home to Jesus in splendid
style. The women wore the kind of hats you used
to see at Easter, heavy with birds and flowers and
ribbons, so that the weather-beaten room looked
like a gaudy garden. The music shook the rafters,
and the people spilled out of the small church
onto Sixty-second Place. Pastor Karen officiated,
which sent a buzz through a congregation that
thought women should be silent in church, but
Sister Rose was firm. This was what Miss
Claudia had wanted.

Curtis Rivers came to the funeral, along with
his two chess-playing pals. The three men wore
suits, and I didn't recognize them at first. Sister
Carolyn and her other sisters from the Freedom
Center were there, singing gospel as energetically
as any of the regular members of the congregation. Even Lotty and Max came, to show their
support for me.

Miss Claudia lingered for almost two weeks
after I had found the negatives in Lamont's
Bible. I tried to visit her most days, just to sit
with her, talk to her quietly, sometimes about my
ongoing search for Lamont, sometimes about
nothing much at all.

Harmony Newsome's murder had become
page-one news once again. It seemed as though

508

the whole country was glad to feast on Chicago's notorious corruption. We were a welcome break from the grim economic news and the predictable disappearance of the Cubs.

Bobby Mallory was at his bleakest during those weeks. He was taking part in a special housekeeping task force, and, from everything I was hearing, he was unsparing in his investigation. But it was painful for him to have to recognize the history of corruption and abuse among the men he'd spent his life with.

Dornick and Alito were by no means the only culprits. They could never have treated suspects so vilely without active collusion up and down the chain of command. Sixteen other officers who'd served at the Racine Avenue station came under federal investigation for allegations of brutality. It was shocking to see that the torture of suspects had continued at least into the nineties. Given the climate of torture cultivated by the U.S. Department of Justice in recent years, some cops apparently felt they had no reason to hold back on their own forays into 'extreme rendition.'

Bobby wouldn't talk to me about it directly, but Eileen Mallory came over to my apartment one afternoon for coffee and told me how betrayed he felt by the relentless revelations of abuse. 'The department's been his whole life. He's feeling that he dedicated himself to, I don't know, you could say to a false god. And besides that, he always measured himself against your father, and he feels it deeply that Tony was willing to write a letter protesting the torture and that he, Bobby, did nothing but request a transfer so he wouldn't have to work with Dornick or Alito. That letter ended your father's career, you know. He never got another promotion after that.'

'But Tony didn't stop it!' I burst out. 'He watched it! He went into the room and told them to stop, but Alito said, 'We're doing it for your brother. For Peter,' and Tony walked out again.'

Eileen reached across my coffee table to put a hand on my knee. 'Vicki, sweetheart, maybe you would have gone in and made them stop. You're courageous enough, reckless enough. You're truly your mother's child that way. But you don't have a family to support. Families are terrible hostages for men like your father. What other work could he get to support you and Gabriella where he knew your health and welfare would be taken care of? Your mother, God rest her soul, she wore herself out giving piano lessons to little girls for fifty cents a week. You couldn't live on that. Tony did the best he could under very painful circumstances. He spoke up. Do you know how much courage that took?'

After she left, I took a long walk with the dogs, trying to digest Eileen's words, trying to reconcile the idea of the father I loved so intensely with the man who'd been a cop, done a job, knowing he was working with men who committed torture.

I remembered the letter he wrote me when I graduated from the University of Chicago. It was still in my briefcase all these weeks later, waiting

510

for me to get it framed. Back home, I pulled it out and reread it.

I wish I could say there's nothing in my life I regret, but I've made some choices, too, that I have to live with. You're starting out now with everything clean and shiny and waiting for you. I want it always to be that way for you.

After a time, I walked down to Armitage and gave the letter to a framing shop. We picked out a frame in green, my mother's favorite color, with a gay pattern around the edge. I could read it and feel well loved. And know what he regretted, and mourn that. And try to realize that you never fully know anyone, that we, most of us, live with our contradictions. I, too, have my flaws, the hot temper he'd also warned me about in the letter, the temper that had frightened my cousin so much it almost cost her her life. Could I learn from that terrible mistake?

Of course, I wasn't the only daughter trying to come to terms with a flawed father. My cousin had more serious issues to face than I did. At least Petra had her mother and sisters to help her try to cope with the shocks they'd all suffered during the last month. The day after our marathon night at police headquarters, Petra flew down to Kansas City to be with them.

My aunt Rachel was bewildered and unsure of what she wanted to do, whether to support Peter through his upcoming legal travails or take her girls and start over without him. Peter was

511

staying in Chicago for the time being, renting a studio apartment on the Northwest Side. Petra wouldn't talk to him, and he and Rachel weren't talking often.

When Petra decided at the end of a week that she wanted to return to Chicago, Rachel flew back with her to spend a few days with her at her loft. My aunt made me take them to see Kimathi at Curtis Rivers's shop. Rachel wanted to see for herself the person who had suffered on Harvey Krumas's behalf. Kimathi was in agony in our presence, and Rivers ushered him out after a few minutes.

'I'm so sorry,' my aunt kept whispering. 'I'm so sorry.'

Rivers nodded with his usual grim expression and didn't say anything. Rachel blinked at him helplessly. She finally asked if Kimathi needed any financial help . . . would they send him to a good therapist or find him an apartment if she footed the bill?

'We're looking after him. He doesn't need your help.'

Rachel turned to leave, her legs unsteady as mine when I'd been with Kimathi and Rivers. I followed her, and was startled when Rivers touched my arm just before I triggered the train whistle.

'That red bag, Ms. Detective. It's working well for you, is it?'

I nodded warily. I had brought the bag with me, and a check for five hundred and thirty dollars, which I'd laid on the counter while Rivers was taking Kimathi into the back of the shop.

'You earned it, I figure. Use the money to help some other poor bastard.' He stuck the check into one of the bag's outer pockets and pushed me through the ropes before I could say anything.

My aunt was silent while we drove back north, but when I stopped in front of Petra's place she said, 'It's so hard to know what to do. You think you've married one man and it turns out to be like one of those bad movies where Goldie Hawn learns the man she thought she married was someone completely different. I'm so . . . so *derailed* in my life, I hired a detective to make sure Peter and I were legally married. Peter'd concealed so much from me, I thought he was capable of hiding another wife and family.'

'What will you do?' I asked.

She shook her head. 'I don't know. It's such a cliché, all these wronged women who stand by their men, like the New York governor's wife. I'm furious with Peter! I don't want to stand by him. And then there's the money. We make so much money, we have so much, and it all came to us because a man was tortured. Peter got rewarded for that poor man spending his life in prison, and turning into that . . . that pathetic — ' Her voice gave way, but she controlled herself and then went on with an effort. 'Petra . . . She's always been so much Peter's child. He wanted a boy, he was sure she'd be a boy, so he's always called her Petey, and taken her hunting and so on. She was always bolder than her other sisters, the four that followed her, until I told him he had to cherish his girls, he couldn't be imagining they were less

513

than a boy would be. And now Petra is having as much trouble as I am trying to figure out who she is, what she thinks about him.'

She gave me a painful smile. 'You did so much for Petra, and you got badly hurt yourself. Your body, that is. But I know you're suffering inside over what your father did. I think all Peter's and my money is dirty, but I want to pay you for your, oh, your time and trouble. I know you're not getting a fee for all the hours and days you lost because of us. And while I'm still married and have that joint account, you should have some of it.'

She handed me an envelope. Later, when I opened it and found a check for twenty-five thousand, I almost threw it out. The money was tainted, I told Lotty. I couldn't possibly accept it.

'Victoria, all money is tainted.' Lotty smiled faintly. 'Especially reparations money. Take it. Pay your bills. Go back to Italy, do something for yourself or something for Mr. Kimathi. It won't change his life if you have to file for bankruptcy. And cashing the check doesn't put you under any obligation to your uncle.'

I cashed the check and gave part of it to the Mighty Waters Freedom Center. But the rest I was thankful to use on my bills. Rachel returned to Kansas City and her other daughters, but Petra stayed on. She couldn't go back to the campaign, and not just because she didn't want to be around the Krumas family. Brian Krumas shut down the campaign once all the charges and countercharges began coming to light.

His Bobbyesque hair in his eyes, Brian stood

in front of a bank of cameras and said he couldn't possibly be a good public servant when his family had colluded in torture to save themselves from the consequences of their own role in killing a civil rights worker. Of course, he looked heroic on television, and those of us cynics watching felt sure he'd be back on the campaign trail sometime soon. Still, it made me think well of him.

Meanwhile, Petra was at loose ends. She spent hours every day running with the dogs and watching horse races with Mr. Contreras. One afternoon, she tentatively broached her earlier suggestion that she work in my agency for a time, but I didn't think either of us was ready for that. I needed a vacation from my family. Finally, I sent Petra over to Sister Carolyn at the Freedom Center. Petra owed Elton a new home, and Sister Carolyn was able to recruit some people from Habitat for Humanity, who showed Petra how to construct a simple place on the river where his old shack had stood.

Carolyn had wanted to give Elton Sister Frankie's apartment as soon as it was fixed up, but Elton's brief moment of heroism hadn't worked any miracles in his ability to be around other people. He wanted to be alone, away from the sounds and smells of others at night. Still, we capitalized on the desire of every public official in Chicago to show what good guys they were — we got the city to donate a piece of land, the equivalent of a quarter of a city lot, down by the river where Elton's shack had stood. And when Petra and Habitat had finished his little house, we even got Elton hooked up to city water.

Petra still didn't feel comfortable talking to her father, although he was cooperating fully with both state and federal authorities in the numerous investigations that were taking place. Some were looking at the cover-up of Harmony Newsome's murder. Others were looking into the allegations of torture at the Racine Avenue station. And, of course, there was Larry Alito's murder. And Sister Frances's.

Later that fall, as Peter started telling his side of the story, he claimed it all started when Dornick found out that I was trying to find Steve Sawyer. When Harvey realized what Petra was saying at the Navy Pier fundraiser, he'd gone at once to Les Strangwell. Although Krumas was afraid his own role in murdering Harmony Newsome might come to light, Strangwell's only concern was to keep everything buried until after Brian made it through the primaries and the general election. That meant trying to keep the story under wraps for over a year. All summer long, while I had felt I was spinning my wheels in my search for Lamont and Sawyer, Strangwell and Krumas thought I was getting too close to Sawyer for comfort. And so they called on George Dornick.

Dornick, with his sophisticated technology and a crew trained at the School of the Americas in every known form of combat, surveillance, and torture, was happy to come to Harvey's rescue once again.

At the end of the summer, as they were coercing Petra into helping them break into my home and office, Dornick had become more brazen and more violent. When Peter and Rachel came to Chicago after Petra disappeared, Dornick told them that their other four daughters were as good as dead if either parent told anyone anything about the Newsome murder, the Sawyer torture, the death of Sister Frances, the coercion of Petra. Rachel flew back to Kansas City and went into hiding with her girls.

All this emerged slowly, of course, but Terry Finchley called me periodically to brief me. As the fall wore on, a prosecutorial dream came true: Harvey and Dornick began attacking each other. Harvey claimed it was Dornick's idea to blow up Sister Frances before she could confide in me. Dornick claimed he knew nothing about it, that Harvey and Strangwell had employed Larry Alito, a loose cannon, an alkie — Dornick had warned them that Alito was unreliable — while Strangwell said Alito was Dornick's go-to boy anytime he needed heavy lifting that he wanted to keep private.

After a lot of hemming and hawing and horse trading, the State's Attorney's Office brought charges against Krumas for second-degree murder in connection with Harmony Newsome's death. Krumas's lawyer had been pressing for involuntary manslaughter and probation, but as the national spotlight started shining on Chicago's finest, the state's attorney realized he couldn't afford to let Krumas off with nothing but a rap on the knuckles.

Dornick's situation was more complicated. He

hadn't helped kill Harmony Newsome, but everyone, including Bobby, believed Dornick had engineered the subsequent cover-up. Peter sang loud and long on that theme. Then there was Sister Frankie's death. Detective Finchley's team traced the Ford Expedition that the bomb throwers drove to one of Dornick's personal crew. And Finchley was willing to believe that Dornick had shot Alito out of fear that his old buddy would crack and flip for the state if the heat got too intense.

51

Gabriella's Voice Returned

In the weeks before Miss Claudia died, I was racing the clock, hoping to find out what happened to Lamont. The day I took my aunt to Fit for Your Hoof, Curtis told me he'd persuaded Johnny to talk to me.

'He needs to get it off his chest and tell someone, and I told him he owed it to Miss Claudia. She needs to know. She loved that boy. Now, Miss Ella, if Lamont had gone on, like our physics teacher wanted, been a college professor with degrees after his name, she'd still have labeled him a failure. But Miss Claudia was pure love down to her bones. She deserves to hear, and I've made sure Johnny'll tell you.'

I wanted to know how Curtis and Merton communicated. I wanted to know if secretly, after all, Curtis was a high-ranking Anaconda. But something in his face told me I'd better not push my luck.

I got Yeoman to organize an emergency visit to Stateville for me and met with Johnny in the dingy lawyers' room one last time. I'd brought one of my photo books with me and laid it between us on the scarred deal table.

'These are the pictures Lamont took,' I said. 'I guess Curtis told you I found the negatives?'

Merton nodded.

'He showed them to you the night before he disappeared, didn't he?'

Merton nodded again, shut his eyes, took a breath: another one getting ready to jump off the high dive for me, or at least for Lamont and Miss Claudia.

'My man came to me at the Waltz Right Inn, just like Rose Hebert told you. He had a set of these prints here, and he wanted to go to that piece of shit representing Steve, show him that some white boy killed Harmony and some cop pocketed the evidence. We talked it over, him and me. We knew what went on at the Racine Avenue station. We knew the risk he was running going in there at all, but we agreed he'd better speak up. But I told him to take prints in, don't let them have the negatives. If they destroy those, there's nothing left.

'So off he went the morning the big snow started. And the day after it ended later, when you could go outside again, there he was, in my backyard, dead. His ears had been cut off, but he'd been killed before that.'

'His ears!' I said. 'So, Dornick and Alito killed him. Or someone at the station did. And they planted his body on you. And if you called the cops, everyone would agree that it was an Anaconda hit. Dornick would say Lamont had turned state's evidence against you and that you'd murdered him in revenge.'

Johnny gave a sour smile. 'You're not so stupid after all, are you, white girl?'

'I have my moments,' I said drily. 'What did you do?'

'I took Lamont inside with me and sat with him all day — sweating blood, you'd better believe — thinking every second that the cops were going to come tear my door down. I wouldn't let my wife or my little girl in. I made up a big lie, a big story, and it cost me my marriage. My wife, she thought I had some other woman in there with me. She left in a hurry, went to her own mama's. I guess because of the storm, all the cops were on emergency duty. Not even that shitbag Dornick could come around to check on me and Lamont for three days.

'A big warehouse blew down on Stony the day before the snow. As soon as it got dark, I carried my brother down the stairs. I got my little girl's sled and pulled my man along, wrapped in blankets. Three miles, that was, hard walking, scared every five minutes some damned cop would stop me.

'Don't you ever repeat that out loud, white girl, that the Hammer was terrified.' He gave a mirthless bark of laughter and flexed his arms so that the snakes rippled under my nose.

'Anyway, I dug through the snow, buried him in the foundation of that place on Stony. No one ever looked in there after the storm. I sat by the newsman every day at three when the early edition hit the stands, looking, but they just built right on top of my boy. They never looked, they never found him. Day three, up comes that shit Alito, merry as can be, acting on a tip that I had drugs on the premises. They had a warrant and they searched high and low, but you'd better believe the crib was clean. I scrubbed that place from window to floor — and more than once, too — and I had Curtis there to watch they didn't plant nothing. My only joy was knowing they were going crazy, trying to find out what happened to the body. They were pissed as hell that the place was clean, but they finally took off. For months, Alito would stop by, or sometimes Dornick, now and again. But after a while, it all died down . . . all died down until you came along, nosing into it.'

'When I looked at the pictures, it seemed to me you might have saved Dr. King's life.' I opened the photo book at the shot that showed the tattooed arm shoving King's head down.

Merton's mouth set in a bitter line. 'I saved him for some white punk to put a bullet in two years later, that's all. And what did it cost? Miss Harmony died, took a lot of light out of the South Side when that baseball hit her in the eye. Steve — Kimathi, he calls himself now — they rearranged his privates and his brain for him. And they killed my man Lamont. That's a high price my homeys paid for one little shove of my arm.'

'Your daughter might like to know,' I ventured.

The anger that was always smoldering behind his eyes lightened slightly. 'Yeah, take the tale to Dayo. Let her know — how did you put it? — I 'had my moments,' too.'

Against all protocol, I leaned across the table and squeezed his hand where the tongue of the snake licked his knuckles.

When I got back to the city, I took the story to Bobby. But he said he had enough going on

522

without digging under a building on Stony Island looking for one more dead gangbanger. 'Even if Lamont Gadsden's there, even if we find him, what am I going to do about it? It'll be Merton's word against Dornick's, and even if for one day out of my entire forty years on the force I am willing to believe a gang scum over a cop, I'd never sell the state's attorney on it. Dornick has plenty on his plate. Let it ride, Vicki. Let it ride.'

I let it ride. But I did cash in some old chips of my own with the state. I didn't try to get Johnny's sentence reduced — he was in prison for serious and well-documented crimes — but I did see that he was transferred to a less punitive part of the system. And I let Dayo see the photos, let her see her father had saved Martin Luther King's life that hot August day forty years ago.

I was also able to tell the story to Miss Ella and to Miss Claudia before she died. Miss Ella seemed almost sorry that I'd found her son. It took away one of her pleasures, the pleasure of complaining that I was taking her money and not delivering. But Miss Claudia, in one of her final lucid moments, told her sister to be ashamed of herself.

'Hate and bitterness, always wrong, Ella. Always wrong. Lamont with Jesus. I know it, I know in my heart. White girl, you did good job. Hard, I know. Hurt, burn, beaten, you stay working. I know, Pastor Karen tell me all. Good, good girl.' She pressed my fingers as hard as she could and then lay back against her pillows.

At first, I thought she'd fallen asleep. But she was just mustering her strength, this time to tell us she wanted Pastor Karen to preach at her funeral. And when Ella harrumphed about women being silent in church, Claudia said, 'Men kill Lamont. Men hurt world, do war, do torture. Pastor Karen preach.'

That was the last time she spoke. She died two days later without ever regaining consciousness again. After the funeral, after the supper in the church hall with everyone's favorite casserole, and ham, and the black-eyed peas with chitterlings that Miss Claudia so loved, Max and Lotty took me away with them for a long weekend in the country.

The day after I got back, Jake Thibaut knocked at my door. I'd seen him a few times just passing on the stairs, him liking to joke about whether I needed him to get a clarinet case or something to carry my body around, but we hadn't really talked.

This evening, he had a CD in his hand. 'Those tapes you gave me — your mother singing — I had them professionally mastered for you. She had an amazing voice. I'm privileged that I got to hear it.'

I had forgotten about the tapes, in the chaos I'd been living in. Now I put the CD in my stereo. As Gabriella's voice, that golden bell, filled my home, I felt so overcome with all the grief and loss of the last forty years that I could hardly bear to listen.

'*Forse un giorno il cielo ancora/Sentirà pietà di me.*'

(One day, perhaps, Heaven again / will feel pity for me.)

I played it over and over while Jake stood awkwardly by. At one point, he disappeared, but then returned moments later with his bass. He played the aria through, first in company, then in counterpoint, with my mother's voice. After that, it seemed natural to bring out her red wineglasses and toast her memory, and exchange our life stories, and, finally, to lie together on the living room rug while Mozart and my mother filled the room.

We do hope that you have enjoyed reading
this large print book.

Did you know that all of our titles
are available for purchase?

We publish a wide range of high quality
large print books including:
Romances, Mysteries, Classics
General Fiction
Non Fiction and Westerns

Special interest titles available in
large print are:
The Little Oxford Dictionary
Music Book
Song Book
Hymn Book
Service Book

Also available from us courtesy of
Oxford University Press:
Young Readers' Dictionary
(large print edition)
Young Readers' Thesaurus
(large print edition)

For further information or a free
brochure, please contact us at:
Ulverscroft Large Print Books Ltd.,
The Green, Bradgate Road, Anstey,
Leicester, LE7 7FU, England.
Tel: (00 44) 0116 236 4325
Fax: (00 44) 0116 234 0205

BLEEDING KANSAS

Sara Paretsky

Two families have been farming in the Kaw River Valley for over a hundred and fifty years, their lives connected through generations by history and geography. Then Gina Haring, bringing with her the liberal air of the big city, moves into a dilapidated house near both farms. Almost every one of the Grelliers is drawn to her, but it is Susan, a woman of ephemeral passions, whose involvement stirs up the wrath of the Schapen clan. The results for her own family will be cataclysmic . . .

FIRE SALE

Sara Paretsky

South Chicago is a neighbourhood private investigator V.I. Warshawski left long ago; it's a dangerous place reeking with bad memories. But now she has returned to the streets of her childhood to do a favour for a friend. It was never going to be easy — and when the mother of a local girl asks her to investigate claims of sabotage at the factory where she works, V.I. finds herself caught up in something more sinister. They say home is where the heart is, but now, as she lies by the roadside with a piece of hot, twisted metal embedded in her shoulder, looking up at the factory's smouldering remains, Warshawski wonders whether a trip down memory lane was such a good idea after all . . .